I

MW01127206

Published by Crystal Lake Publishing
www.CrystallakePub.com
www.facebook.com/Crystallakepublishing
https://twitter.com/crystallakepub

Edited by Ross Warren

READ ORDER

85 (10)	113	1	163	127
45	361 (14)	95	243	195
183		227	19	329
305		263	57	
317 (12)			281	
			375	

A word of thanks from the Publisher:

Thank you, dear reader, for allowing us into your home and mind. Just knowing that you are holding this book in your hand right now makes me grin with pride. Writing, like most art, begins as a solitary act, and ends up being shared by thousands. I am grateful for your part of this wonderful adventure.

I'd like to thank the writers I've met throughout this project. Writers seldom get the praise they deserve. They are amazing men and women, all with their own problems, schedules, sicknesses and real life interruptions (and most of the time day jobs). I've even met a few writers living in physical and emotional pain, yet they still get the work done on time, never wanting to disappoint their fans. Always professional.

As you can see, writers seldom write under ideal conditions.

Writers are not just dreamers, we are doers. Passionate creators in our own right.

Personally, I've enjoyed scary stuff since I was a young boy, whether I did the scaring or something scared me. It's an addictive adrenaline that most don't understand, but they always go back for a second helping. Why else would you be reading this book?

I'd also like to thank all the amazing people who have contributed to this collection, directly and indirectly:

The writers (again), you are all amazing and I wish you all the success in the future. Hopefully the readers will take the time to take a look at your other works.

Thanks to Ross Warren, for agreeing to undertake the enormous job of editing this tome.

Thanks to Ben Baldwin, without whose incredible art work I'd never have been able to draw so many authors to this anthology.

This might seem weird, but thanks to my day job, for the money to get this project off the ground. I knew you were good for something.

I'd also like to thank Robert Swartwood, for his professional eBook formatting services.

And how can I not take the time to thank all the reviewers, bloggers and internet surfers for spreading the word, even the proof-readers for each individual writer.

Finally, thank you to my friends and family, for understanding my drive and passion enough to let me disappear for hours every day into my own, extremely vast, world.

So, dear reader, I hope you'll join all our adventures into the unknown and the bizarre, where you will not only glimpse through a crack in the veil at the on-going battle between good and evil, but help me discover the horror heavyweights of the future.

Long live Horror!

Joe Mynhardt
Bloemfontein, South Africa
24 March 2013

Content:

His Own Personal Golgotha by G. N. Braun   1

21 Brooklands: Next to Old Western,
Opposite the Burnt Out Red Lion
by Carole Johnstone   19

The River by Armand Rosamilia   45

God May Pity All Weak Hearts
by Daniel I. Russell   57

Darker with the Day by Scott Nicholson   85

In the Darkest Room in the Darkest House on the
Darkest Part of the Street by Gary McMahon   95

Till Death by Joe Mynhardt   113

On a Midnight Black Chessie by Kevin Lucia   127

Father Figure by Tracie McBride   163

Room to Thrive by Stephen Bacon   183

Hungry is the Dark by Benedict J. Jones   195

Eternal Darkness by Blaze McRob   227

This Darkness... by John Claude Smith   243

Lost and Found by Tonia Brown   263

Mr Stix by Mark West   281

A Snitch in Time by Robert W. Walker   305

Shade by Jeremy C. Shipp   317

How the Dark Bleeds by Jasper Bark   329

Don't Let the Dark Stop You Shining
by William Meikle   361

Where the Dark is Deepest by Ray Cluley   375

Introduction by the editor:

Achluophobia, Nyctophobia and *Scotophobia* seem such overly complicated words for what is such a simple, primal fear as that of the dark. For most of us there will have been a point in our childhood when we became anxious about turning out the light for fear of the monster under the bed or the fingernails tapping upon the window pane.

In all but the most severe cases it is something we grow out of as we move into our early teens much like other things, such as personal hygiene and listening to our parents. However it doesn't go away, it just lies dormant within us waiting for its opportunity; a deserted multi-storey car park late at night perhaps or an evening home alone when a spouse is working away. The fact it remains is beneficial to the writer of horror and dark fantasy though, as it acts as a well spring that we can return to both for ideas and to remember the emotional and physical reactions it provoked.

The authors of these stories all take fear of the dark as a theme, but far from being twenty similar tales there are a vast diversity of styles and approaches in evidence. You will be taken back into the past, down to the depths of the ocean and across the borderline between our world and the next. You will see snapshots from the lives of small children, old-time cockney gangsters and aimless stoners. You will journey into the darkest house on the darkest street, wander hospital basements and take a flight in the comfort of first class. You will meet Mr Stix.

But remember through the horrors and dangers you encounter in these twenty stories, by some of the most talented writers at work in four continents, the dark is just an absence of light; an intangible thing that cannot really hurt you. Can it?

Ross Warren
Cheltenham, England
March, 2013

His Own Personal Golgotha
G. N. Braun

gol•go•tha (n). A place or occasion of great suffering.

Darkness and dirt.

After he'd woken in the small, muddy cavern, he'd scrabbled uselessly for what felt like hours, but it was all still darkness and dirt.

He didn't want to die today. He'd find out soon enough whether the choice was his to make.

His fingertips scraped against something unusual in the earth as he struggled in the direction he hoped was up. Smooth and rounded, it came free as he pulled at it. In the darkness, he couldn't see what it was, but later, as he climbed back down to rest for a moment, he grabbed it from the floor. He scraped enough dirt from it to feel eye sockets and teeth. It was a skull, small enough to be that of a child.

He placed it back on the floor, and continued his journey to the surface.

He clawed at the earth, still hoping he was heading in the right direction. The longer it took, the harder it was to breathe, and the dirt around him seemed to draw closer. He felt the knot in his chest tighten as his lungs cramped and his heart pumped faster. He had to get out. He increased his effort, until he broke through to the world above. Still, darkness reigned.

He'd been without light for so long that he could see fairly well. Everywhere around him, nothing but gravestones.

Low hills surrounded the valley that held the graveyard, and the dead, ragged trees that crested the hills appeared as skeletal hands reaching for the stars.

He dragged himself out of the grave, and tried to brush the clay from his rumpled trousers, but the cloth was covered in it. He was shirtless.

Near him was a headstone.

Words were engraved upon it.

Unum Qui Patitur
'One who suffers'

Suffers?

He cringed without knowing why.

He looked up at the night sky, unsure of just where he was and hoping the pattern of the stars would look familiar. No such luck.

A blood-red moon hung low in the sky, silhouetting the scraggly trees that lined the distant hills. He had a lot of walking to do, and wished he knew which direction to take.

All around him, decrepit gravestones lurked in the dark like murderers, huddled and hunched, waiting for unsuspecting victims to stroll by. He could just make out the words engraved on the ones nearest where he stood.

Caput Mortuum
'Worthless remains'

In Parva Mors
'The Little Death'

This second phrase was engraved on a smaller stone than the others. He looked around and saw that most of the nearby graves were child-sized, covered in images of tragedy and loss. As he moved closer, he saw on one the image of disembodied hands from Heaven reaching down to pluck flowers from the earth; on another, small lambs, lost and alone. Cribs were carved on a third grave, one that was laid out in size as though for three children. The cribs on the edges held images of sleeping children while the third was empty. On the ground beneath some of the gravestones were toys: raggedy dolls and faded doll-houses; wind-up metal cars now rusted or with paint peeling; in front of one, an old-fashioned spinning top with a spiralled auger.

Ravens rested on some of the headstones, a glint of red shining in their eyes as they watched him trek through their home.

Gluttons. Harbingers of death. He could recall no more.

Why can't I remember?

He looked behind him to the earth he had clawed his way out from under, and found another small grave. No image or text on this one. No toys at the base.

He shook his head, and followed a sudden compulsion to move on, to move away from where he was standing. He walked slowly forward, along a roughly-defined path that had to lead somewhere. He didn't know where he was going; he just knew he had some destination in mind.

As he moved through the graveyard, he gradually found his bearings. Some hills lay ahead. They looked like a scabrous spine exposed in a shallow grave, the bony processes regular and symmetrical. Beyond the third vertebra from the left lay a light. It was a glow rising beyond the hill, a sign of life and a possible destination. He knew what it was, somewhere deep in his mind. A name floated up from the depths of his memory: *Necropolis* – City of the Dead.

Home. I think its home. A way to the truth. A place of knowledge.

He yearned to know.

Desiccated leaves littered the path he walked. Every footstep crushed more of them into dust; red, brown and gold. Slush-piles of dirty-white, half-melted snow lay here and there between the graves, a sign of impending winter. Sudden flashes of an image invaded his consciousness; a young girl, clad all in white, almost glowing, skipping though an orchard on an autumn day. The leaves scattered with every step she took; red and gold and brown, to match the leaves he walked through now. The vision vanished, yet something remained with him. *Regret? Desire?* He wasn't sure.

Shaking his head and sinking back to his own reality, he lengthened his stride, heading toward the spinal hills and the light in the distance.

So far, yet too close at the same time.

The leaves fell behind him and the snow became more prevalent. Goosebumps rose on his torso, and he found himself wishing for more clothing. He wanted to feel warm, for once in his miserable memory.

A tickle in the back of his throat caused him to cough. After a second, it formed into a hard lump, packed in his throat and blocking the air from his lungs. Gagging, unable to breathe, he dropped to his knees. Leaning forward onto his hands, he tried to hack up whatever it was, and grew dizzy from lack of air. Finally, with one harsh, wracking cough, he felt it move inside his neck and brush the back of his soft palate. He strained to open his mouth as far as he could and reached inside with a muddy hand. He managed to grasp something soft and fibrous. He dragged it out, inch by painful inch. White fabric; lacy cotton. At least fifteen or twenty inches of what seemed to be part of a dress. A few blowflies were caught in the material, buzzing weakly.

One last lump remained in his throat, and no matter how hard he tried, it wouldn't shift. His lungs were bursting, and his head spun. Darkness started to seep into the edges of his vision, and he fell forward onto his hands once again. No matter how much he tried, he couldn't breathe. Darkness engulfed him.

He awoke in agony, his throat burning but now clear and empty. He was in the mud where he had fallen. His nose was filled with slime, and he could barely draw breath, but he had more oxygen than he'd had just before he blacked out. He lifted his face, and snorted his nostrils clear. Pain streaked through his neck, and his breathing was ragged and shallow. It hurt to breathe too deeply.

Gradually, his mind cleared and his heartbeat slowed.

He looked around to gain his bearings, and was

taken aback by the changes.

How long have I been out? Where am I?

Red was everywhere. Red leaves now littered the ground, and lay over the gravestones that surrounded him. The blood-red moon had sunk lower in the sky, yet seemed to have grown. It looked so close he imagined he could reach up and touch it.

A childish giggle rang out through the still air, echoing amongst the graves and the crypts, making it impossible to identify its source.

"Who's there?"

"Caitlin..." the wind carried a whispered name.

The smell of roses wafted through the air, underscored with the pungent aroma of musk. Potent yet seductive.

Another giggle rang out, more blatant than the last, from a different location. He whirled toward where he thought it came from, but again it was impossible to pinpoint.

The scent of rose and musk grew stronger, visceral and sweet. He felt a stirring in his loins. He looked down at his erection in wonder. It was a physical reaction, but to what, he had no idea. The combination of the innocent laughter and the sexual undertones of the perfumed air aroused him. His penis tingled and grew even harder, to the point where it became painful. He reached down and unzipped himself, freeing his engorged member. It throbbed as the cold night air hit, straining to grow beyond its limits.

The smell grew stronger, now infused with vanilla and the scaly smell of old semen, and swirled through the air, almost visceral enough to touch. The temperature suddenly dropped even more. Cold seeped into every inch of exposed skin, causing his erection to shrivel and die.

"No. Please. Stop. You're hurting me..."

The voice was now distant and pleading, where before it had held a more mocking undertone. This part of his journey was nearing an end.

Where did that thought come from?

What journey?

Another peal of laughter, even more distant, tinkled like bells in the now-frigid air, followed by a fading voice.

"No more. Please, just let me go. I won't tell... I promise."

A sudden red desire ran through him in a wave, followed by a sense of regret.

Follow the voice!

He took a step towards the direction he guessed the voice had come from. Toward the hills. Toward the glow of Necropolis.

Toward the truth.

#

Hours later, the graveyard showed no signs of ending, yet the vertebral hills seemed closer, the glow more palpable.

His feet were beginning to ache. He'd need to rest soon. He'd hunted the girl more than halfway toward the hills, but the nearest he had come to finding her was bubbles of tinkling laughter floating through the air.

The landscape had changed as he neared the hills. Palm trees spaced here and there between the graves. Once, he had seen a bonnet spiralling in the wind, drifting aimlessly through the sky.

Soon he could walk no further. He slept for a while, exhausted.

He dreamt he sat inside a cage of bones.

Outside, a young blonde girl sat amongst dogwood trees, eating sweet, red berries and watching him.

"Who are you?" he asked.

"I am the victim of your desire," she answered. "I am your lust, and I am death. I am named Caitlin."

"I don't understand," he said, although he thought maybe he did, somewhere deep inside his heart. His mind rebelled at a memory he couldn't quite grasp.

"You hurt me very much," she said. "You took from me that which I didn't want to give."

"What did I do?" he asked.

Caitlin parted her lips to answer, but no words came out. Instead, she closed her eyes as a fountain of deep red blood poured from her mouth and nose. Her jaw stretched wide, and then even wider, accompanied by the cracking of bones and the snapping sound of ligaments stretched beyond their limit.

He stared in horror as her chin bent down far enough to touch the lacy collar of her pristine white dress. A scream built up in his throat, but refused to be voiced.

The blood spilled down the front of her dress, soaking the fabric and turning it a vivid red. She opened her eyes. They were as red as the blood; no white of sclera, no black of pupil. Pure red.

He looked at her. She looked at him.

She leaned forward and passed something between the bones of the cage. He managed to break away from her gaze, and looked down to find that he held an old stuffed toy. An owl; tattered and torn.

"For wisdom," she said. "For redemption."

By the time he looked up, she was gone.

Everything was gone: the cage; the girl; the blood; everything.

He awoke, lying on his back and staring up at the stars. They still didn't look familiar, but he had a sense of *déjà vu* that almost crippled him with its strength.

Why am I here? What have I done?

I'm sorry.

This last thought hit from nowhere. He felt a twinge of regret, but wasn't sure he was ready to face what it was he regretted. He felt shame.

He stretched and sat up. Looked down. By his side was the owl from his dream.

He reached down and picked it up. It was old. Two worn and chipped buttons represented eyes. Rough stitches held it together, now ragged with age. There were spots the colour of rust here and there on its body.

Blood? It looks like blood.

He knew he'd seen it somewhere before.

Where?

He remembered an orchard in autumn. Leaves covered the ground between the rows of apple trees, and shrivelled pieces of fruit lay forgotten from the harvest. He remembered the red, the blood.

He could recall nothing else, but he knew that, in time, it would come to him.

Standing up, he stuffed the owl under his arm and walked toward the glowing hills.

#

He walked for what felt like a full day this time, and drew closer to the hills. Sweat hung heavy on his brow, despite the coolness of the air. Still no sign of dawn. Nothing but endless night and an ongoing desire to reach the far side of the vertebra hills.

He had a sense that his desire was to be avoided, but he couldn't control it. Somehow, he knew it would be more trouble than anything, but he had always been weak in the face of his longings.

Another few hours, and the graves had started to thin out. Finally, there was nothing between himself and the hills but a vast meadow, laced here and there with apple trees. He wondered if this related to his memory.

Have I been here before? Will I be back again?

Why did he think that? It made no sense. Nothing made any sense.

Who was he? Where was he, and where was he going?

The vertebral hills lay ahead, much closer now. The light behind them was brighter. It was a soft, pearl-like colour, with traces of red and black around the edges. Like no light he had ever seen before.

"Don't. Stop. Don't stop."

It sounded like Caitlin again. She seemed a fair

distance away. Somewhere in the hills, up near the ridgeline. He pressed on, determined to find the source of the voice.

He reached the end of the meadow. The apple and cherry trees had given way to silver birch. Sparse patches of shrubs poked up above the grass here and there. The hill itself, the third from the left in the range, seemed made of rounded, strangely-uniform white rocks.

It was only when he got close to where the grass ended that he saw what the hill was really composed of.

Skulls.

Thousands, tens of thousands, maybe even millions of skulls. The hill was a pile of bone two hundred metres high. He looked left and right, but the other hills in the range seemed normal. They were covered in grass, and the silver birch continued up the slopes. This hill, the one he needed to climb, was a barren pile of skulls.

Interlaced within the pile were other bones: long, thick femurs; delicately curved ribs; flat, axe-like shoulder blades; and stumpy spinal vertebrae. Millions of bones, piled high enough to contain every skeletal structure from every grave in the endless cemetery he had walked through to get here.

"Don't stop. Keep going. Climb and achieve knowledge. Face the truth that lies within."

Again, that voice called out to him. Again, the compulsion pulsed though him, an almost sexual feeling that stirred his loins and raised the hairs on his back and neck.

"Keep going and you shall find the meaning and the memory. Don't forget the owl."

He still held the stuffed toy in his hand. He'd almost forgotten it was there, but he'd managed to keep hold of it.

He looked up toward the crest of the hill. There seemed to be a large white box there, the size of a coffin. On it, a white figure reclined.

"Keep going."

He stepped onto the first of the bones, expecting them to shift beneath his feet, but they proved more solid than he expected. It was as though they were firmly fixed in the ground underneath; purely a decorative layer.

"That's it. Come to me. Don't stop."

"Who are you?" he cried out.

"I am temptation and punishment. I am your weakness and your desire. I am what lies within. I am innocence lost and the child of stolen dreams. I am diminished by lust."

A hidden memory surged forward at these words.

[flash] Stalking her, stealing her, taking her amongst the budding apple trees.

He came closer to remembering what he had done. The details still escaped him, yet he was nearer to the truth. He dropped to his knees, shame and regret warring inside.

What am I? How could I?

After a while, he came back to his senses. He had to make amends. He had to make things right. He had to find Caitlin.

"Where am I?"

"Where you need to be."

"That answers nothing," he said. "Where do you lead me?"

There came no reply, and the figure stood up from what he now saw to be another grave. It turned away and walked down the other side of the bone-hill. The last he saw, her fine golden hair was billowing as though wind-blown, yet there was no breeze.

"Caitlin," he called.

There was no response as the figure disappeared over the crest.

"*Caitlin!*" he called louder. Nothing. She was gone.

"I'm sorry," he whispered.

He increased his pace, and soon enough he reached the tomb she had been sitting on. A square of white stone, large enough to hold a coffin and protect it from the elements. There was no headstone; just one word engraved on the top slab.

Tu
'You'

Me?

Beneath the word was a carven symbol – a serpent, in the form of a circle that was swallowing its own tail. He had seen it before, but had no idea what it signified.

Rebirth? A cycle?

The tomb was sealed. He had no desire to open it. The very idea terrified him even more than he already was, if that were possible. He turned to follow the girl. He reached the crest of the hill and stopped, staring in wonder at what lay before him.

A massive city, marbled and lit throughout by what appeared to be torchlight, lay in the valley past the hills. It went for what seemed to be miles; houses made of stone interwoven with crenelated towers and castle-like fortresses built of massive basalt blocks. He could see movement in the distant streets. Crowds washed through them like water moving through a series of creeks; fluid and full of motion. Surrounding the city was a towering wall, segmented by gates that stood at least thirty feet high. All seemed closed except one, which stood at the termination of a snaky road that led from the base of the bone-hill to the city itself. It was lined with torches and strange-looking trees.

Necropolis. *City of the Dead.*

He didn't know how he could be sure, but he was still certain this was the city's name.

A breeze lifted the hairs on his head, cooled the sweat on his brow. It carried with it the scent of vanilla and old sweat. Somehow, it seemed both arousing *and* abhorrent now.

He started down to where the road began at the bottom of the hill. He was close now – he could almost feel the possibility of resolution. The toy owl dangled from his hand as he scrabbled down the bone-hill.

Soon, I will know who I am and accept what I have done. Soon I will be whole again. Soon, I will live again. Soon, I will say I'm sorry, and she will know I have found the way.

He reached the base of the bone-hill, and looked

along the road. What he had taken for trees were actually poles, wrapped around with barbed wire that held up many childrens' toys. The poles were spaced about a hundred feet apart, all the way to the city.

A voice whispered in his ear.

"Look at me. I'm bleeding."

He whirled, trying to find who had spoken.

"I'm bleeding for you*!"*

He dropped the owl and clutched at his ears, spinning again, but there was no-one around. The breeze picked up, strengthening the smell of vanilla and sweat, but this time it was laced with the tang of copper and old blood. Still, it managed to arouse him once again. His penis grew erect, and sweat sprang from his pores.

He stumbled along the road for a few metres before he remembered the owl. He went back to grab it. It looked different. He couldn't work out what it was for a second, and then noticed the eyes. Before they had been old buttons, but they were now tarnished pennies, sewn on with metallic thread.

Pennies for eyes, or to pay the Ferryman?

He walked toward Necropolis. *Not far now. I'll be there soon. I'll find out what lies beneath the bones and the blood and the dreams and the graves. What lies beneath the earth. I'll remember what happened, and I'll find a way to change it all.*

"Soon. You'll have it all very soon. This time, things will be different."

There was that voice again, but this time he ignored it. He cared for nothing but to reach the gates and find that which he sought. Knowledge.

He walked past the barbed toy-trees and the lit torches; he walked until he reached the city gates. They were closed, although he was sure they had been open when he had gazed down from the bone-hill. Old and worn, the wood they were made from looked ancient, yet they seemed solid. The gates were black and arched, and were graven with one phrase repeated in many different fonts.

Virginis Portam
'The Virgin's Gate'

He pushed against them once, and then again, but there was no give. He took a step back and kicked at them. Nothing.

"If you want to enter, you must take them by force! The city does not want you to enter. I don't want you to enter. I want you to not want to enter."

Caitlin's voice, saying those words, brought back everything in stark detail. He recalled walking through an orchard. He remembered seeing her walking alone one row away from him, maybe on the way home from school. He remembered his lust, and he remembered what followed. He remembered... God, he *remembered*.

Anger and shame ripped through him. This was a lie. *He would never do that, would he?*

He charged the gates with all of his strength, uninvited yet undaunted. Angry and suddenly unrepentant.

At the last second, just as he reached them, he heard the voice once more.

"We all must bear the burden of the choices we make."

He tried to pull back.

No! I won't do this, he thought, but it was too late. The gates flew open. He fell through them, into darkness.

#

Darkness and dirt.

After he'd woken in the small, muddy cavern, he'd scrabbled uselessly for what felt like hours, but it was all still darkness and dirt.

His fingertips scraped against something in the earth as he strived in the direction he hoped was up. Smooth and rounded, it came free as he pulled at it.

Caitlin? Why did that name spring to mind?

He placed it on the floor, and continued his journey to the surface.

Soon enough, he broke through to the world above.

Still, the darkness reigned.

Behind him was a headstone. Words were engraved upon it.

Fatum Circuli
'Fate Circles'

He leaned forward and laid the stuffed owl at its base.

He didn't want to die again, and hoped this time would be different.

redemption (n). The act or process of redeeming or of being redeemed.

21 Brooklands: next to Old Western, opposite the burnt out Red Lion
Carole Johnstone

We're rarely all in the house together. Not even to sleep. Whenever we are it's by accident; none of us mean to be. Families aren't supposed to like each other, are they? I don't see how they can. They save the worst of themselves for themselves because everyone needs a break from pretending. I wrote that in an essay last year and Mr Ingles gave it a B plus before making me stay behind after class to ask if I was alright. I said yes, why wouldn't I be?

I only came back at all to pick up some stuff before going back to Julie's: underwear, some food, more smokes, because she's been getting a bit pissy about stuff like that lately, and I like staying over at her bit. It's as shit as mine, as all the houses around here are – wooden two bedroom bungalows that started out as holiday chalets for rich people – but it's just her and her mum. And as far as families go, they've more energy for pretending. And they've got cable.

Mum caught me stealing the food because I rooted about in the fridge for ages – there wasn't much in there worth stealing – and I forgot about the beep it makes when you've left the door open too long. She didn't get up, she never gets up, but her thin scream forced me into the front room. She made me sit down and wait for Dad. I could've just left, I guess, it's not like she's ever going to be able to stop me, but I knew I'd pay for it later if I did.

Me and Mum don't speak. We must have done once, I suppose. On days when I'm pretending that she's not pretending, I blame her drowning lungs. I sat on the sofa, she sat in her armchair opposite Dad's, and some five o'clock quiz show buzzed and applauded between us. She watched me for a bit, but I didn't look at her because I don't do that anymore either. It's not just that she's all sucked in and wrinkled like a deflating balloon now, it's more than that. I'm scared to look. When she does speak to me at all, even in those two or three word breaths that rattle in their beginning and end, I can hear the bile in her. She hates me and I don't know why.

The back door bangs, creaks open – squeals open – and then bangs harder again as it shuts. We never use the front door; I don't even know if it works. The back door you could hear working from three or four streets away. I think it's Dad, but it isn't, and I'm nearly disappointed. A stay of execution isn't much better. Sometimes it's worse.

It's Wendy, which is nearly as bad. "Hey, Mum. Where's Dad?"

A dry and rustling shrug as familiar as bad breathing.

Wendy tuts. "Pub then, shit. Shit!"

Silence apart from the applause, and then, "Thought you was... stayin... with Mick to–"

"Well I fucking was, but his shitheap got a flat on the Sands and we need a spare." Wendy comes into the front room, stands in the middle of it. "Think Dad's got a spare?"

Mum swallows hard. It's a dry, noisy click. "Might

have." Mum doesn't like Wendy much more than me I don't think, but it's enough to speak to her. It's enough to say *might have* when we all know that even if he does Wendy won't be getting it.

The door bangs open, bangs shut. Mick's heavy footsteps fill the quiet and then his bulk fills the doorway. He winks, he grins, scratches at the big black tattoo on his shoulder. "Evening ladies. Where's the man of the house then?"

Wendy tosses him a look. Her hands stay on her hips. "Pub."

He comes in and sits on the arm of the sofa furthest from me. Grins. "Haven't seen you here in a bit, gel. What's up?"

I'm grateful that someone is finally looking at me, but not enough to answer.

"She's waitin... for her dad."

"Oh yeah?" Another wink, another grin. "What you done then, gel?"

"She'll have been stealing," Wendy says. "That what you've been doing?" She stays in the middle of the front room, shaking her ugly hair like a prize stallion, not even looking down on me because that would mean looking. Wendy calls herself a hairdresser, but all she does is put rollers in cauliflower heads in the back room of Bobby's Bingo. Mick's a drug dealer but everyone pretends he's a fisherman.

"I was just getting food out the fucking fridge," I mutter.

"Stealing it more like," Wendy says.

Can you steal food out of the fridge in the house

you live in? It doesn't matter that I was doing exactly that, not really.

Mick gets up. "Jimmy's not goin' to give us a tyre, Wends. C'mon, I'll pick one up tomorrow."

"And how are we going to get back to yours, eh? If you think I'm walkin' back through this estate in the middle of the fucking night, you're thicker than you look. I keep tellin' you to sell that shitheap for scrap and buy something that'll actually go. It's not like you don't have the money, Mick."

"The Baron is not a fucking shitheap. And it wasn't a fucking flat. You leave anythin' on the Broadway more than five minutes these days and it's nicked, fucked or slashed dependin' on the weather." He laughs like this is the funniest thing he's ever said.

I believe him though. It probably wasn't a flat. It isn't the middle of the night either; it's five p.m. But the Baron is a shitheap. Occasionally Wendy has to be right about something.

The back door bangs, screams open, bangs again. We all hold our breath, Mick included – in that we have about as much choice as Mum does.

Dad takes a long time getting to the front room; I hear him swear at the kitchen table when he walks into it. "Ah, what the fuck is all this? What the fuck you all doin' here?"

Like I said, we're rarely all in the house together, and whenever we are none of us mean to be. None of us want to be.

"Mick got a flat on the Sands, Dad. You got a spare that–"

"It wasn't a fuckin' flat, Wendy, Christ! You know

what the Broadway's like, Jimmy. Some bastard–"

Dad staggers through the door, past Wendy and into his beat up armchair. I can smell him: lager, sweat, chilli and the cold. When I get brave enough to look up, I'm relieved that his red-faced, thin-lipped rage is only for Mick.

"Fuck off, Michael Whitney. If someone did for you or your fuckin' beat up Beamer, lit up red as the fuckin sky at night, then it's for good fuckin' reason." He closes one eye, but its neighbour stays half open. "Fuck off out my house."

Dad's like all the olds around here: he doesn't care that he lives in England's povviest town; he revels in it. Mr Ingles calls it the Indices of Multiple Deprivation. He showed us a spreadsheet once with entries for income, employment, health, disability, crime and living standards. Of nearly thirty three thousand neighbourhoods, we were (in his words, and with one of his sad chuckles) literally streets ahead. Dad doesn't see it that way. When they tried to bulldoze the chalets before I was born, he went to court with all the other residents and won. I think it's the only thing he's proud of. I can't ever remember a time when any of the shops on the Broadway were anything more than shuttered, graffitied spaces with names I can't read, or when a new burnt out anything made me stop and look, or a winter where our wooden houses didn't flood; our walls are patterned with varying tidemarks and Mum knows the year of every one of them. Dad's still proud of it all. He calls it self reliance. But he needs a lot of drink to say so.

"Dad, we need a spare."

He hauls himself out of his armchair. "Well, you ain't gettin' one. Fuck off, the lot of you." He looks at me then, his still awake eye getting wider. "What's she done?"

I hear the louder hiss of Mum's oxygen cylinder when she turns it up; I can imagine the rise of the bobbing red ball inside its gauge. "She was... stealing food... for the... Martins."

"I wasn't!" My hands are angry fists until Dad starts coming towards me; I have to let them go so that I can try to get away. "I wasn't. Dad, I wasn't!"

His shadow makes me cringe and I stop trying to get up. He's too drunk to hit me right, but he still gets that soft spot just below my temple and my teeth rattle together, trapping my tongue. I make a stupid sound, like a dog that's been kicked in the ribs, and then I put my hands up in time to protect myself from the next punch. Dad's lost interest anyway; he backs up, staggering again on his way back to his armchair.

I cough, spit and it comes out red.

"Ugh," Wendy says, still not really looking.

When no one else says anything at all, I get up and run out the front room, around the narrow bend of hall and then into the bathroom. I lean over the sink and spit red again before rinsing out my mouth. I'm examining my tongue in the mirror, trying to find the bite that I've made, when Mick comes in. He looks at my reflection and winks. Grins.

"Seems a shame to waste the opportunity."

I elbow him in the chest when he tries to touch me; when his cold hands grab at my waist, when his fingers pinch at my nipples.

"C'mon, Suse, don't be a bitch about it."

His hands slide up inside my T-shirt. I bite down on my swollen tongue again. Our faces look ugly in the mirror, so I stop looking. I try to push him off, try to reach the door, but he follows too fast, never letting go of my shirt, pushing me back against the tiles. His breath is hot, the bristles of his stubble spiky, his tongue hard, erect.

"You taste good."

I taste of blood.

He yanks down my jeans without undoing them and then my knickers, kicking my feet apart, making me grab hold of him for balance. He thrusts one finger inside me, then two.

"God, you're always so ready." He says it like the idea revolts him, but he's still smiling. Still grinning. He starts moving his fingers in and out, fast then faster. "You like that, don't you, bitch?"

I don't want to, but I do. I don't want to like the words he uses and the way he always uses them, but I do. Maybe it's because I've watched him for years from my bedroom window, washing down cars in the street, his shirt tucked into his back pocket, his tattoo black against the white of his skin. It's more than that, I know. It's because he's with my sister.

The tiles are cold, cold against my shoulder blades and back as he shoves into me. He never uses a condom, and I never ask him to. I try not to cry out; I try not to wonder where everyone else thinks he's gone. I try not to listen to the filth that he hisses into my ear.

He never waits for me to come. Maybe he doesn't

want me to. If it's a consideration at all. And maybe I'd like myself a little more if I didn't. But I do. Almost every time.

Mr Ingles sometimes lends me books on the sly. He says I'm the only one in any of his classes that could make it out of this town. They're not the books the school makes us read. They're just as old, just as hard to read, but the difference is I want to. Some of them are pretty dirty, but the people in those books don't have pricks or cocks or gashes or cunts. They don't come, or worse *cum*. They spend. It's a far better word for it. As if every one of my ugly and violent orgasms has cost me something.

This time it doesn't cost me anything at all. Or Mick. Because the lights go out.

He lets me go straightaway, swearing when he pulls out of me, still swearing when he zips up his jeans. I try to do the same but I'm shivering in the sudden cold, sweat drying to an itch.

"C'mon, Suse! You decent?"

I don't answer him. I can already hear Wendy shouting his name.

"C'mon to fuck, Suse. Right, I'm goin' first, alright?" He pushes me back against the tiles. "Wait a few minutes, alright? Alright?"

"Alright."

I hear him swear a bit more as he feels his way towards the door; hear the lock pop, the door creak open, letting in no new light at all, and then close again behind him. I stand shivering in the dark, the tiles still cold against my back, but while they're still there I know where I am. I start counting in my head but soon give up. I can hear them all still in the front room, swearing, shouting. No one is shouting for me.

I don't like the dark. I've never liked the dark. Wendy loves it, maybe because it was her right hand man when we were kids. But even when she was torturing me she never really got it. It's not what's hiding in the dark that scares me. It's just the dark. It makes everything small. It's heavy and thick and it's all you can see, all you can breathe. It makes a bathroom feel like a coffin.

I run out into the hall too quick and bounce off the corner of the front room wall, banging my head, my left shoulder. It hurts, but not enough to make me stop. The hall feels as small as the bathroom. Smaller. I grope my way along the wall, following the sounds of my furious family. When my fingernails stick inside the hinge of the front room door, I hiss, bringing them up to my sore mouth, and then I stumble in, nearly crying with relief.

Wendy is still standing in the middle of the room. She's holding up a fake Zippo that blows left and right in hidden draughts, pulling ugly at her face. Dad's swearing so much I don't need to see him to know that he's still in his beat up armchair.

"Think the lights are out on the whole street," Mick says, and I hear the squeak of his arm against the window. "Which ones still got folk in 'em, Jimmy?"

Dad belches and swears some more. Not many, is the answer. The Old Lion pub across from us was torched nearly three years ago because of all the drug dealing. Dad hates junkies and flash gits like Mick, but he hated losing his local more. Now he has to go to The Mermaid, which is nearly on the front. More than half of the houses on our street are boarded shut with graffitied steel; half again are as burnt out as the Lion; of the remaining three, only one is anywhere near to us. I don't know what happened to most of our neighbours – where they went before or after their houses were destroyed. They just go. People do that all the time. They just up and go.

"Fat Bob's is two houses left," I say.

Another squeak. "Can't fuckin' see. Might be out too."

"Christ, Mick," Wendy snaps. "Why d'you have to get a fucking flat? I hate this place!" The last part comes out as a screech, which only stops when we all hear the nasty creak of Dad's armchair.

"Well fuck off then, gel. Fuck right off. No one here'll be stoppin' you."

Wendy doesn't move, but she looks over at me. I wonder what she sees. To me, she looks like a tall-booted mannequin glowing orange. I'm probably just a shadow.

"Think I can see lights out on Breckfield," Mick says. "Nothin' closer."

We've never had pavements or street lights on Brooklands, but we're luckier than most. The council stopped repairing a lot of the roads a few years back and they're either narrow dirt tracks or potholed and cracked tarmac. Some of the chalets out on the Flats don't even have mains sewerage.

Mick chuckles, his voice getting closer. "You pay the electric, Jimmy?"

"We're on a fuckin' meter, wise guy," Dad says,

and if I was Wendy I'd have shut my lighter, because his voice is turning back into the one that wants to hit someone.

No one says anything for a bit. I think about trying to phone Julie even though the signal's always crap, but then remember I've no credit. We don't have a landline either; kids kept chucking tied trainers over the wires, and when that got dull, they just knocked the poles down. Dad said he'd rather spend the line rental down the pub.

When no one says anything for even longer, it gets a little spooky. I'm dead aware of the dark of the hall pushing at my back, so I creep into the front room a bit more, even if that means I don't have anything to hold onto anymore. I can hear Wendy and Dad and Mick breathing; I can hear Mum trying to. The hiss of her oxygen cylinder is the loudest of all.

I jump when Mick says: "You got any candles, Jeanie?" So does Dad, I think, because I hear a thud in his corner and then a curse.

"No... candles."

"Right well, we can't just sit in the fuckin' dark. What about makin' a fire? You still got that old barbecue out back, Jimmy?"

I don't want Mick to go out back. Don't want that at all. I start feeling my way closer to his voice, but it's harder to follow than I thought it would be.

"You ain't makin' no fire in my fuckin' house, Mick."

"Right, so what, we do just all sit in the fuckin' dark then? You know no cunt's goin' to jump in their van and nip down here to fix whatever the fuck's gone wrong, right?"

"We could... go... to bed."

"It's dinner-fucking-time!" Mick bellows, and I'm surprised to remember that he's right. It doesn't feel like dinner-fucking-time. The dark is so absolute it might as well be the middle of the night.

I'm still shuffling towards Mick's voice – it's easier now he's shouting – when Wendy sparks up her lighter again, so close to my face that I can feel its heat enough to shriek.

"What the fuck're you doing?" She's looking at me now, but even though she's the only thing I can see, I don't look back.

"Trying to sit down."

She waves the fake Zippo high enough to expose the angry shadow of Mick near to the far end of the sofa. I grope for the closer edge of it and sit down. I hear rather than feel Mick doing the same; we're too far away.

"This is the third fuckin' world right here," he mutters, but maybe not loud enough for Dad to hear him.

If this was one of those crap TV movies Mum watches on Channel Five every afternoon, we'd be minutes away from huddling close around Wendy's fake Zippo; Mum and Dad sharing forgotten memories from our childhoods; Mick proposing to Wendy or professing undying love for me like in Mr Ingles' books; all of us realising one way or another that we love each other really. I'm not holding my breath, and Mum couldn't even if she wanted to.

It's just so quiet, that's what I don't like the most.

Worse than even the dark. Maybe. Usually the lights and those quiz shows hide the outside enough I forget it's there. The real outside, I mean. I forget we're nearly on our own now.

The worst day was the one when I realised Old Western had gone. He'd lived next door to us all my life. Even Dad liked him. On the last Friday of every month he'd bring Mum daisies and Wendy and me sweeties and Dad a bottle of white rum that they'd both drink out back or in the front room depending on the weather. He used to own the whelk and jellied eel shop on the promenade, and when he lost that he sold them door to door instead. Dad said he got good rates from the shore boats and he was a stand up fella because he always passed them on. Unlike Mick, Old Western really had been a fisherman once.

His house didn't get torched. A few days after he'd gone, some men in a white van came and put in the steel shutters and doors instead. A few days after that a letter came through the back door addressed to me. I stuffed it in my bag and waited to get to school to read it. I went into the toilets at morning break. There was nothing inside the envelope except a crumpled up bit of paper. In printed black letters:

19 Brooklands: next to Chappels, opposite the burnt out Red Lion

And then underneath that, in Old Western's scribble: Careful of the Dark Susie x

After I'd read it, I flushed it and the envelope down the toilet because I was still angry that he'd gone. Or probably that he could. They got stuck; I could still see the black print even when the toilet started filling up to the top, spilling dirty water onto the tiles.

A few days after that the graffiti started. Everyone knew Old Western, so his was a popular spot. Dad went out on a Sunday and spent two hours cleaning a big red-painted PEEDO off Old Western's porch, because he said it was the only one that wasn't true.

When Wendy suddenly shrieks, I nearly shriek myself. I nearly stand up; I nearly lunge towards Mick.

"What the fuck, Wends?" Mick growls.

"Mick?"

I can hear her moving and moving quick. I feel the cool whisper of her body as it passes near to me; hear the gassy burst of her fake Zippo. I still flinch from the light and her lunging face.

"What is your problem, Suse? What–"

"Jesus H Christ," Dad mutters, and I can tell by his voice he's been sleeping.

"You think it's fucking funny, Suse?" Wendy's face throws even uglier shadows. "You think it's funny to creep up behind me in the dark, tryin' to fucking scare the shit out of me?"

Like she used to, I think. But I can tell from her face that she knows it wasn't me. I haven't moved since I sat down.

She looks back over both shoulders, but doesn't move the flame from my face. "If it wasn't Mick it was you!"

I wonder why she thought it was Mick before she thought it was me, and then I see her free hand and forearm clamped hard across her breasts. We both hear movement in the corner where Mum sits at the same time. Wendy spins around, shooting out her lighter arm towards it.

"There's... someone... here."

None of us move. I can hear Mum's breathing getting faster, wheezier. I can hear the loud hiss of her oxygen because no one else is making any kind of noise at all now.

"There's someone here... someone here someone–"

Her oxygen cuts out like she's shut off the valve. That only ever happens when the district nurse needs to change an empty cylinder for a new one. The weird silence frightens me even then – now it stands up the hairs on the back of my neck and scalp in bunches.

Mum doesn't try to say anything else, which is worse. I stare at Wendy's drunk flame, and then I try to stare past it towards Mum's dark corner. I think I hear something – a muffled something – and even though I keep trying to hear whatever it is, I want Dad or Mick or Wendy to start shouting and swearing so I can give it up.

Finally, it stops. That muffled nothing becomes complete nothing. I can't hear anything at all.

"Jeanie?" Dad. The creak of his beat up armchair. "Jean?"

I screw my eyes shut black. Open them. Black.

Wendy shrieks again when something thuds without echo on the carpet. I watch her flame drop down to the floor, exposing her scuffed leather boots. Exposing the thrown armchair cushion less than two feet away from them. She doesn't move; the fake

Zippo doesn't move. The cushion was a Christmas present to Mum. I made it in Home Ec. three years ago. Wendy's light shakes over the little stone cottage next to a silver rope of river.

And then I can't see either anymore. Only dark. Wendy shrieks again and her fake Zippo flies in a feeble arc: up and then down. It goes out.

I hear a little thud, a whimper. The creak of Dad's beat up armchair again, his curse – but it's pitched high and alien – and then Mick's better one and the feel of moving air, maybe his fist. Another thud. I'm still on the sofa, but I've started trying to climb up towards the back of it, my sore fingers gripping at its spine.

Someone taps hard on the shoulder that I banged into the wall. It sends shocks down my arm and into my fingers. I let go my right hand and my body spins round. I stare up into the dark. All I see is the dark.

I get up. My thighs are shaking. When I step away from the sofa, I immediately forget where I am. Where the door is. A hand drops onto my good shoulder. It's heavy. I feel the weight of someone behind me, though they don't make any kind of sound at all. They walk me forwards a few feet. Another hand drops onto my bad shoulder. Both start pressing down hard and I drop to my knees before I get that I'm supposed to. I hear another too close sound – a whimper – and then realise that it's me. The hands disappear.

I'm breathing so hard that it takes a while for me to realise that I'm not the only one doing it. I reach out – flail out – and hit Wendy's leather jacket on my left;

Mick's bare arm on my right. I can smell Dad dead ahead: lager, sweat, chilli and the cold. And something else – something he's never smelled of before.

I whimper. Wendy whimpers. Mick and Dad make no sound at all. I don't need light to see us kneeling on the front room floor, facing one another inside a tight square. I can feel the heavy air behind us move, pressing us closer. I can feel it pace around us like a restless lion. Black inside black.

Minutes pass like this. None of us move; none of us speak. The owner of the hands paces faster, even though I can't see him, can't hear him.

Finally Dad clears his throat. "You got the wrong house."

Silence.

I hear him shift his knees; I smell his sour breath. "I own this shithole outright, fellas, so if you're them come lookin' for back rent, you got the wrong fuckin' house."

It's not fellas though; I can tell Dad knows that as well as me. It's not even fella.

There's a sudden scuffle where Dad is. I hear him start to curse and then his voice doesn't so much stop as run out. It gurgles. Wendy screams; I hear the slap of skin against skin and only realise it's her palm against her mouth when her scream muffles, chokes. There's a new smell. It's like the pork sides Dad sometimes brings back from The Mermaid. Another thud – a big one. I only realise that my hand is covering my mouth too when I try to breathe and can't.

I need to get up. My crotch is still damp. My knickers are twisted inside my jeans, cutting into my groin hard enough to give my left leg pins and needles. "Mick?" I whisper, looking right. "Wendy?" Left.

They don't answer. I know they're there: I can hear them, feel them, but they're too afraid to answer me, even if they know that it doesn't matter; even if they know that the someone in here with us knows exactly where we are. Where he put us.

I feel a whisper of cool air at the back of my neck, moving left to right. Towards Mick.

"Fuck this." Mick gets up – I feel it in a fast whoosh of coppery air to my right and then faster still in front of me. I start trying to get up too, but my dead left leg drops me onto all fours. Wendy starts screaming for Mick to take her too, but I know he won't. She pushes against me as she struggles to get back onto her feet – the someone kicks her hard enough that she falls forward into me instead, sending us both sprawling onto the carpet. It's wet. It smells.

Mick makes it as far as the kitchen, maybe even the back door. His scream is far away, but I can hear the dismay in it before the horror gets louder. And then nothing. More silence.

Wendy is sobbing when the someone comes back. We still can't hear him, can't see him. And now we can't even feel him. But he's still here. He's here.

Would this be when Wendy and I hug and clutch at each other like we never did when we were kids? Is this when we realise that there are worse things than each other? I grab for her when she gets up; I scream for her, because my leg still won't work and she's my big sister whether she wants to be or not. I remember the books Mr Ingles gave me; I remember him telling me that family is the worst and best of everything – that it's why we exist at all.

Wendy screeches and falls back against me again, scrabbling for a hold of my sweaty cold skin. I shoot out my good arm and it slides through the hot slick wet of her chest. I don't scream. I don't take my hand away. Instead, I half kneel, my heels digging into my numb bum, my free hand drawing into a fist. I feel Wendy die: she runs over my good hand in hot hiccups. I hear her die in frothy breaths that are still trying to scream.

After, I don't try to get up because there's no point. I can't smell pork sides anymore. Just blood. I know the someone is still in here with me. Prowling around the front room. And I don't much care. We're despicable, is that it? Is that why? If it is, then it's a worse reason than no reason at all. It's worse than jacked up kids knocking down telegraph poles; worse than the olds setting fire to everything they hate; worse than drunks beating up their useless wives and children, or jealousy spent through ugly sex, or councils making fancy spreadsheets and calling dirtshit poor something no one else can pronounce. Worse than the good ones jumping ship and leaving the rest of us behind. Worse than teachers pretending that there's something else, something better. *Somewhere* else.

Eventually, I lean back, wiping Wendy on my jeans. My hands are still shaking, but it's not because

I'm scared. Not anymore. Even I can see that despicable people can only breed despicable people. It's no reason at all.

I reach out my palms so I can stand, and my fingers brush against metal. Wendy's fake Zippo. I pick it up. It feels very cold. I thumb the wheel once, twice; the second time it sparks but doesn't take. I stand up slowly. Swallow. The third turn bursts into bright light. I hold it up and away from me. Dad and Wendy are sprawled on the carpet: Dad on his back, his neck a red smile; Wendy on her side, still letting out hiccups of blood. Her skin is pulled back in one big flap, and I think there's the white of her ribs inside it. I can see the shadowed, open-mouthed gape of Mum in her armchair. There's no blood on her at all.

I turn the light towards the front room door and the someone scuttles across it on all fours. I balk before remembering that I'm not scared. I step around Wendy, being careful not to stand on her outstretched fingers. I finally hear a sound, but it's not one I like. My imagination thinks it's a chuckle, but it didn't sound like one.

I creep towards the door, mainly because I'm being allowed to. Is it because I'm not as despicable? Maybe the someone doesn't know about Mick or all the stealing. I hold the lighter high and out, and it makes me feel safer even if it only exposes me and more shadows; even if it only makes the dark around it darker. It feels like a torch, a priest's cross. I feel for the door's edge with shaking fingers. I step into the hall.

I smell the petrol before I feel it splash against my

skin. I've flung the lighter forwards into the kitchen before I start screaming. It lands on its side on the lino, flame hissing bigger, exposing Mick's curled up body against the kitchen unit under the sink, pulling his face about. His cut out eye dangling against his cheek.

I forget that I shouldn't be screaming. I forget that I'm not scared anymore. And then the petrol hits my face like it's been thrown from a bucket and I gag instead of scream, trying to turn my body away. More petrol hits my shoulders, my back. Another throw soaks my jeans, sucking them in against my shaking legs. The stink is bad – the stink is terrible – but the threat of it is worse.

I don't try to run back into the front room because I don't want to die with my dead family, and I don't run down the hall towards the bedrooms because I don't want to die anywhere else. I don't run towards the front porch because the door is always locked and I don't know where the keys are. My only escape route is through the kitchen and the back door, but the still lit fake Zippo is there, spitting and hissing, barring my way. And I know – I *know* – that the someone is there too.

I cough, try not to choke. Try not to cry. I edge my way into the kitchen, my soggy feet squeaking on the lino. The fake Zippo is lying right in the centre of the room and it's not a big room. I pretend that it's my only enemy because it might as well be.

A couple of feet in and my hip bangs hard against the kitchen table, making me shriek. I grab for its edges with my sore fingers, never taking my eyes off that hissing flame. The table pushes me out towards it, but I let myself get no closer than I have to, even though I just want to run – to take my chances and run for the kitchen door and the back door a few feet past it. I don't. I'm too terrified of what it'll feel like to go up like a bonfire. I know it'll hurt a lot worse than having my oxygen cut off or my throat slashed into a smile.

I try not to look at Mick either as I keep on edging towards the door, and that's easier to do, even though the fake Zippo keeps catching the dangle of his eyeball, making me think that it's still moving.

The kitchen door is very light – I don't even think it's proper wood – when I hit it with my shoulder, it starts swinging shut. I grab for it with a nearly quiet shriek, yanking it back too hard, banging it off the table. I make my hands into fists and stop its backswing with my foot. The fake Zippo is now far enough away that I can move out towards the space that the open kitchen door has left. The back door is less than two feet away.

The someone stands up. Like he's been crouching on all fours inside the kitchen doorway, waiting for me to think that he's gone. I still can't see him, but I can hear him in a slow whoosh of air rising up from the lino. And I can feel him. He doesn't breathe, he doesn't sweat. But he's there. Inches away.

Two hands punch against my chest, staggering me back into the kitchen. Towards Mick. Towards the fake Zippo.

"No, please. Nopleasenopleaseplease."

He stops pushing long enough for me to run as far

away from him and the fake Zippo as I can without giving up any more ground. I smack hard into the kitchen table again, doubling myself over it, whacking my chin against its top, my teeth cracking together, singing high inside my head. I spit what tastes like more blood, and then turn around.

The light from the fake Zippo has gone. I don't know if it's because it's really gone or because he's standing between me and it. I try to listen for its hiss, but all I can hear is my own breathing and the blood rushing through my ears.

And then I hear a muted thump, maybe a kick. A groan. I bite down on my swollen tongue again. The groan is Mick. Mick isn't dead.

Another kick. Another louder groan. *Mick isn't dead.*

I imagine eyes looking at me in the dark. My heart kind of stops, and then starts banging too hard and too fast, making me feel sick again. I suddenly realise I'm being offered a choice. Mick and me. Or just me. In Mr Ingles' books, the main character always knows what to do. In the end, they know what is the right thing to do. I don't. And not just because the petrol and the fear and my heart are making me feel sick and a bit dizzy. Not just because if one of them was still going to be alive, I'd want it to be Mick.

If the someone is a vigilante like the olds down the Mermaid and Bobby's Bingo, he wants me to leave Mick behind. But if he's the Devil like in Paradise Lost, and God is waiting to see what I'll do, then I'm supposed to take Mick with me. And if he's just a man like Dad said – a man come to get money or his kicks

– then I'm fucked whatever I do. But he's not just a man. I know that at least.

A finger – I think a finger – traces the left tendon of my neck, down to my collarbone where it digs in. I hear the raspy turn of the fake Zippo's wheel. I see its brief spark inches from my face. And as far as I care, it takes away my choice.

I turn and run. I run into and then around the kitchen's flapping door, my wet feet skidding on the lino as I grab for the doorframe, bending back my nails. My sore fingers scream. The back door feels cold against my skin. I scrabble for the handle even as I hear Mick's groans getting louder, more awake. For a few seconds I think that it's all a lie – that the door is locked; that I never had any kind of choice at all – and then the back door gives in its usual bang, and cold briny air rushes in, pushing me backwards.

Not for long. I lunge through the new space, ignoring the door's stupid loud creak. I'm already down the steps, around the house and into the street when I hear the bigger bang as it shuts again. Mick screams high and long, but I pretend it's the wind. It could be – the wind off the Sands is as sharp as a bitch's tongue, Dad says.

I stop running when I reach what I think is the middle of the street. I stand shivering instead. There are no lights anywhere in Brooklands. I look right, where I know the black skeleton of the Red Lion is, but I don't go towards it. I look in the direction of Fat Bob's chalet, but I don't want to go there either. If I squint, I can see the lights that Mick saw out on Breckfield, but that's far too far away. I look back at the dark of my house.

I should be running, I know that. But I can't. This is my home, and it's surprisingly hard to leave it. I don't know what it was all for – what it *is* all for. Am I safe? And if I am, what do I do? Where do I go? What do I say?

I'm still shaking so hard that my knees keep nearly giving way, pushing my bum out, making me flail about for blind balance. I can smell the sea, which should be impossible because I'm still covered in petrol and Wendy's blood – but I can smell it all the same. I can even hear the crash of waves out on the Sands.

He comes out through the back door. It doesn't bang or creak open. It shuts with a tiny snick that I still hear. Over the wind, the waves, the shaking chatter of my teeth, the stutter of my breath.

I imagine eyes looking at me in the dark again. I imagine that dark sucking close until nothing else is left between us. I push my sore tongue against my incisors.

A hand grabs at my wrist, bringing it up in front of my chest. Fingers prise mine open and something crinkles inside my palm. When my fingers are forced shut, the round feel of it scratches at my skin.

I feel a breath that isn't a breath. A chuckle that isn't a chuckle. A threat that isn't even a whispered word. And then my fist is let go – dropped like a stone against my sore thigh.

I close my eyes because they won't stop watering. I take one breath and then another.

"Go away." But I don't think I say it. And no one is

there to hear me even if I do.

He's gone.

I stand in the middle of Brooklands for a long time. Long enough for clouds to move inland, first spitting against my skin, and then beating down hard enough to echo inside the Red Lion's ribs and against steel shutters.

The sound wakes me up a bit. Or maybe it's because the worst of the petrol is washing away in the rain. I lift up my fist and let my fingers fall open. The paper doesn't crinkle so much now it's wet. I think of playing rock, paper, scissors with Old Western on the front porch as I peel it away from the rounder thing beneath.

I know what that thing is, of course. I let my numb fingers slide over its slick, bumpy surface for a second or two, and then I push it into my jeans pocket. I don't know why. Maybe because it belonged to Mick.

The paper is wet and getting wetter. I try to smooth it out, but I don't know why I'm bothering. I can't see it any more than I can see anything else. And I know what it says –I can *guess* what it says.

21 Brooklands: next to Old Western, opposite the burnt out Red Lion

I screw it into a ball between my palms, and my skin is now numb enough that it doesn't hurt at all. I throw it into the dark.

And I start walking back towards Julie's bit.

The River
Armand Rosamilia

Harlan heard the body before he saw it. Bloated with flies and critters, the cacophony echoed through the strip of forest that was left, keeping up with the fast-moving cars on the overpass ahead and the shallow river gurgling along its dying noise as the sun drained it drop by drop. *It's not the heat. It's the humidity*, his granny used to say to them. Harlan believed it, covered in sweat and now in no mood to go fishing before it became a mud hole.

The banks sloped down, wet and brownish black, into the water, the sun attacking spots it hadn't touched in decades. Momma said this was the worst drought in fifty years, but Harlan was only eleven and had no idea if she were right or just exaggerating like she was apt to do.

Harlan got as close to the muddy bank as he dared.

He didn't think she'd been dead long. She still had skin and hair and teeth, although her eye sockets were empty. Half submerged in the muck about twenty feet from the sloping bank, with a thick chain around her waist and threading up around her neck and down to her wrapped feet, she was jammed under a fallen tree branch as thick as Harlan's body. He glanced up at the whizzing cars and wondered if anyone could see her down here, if anyone had stopped or even noticed in their rush.

The flies were surrounding her in angry waves. The stench was strong but he didn't know if it was the body or just the muck of the river drying out.

Harlan felt sorry for the girl, whoever she was. His impulse was to slide down the bank and approach her, but he knew from watching Momma's television reality shows that you never messed with the crime scene. He suddenly felt very sad for the girl and began to cry.

#

Harlan wiped his muddy sneakers on the worn welcome mat outside the kitchen door, put his fishing pole against the house, and hoped lunch was ready. Most days Momma was in the living room, watching her stories, and he made himself a sandwich.

Not today.

"Hey, Son," his daddy said with a warm smile. He was seated at the kitchen table eating a ham and cheese sandwich, a cold glass of sweet tea in his hand.

Momma, beaming, put a napkin in front of her husband. "Harlan, honey, your daddy is back."

"For how long?" Harlan asked and refused to enter the kitchen. He hadn't seen this man in four years and now suddenly he was back and eating a sandwich.

"Forever, Son." His daddy pushed the chair next to him out with a foot. "Sit with your old man while I eat. Man, you got big, Harley."

"No one calls me that. My name is Harlan, or did you forget?"

His momma raised her hand as she wheeled on him. "You show some respect for your daddy and for an adult, do you hear me, young man?"

Harlan's daddy put a hand up before she could slap her son. "It's fine, I deserve that." He smiled again and took a sip from his sweet tea. "Come and sit with me, Son." His daddy glanced at his momma and she retreated to the living room.

Reluctantly Harlan obeyed, but pulled the chair as far away as he could. He remembered the beatings his momma would take from this man when drunk, and the last night before he stumbled out when he sliced Harlan with the broken beer bottle. Harlan rubbed his thumb against the scar as he stared at the man.

His daddy lost his smile for a second but recovered. "I'm really sorry about that, buddy. I was a different man back then." He took the last bite of his sandwich and talked around his food. "I swear to God I haven't had a drink in four years, and don't want to." He looked away and seemed to stare at the cheap painting on the wall. "I've learned so much and made peace with all my mistakes." He turned back to his son. "I know I have so much to prove to you, little man. And I intend to, trust me. Your momma is just happy I'm home; I know she's been struggling without me here. But you... you're just like me, boy, you need someone to prove to you they've changed. I intend to do that."

Harlan liked the words but knew enough about people already in his short life to remember the old man, drunk and raging around the kitchen, threatening to kill his momma.

"I'll tell you what: tomorrow we'll toss the ball around. When I left you were too young to get in a good game of catch, but now we can do all the things we missed. Can you ride a bike?"

"I don't have a bike."

"Well then the first thing I'm going to do when I get me a job is buy you one, a brand new bicycle and we'll go for rides together. How does that sound?"

Harlan smiled despite his reluctance to believe his daddy.

"We'll go into town and see a movie and get out of the heat, too. Wouldn't that be nice? I'm sure your momma would love to see a romantic comedy." He smiled at Harlan. "Sometimes, Son, you have to watch a Jennifer Aniston movie to keep on the good side of a woman. That's a lesson for you, right there. No more bad lessons from your old man, got it? I'm only going to teach you the proper things to do in life. Like treating women with respect, or working hard for what you want instead of trying to take it. I've been given a second chance with you and your momma and I won't ruin it this time."

"Can we get a swimming pool?" Harlan asked.

"Sure. It might be a small one but it will keep you cool with this godawful heat."

Harlan thought of the girl in the river again but didn't want to say anything just yet. He knew he should say something, especially to an adult, and if it was just momma here he would have told her the whole story as soon as he came home. But he had no connection to this smiling man sitting at the table with him, drinking sweet tea instead of beer. "The river is almost dried up," he finally said.

The anger on his daddy's face was sudden but familiar. He pointed a meaty finger at Harlan as he pushed back from the table, scraping the chair across the linoleum. "Stay away from that river, got it? There's nothing there for you." He took two steps back and leaned against the refrigerator, looking deflated. He put on a smile even though his eyes looked fevered. "First thing tomorrow morning I'm going into town to find a job and buy you a swimming pool so we don't have to worry about this heat or the river again. How does that sound, little man?"

#

Harlan spent the next three days in his new pool. A small blue plastic cut-out with smiling octopi and grinning fish. If he got into the fetal position he could get half of his entire body underwater, one eye skimming the water line and the other underwater and watching his plastic toys floating.

"Momma, wanna swim in my pool?" he called to her as she hung wet clothes on the line. "I'm getting bored."

"Go find some of your friends, Harlan. When Daddy comes home from work he said he'd have another present for you so don't go far."

Daddy had gotten a job at the sawmill up the river and was working twelve hour shifts. Since his return he'd fixed the squeaking board on the porch, the back porch light, the toilet that wouldn't stop running and the dishwasher.

Harlan was also positive they were doing grownup things at night that he didn't want to know about, and he put his pillow over his ears to keep the groaning noises out of his head. Even now, sitting in the warm water of the pool, he tried to think of something else, anything else...

"Stay away from the river," his momma was saying as she hung his white underwear on the line. He hated when she hung his tighty whities.

"The river?" he asked, her words hitting him. In all the excitement of the pool and a new baseball mitt and Daddy being home and spending time with him, he'd forgotten about the river and the girl.

"Daddy said they found a dead girl in the river near the sawmill the other day and it's dangerous to go down there, with the drought and the muck like quicksand. Poor girl drowned in a foot of water."

"Was it in the paper?" Harlan asked as he jumped out of the pool, his skin immediately drying in the nearly hundred degree heat. If she were found he wanted to know who she was. Harlan felt guilty he'd already forgotten about the girl and all it took was a plastic swimming pool.

His momma shrugged her shoulders. "I don't know about the papers, Harlan. Your daddy told me."

Harlan went inside without another word to get dressed. Something wasn't right, and he wanted to check it out. The girl was nowhere near the sawmill, which was set at least four miles upriver. Daddy was lying.

#

She was there like the other day, covered in mud and sunken up to her chest now. She'd moved and was now facing directly at him but hidden under the log.

Harlan was sure no one from the overpass would be able to see her, even if they stopped their car, got out and hung over the safety rail.

He wondered why his daddy had lied to him and what he had to do with this poor girl chained up and tossed in the river like garbage. Harlan began to cry and could imagine feeling her pain as she was forced here, the chains strewn across not only her body but her very soul, binding the flesh and the spirit together for all eternity in this watery grave.

She had a small voice, she was only fifteen but worldly, a wanderer and runaway from Jacksonville, just wanted to escape the beatings from her daddy and her absent momma, the men who came to her in the night and paid her daddy lots of money she never saw, the things hurting her, all of them breaking her, ripping her apart and trying to find her soul but she wouldn't give it to them, wouldn't stop fighting, had to flee, had to escape and get as far away as the stolen money from Daddy's wallet would get her, a Greyhound bus and then hitchhiking, stopping on the overpass and wanting to drink from the cool river, it looked so inviting, she was so thirsty, so very thirsty...

A car overhead beeped its horn and Harlan stopped moving. He was ankle deep in muck, only ten feet from her now. Her barren eye sockets were dark, too black, especially with the sun beating down on them. The flies took flight in an angry swarm and Harlan turned and ran away, slipping and sliding in the brown slop as he moved.

\#

His daddy was waiting on the back porch, a brand new bicycle with a red bow on its handlebars. Momma, excited and dancing from foot to foot, squealed when Harlan came into view, covered in mud.

Daddy's smile dropped and he turned to his wife. "Go inside. I need to talk to Harlan first. Alone. Go."

She obeyed and Daddy rushed to Harlan in a run, getting in front of him. "Where have you been?"

Harlan was scared and wanted the safety of his mother. He just wanted to take a cold shower, work the grime off of his body. He felt dirty not only physically but down to his soul. And he was mad as he looked at his daddy now, who was trying to buy his silence with bikes and pools.

"You know where I've been."

His daddy grabbed him by the arm as he tried to pass and squeezed, fingers digging into Harlan's skin. "I told you to stay away from the river."

"Why did you lie to Momma?" Harlan asked, trying in vain to get free.

"What?" His father looked confused for a second but didn't release his grip. "I told her that so she'd keep an eye on you and keep you away from the river."

"And make me think she was found?"

His daddy's eyes lit up. "You don't know anything, and you're not going to tell anyone about her. Is that understood?" He leaned into Harlan. "If you tell your momma, after all I've been through these last four years, I will hurt her." Spittle formed at the corners of his mouth. "I will drown your momma in that river. Do you understand?"

#

"You haven't eaten your breakfast, Harlan," his momma said to him. "Did you sleep well?"

Harlan put on a fake smile as his daddy came into the kitchen and kissed his momma, glancing at Harlan and winking at him before sitting down.

"You look tired," his daddy said.

"That's what I just said to him." A steaming cup of coffee and a plate of scrambled eggs and sausage were put before Harlan's daddy. His momma smiled. "I'm so happy to have both my boys here again. These have been the happiest couple weeks of my life, honest to God."

"Mine as well. Glad to be back." His daddy stuck a fork into his eggs and held it in front of his mouth before looking at his son. "Glad we're one big happy family. How has your last week been, Son? Riding your bike?"

Harlan's last week had been hell. Whenever he closed his eyes he could see her and feel her pain. In his dreams she called him into the muck to save her but with each step he sunk deeper and deeper, clawing and scratching to reach her and release her from the chains and her prison. She'd be free and maybe then his conscience would then let him sleep, but he could never reach her. She sank deeper into the mud and with every inch he moved she got two inches farther away.

The touch of his daddy's hand on his shoulder made him jump.

His momma sat down at the table with her own

coffee and breakfast but frowned. "Are you sure you're alright, Harlan?"

Harlan stared at his daddy's face and smiled. "I'm fine. I'm going to ride the bike today. Can you bring home a football after work today?"

His daddy smiled and tousled his hair. "Of course I'll bring home a football. The day boss says I'm a fast learner and I'll be up for a raise soon. Might even be a foreman myself in another year. Then I'll buy you whatever you want."

#

It had started to rain, a light mist draping gray clouds. Harlan woke from another of the nightmares and knew what needed to be done. By the time he dressed and was out the door, it had started to come down harder. Harlan hopped on his bicycle and was halfway down the driveway before the porch light came on behind him. He didn't stop, pedaling as fast as he could.

If it rained as hard and steady as it was right now, the river would fill and rise within an hour and she'd be gone. Back under the water, back hidden forever. What his daddy had done would be erased, all evidence washed away. Harlan should have gone to the police or told another adult what happened.

As he stopped his bike and dismounted at the edge of the banks he could hear the noise of the river as it began moving, the rain filling in the pools and dried cracked earth.

She was there, her head just above the water, straining to stretch her neck so Harlan could find her.

She was scared, she was drowning, she needed to be unchained and dragged from the river before she was gone again, submerged and trapped in her mud prison, and she called Harlan to her.

Harlan heard the call from his panicked father on the riverbank but it sounded so far away with the noise of the downpour as the sky opened up.

Harlan waded to her in water over his belt, bracing against the log and lifting her head as water splashed around them.

She smiled.

He saw his daddy, chained to the bottom of the log as the water subsided and dried and he called to the runaway girl to save him. But it was a trap and he was freed. Four years he'd been tricked into the prison, four years to think about what his life had become and the mistakes he'd made to his wife and only son.

Just as the girl was now freed, and she let the bubbling river carry her downstream, away from the poor little boy now trapped in the chains, and his familiar father, screaming from the riverbank.

God May Pity All Weak Hearts
Daniel I. Russell

July 15th 1905.

It was in the carriage that my doubts consumed me, and as the recently lit streetlamps passed by, I could not shake the horrifying images that filled my thoughts. It is said that the husband is the master of the house, and in our modern society this holds true; yet there must always be an exception to the rule, no matter how sagacious the order. Your typical man, and certainly the educated men of science I have spent my career working alongside, would label me foolish for allowing my dear Cora the power to secure our newest lodgings. However, my wife has much more the creative eye, and I raised not a single protest as she began preparations. Rather I spend many an evening in a house of character than the clerical and functional abode I surely would have orchestrated. Yet what terrors could a woman born of the music hall stage inflict on a home? I feared I would be spending my days in an abode fashioned in the style of a lady's boudoir!

I disembarked a little ways before my destination, choosing to enjoy the balmy summer dusk. The smog of London has lessened since our arrival eight years ago, allowing for pleasurable evening strolls. The street in this quiet suburb still held its activity against the deepening shadow: late workers hurried home for their suppers, and children busied themselves with one last game before heading home to irate mothers.

I approached our newest place of residence, thirty-nine Hilldrop Crescent, just off Camden Road. I stood for a moment, taking in the charm of the house, of which there was very little – much to my approval. My wife had dumbfounded me, as this was no residence set within a community of artists and musicians of which I expected, nor did the walls and windows reflect her grandiose, her larger-than-life disposition. Rather, thirty-nine Hilldrop Crescent appeared a working man's house that had neither the shine nor sparkle of a diamond, but the modesty and function of a piece of coal.

Carrying my few personal belongings in my case (Cora had used an expensive firm to move the rest of our possessions previously) I stepped through the open wooden gate and up the neat paving stones to the front door, where I gently tapped for fear of disturbing our new neighbours. Cora is not the most attentive of minds. Without a reply I tried to rouse her again, for surely my wife would be enamoured with the idea of showing her husband the fruits of her labours from the threshold.

Without a sound from inside, I ventured to the dark window, but even shielding my eyes from the streetlamps and pushing my face to the glass revealed nothing within the murk. Deflated and unsure that I had, indeed, arrived at the right address, I tried the door a third time to disturb Cora, whom I thought was asleep within.

Startling me, the door swung inwards to reveal a bare hallway that contained the deepest shadows and a staircase, rickety and narrow. I am not one for fanciful stories and the silliness surrounding ghosts and devils and the like, but I will admit my trepidation. Calling for Cora, I stepped inside the house and hastily lit the first of the lamps along the wall. Secured by the golden circle that held the darkness at bay, I dared my feet to carry me to the next lamp and so forth, until the hallway was filled with a cheerful glow. It was from this haven against the shadows that I explored my new home, and sought to discover the whereabouts of my darling wife.

July 16th, 1905.

Regarding relationships, I believe that the mind records events like this diary holds these very words. Of course, any relationship has a beginning: the moment you set eyes on the young woman who is to be your wife, or the first time you set about your duties for a new employer. Even now, I recall with clarity my initial days at Dr. Munyon's Pharmaceuticals, meeting with the good doctor and enduring his analysis of my character. Munyon sympathised with my annoyance and disappointment that my own qualifications, acquired with highest honours back in the United States, were not to be recognised by the College of Medicine here in England. Yet he offered me employment in the vending and distribution of patent medications. Alas, as previous entries in this diary have stated, my lasting employment with Munyon was not to be, due to the ever-increasing demands put upon my time and finances by my wife's stage career. Yet I do not hold any ill will towards the good doctor. Some relationships prosper, others wither and die.

My relationship with this house began on a sour note. Last night, having explored the ground floor of this exceedingly mundane abode, and determining that Cora was not to be found in the kitchen, pantry or lounge, I ascended the creaking stairs, warding off the darkness before me with a lamp.

On the second floor, it transpired that my wife was absent, yet her touch on the house was not. While the exterior and ground floor were to my taste, basic and practical, the upper level had succumbed to Cora's eye and hand. Thick carpet covered the hallway boards, and the walls sported a few framed news clippings of my wife's performances, regardless of their words (*mem*. Truth be told to this journal alone, Cora's vocal talents leave a lot to be desired, and this has been remarked upon in the local press). As I entered the master bedroom, my mouth fell open at the spectacle that met me. In its entirety, the room had been decorated pink!

Shaking my head at this latest absurdity, (for a man of medicine sees not the colour of a delicate rose nor the gentle hue of a sunset, but the glow of a fever or a mix of blood and saliva) I placed my lamp on the dresser and sat on the edge of the bed, which was also adorned with pink sheets, pillows and valance.

It was from there that I noticed the imperfection in the wall opposite. Had Cora sought the advice of a surveyor or architect before signing our names on the lease?

I approached the wall and ran a finger along the crack that ran across the plaster like a Caesarean scar.

Adding to my dismay, I saw how the flaw had been recently painted over in the ludicrous pink, only to become opened once more. Even as I continued my examination, more flakes and clumps of plaster fell away beneath my skin and drifted to the floor.

And so with this latest disappoint, I made my toilet and readied for bed, anticipating the late arrival of my wife while I update these pages. It had become apparent that a change of homestead had not changed habit, for Cora must be about town with those of the Music Hall Ladies Guild, and she shall return in the early hours full of merriment and the stench of gin.

I shall remember the damaged state of the wall for another day, upon which Cora may be of a more sober disposition to discuss such matters.

September 2nd 1905.

It has been just under two months since we relocated to Hilldrop Crescent, and I feel my good spirits are waning. While the faces that pass by the windows are different, as too are the street names and walls and shingles, I know that nothing has changed in the day to day business of my affairs. Gracious! How my words are steeped with indigence.

My work at Drouef's Institute for the Deaf remains challenging, helping those less fortunate than myself, and I return home on an evening tired yet satisfied, for the aid of others is good for the soul. I also appreciate my time with dear Ethel Le Neve, a young girl who has recently been appointed the post of my assistant. Ethel is quite the English rose among her more brazen species, and attends her duties with efficiency and a silent determination. The young lady has become a dear, dear friend.

Of my wife, I record a diminishing relationship, as I spend less time with Cora and more so that of her stage persona, Belle. Her laughter and joking fills these rooms, and her voluptuous frame dances and sings through the halls and the gardens. I adore the light she brings to this place.

However, supporting the career of a star of the music hall is a burden on the finances, and for one on such a meagre wage as Drouef pays, I have found myself advertising for lodgers to supplement our income.

And as for my other problem, the poor workmanship regarding the wall of our bedroom, I feel the mystery deserves a little more space in my journal to document its intricacies!

I will recall a few nights previous, upon which Cora had retired early to bed following a performance that same afternoon. After concluding some business for the Institute and ensuring the house was in order, I too ventured up the stairs and into our bedroom. I found my wife already fast asleep, lying on her back and snoring quite stridently. I placed my lamp upon the table by my bedside and readied for the night, eventually climbing between the sheets and extinguishing the flame.

At some point in the night, and for lack of a time piece I cannot be accurate, I registered an odd noise from the other side of the room. In the sensible light of day, one could easily dismiss this as the scraping of a tree branch against the window, but lying in the darkness, the horrid sound filled my head with giant rats scratching and gnawing within the very walls! I do not admit to a phobia of the vermin, though I will abide them not, for they are carriers of pestilence and rodents by the Thames can grow to the size of cats.

Being careful with my actions, I reached from the warm sanctuary of the bed sheets and lit the lamp beside me. At once, the dry, abrasive noise came to an abrupt end, leaving me feeling foolish; an educated yet terrified man fearing noises in the dark, as a child would cower in a storm!

It surprised me little that the source of the commotion had been the thin fissure in the wall, which had grown in size over the last few weeks. Even as I watched, another chunk of plaster fell from the crack, revealing more of the darkness within. Surely, some activity would have disturbed this plasterwork? Damning my fright and even more so my languor in repairing the blasted wall, I turned down the lamp and tried to sleep, vowing to seek a tradesmen at the soonest opportunity.

December 6th 1906.

I write these words with a shaking hand, a numbing combination of brandy (of which I do not usually partake) and anger that boils through my veins like lava. I shall start at the beginning of this cursed day.

With the festive season fast approaching, my wife has seen her bookings almost double. While her singing voice is far from the most eloquent, her buxom personality and rosy way are a much sought after commodity in this time of good cheer. This increase in fortune has snatched what time I would ordinarily spend with my wife, leaving me with little more than tending to the lodgers and my work at the Institute.

Just this morning, I found myself staring at my wearisome reflection in the bathroom glass. A serious man stared back through the tiny lenses of his spectacles, fine moustache hiding the straight line of his mouth. I pitied this poor soul. I wondered, what visage would stare back at me should this man find his situation changed? For a moment, in which God would have looked away and the Devil clapped his hands with delight, I considered a life with my dear Ethel. A quiet girl as opposed to a wife who is both loquacious and promiscuous! Would such a life bring a smile to this serious man's lips, or a sparkle to these lacklustre eyes?

Nonsense, I told my reflection. Ethel is but a girl and would have no interest beyond that of friendship.

I finished my preparations for the day and departed for the Institute, wherein my duties proceeded as usual. It was upon my return home that my troubles began.

One of our more recent lodgers, an older gentleman by the name of Hodges, was often to be found loitering about the house before he ventured out to attend business of his own come evening. I know not his career, but allow that he is an early riser and his lodgings are paid in full. A private man, something of which I can relate to, Hodges has never been a cause for concern.

Upon my return home, I noted that Hodges' door,

which led directly from the hall, was ajar and on my approach, was knocked closed. This was no surprise to me, as I say Hodges is a reserved fellow. Allowing him his solitude, I passed by his room and on to the kitchen, wherein I prepared a pot of tea. To give the drink time to cool, I headed to the master bedroom with a mind to examine the fissure in the wall further. The prices demanded by some of the tradesmen I had spoken to were a little too steep for our meagre income, and I aimed to attend the job myself, another for the list of chores supplied to me by Cora.

The enigma around this strange feature continues! Opening the curtains to allow the maximum of light into the room, I saw with some dread that the crack had widened further still, as if a seismic force had shaken the wall during my hours at the Institute. The jagged edges of plaster lay a good inch apart, wide enough for my probing fingers. I found nothing inside, and even holding a lamp up to the wall and peering inside the gap revealed nil. The darkness held, resolute against the pressing light. I considered the layout of the house and anticipated that the wound in the structure would pass into the bathroom.

It was at that moment that I heard hushed voices from below, followed by a feminine laugh like the call of a tropical bird. At least one mystery was solved. It is without question that Hodges would demand his privacy; he had the company of a lady within his chamber!

I judge not lest I be judged. In my consideration, business within his room, signed for and paid in full, shall be his own concerns and not my own. While acting before wedlock is indeed a sin, I have seen much worse atrocities committed following the bond of marriage. I believed Hodges to be a mature man of level head and good intentions, and I left him to his devices, but remembering the tea and bitterness over the ever increasing fissure in the wall, I returned downstairs.

It was here that I discovered a puffed Cora, red of face, slipping forth from Hodges' room. While my heart denied what so blatantly stood before me, my reasoning I could not ignore. To perform such deceitful and lusted sin beneath our roof pushed the boundary of my own tolerance. I have been too long impotent in the face of her cavorting.

Hodges, that coward and scoundrel, remained locked in his room while we argued. Cora, as stubborn and dramatic as is her way, challenged my sobriety and routines and despite the hours and finance invested in her career, she accused me of becoming obstructive to her ambitions.

Stung by her words and actions, I left that cursed house in a temper. My dear Ethel would listen, for what she lacks in age and experience, she makes up for in a listening ear and kind heart. Oh dear Lord, how cruel you must be to allow my marriage to this tyrant while such a fragrance goes unsavoured!

December 7th 1906.

My pen causes long shadows across this page, thrown by the morning sun that creeps over the rooftops. My curtains are drawn to allow that welcoming light inside.

I have slept scarcely a wink since the early hours. After my long talk with Ethel, I visited a local tavern for what is known as Dutch courage before returning home. My wife can be such an intimidating woman.

Worse for wear, I stumbled back to 39 Hilldrop Crescent, expecting to find Hodges and Cora once more in relations, however, Hodges had since made his leave, his rented room open and stripped of any effects. At least the man had the sense to move on to pastures new. As for Cora, she too had vanished. With Hodges? I knew not at the time, nor cared. Unsteady on my feet, I lurched up the rickety stairs and into our bedroom, collapsing upon the bed.

It began with that damned scratching sound.

Rousing me from my ragged slumbers, the rats I imagined clawed and gnawed from behind the wall, no doubt adding to the width of the ever widening crack.

I sat up, reached for the lamp on my bedside table and lit it for its meagre glow.

The damage had indeed worsened. A crack now ran vertically through the middle, like the plaster was mere skin that had been sliced with a scalpel and peeled back, revealing a dark pit at the centre. From within came the sound of vermin burrowing, ever burrowing. It echoed out of the hole as if from the depths of a well.

Still in my day clothing, for the alcohol had taken the effort to undress, I swept my legs from the bed. The moment my shoes touched the carpet, the noise ceased.

At first relieved that the rats had taken their leave,

the sudden silence seemed to snatch the air from the room, leaving me to stand in a vacuum, hairs standing up along my arms, the flame of the gaslight flickering.

I slowly approached the wall, my light held aloft, each step bringing a surge in trepidation, a magnet whose repulsion increased with proximity.

In hindsight, I believe it was the remnants of whiskey still floating in my system that leant me the bravery to gaze inside the dark depths of that hole, yet my efforts proved fruitless. Despite the extra width, the contents of the fissure remained in secret.

My education lies in the field of medicine and alas I am no expert in the area of physics, though surely the knowledge of any man of sound mind will report that darkness is to be gone on the presence of light!

What lay beyond my wall did not obey any laws set down by man or God.

The darkness held thick as oil.

Filled with such unbridled horror, I retreated from the wall and fell back onto the bed, holding up the lamp like it had been blessed by the Lord himself and would keep any evil at bay.

I pray that this diary falls not into the hands of another, for they will surely brand me a lunatic for the following. Even now, sitting in the brightening morning, the image is at the forefront of my thoughts and cannot be burned away. I know that this was no bad dream, alcoholic delusion or mental reaction to the tribulations of the day.

For a moment, I believed I caught motion within that dark world, but this merely distracted me from the real fright that clung to the edges of the cracks.

Two hands, both pale as a cadaver's, gripped the wall. Thin fingers were curled out of the shadow like worms from some dank underground cave where light is an unknown concept. Fingernails pressed into the plaster.

I gasped and nearly dropped the lamp.

As a landed fish may silently slide back into the murky depths, so too did these ghastly hands, their nails leaving the tiniest of paths along the wall.

For a long time, I sat perched at the edge of the bed, staring into that abyss, waiting for the rest of the horror to emerge.

What to do in the face of this dilemma? The beast appears dormant in the day time. As the sun rises and my confidence grows, I shall move the heavy wardrobe to prevent any further activity and consider my next move.

December 20th 1906. (extract)

How very foolish of me! I have reread my previous entry, which was barely legible due to my erratic hand, and have dismissed my recollections. A sad result of a very upset mental state, I adhere. Behind the wardrobe, the hole in the wall has not emitted the slightest of sounds, and every night I retire following my work at the Institute and my rest is undisturbed. Beast indeed!

Still no sign of Hodges, to my relief. His replacement, Rothering, a young man who works at the foundry, appears honest with no... tendencies towards my wife. Cora herself is busy as ever with the festive period, but I find her returning home at a reasonable hour and of acceptable sobriety. I believe she feels the guilt of her actions and has turned over a new leaf.

March 16th 1907 (extract).

As with Dicken's ill-fated Scrooge, I have become tormented by festive ghosts. With Christmas and New Year many weeks in the past, it seems the period still is not over. Cora's bookings have not shied over the cold winter, and she spends more and more of her time with those harpies at the Music Hall Ladies Guild. Her new found decency is lacking, with my occasional night spent solitary as Cora socialises well into the night, only to stumble home the following morning, still singing and intoxicated from the night's adventures.

I fear we are slipping back into our old ways. Only yesterday, I attended the tailor to acquire new clothing for my work at the Institute. Cora too attended and after my measuring, informed the tailor of the material and colour which I desired! I will admit that I felt hurt and angry by her seizing of my affairs, yet held my tongue to prevent our discussions in public.

There is also rumour of Cora being seen with a man about town. I am yet to confirm these allegations and until that time must trust in the fidelity of my wife.

Sweet Ethel requested that we take a stroll through Hyde Park this evening, as she felt my disposition has been a little dark of late. While my heart flutters at the thought of such a rendezvous, I reluctantly declined. While Ethel is very dear to me, I am still a married man and must put all thoughts of romance aside. I will not lose Ethel as my closest friend, despite the sparks I feel as she takes my hand in those private moments. In these dark times, one must remain good and noble.

Mem. Must ensure I bait the traps. It would appear the rats are in the walls again. I can hear them at night.

November 2nd 1908.

It amuses me bitterly as I flick back through these pages and find these entries of a soul bared among the mundane lists of tasks and numbers! It paints a very sad portrait should you sift through the daily trappings of my day to day business and put the pieces together.

Just as the days follow their circle, as do the months and seasons, my marriage has once again come around to this. Cora has admitted, quite flamboyantly, that a string of lovers have passed through her life in recent months, lavishing upon her various trinkets and passions.

Like the patent medicines I so fervently promoted in my days with Dr. Munyon's, sometimes the impact can be lessened with prolonged courses, and the body requires a larger dose to respond. My Cora, she has exposed me to her exploits for so long that nothing surprises me. Rather than react with the previous shock and heartbreak I have logged within these very pages, my response is hum drum. Cora's constant perfidy has become the equilibrium.

So what now for the future? My righteousness and loyalty are crumbling, as is the wall of the bedroom, which deposits dust and plaster behind the wardrobe on an almost daily basis. I watch Cora as she sleeps. I do not take my wedding vows lightly, yet I lie in the dark, listening to the rats gnawing at the foundations behind the wall, and I dwell on the current state of affairs. While I grow tired of her wayward actions, which at times feel befitting to a woman half her age, I see now that Cora is happy, while I, on the other hand, have grown stagnant in my routines. I am not hurt directly by the adulteries of my wife, rather it is my own missing desire that pains me so.

Today, I may put to my dear Ethel to take a walk with me following our work together at the Institute. How my mouth goes dry at the mere thought! A girl so pure and kind may very well refuse my proposal, but I feel in my starved heart that she is to be the piece that is missing. May God give me strength for what I am about to do. While He shall surely disapprove of this affair, I trust the Lord shall see this is a matter of love, and lend me the courage to see it through.

January 5th 1909.

The oddest thing happened this evening. The theory of out of sight out of mind no longer applied regarding the growing hole in the bedroom wall. I have no idea how Cora can sleep through such a racket. The vermin inside attend their demolition work nightly, as if they are rushing to meet some deadline known only to themselves.

While Cora was out on one of her many exploits, I concluded my business for the evening and enjoyed a cup of tea before attending my night's work. With some effort, I pulled the cumbersome wardrobe aside and studied the revealed wall.

The radius of the hole appeared the same and this didn't account for the sound of gnawing nor the amount of dust that had fallen to the carpet. I initially deduced that the fissure had not overtly widened, but perhaps had *deepened*. However, there had been no sign of damage within our bathroom, which was the next room. Considering this queer problem, I lit the gaslight and peered into the darkness.

Once more, the light did nothing to shift the shadow. It was easy to imagine one looking through a window into the deepest reaches of space, a destination no telescope had the power to observe.

I reached out to sample the depth of the hole, but refused at the last moment. Something about this anomaly – the density of the darkness and a fleeting memory of dead fingers curled around the edge – refrained my hand. Instead, I listened for evidence of the long-tailed workers that coordinated such wreckage. Only silence reigned within.

Uncertainty gnawed me. It felt that this transgression against light had become my own personal affair, and I was unsure of the appropriate steps to take. It had become clear that some fiendish will was at play, and I had the suspicion that should I find the funds to have the hole repaired, the fissure would appear again, costing me of pocket and mind.

It was then that something revealed itself in the darkness, although to keep a true account I have to confess that the sight was glimpsed for but a second, and due to its nature, I cannot vouch for its authenticity.

Outlined deep within the darkness glimmered two

small circles of gold. I gasped, believing that some hellish animal had been lurking in the shadows all this time, scrutinising me and drawing its malevolent plans.

To the relief of my beating heart, I realised that close to being a set of eyes, the golden object I had seen had been a pair of spectacles, similar to my own.

As I stared into the hole, the sight now a mere memory like an after image of a bright sun, I held that not only had I witnessed a pair of small golden spectacles within the wall, but also a long moustache below and thinning hair above! How foolish of me! Driven to terror by my own reflection!

I surmised there had to be a mirror or at least a pane of highly polished glass within the wall. How it originally came to be inside the wall, I have no idea. However, as I raised the gaslight to seek out a second glimpse of this reflection, I found darkness.

Only darkness.

I replaced the rotten bait on the untouched traps and pushed the wardrobe back against the wall. This house deepens my curiosity once again.

July 27th 1909 (extract).

I must make efforts to secure this diary in future. I fear Cora suspects my growing intimacy with Ethel, and these words will betray me should her eyes fall upon them. Troubled sleep these last few nights. Hearing scratching and banging in the early hours that stir me from my nightmares. I worry the strain of my romance is beginning to tell. I am a doctor and a gentleman, and am not cut out for such secrecy! At times I pray to God for assertiveness in these troubled times.

October 2nd 1909 (extract).

My position grows ever more precarious. While Cora continues her gallivanting about town, irrelevant of company and marital honour, her suspicions have narrowed on my romance. She demands to know why I spend much of my time with, in her own words, that slip of a girl. Lord knows that I wish so much to confess all and end this unfortunate charade. But that won't do at all. My reputation and limited means, which I have striven to achieve over this last few painful years, my wife shall surely take from me.

Just this morning, sweet Ethel suggested we elope and leave this God forsaken city and all who dwell within it, perhaps catch a ship back to the United States. Return to my homeland, to practicing medicine. How dear her naivety! I understand the intentions of my wife. She is comparable to the schoolyard bully who demands all the toys to herself, and shall not allow any of the other children a sliver of happiness. Should I indulge Ethel's request – and how I have lain awake and considered it so! – this dark cloud will pursue me to any horizon. At times I contemplate ending my affair with Ethel. She deserves this not, and can find love with a more simple man in accommodating circumstances. Yet I know this could never be the case. It destroys me to picture her on the arm of another.

This sleeplessness is affecting my work at the Institute, and I worry that Drouef has taken note of my fatigue and lack of concentration. How can one attend such trivial duties with such a tempest swirling in one's thoughts?

I have resorted to sampling my own former wares, purchasing vials of Hyoscine from old contacts to aid my rest. I fear the delusions brought on from such medicines, as once again, I am finding terror within the hole in the wall. On a few occasions, in the early hours of the morning as my lodgers sleep soundly in the rooms below and my wife is attending parties, I grip the sheets, too afraid to move. At the far side of the room, I believe I see the wardrobe rocking back and forth and a heavy weight is pounded against it. The great wooden frame becomes pushed aside, its legs scraping fresh trails in the spilled dust and plaster on the floor.

Alone, whimpering in the dark, I watch the darkness spill from that wide cavity like ink dispersing through water, and the brute that abides within curls his ghastly fingers around the lip, pulling himself from the shadowy miasma.

I wish for death and curse those damned medicines that have delivered these macabre visions.

The fiend stays within the darkness of the wall, watching me as I cower on the bed. The weak glow from my gaslight reflects in its gold-rimmed spectacles, and its mouth remains a rigid and serious line beneath its lustrous moustache. Every part, this is my doppelganger.

In the reassuring light of day, I reason that this is my subconscious emerging through the gateway of my troubles and drugged mind. I am no doctor of the human psyche, but I stare back at the tormented soul within the wall, and despite my horror and revulsion, I pity the fellow, for he appears trapped inside his darkness and seeks only a way out of his prison.

January 25th 1910 (extract).

Night terrors increasing despite removal of medication, which I have deposited under the bathroom sink. Ethel's unease is growing, having found my wife waiting for her outside the Institute on two occasions. I dread our affair has been discovered regardless of our precautions. While this relieves a part of my heart, for at least this lengthy ordeal shows signs of finality, I am anxious for the coming storm we must sail through before safely arriving at port.

For indeed, while Cora – during the few hours we spend in each other's company – has not yet approached the subject, her behaviour has become increasingly more erratic and promiscuous. She plans to throw a party of her own this next week. How I loathe her demands that I attend on the grounds of presenting a happy and content marriage to those she seeks to impress for the sake of her failing stage career. This gathering is set for the 31st of this month. I reason that should I abide by her wishes, that this will grant me favour with the officious woman my wife has become over these last few years, and may calm the turbulent seas somewhat.

If only I could sleep! My thoughts deceive me.

January 30th 1910.

Cora has dominated my time in regards to this

foolish party. I have had barely a moment to meet with my love, who has been sympathetic and patient throughout this business. I assure her that this party is not a social occasion, merely another stepping stone to our future happiness. She believes my intentions, which causes me to love her all the more. Dear, sweet Ethel! I promise you we will be together soon. She requests that I meet with her briefly tomorrow afternoon, for she has news that would interest me greatly, and she does not wish to discuss our affairs at the Institute.

How I would suffer a hundred of my wife's ludicrous parties for just one moment with my Ethel!

Now I must continue the preparations for tomorrow. Cora appears to have invited all the performers in London to our modest abode.

31st January 1910.

Within these walls, I have seen the darkness of Hell. I know not what I have done.

29th July 1910.

It is with great trepidation that I return to these tainted pages after so long, but my intention is pure and virtuous. Should you, dear reader whom the future hides from me, be reading these entries, then my crimes will have been discovered, and no doubt my thoughts and actions will be presented as evidence should I be caught. To you, Sir, I have no regrets in the keeping of this diary. Many a criminal has found himself caught short following some foolish mistake or neglected cover up. Why would one record, in his own hand and voice, such a document as to condemn him?

I make no excuses for what I have done. While my memory remains fogged regarding the events I am about to document, I fully admit the resultant scheme to flee across the Atlantic is entirely my doing. Let it be known that Wifie, my Ethel, had not a hand in this, and she accompanies me as my loyal partner and mother of my unborn child, not as an accomplice.

Indeed, the mother of my child, which is the pressing news she so joyfully divulged that afternoon before the party.

I aim to record the events leading to this morning, where I sit at Antwerp docks, watching the sea, my new wife beside me as I jot this down while we await the liner *Montrose*. We will seek our refuge in Canada, away from this plight. I believe there has been some... contact with God only knows what, and I shall keep my records complete for reference, should this strange phenomenon occur once more.

For the sake of my Ethel and unborn child, I pray this will never be the case.

I had attempted to retire early the night of the party. Cora had once again become intoxicated on gin and cheap wine, insisting on serenading the attendees throughout the occasion. Our lodgers had vacated the house for the evening, leaving the more colourful of performers – mostly fellow Music Hall performers, musicians and dancers – full reign of Hilldrop Crescent. Cora had taken offence of my bid for privacy, and her mood, slowed by alcohol, quickly darkened.

How I hate her still, that foul pig of a woman! She had indeed approached sweet Ethel with her accusations and declared to her friends how she had driven the seductress away. My husband can barely satisfy one woman, let alone two, she had joked, much to the amusement of the fame-hungry gathering.

Trying to escape her mockery and the public discussion of my most secret business, I fled up the narrow staircase, ploughing through the darkness, unconcerned with lighting the lamps on my journey. I needed the shadows to hide me from their laughing eyes. I demanded seclusion.

Inside our chamber, I sat on the bed, my head in my hands. I remember contemplating leaving the house in a temper. Packing a bag and leaving the damned lot of them behind. Yet, something eased my rapid, undeveloped thoughts. I felt somewhat relaxed for the first time in weeks.

I... sensed *his* coming, rather like the way the air becomes heavy and charged just before a storm. Three loud bangs echoed in the room, the wardrobe shaking with each blow. This worried me not. I felt no threat from the beast inside the walls, having been subjected to his mischief for some time now. On the contrary, and I find this hard to put into words, I welcomed his arrival. Perhaps because Cora had discovered most of my secrets, and while the darkness and the thing it contained revealed itself only to me, I felt the power I had over her. She couldn't take *all* of my mysteries.

In point of fact, she would take nothing from me. Not my dignity. Not my love. Not my child.

It was then that the wardrobe was eased aside. It

emitted a squeal as its legs scraped across the floor. The shadow spilled out once more from the hole in the wall, reaching for me with tendrils of shadow. A living void. A swirling shade.

I sat up and stared into its black depths, becoming lost in the turbulent eddies of the abyss. Deep within, glittering like treasure found in the darkest depths of the ocean, the golden rims of my twin's spectacles shone.

He had arrived, and that night, I would aid him in his escape.

I crossed the bedroom, ignoring the sounds of frivolity and Cora's loud, grating singing voice, and approached the hole. The darkness hung about me like fumes from hot tar, and I shivered, the deep swallowing the very heat from my breath.

I gripped the edge, where my counterpart had clutched the plasterwork with his pale talon-like digits, and leaned ever closer, bring my face to the churning surface of shadow.

Inside, the ghost's hanging moustache parted in a ghastly smile.

And then? I can recall nothing, like the spectre had hypnotised me into a state of restless slumber.

However, as with any nightmare, I remember a few details on waking. I heard Cora stagger into the room, the bedsprings squeaking as she collapsed her ample and drunken frame atop the mattress.

"I have had too much wine to sleep," she mumbled. "Give me something. Be of some use, you pathetic man."

I opened my eyes, trying to shake my drowsiness

and attend her needs. Hyoscine remained under the bathroom sink in generous quantities, and it would be a small chore to provide my wife with a dose to aid her rest.

Yet, it was not me to whom she spoke, or rather, it *was* me! I watched myself leave the room, and just as I intended, return clutching a large bottle of the drug and a syringe.

Alas! It was I that administered drug in great quantities, displaying complete dominance over my dozing wife!

My thoughts grow increasingly cloudy the more I try to arrange them. It was not I that administered that lethal dose of Hyoscine, but without doubt the forensic scholars at Scotland Yard will find my fingerprints on both the bottle and the needle.

My next coherent memory was of awaking next to Cora, my wife of many years already cold as the first sunlight began to creep underneath the curtain. The wardrobe had returned to its position against the wall, and upon inspection, the wall and its pink paint were flawless behind.

The suggestion was almost too much to bear, that I had callously murdered my own wife. Only the entries in this very diary have saved my sanity, that Cora did not die at my hand, not that any investigator would believe such a wild story.

Coincidentally, knowing my story would not be considered and I would be sure to face the hangman's rope, I disposed of Cora's body later that morning once I was safe in the knowledge the lodgers were at their employ. Despite my will to record the facts, I choose to refrain from writing the details of my method of removal of Cora. Some horrors are... to be left unsaid.

While Ethel and I lived on at Hilldrop Crescent for some time, spinning falsities in regards to Cora's return to the States to maintain our freedom, we became hounded and fled. It is without question that the authorities will be searching the house, perhaps as I write these words.

I see smoke on the horizon, the approaching steamer, and Ethel is smiling. One last obstacle and beyond that, the future. *Our* future.

For the first time in many a year, hope is a concept not so futile.

God may pity all weak hearts after all.

Dr. Hawley Harvey Crippen.

Darker With the Day
Scott Nicholson

It's black and I remember now.

No, that's not right. I remember before. Not *now*.

I remember the laboratory, the fire, the war, and I had a name. It was a long name. Lt. John Sorenson.

And I can only remember it after I have fed and the light of wisdom flows through me.

So thank you, Corporal. Whatever your name is. Maybe they'll collect your bones and put you in the Tomb of the Unknown Soldier.

And bless this meal, O Lord, that I have received from your bounty. Except maybe I shouldn't say Grace, no prayers for the thoughts that have returned. Better to be confused than to see all things clearly, especially when my hands are red and my skin is gray and my heart is an open sore.

The street smells of gasoline and smoke and broken things. If not for the odor of meat on my face, I could find my way home. Because home is where you go when you have trouble, home is where the door protects you, home is where she is.

John Sorenson. A name too good for the thing I have become.

John was the one testing the retroviral serum, a trial so obscene it had to be sequestered in a private D.C. lab. Top secret, Capt. Hayden said. In the chain of command, the lower ranks never ask questions. Right, Corporal?

At ease, soldier. You have served.

So John asked no questions when ordered to inject the serum into corpses. Did you, John?

It seemed like an exercise in futility, because everyone knew dead people couldn't pump blood through their veins. But when the first one began stirring, when the lump under the sheet twitched on its steel trolley, even Hayden was shocked. Humans had meddled in the domain of God, and we know the consequences of such vanity. But it was an act of love as much as it was defiance, and love is all we have left now.

And I wanted to tell her about the mystic wonder we had discovered, but others found it abhorrent and sacrilegious. The lab exploded. Domestic terrorists, probably. Either way, Pakistan took the blame, eager to offend the country that had been massing troops at its borders. But that wasn't the worst thing to come from the attack on the lab. Subject 37 shambled out of the observation room when the glass shattered. Thirty-seven got Hayden, latched onto his neck while he was stunned. I tried to help, and that's when it got me.

That's when *this* got me.

I remember it all, now that my belly is full and my brain is working again. I remember calling her and telling her to take Dolores and run. Drive for the cabin in the Pennsylvania mountains. Wait until I get there.

I'm not there yet. The war got here first.

But I keep my promises. When you love someone, you owe them that much.

And so it's time to leave this cold room and this stack of wet bones. Time to walk the dark and go home.

The air outside the room is different. I can't taste it or breathe it, but I feel it on my face. The cruelty of my condition is that I know exactly what I'm missing. I am aware my heart no longer beats, though my heart still holds her face. It is a love that surpasses all understanding.

The night is lit by distant fires, the hell of war licking the horizon. Behind the gates I feel them moving. If my belly were empty, I would go to them, love them, use them. But if I were hungry, I wouldn't know it. I'd forget again and then I would be like Subject 37, nothing but a mouth on legs. Eating without conscience or consciousness, nature running in reverse. No chain of command, no law except supply and demand. But my demand has been supplied and so I move through the dark, onward, the shapes in the shadows nothing to me now, his flesh thick on my swollen tongue.

The city is shattered, no electricity, the streets clogged with silent hunks of wheeled steel. Even the sirens have gone quiet amid the low rumble of falling buildings. The supper of soldier sits heavy on my gut, infectious acid dissolving the stray bones. I'm not sure how many I have eaten since I stopped being John Sorenson, but the war has seeped deeper and the nights stretch longer and I'm still miles from her.

I pass a dog in a puddle, the milk of the moon reflecting on the water. It paws at the pavement, whimpering, seeking traction, but the weight of its useless back legs holds it down. I ate a dog once, or maybe twice, when the need came on. The communions are lost in the haze of fever and hunger, but the rich, coppery nutrient and the vibrant twitch of living flesh always jolt me to memory and a sick mockery of life.

Waking from rapture to a deeper rapture.

And my fingers clutching the entrails of prey.

Dogs... and sometimes people.

Like the corporal, like those who even now scurry behind the walls and inside buildings, knowing my kind is out in the streets. Our kind.

I have already fed, so I leave the dog to its futile struggle. Maybe it will feed another, and that subject will remember its own life and accept the joy of its new existence.

In some ways, it's more honest than my previous life, one of brass tacks and polished shoes and shaves and salutes. A world of us against them, with the lines ever shifting toward whatever best served those in power. I never questioned that structure, not then, not as an army biologist, a family man, a God-fearing member of the human race.

It took *this*–a Lazarus miracle, a demonic possession–to help me fully understand. Tender are the mercies of God, and all the silly squabbles over good versus evil crystallize. Only a brain fueled by the profanity of living flesh can comprehend the beautiful design of this new order. It was never "Nature versus nurture," as the psychologists used to say, though I notice they're not saying much these days.

No, it's nature/nurture, the same thing. Eat and be fed, take and be fulfilled, kill and let be dead.

Again I salute you, Corporal, as I move my legs and slide my torn feet across the rubble. Through you,

I have partaken of the forbidden fruit from the tree of knowledge, and I walk through the valley of the shadow of death in the Garden of Eden. My Eve is out there, though despite all the things I remember, her name still eludes me. Omniscience in all things but this lingering, consuming love.

And all around me, the world goes on, campfires on the rooftops, a gunshot echoing down a distant alley, the wail of a scared infant. The financial section lies in ruins, the security gutted. I know this avenue, though its lanes are cracked and cool, the vehicles no longer crowding one another. I pass a stalled taxi and at the wheel is a dead man in a turban, the flies buzzing his flesh. He holds no appeal, because his blood is turgid and coagulated. An injection of the retroviral serum would restore him, would make him one of us, but those who have entered paradise are prone to locking the gates behind them.

Ahead lies the cathedral, a great spired testament to mortal fear. The windows have been shattered, by bombs, vandals, or infidels, it makes no difference. Stained glass glints like a billion angel eyes. My bare feet crush them and move on.

I remember those pews, the soft crushed velvet, the hard oak flooring where the sinners hit their knees. I turn, the wind carrying a trace of smoke across my face. I am called to the door. Memory pulls at me, compelling me onward, but this diversion is momentarily stronger. When God commands, only the dead ignore, and I'm not dead yet.

On the steps lie the bones of a provider, cracked and polished by the moonlight. The alcove is an onyx box, inviting those who worship by night. I was married here. I walked up these steps a free man and down them with a mate for life. Now I am free again but the climb takes longer this time, my feet slippery with the fluids that ooze from my ripped soles.

Ripped souls.

I would never think things like this if not for the change. Now I know why Lucifer rails against the Father–to have all this and then have it taken away. God is merciful, say the robed and celibate men who stand in this altar, but He also tolerates necessary evils. I wish one of those priests were here now, I would break his skull like an egg and suck the sweet marrow of his brain, all those secret thoughts now mine.

As I shove through the door, the smell of wax assails me. The orange bulbs of candlelight flicker and bob from the breeze I have allowed into the sacred space. My senses are heightened, the glorious electricity of my condition tingling through my limbs. Someone is here, someone with warm blood and red meat and misplaced faith. I have known them all, junkies and whores, bartenders and warriors, poets and housekeepers. They each have a flavor, but in the end taste the same, and my love grows larger with their sacrifice.

Christ could take the nails, but anyone can die for somebody else's sins. The true test of faith is living again, rising up and walking among the people, carrying the message to those who flee your approach.

This one, hiding in the church, does not flee.

My feet are loud and wet in the dimness. I go

toward the small curtained chambers lining one wall. Confession may be good for the soul but not for the flesh. Already I feel my thoughts racing, crashing one upon the other like waves in a hurricane, losing their order beneath a larger force. If I don't feed again soon, I will forget, and then she will be farther away and I won't be able to love her.

It's the one curse of this condition, that I know it will pass if it is not fed. I am drawn by a need as old as time, an instinct for survival, a craving to consume. The attraction is like an obscene magnetism, my teeth aching, the rancid juices of my bowels gurgling and leaking down my corrupt legs. The church is a sanctuary, and all is forgiven here. The throbbing heart accelerates, giving away its position. I grip the curtain with ragged fingers. I want to remember this moment and all the moments to come.

To do that, I must eat.

Because already I am forgetting. John, was it? John the Baptist, John the dentist?

If I could talk, I would say a prayer and bless this gift I am about to receive from Thy bounty. I tug the curtain and the candlelight swells, the woman's eyes are closed and she is saying Hail Mary Full of Grace and I moan the words along with her, lost in the rhythm as I lower my face to her throat and then the words slide into a shriek and then a moist sigh and I remember now.

Thank you, woman. You might have been a nun or a mother or a teacher or a scientist, but now you are free from sin and your bones rest on consecrated ground. And I am condemned to walk on.

Home. I remember now.

She will have left long ago, just as I told her, before the bomb and Subject 37 and the fever and the state of enlightenment. I gave her a ring that had three diamonds, and she gave me a daughter. The girl's name is Dolores and she is a child of God.

No, that's not true, she is my child.

Maybe I am God now.

Maybe I know too much.

Eat and remember, starve and forget. It's a matter of will. And all the world is a mouth.

The street is gray now, the sun making a pink nest in the East. I know the way. I turn, and there are soldiers in the alley. I raise my arm to salute and strings of shredded intestines slide from my fingers. One of the soldiers shouts and I wish I could tell them we are on the same side, but I feel a different truth. A gunshot rings out and the slick bit of metal whistles past my head. I don't see how he could have missed at such close range. My brain has expanded, fat with the worship of dozens, a soup of souls.

I should hate that which seeks to destroy me, but my quiet heart has no heat for hatred. Acceptance is a flagstone on the road to enlightenment, and all seekers must leave behind the desires of this world. And the last thing to lay aside is my love for her, and I can't rest in the bosom of my Lord until I know she is saved.

The soldiers run down the street, and no more bullets come. There must be many of us now, more of us than there are bullets, more rotted palms than every nail in the world could pin to wood. The shadows seem shorter, the concrete glistening with the first rays of dawn, a rising hope and promise. I am nearer my God to thee.

And this was our street, is our street, I remember now. Houses arrayed like wooden blocks that Dolores plays with, the ones with letters of the alphabet. Symbols to make larger symbols to explain larger mysteries. Books and scripture and prayers and this deep, hollow hole inside.

Forty days in the desert, I walk with God.

Or maybe it is the third day, a time of rising.

And the sun is high and it might be tomorrow or a week from now and the hunger is growling inside me, fallen angels clawing up from the depths. You are what you eat.

And we are legion and food is scarce.

I was John Sorenson but when God calls, you remember.

Remember what?

Here I am.

Home. I see it now and I remember how I used to pull into the driveway after work, and she would be there, waiting at the door. I can almost see her face, waiting.

Almost.

And I am closer but I am farther away.

Did I tell her to run?

Or is she like the others?

How strong is her faith and love?

Would she be waiting still?

Would who be waiting?

God, why has thou forsaken...

A door.
Heart beating.
Love.
Her.

In the Darkest Room in the Darkest House
on the Darkest Part of the Street
Gary McMahon

Kept in the dark.

It's a common phrase, a saying that's been worn thin by overuse, but which of us can honestly say that we understand what it means? To be shut away in a lightless place, where you are shunned and hidden from the rest of the world.

Kept.

In the dark.

#

"I have an idea."

I glance at Brenda, wondering what she's been up to this time. I like her a lot – maybe even love her, in that clumsy and intense way that teenagers fall in love – but sometimes she makes me nervous.

"Wanna hear it?"

I nod. "Is it safe?"

"What do you mean? Of course it's safe."

"You know exactly what I mean. Your 'ideas' usually involve some kind of physical risk. Remember that time you convinced me to steal a car"

"That was ages ago. I was young. I didn't have a clue what I was doing."

"And now?" I smile, just to let her know that I'm at least half joking.

"Now I know more." She grins. "At least thought I

did, until I had this idea..." She slides off my bed and walks to the centre of the room, adjusting her skirt. Her long legs are lightly tanned. She always looks so healthy, so vibrant. Sometimes it feels like my entire body aches for her.

I stand and stare at her. "Okay, then. Let's hear it."

"That house. You know the one..."

I start to say the old rhyme: "In the darkest room..."

"In the darkest house..." continues Brenda.

"On the darkest part of the street..." I stop there, unable to remember the rest.

Brenda is still grinning. "How the hell does that end, anyway? I always forget."

I shrug. "Beats me. I haven't really heard that stupid rhyme since I was a kid."

She drifts over to the window, pulling apart the curtains and staring out into the street. The streetlight catches in her hair, making it glow. I can see the top of the tattoo on the left side of her neck; a single curling black squiggle. "It's empty now," she says, lowering her voice. "They're tearing it down a week from today. Flattening it. Nobody wants to be reminded of what happened there."

"Can you blame them?" I'm whispering, too, but I have no idea why. Maybe it's just the mood.

"I think it's fascinating." She turns away from the window, facing me. Her eyes are huge; her lips are full and dark; her skin seems to shine. "I always wanted to get inside, to see what's in there."

I shake my head, raise my arms. But even then I know that I'll do whatever she asks. I always do; she controls me without even trying.

"Come on, Mark. You and me... we'll break in there, have a look around, see what's what. We might even be able to bring out a souvenir and sell it on eBay."

"Okay," I say, shaking my head and wondering why the word didn't come out as "No," the way I'd intended.

"Great," says Brenda. "That's great. Meet me at the end of the street about ten past midnight." Then, before I have the chance to change my mind, she skips over to me, kisses me on the mouth, and leaves the room. I stand and listen to her footsteps as they pound down the stairs, still tasting her on my mouth. When the front door slams shut, I wince, as if I've been struck.

In the period immediately following her departure, the house seems too quiet. My mother is away for the weekend, visiting a second-cousin who's dying from some form of cancer. I spoke to her this morning, listened to her cry down the phone. Even though I'm not comfortable showing affection towards my mother, I miss her. I want her back, if only to let her know how much I actually care.

I sit down at my desk under the window. My laptop is switched on. I jiggle the mouse to bring the machine out of sleep mode and log on to Facebook. I scroll down a screen filled with vitriol, and then shut down the browser. Social networking depresses me. Everything depresses me... everything except Brenda. But even she makes me sad, because I know I'll never really have her. All I am to Brenda is a quick fumble and some company on her silly escapades. I'm some kind of emotional crutch; she needs me like a pet owner needs a dog.

I will never be anything more than that.

Outside, the wind stirs the leaves of the trees in the garden opposite. Litter scurries along the gutter at the side of the road, and a solitary man walks past with his head down, shoulders hunched, and his hands stuffed into the pockets of his long black overcoat. Someone coming home from the pub, half pissed and battling the angry wind.

I look to the right, beyond the end of the street, where the post box stands like a dumpy red sentinel. Over the junction, and about half a mile along the next street, is the house.

The skipping rhyme we tried to recite earlier predates the events that happened there, but it will always be associated with the place. In 1996, the bodies of three women were found in a small box room at the top of the house. The house had been empty for over a year at that point, and it took them a while to track down the man who'd lived there.

The killer was called Marty Benson. He was a factory worker. He kidnapped the women, locked them in the room, and then strangled them one by one. He forced two of them to stand facing the wall in opposite corners of the small, dark room while he killed the first. Then he called the next one over and killed her. Finally, he throttled his last victim. Then he carefully undressed them and raped them. Afterwards, he dressed them again. He positioned them in separate corners of the room with their legs open and their hands clasped loosely in their laps, and sewed up their eyes and mouths with fishing line.

By the time they were found – by a local housing officer who realised that nobody had checked the house since the last tenant moved out – they smelled pretty bad, and the rats had been at them. According to the popular account, the one whispered by school kids and chatty old ladies, the room was filled with flies. The sound of their buzzing was deafening. They'd laid their eggs in the stitched up eyes and mouths, and maggots writhed between the thick, clumsy stitches.

I'm not sure how much of the story is true and how much of it is generated by urban myth, but I do know that the house has been empty ever since. Marty Benson hanged himself in prison while he was still awaiting trial. The council boarded up the house and left it empty, allowing it to gain notoriety and take on the swollen aspect of nightmare. And now they are going to demolish it.

Local kids make up stories about the house, chant the old skipping song, and dare each other to approach the front gate, but nobody I know has ever been in there. Now that I'm older, the house seems less scary and much more tragic. The psychic vibrations of what happened linger, breeding a sense of despair. I suppose that it's all part of growing up: setting aside those silly childhood fears and replacing them with adult ones.

Down below, the street is empty again. The man I saw earlier has vanished. Even the wind is dying down, allowing the litter to settle and the trees to regain their stillness. I put on my headphones and listen to some music. Before I even know I've been asleep, I wake up with a pain at the base of my skull where it's been resting against the back of my chair. I sit up. The headphones have fallen out; I can hear tinny music coming from the approximate area of my crotch.

I check the clock. It's just after midnight. Brenda is expecting me. I stand and grab my jacket from the hook on the back of the door, and leave the room, shutting the door behind me. I glance along the landing, at the door to my mother's room, and wish that she was behind it, asleep in her bed. Then I go downstairs and out into the night.

A slight breeze follows me along the street. I can see Brenda waiting for me at the post box, leaning against it and smoking a cigarette.

"Hi," she says as I get close. "You all set?"

"I suppose."

"Don't be such a wuss." She pushes away from the post box and flicks the stub of her cigarette into the road. The lit end describes a fiery arc. On her back, Brenda is carrying a black rucksack. She is wearing a long black turtle-neck sweater, black leggings, and a pair of grubby army boots. She shouldn't look sexy, but she does. She always does.

I follow her across the road and along the street, drawing level with her as we walk. Her heavy boots scuff the paving stones.

The streetlights outside and to each side of the house are broken, so this part of the street is in darkness. These lights always seem to be off. No matter how many times the council workmen come along and fix them, within a week they're broken again. It's as if the house prefers to sit brooding in the dark.

"Wait here," says Brenda, grabbing my arm. I stop and look down at her hand. It looks white and bloated in the darkness, the fingers wriggling like fat maggots.

We are standing just beyond the patch of darkness on the pavement outside the house. Brenda slips off her rucksack, unzips it, and takes out a short crowbar. She hands me the tool and puts back on her rucksack.

"What's this for?"

"Well," she says, glancing at me. "It isn't a back-scratcher, is it?"

"Sorry." I heft the crowbar. "I'm nervous."

She smiles, winks. For second, I think she is going to reach out and ruffle my hair.

I'm not sure if I want to slap her or kiss her. Instead, I do nothing. I just look down at my shoes and wish that I had the courage to tell her how I really feel.

"Come on, scaredy-cat. Let's get in there." She darts away from my side, entering the block of darkness between the broken streetlights. As she passes from light into dark, I experience the sensation that I am losing something for ever. Then, pushing the thought aside, I follow her.

Brenda is already halfway along the garden path to the front door. She ducks down and scurries along the side of the house and waits for me in the shadows. I move quickly, not wanting the distance between us to become too great, and crouch down at her feet.

The houses on either side of this one are both empty. Nobody likes to live next to the house. It has bad juju. Nobody can ever be happy this close to the site of such atrocities.

"This board, here. It's loose. Do you see?"

I look up. She has pulled the timber panel slightly away from the window. There's enough of a gap for a small hand to slip behind the board.

"Yeah." I rise and shove the end of the crowbar between wood and wall, then yank it outwards. The wood makes a loud splitting noise, but it comes away easily, the screws holding it to the wall popping out and scattering on the ground. It takes us seconds to prise the panel fully away from the wall, and before long we are looking at a window.

The dusty glass is still intact. Brenda once again removes her rucksack and opens it. This time she takes out a pair of heavy duty leather gloves, the kind people use for gardening. She slips them on and pushes me out of the way. Glancing around to check that there's nobody in the vicinity, she then pulls back her right arm and sends her fist through the glass. The sound of cracking glass is quieter than I expect; it's a clean break. She picks the remaining shards out of the frame and sets them down behind us, and then returns the gloves to her rucksack.

"Simple," she says, glancing at me. Her pupils are dilated. I can smell a musty aroma, like cannabis, on her clothes. I wonder where she was before she came to meet me. I know that she has other friends – other guys she likes to see – and a few of them are into the drug scene. I've never met them; she won't allow it, tends to keep our friendship exclusive for reasons of her own. Because I'm so caught up in her mystique, I go along with it. I don't question her motives, and am just happy that I get to spend so much time with her.

She once told me that fucking on cocaine was brilliant, but all I could think about at the time was who she might have done it with.

"I'll go first." She manages to get her knee up onto the window sill. Gripping each side of the frame, she pulls her body inside. I watch her as she is swallowed up by the intense blackness inside the house, and consider running away. What the hell am I doing here, anyway? Why am I trying so hard to impress a girl who has little interest in me, and who will never consent to forming any kind of serious relationship?

"Get in... quickly." Her voice comes from within. I can't make out her face, no matter how hard I try. There's just that disembodied voice. It could be anyone; it could even be someone impersonating Brenda to lure me inside.

I climb over the window sill, stumbling as I slip inside. I fall onto the floor, jarring my knees, but don't call out.

"You okay?"

I nod. Then I realise that she can't see me. "Yeah... I'm fine."

There's a quiet clicking sound and Brenda's torch flickers on. The light is meagre; it barely penetrates the thick, oily darkness. This strikes me as strange, but then I tell myself that all the windows are boarded up and the lights outside are broken, so no external light is able to access the interior. Of course it's dark; it has to be.

Brenda's clunky boots make the floorboards creak

as she walks across the room. Her silhouette looks bulky at the back because of the rucksack. I get to my feet and follow her. "Do you have another torch?"

She stops, turns. I can't pick out her separate features in the dark; her face is just a floating black lump. "You mean you didn't bring one?"

"I didn't bring anything."

"Jesus, Mark... do I have to do everything for you?"

"Sorry. I fell asleep. I didn't have time to sort out any stuff."

"Well, I only have the one torch, but if you stay close to me we'll be okay. Just tread carefully... some of these old boards might be rotten. I don't want one of us going through the floor and breaking an ankle."

She starts moving again, towards an outline that looks like a doorway. I can't see any sign of a door inside the frame, even when the torchlight manages to reach that far. We are in what seems to be some kind of reception or dining room. There's no furniture. The walls are clean and unsullied by the kind of graffiti that usually appears in abandoned houses. The floor is bare.

"It's weird in here." I don't like the way my voice sounds: all light and distant. "It's too... clean."

"They must have taken everything out years ago, just left the shell."

I follow her voice, catching up with her at the empty doorframe.

"Through here," she whispers.

We move out into a narrow hallway. My nostrils twitch, filled with the musty smell that always accompanies empty houses, buildings that haven't been lived in for a long time: the stench of abandonment, of quiet despair. The same odour I picked up on Brenda's clothes outside. I try to tread lightly, softly, in case I step on a shattered board. I reach out on either side of me and feel the walls. They are smooth and dry. There are no pictures hanging here.

"Which way?" I say, knowing exactly what the answer will be but asking the question anyway, just to hear the sound of my voice.

"Up. We're going upstairs... to the room at the top of the house, the one where he did it."

I've seen Brenda like this before. Once she catches the scent of adventure, she won't give up. She enjoys the thrill of danger. She is always the first one to follow through on a dare. I admire her for her courage, but I also fear her. No, not her exactly: it's more that I'm afraid of what she might do, or might make *me* do alongside her.

The stairs creak and groan as she starts to climb. Wood pops loudly, the sound like that of popcorn thrown on a fire or shots fired from a small calibre handgun. I climb behind her, watching her slim back, the curves of her thighs beneath the tight black leggings. I want to reach out and touch her, but don't dare. She's beyond me; she lives in a cold, dark place that I can only ever enter when she grants me permission.

At the top of the stairs she turns right, following the landing around a tight bend to a second set of stairs. We stop here, examining our surroundings. The landing is wide, with doors along it on each side. The doors are all closed. I imagine people behind them, sitting quietly on their beds or standing motionless before dirty mirrors, waiting to be let out into the greater darkness of the house...

"Just a minute." Brenda reaches out a hand towards the wall. I hear the dry click of a light switch but nothing happens. "Well, it was worth a try," she says. Then she continues around the bend and starts climbing the second set of stairs, the ones that lead up to the roof.

"I'm not sure about this," I whisper. "What if someone's up here?"

She stops. "Who the hell would be up here, Mark? Don't tell me you're afraid of ghosts." I sense her smile; I can't see it, the torch is pointed upwards, painting the walls and the few steps ahead of us yellow.

"No, of course not..." I swallow with difficulty. "But what if a tramp has made his bed here, or some junkies use it as a shooting gallery?"

"There's nobody here."

"How do you know that? How do you know for certain?"

She leans against the wall. The torchlight dances across the walls, the stairs, the crooked wooden handrail. "Because I've been watching. I told you I wanted to come here for a long time, didn't I? So I've been staking the place out, making sure nobody's here." She turns and looks down at me. Torchlight glints in her dark eyes, making her look like a stranger. "Feel better now?"

I nod. It's a lie. I feel even worse.

She continues to climb.

As I often am, in that moment I'm struck by her grace, the way she moves so sensually through the dark. I'm sure she once told me that she used to dance, perhaps when she was a child. I can see the music in her movements; she skims through the air rather than plodding heavily along on the surface of the earth like the rest of us.

"I think it's this way," she says, drawing me out of my thoughts. "Right at the end." There's another landing, this one much shorter and narrower. To the left, there are two rooms, again with closed doors. To the right, at the very end of the landing, there is a much smaller door. "It's that one..."

I know she is right. I can feel it; a strange pressure. I remember the fragment of childhood rhyme: *In the darkest room, in the darkest house, on the darkest part of the street...*

It doesn't make me feel any better. Somehow I think that if I could remember the rest of it, I might be able to banish my fears. It's unclear to me exactly what I am afraid of, but I'm certainly afraid of something. Is it Brenda? Perhaps; she's intimidating and near-psychotic in the way that she pursues whatever she wants. Or maybe it's just the darkness, the darkness that moves and twitches and envelopes us like a physical thing.

I follow Brenda along the narrow landing. Her boots thud on the boards; the timber groans. I reach out and steady myself against the wall. The ceiling is low; after a height of about a foot the walls taper steeply upwards, formed from the rafters There's a single window at the end, not far from the small door, but this one, too, is boarded over.

"It happened here," says Brenda. "It all happened here. He took the three of them, dragged them up those stairs, and locked them inside this tiny room. They cried, they screamed, they banged on the door and on the walls, but nobody came to save them."

"Is that why you're here? To save them?" This stunning psychological insight sounds so damned trite when I say it out loud.

She laughs, but it isn't a pleasant sound. "Don't be silly. It's far too late for that. They're dead. He killed them. He throttled the life out of them and defiled their beautiful bodies."

She stops when she reaches the door. It's roughly three feet high and a foot wide; what lies behind it must be more of a storage space than a room. I watch as Brenda runs her hands along the edge of the frame, presses the tips of her fingers against the top of the door.

"They were in here for days, starving and thirsty. Not much air. Holding onto each other for comfort... in the dark, in the absolute dark." Slowly she lowers herself to her knees and presses the side of her head against the door, listening.

"I can hear the echoes." She reaches behind her and grabs me by the arm, pulling me towards the door. "Listen."

I let her push my ear against the hard, rough wood, and I strain to hear. There's a soft click and the torchlight goes out. I close my eyes. She grips me tightly. I hear a faint scuffling sound, like feet moving tiredly against the floor, and then something that might be a whimper. Brenda lets go of my arm. The light doesn't come back on. I want to open my eyes but I'm too afraid. I'm not sure what I might glimpse, on the landing, in the darkest room, in the darkest house, on the darkest part of the street, if I do.

Then I hear another whimper, softer than before, as if someone is forcing out their final breath. This is followed by a gentle buzzing sound.

I open my eyes and draw back from the door. I'm alone on the landing; she has left me here, helpless in the dark. I push against the small door, just to enable me to move away from it quicker, and it snickers open. I stare in horror as the door moves slowly inward and a wide band of black develops at one edge of the frame. From inside, I hear the frantic buzzing of flies.

I hear the sound of footsteps behind me. Someone large and heavy is climbing the second set of stairs, coming towards me. He knows I'm here. The killer has returned. Despite all the stories, the Chinese Whispers passed between children during school playtime, the man who killed those women is still alive, still on the loose... and he's come back to kill me, too.

A small white shape writhes out of the darkness of the small room. It's a woman's hand, beckoning to me. The fingers open, make a come-hither motion, and without thinking I step inside, pulling shut the door behind me.

It's cramped in here; not much room to manoeuvre.

The flies bat against my face but I'm too nervous to raise my hand and flick them away. Somehow I manage to get myself turned around, and I back up against a wall. My flailing hand brushes against something that feels like an arm or a leg, only looser, with hardly any definition. "Brenda?" My voice is faint, a ghost of itself.

"I'm here," she says, but her voice seems to be coming to me from a great distance and it's rendered vague by the droning buzz of the flies. "I'm finally back where I belong, with my sisters."

On the other side of the door, I hear footsteps. The door rattles in its frame. Somebody chuckles softly. Then the footsteps move away, before stopping altogether. I don't hear them descend the stairs. Whoever is out there, he is waiting on the landing.

I think about Brenda and how she's never let me meet her other friends; how she spends most of her time with me; how I've never seen where she lives. I've known her for a couple of years now, but not once has she asked to meet my mother, or shown any interest in the other people I know outside the confines of our relationship.

She's always kept me close while at the same time maintaining a distance. I realise now that it was all leading up to this night, when she could return here, with me for protection – or perhaps as a diversion to distract whoever is on the other side of the door.

My breathing is ragged. My chest hitches uncontrollably, as if I'm on the verge of an asthma attack. I try to calm down. I close my eyes and start slowly counting to ten. When I reach the number eight

I hear the soft click of the torch next to my ear as it's turned back on.

I hold my breath and continue to count. But when I reach ten, I don't open my eyes. I keep on going. I do not want to see the other three occupants of the room, and what has become of them.

I don't want to know whose soft, spongy hand has just slipped into mine, or gaze into the stitched-shut, maggot filled eyes of my beloved.

Softly, and to offer us some sort of comfort in that tiny room, I begin to whisper the old rhyme.

I only wish I could remember how it ends.

Till Death
Joe Mynhardt

Darkness – its impenetrable black veil had reigned over the last six months of Derek's curbed existence. His prison, a rectangular living room with one closet and one bathroom for all five of its captives, experienced more than sixteen hours of darkness each day, and there were thousands just like it.

Derek lay on a thin layer of carpet beneath the dining table, shrouded in darkness, doubting whether he was asleep or awake and for how long. Perhaps he was dreaming right now. Was it possible he was still in his house, before the living nightmare started? Before *they* came.

#

Derek had been watching late–night television that night, his teenage daughter Meghan moments away from falling asleep on an adjacent couch. He'd reached for the stack of plates and cutlery on the small table between them and the television.

"Leave the dishes, Daddy," Meghan mumbled. "I'll do them tomorrow morning."

A smile inched along Derek's face. A few months earlier he'd hardly known how to boil an egg, yet now he could prepare a meal worthy of praise. Who better to share it with than his daughter? "You sure, honey? I'll just let them soak."

"No. You already make me feel bad for not helping

out enough."

"My steak sauce really does a number on these–"

"Leave it," her voice muffled, yet stern.

Derek smiled once more. He knew she'd say that, and he loved it every time she did. It was their little game. His ex wife hated him for it. She hated it almost as much as Meghan wanting to stay with her dad after the divorce. He found it strange how quickly some relationships deteriorated; how people went from passionate, promise-to-love-you-forever assurances, to screaming, swearing and death threats. Unfortunately, Derek's lack of a job and home–making skills at the time had forced the court to side against him.

"Thanks, honey," he finally replied. "You're the greatest."

She didn't answer. A soft snore and a shudder of her body let him know she was asleep.

A floorboard creaked upstairs. Derek reached for the television remote and brought down the volume, hardly emitting a breath of his own.

He waited, unsure if one creak warranted further investigation or a shrug.

Another creak, this one closer to the stairwell, forced Derek to his feet. In his mind he pictured the intruder creeping down the steps to spy on them, but he didn't dare think what would be going through such a person's twisted mind.

Derek checked if Meghan was still asleep. He tested the lock on the front door, scowling at himself for making the softest of noises as he released the handle. Once he was certain Meghan was safe, Derek grasped a steak knife from the table and tiptoed barefoot towards the staircase, moving slower and slower the closer he got the first step.

He peered up the staircase as it veered off to the right. His heartbeat threatened to reveal his position.

The source of the sound could've been the old house settling for the night, or something as harmless as the wind knocking things over, but he had to make sure. He was always extra careful when Meghan visited. If only he hadn't left his handgun in the safe in his room, at the far end of the hallway.

His grip tightened around the knife. He traversed the staircase, thinking, believing someone watched him. He peeked over the edge of the top step. The dim light of his bedroom lamp illuminated the hallway just enough to cast a few insidious shadows across the walls.

Derek felt like a child forced to run through the darkness.

Just as he decided to make a run for it, a distant scream ripped through the neighbourhood, increasing in intensity and death-encroaching panic before it abruptly stopped.

Derek gasped, then stood in silence. Should he run to his daughter's side? Should he make a dash for the gun? He waited for sound to trigger his next move.

#

The reality of what had happened, too cruel to recall, hauled Derek back to his dark and silent prison. His thoughts muttered themselves out loud and he forced himself not to think about the events of that night...

like he had so many times before.

The room lay in silence, waiting for the day to start.

Derek reached into the darkness. His fingers cradled the leg of the dining table – gripping on to his sanity or whatever sense of reality he could grasp.

He wondered how many people also lay awake, staring into the black abyss for any sign they were still there. Not just in this room, but in all the others he knew existed. Thousands of people, just like him, unable to rest. They'd also think about the attack. About their absent loved ones. About an absolution they prayed would come.

Could Meghan be one of them?

Most nights fear kept Derek awake, fear and the possibility of catching one of the bastards that had forced him to share a room with four strangers. He wondered if any of the creatures were in the room at that moment. He'd never seen them before, but he had always assumed their presence. What good would capturing them do, anyway? A feast for his imagination was all it could ever be.

Something shifted across the carpet towards him.

Derek froze while his body overdosed on adrenaline. One of those things was in the room and had, by some bizarre fortune, given away its position. Sound was the only proof he had.

A solid object, metal on wood, scraped on the table top above him, followed by faint footsteps moving away from the table.

Derek clenched his fists, ready to strike. His tongue flicked out to wet his dry lips and he swallowed hard past the dryness in his throat.

A whimper seeped through the black and someone gasped for air.

Derek sat up to listen. He searched for the source of the panic.

A sudden, yet soft, shriek of pain. The whimper turned into a quiet, lonely sob.

"Wake up," Derek called to the others, loud enough to wake them yet careful not to shout. He didn't want the lights to come on. Not again. "The girl. Get to the girl."

The other three occupants stumbled through the darkness in search of the distressed girl, while Derek crawled towards the corner, the last place he recalled seeing her. He was careful not to bump into any of the furniture. Once the lights came on, there wouldn't be time to rearrange.

"Where is she?" an adult woman asked somewhere behind him.

"Over here. I'm almost there." Derek's hand pressed into a moist spot on the carpet seconds before he found her squeezed into the corner of the room. "What have you–"

The lights flashed to life.

Derek shielded his eyes from the crushing brightness. A blurry vision of a white dress was all he could make out. That and the river of red staining her arms. His hands fumbled to find the teenage girl. He had to find the source of her injury within the torrent of blood – had to clog it before it could spill the last of her life blood.

The other two children cried through muffled

screams. They'd bring the creatures, the pain and the true darkness. Times like these the light proved much worse than the dark; you could get used to the dark.

"Quickly," Derek said.

"Oh, no," the woman cried. "What do we do? What do we do?"

"What we always do. No matter what. Now get to your places." Derek fumbled for a cloth or sheet to tie around the girl's slit wrists. They had tried previously to hide the knives or other sharp objects from her, but the monotony of their everyday ritual made them all forgetful.

The kids cried louder, uncertain what to do or how to help.

Derek motioned them to the table. "To your chairs. Quickly." He tore a piece of cloth from his shirt and bound it around the girl's wrists like cuffs and pulled it tight, her arms pressing together at an awkward angle. He wiped as much blood from her skin as possible and carried her to the table. "Stay with me." For a few moments he tried to recall her name. Since their capture, Derek had only had time to think of his own, real, daughter. "Don't fall asleep." He sat her in her usual spot, hands on her lap, angling her so she wouldn't topple over or slip down the side.

The pretend wife of Derek's pretend family tossed a rug over the crimson battlefield and took her seat at the table just in time. The machines within the walls rumbled to life.

Derek straightened his suit, clipped on the tie he kept in the breast pocket and took his place at the head of the table. "Wipe your tears, now. And remember to smile."

The shutter shook with a screech of steel on steel. It inched towards the ceiling, allowing the rays of sun to stretch across the carpet towards them.

The final bang of the shutter settling into place forced Derek's gaze to the plastic food before him. The sounds and shadows and vulnerability of being watched, like every day before it, pulled him back to the night it all started. Before he was turned into a window display.

He tried to recall the good times he had spent with Meghan before the invaders came, but his analytical mind insisted the story run its course. He...

#

... had stopped at the top of the stairs to listen for the position of a possible intruder.

He inched forward and peered into the first bedroom. A bright light, moving in irregular zig–zag patterns, flashed past the window. Derek jerked into motion and he ran down the hallway. At each side doorway he cringed away as if he expected something to rush out and grab him. One thing he knew for certain – they weren't alone anymore.

More screams erupted throughout the neighbourhood. An explosion followed, setting off a series of eruptions, car alarms and more screams.

Derek's fingers fumbled across the safe's keypad. He grabbed his gun.

Meghan screamed downstairs.

He turned to run. He had to get to her before

anything bad happened. The roof shook as if some unseen hand was trying to lift it like a doll's house.

His heart thumped like fist blows against his chest.

He prepared himself to shoot whatever waited for him downstairs, but at the edge of the staircase an invisible force started to push Derek down, as if the intruders knew the gun was a threat.

Meghan's screams rose up the staircase and willed him on.

He shoved against the intense gravity, refusing to be pushed down. With every inch he moved closer to the ground he forced himself onward, skimming his body down the staircase, pulling forward against the banister.

"Daddy!" Meghan yelled.

A last burst of energy sent him leaping to the bottom of the stairs, where he lay sprawled on the wooden floor.

Two dark beings, tall and skinny and naked, circled Meghan. She lunged at one with the other steak knife. The creature screeched in pain as the blade slashed across its slick grey skin, but did not relent. It merely raised an arm, equipped with blade-like bony fingers and slashed its nails into Meghan's throat.

Derek screamed.

Gasping Meghan fell to the floor, bathed in crimson.

With the gun now too heavy to lift, Derek inched forward and reached for her hand, their eyes meeting. The creatures gouged at Derek's back while he stared into his dying daughter's eyes. His world plummeted into darkness, a darkness he would never escape.

#

There he sat, back in the room at the head of his fake family. A family filled with strangers he refused to accept: a wife who had no idea where her real family were; a young boy whose parents were slaughtered in front of him; a young girl who swore she'd died alongside her family but woke up here with them; and of course, the teenage girl struggling to get over the things the creatures had done to her and her friends before they were separated.

Here they would live, day in and day out, for who knows how long. They'd stare at their plastic food and cardboard cut–outs and put on their cardboard smiles, a window display for the new dominant species. With subservience came real food, served after dark with a pinch of salt and nothing else. It was a small reward for obediently displaying the same scene of an average human day.

A moan escaped the girl's lips.

Derek bowed his head slightly. He kept his gaze on his replacement daughter and the bright light from the forgotten world outside. The creatures were already moving past the window.

A red shadow seeped through the cloth surrounding the girl's wounds, her skin pale and dying.

A few window-shoppers moved closer as they seemed to notice the blood. Derek wondered if they could smell it.

The girl slid down her chair and the rest of the family started.

The long-limbed creatures outside roared in protest

at this change in routine. Why wasn't the human smiling anymore? Didn't she enjoy sharing a meal with her family? What an ungrateful creature!

Derek shook his head at their pitiful exhibition. It had been weeks since they'd even looked at them, yet now they wanted to object. At first Derek and his fake family had been such an amazing display, one of thousands of different ones, yes, but they did what was required of them and they lived. Anything was better than the physical torture these creatures were capable of inflicting.

But then the creatures grew bored, they hardly seemed interested anymore, barely laughed or taunted as they fell into their own daily routine of whatever menial acts encompassed their lives.

More creatures gathered to examine the odd girl.

Derek had contemplated suicide before. Who wanted to live in a world where even superior beings couldn't live free? More than once he thought of murdering his new family. That'd be a show those freaks had never seen before. Or would it?

The crowd beyond the window drew closer, a large shadow eclipsing the sun.

The rest of Derek's 'family' cried in horror, all but the girl, whose blood now flowed freely from her wounds as if there had never been a cloth to stop it. The blood ran down her thigh and plopped onto the off-white carpet.

Derek knew he had to do something to show these things he was more than just a window display, more than just a dressed-up mannequin representing a defeated race. He had to step up and become a new man.

He looked around the table and realised it was time he accepted these people as his new family. He thought back at the months they had spent together, recalled their names and what they had mentioned about their lives before the assault.

He pushed back his chair, fighting off his wife's protesting hands. He slid his arms under the teenage girl's body, cradling her as he raised her up. She rolled her head in the crook of his neck and moaned. Her name... was Carin.

"No, please!" his wife shouted.

His young children shrieked in horror, knowing their punishment would soon be administered.

Derek carried Carin to the window, shouting at them for everything that had gone wrong for himself and the human race. He flicked his hand at the window, sending drops of Carin's blood flying towards the glass in defiance.

Carin's body grew limp and heavy, her breathing shallow.

He doubted if they could hear him, since he couldn't hear *their* screams of shock and anger. Most of them wanted to kill him, but he could see some of them were touched by his actions, those of them who somehow retained compassion. Hope. Perhaps they had learned *something* from observing humans for so long.

The shutter screeched to life. Sunlight retracted across the carpet. The shutter banged shut as it separated the two worlds.

A door slammed open behind him. Footsteps

thundered towards Derek and his family. Their screams filled the room with fear and unrelenting torture.

Derek, refusing to turn, continued to stare into his daughter's fading eyes, ignoring the sounds of tearing flesh and shattering bones behind him. "I'm sorry I wasn't there for you when you needed me most."

Her eyes glazed over as her final breath left her body.

Derek closed his eyes and waited for pain and death, hoping this time it would lead to a more permanent darkness, or at least a second chance.

Animal-like footsteps charged towards him and the creatures lashed their fury onto his back. Derek fell, drowning in the black sea of pain and death. He never let go of his daughter's hand.

#

The abysmal darkness subsided.

Derek opened his eyes. It was dark, but he'd gotten used to this level of obscurity. He was back in the room.

He wondered how long he'd been awake, or if he was perhaps still sleeping. He brushed a hand over his shoulder and neck, feeling for any signs of the bones he knew had broken during the attack and the skin he'd seen peel off. Like before, there were no signs of abuse. Once again, like so many times before, the creatures had tortured them, likely killed them, and brought them back. In a way he was glad to see his family. It wasn't too late to make the best of this life.

For the first time Derek realised why he couldn't get over Meghan's death – she was the only good memory in a sea of suffering, his Atlantis. Perhaps they did bring her back, and she was living with a new family, like his. That didn't really matter any more, not under these circumstances. He hoped she accepted them.

The rest of his family, including Carin, slept in silence as they all waited for a saviour, someone or something to take them away from this prison.

Perhaps old age...?

If they were lucky.

For now Derek would apologise for his actions, and make their lives as bearable as he possibly could.

On a Midnight Black Chessie
Kevin Lucia

Now

Bradley once again turns onto that the strange road bathed in the moon's eerie phosphorescent glow. He recognizes this place, now. Understands what it is, where it came from, and how it came to be.

Ned sits on the passenger side, still drunk, forehead pressing against the window as he gazes at the glowing scenery. "Wow. Am I awake, or dreamin?"

"Neither," Bradley whispers. "Or maybe both."

Towards Ned, he feels a resolved sadness. Bradley no longer hates him so much, but rather pities him, for he's caught up in something much larger than himself, much larger than Bradley, or anything else. And Ned's completely helpless in the face of it.

And as they drive down this softly glowing road, Ned continues to stare. "Geez. Don' recognize this at all. You take a wrong turn? We lost?"

"No," Bradley says as he slowly pulls up to the glowing church at the road's end. "Not at all.

"I'm home."

Three Days Ago
Friday afternoon

Bradley Sanders had just pulled his office door shut and was in the process of locking it when he heard: "Hey, Brad. What's up?"

He breathed deep.

Feeling his insides warm.

And he turned, smiling at Emma Hatcher, a colleague in the Mythology Department at Web County Community College. Young and vivacious but also highly intelligent, Emma didn't fit the role of musty old Mythology professor. Fiery, brimming with energy, she'd proven very stimulating company this past year or so.

Very stimulating, indeed.

He regarded Emma's approach with surreptitious appraisal. She glided towards him. Not swinging her hips, exactly. But swaying in a graceful way that couldn't be so plainly described as "walking." She seemed more suited to Broadway than a backwater community college in the Adirondacks.

She smiled. "Heading home?"
He shuffled books and office keys and his satchel.
"Well. Urm. Yes. And you . . ?" He nodded towards
the exit, feeling both foolish and wonderful.

"Yeah. SO done with this place for now. Especially with summer session starting Monday." She smiled. "Walk with me?"

He grinned like an idiot but didn't care. "My pleasure."

She fell in step with him. "Y'know, some folks from other departments are meeting at the White Lake Inn tonight. An 'end of the semester' mixer. Around nine."

She paused.

Offering him a gentle grin. "Of course, you'll probably be too busy playing with your trains, I suppose."

He snorted good-naturedly and looked down, heat rising past his collar. "I'll have you know, I enjoy many other stimulating pursuits besides model railroading."

Eyebrows raised.

Glistening, playful lips curved upwards. "Such as?"

"Well. Er. There's perusing yard sales. Thrift shops. Of course, my studies. And... well..."

"Hah!" She bumped shoulders with him. He shivered, even at this platonic gesture. "Admit it. At heart, you're a big kid obsessed with his train set."

"*Layout*, Emma. It's a model scale layout of Clifton Heights. A set is something you put under a Christmas tree for children to play with."

She chuckled. "Methinks you've been working too hard on your *layout*. Bit overprotective, aren't you?"

He shrugged. "Perhaps. It's addictive, really. Like building my own world."

"Well, Maestro... if you're not too busy building your own world... tonight. Nine. See you, maybe?"

And with that, they pushed through the exit into the sunny afternoon. Emma glided off towards her white Mazda Miata, looking over her shoulder, smiling, her eyes dancing.

He waved.

Grinning like a fool.

She grinned, waved back, gliding toward her car. She opened the door, tossed her purse and books and satchel inside, and flicked him one more jaunty half-wave.

She got into her car, started it up and drove off.

While he stood there, staring, satchel in one hand, books pinned under his arm, cursing himself delightfully for being a thousand times an idiot.

But a happy idiot.

Until he considered her parting rejoinder, and felt his joy recede.

if you're not too busy
building your own world

Subdued, Bradley shuffled to his car.

Friday Evening

Bradley's train layout filled over half his basement, its wooden tablework skirted with blue cloth that just touched the floor. Underneath he stored his supplies, extra parts and unused rolling stock: boxcars, flat cars, oil tankers, engines and cabooses. Boxes of automobiles. Unassembled houses, gas stations, stores and warehouses. Miles of track, assorted spare parts (organized into rectangular sorters), shakers filled with powdered terrain of all kinds: grass, dirt and gravel. Bags of shrubs and pre-assembled trees of every size and shape and color. Rolls of plaster, tubs of clay for landscaping. Miniature lights for homes and stores and churches.

Everything he needed.

Packed into green totes, stored neatly under the layout, behind the royal blue curtain.

Over the last few years, he'd spent hours casting plaster streets and roads and sidewalks, stringing electrical lines, aligning buildings to scale and landscaping hills and knolls, applying grass and dirt and gravel, bushes and trees where needed.

He'd spent hours down here.

Cocooned in the peace of his basement, every night. On afternoons like this one, weather regardless. On holidays. Weekends. Next to teaching and studying, modeling trains had become his love. An obsession, he freely admitted. He loved every inch of his layout, this version of Clifton Heights that only existed here. Loved it, as a Creator must love His world.

He smiled.

Claiming godship of a model train layout might be petty, but he'd take it.

What else did he have?

But he forced himself not think about that as he poured plaster into the roadbed he'd outlined with molding tape, branching a new road off Front Street, one that didn't exist in real life, advancing into the layout's last bare section, the final thing he needed to finish in his world.

A section of Clifton Heights all his own.

Of his making.

Though he'd intended his layout to generally resemble Clifton Heights, he'd tweaked his version in places. Most of his alterations were cosmetic, accounting for railroad tracks that didn't exist in real life. And, some buildings he'd moved around, simply because he'd thought they looked better this way.

But that was fine. Realism wasn't necessarily *reality*, after all. Realism offered its own reality.

This was *his* world, wasn't it?

So he poured one last drop of plaster. Picked up a

flat, rectangular piece of balsam wood, placed it edge down over the newly-poured street and scraped the excess plaster off the road's surface. He put the wood aside, grabbed the moist towel hanging from his belt, dabbed the plaster that had leaked under the tape. Tomorrow, he'd paint the road black, lay down some gravel for its shoulders, and begin landscaping.

He dabbed away one last spot of plaster.

Stood, and examined the new road. Tucked the damp towel under his belt and grunted. Then turned to his workbench, where he'd laid out the buildings he intended on using. Six different styles of residential homes.

And a church.

But not just any church.

For he'd modified it. Removed the steeple's cross, painted over marks of mainstream faith with a slate gray. Because this was *his* church. This was his world, after all. This church should worship *him*.

He smiled. "The First Congregational Church of Brad," he chuckled.

But of course, he couldn't name a church after himself. So instead, he'd decided to call it "The Church of Luna." Dedicated to the various moon gods and goddesses he'd encountered in his studies. Which made wonderful sense, seeing as how tonight was May 5th, the month's first full moon, which would last until Wednesday night.

His sigil? Carefully painted onto the front and back doors with a toothpick dipped into black paint, a pagan moon symbol:

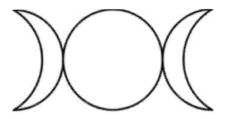

And he knew exactly how he'd arrange things after he'd finished the road and surrounding forestry. Houses on either side, with varying-sized lawns...

And the church at its end.

Yes.

A road leading to his church. The Church of Luna. Because all roads in his world lead back to him, yes? And, as a final touch, he'd already decided on a graveyard behind the church, framed by hills and a forest. Of course, many pagan beliefs favored cremation over burial, but that didn't matter. This was his world, one he'd built with his own hands, the product of his toil and care and sweat, his blood, too.

He could do what he pleased.

He glanced at the wall clock.

It read three.

He thought of breaking for an early dinner; reading from Edith Hamilton's *Mythology* to prep for Monday. After, he'd cut wire mesh for the surrounding hills, mark out building plots and begin laying ground cover: lawns, shrubbery, the forest. Perhaps he'd even tinker with The Church of Luna's graveyard...

Or.

meeting at the White Lake Inn tonight
an 'end of the semester' mixer
around nine, you should come

if you're not too busy building your own world

He rubbed his nose.

Staring at the completed sections of his layout.

At its curving tracks, rolling hills, precise town blocks, brilliantly verdant lawns and forests, and that newly poured road. Thinking about building and molding his world. And about how loud and crowded it'd likely be at The White Lake Inn, how he'd much rather spend the evening here, making a world from nothing... but for *Emma*.

Emma, on one hand.

The train layout on the other.

Everyone needed variety. He was an adult. Capable of balancing more than one interest, and he respected and liked Emma. Wanted to be around her, learn more about her, maybe even...

(take her to bed)

... and he'd begun caring for her, more than as a colleague. That he couldn't deny.

But did she reciprocate?

Could she reciprocate, actually feel attracted to him? He was ten years older. Stodgy. And he spent all his time building model trains, for goodness sakes. Their only common ground was mythology. The idea of a liaison between them seemed far-fetched. What if he revealed his feelings, and she didn't reciprocate?

He'd feel foolish. Also, if that ruined their pleasant friendship, he'd be devastated.

But what if she *did* reciprocate?

What then?

He bit his lip.

Staring at his layout.

And decided that even a Creator could relax. Even a god could take a day off, couldn't He?

But as he left the basement, thrilling at the prospect of seeing Emma socially for the first time (even if in mixed company) he couldn't repress a small twinge as he shut off the basement lights and ascended the stairs, couldn't completely repress his guilt at casting his unfinished world into darkness.

Friday Evening

Bradley sat at the end of the table at The White Lake Inn, staring at nothing, sipping his Heineken occasionally, cursing himself.

For the night had turned out exactly as he'd feared.

It had begun fine. Emma, excited to see him, had squealed, slip-stumbled off her stool and hugged him briefly around the neck with one arm. She'd followed that up with a quick peck on the cheek.

Completely platonic, of course.

As she'd kiss a brother or cousin.

But his heart had swelled with pleasure. And the folks from other departments, whom he didn't recognize, had acted pleased to meet him.

However, after some small talk, Bradley faded into the background, gradually disappearing, like always. Occasionally, Emma glanced his way and smiled, but she seemed far more interested in a young man sitting next to her, a young man with longish, curly black hair and big blue eyes.

So things had transpired as they always did: he became part of the scenery. His attention drifted as they chatted about sports and reality television and the next episode of that zombie apocalypse show; politicians and whether or not the budget will get passed, who was up for tenure, who was a son-of-a-bitch, and which son-of-a-bitch was up for tenure.

An idiot.

An absolute idiot.

But then things changed. Everyone at the table scattered. The women headed to the lavatory and the men either to the bar for more food and drink, or to the jukebox.

Leaving Emma and him alone.

His mind fumbled a dozen witty conversation starters... but failed to initiate one. Luckily, after finishing her current glass of wine, Emma asked, "And how are you managing, Quiet Mouse? Hanging in?"

He shrugged. Pursed his lips, and in a rare moment of inspiration, decided on the truth. "Actually, I'm bored to death. Having a dreadful time." He offered her a jaunty smile that surprised even him. "You?"

To his delighted surprise, Emma snorted and had to cover her mouth with both hands. She swallowed, coughed and managed, "Oh, God. Some of them are kind of shallow, aren't they?"

He opened his mouth, paused, realizing he didn't actually mean that, at all. "No, not really. I'm just a crusty old academic, I suppose. More comfortable in solitary pursuits than I am social ones. I can lecture eloquently about humanity and our hopes and dreams and fears and how those are reflected in our myths and legends, what they reveal about being human, but I'm not so good at acting like one, I'm afraid. Or at enjoying their company."

She gave him a knowing smile. "So not true. Really. We get along, don't we?"

And there it was.

An invitation for him to broach his true feelings. Did he dare? "Well, yes... mostly because..."

But the moment slipped past as she reached over and patted his hand. "I'm sure any single woman your age would be mad about you."

woman your age

And the chance disappeared.

woman your age

As the ladies returned, followed by the men with refilled pitchers and promises of hot wings and chili cheese fries soon to follow.

Quickly, almost as if he'd never spoken, Bradley faded into the background once more, occasionally sipping his now lukewarm beer, feeling numb, realizing he was flirting very near to pouting, and not sure if he cared.

And then Emma yawned, ran a hand through her gorgeous, silky black hair. "I'm done, folks. Bushed. Summer session starts Monday, and I've done nothing to prepare."

Chuckles circled the table. Bradley flickered a smile, though he doubted Emma noticed.

And then, a blessed reprieve. Emma met his gaze, smiled and asked, "Walk me out, Brad?"

He blinked. Stupidly, he felt sure. He did his best not to stammer. "Yes. Certainly. Really, I probably should get going myself."

"I bet." Emma winked as she shrugged into a light spring coat. "Probably eager to get home to your trains, and all."

A slight flush of... anger? pulsed through him. Was she joking, or...

The group's laughter sounded amiable, the young man who'd sat next to Emma – a Math instructor, he thought – saying he'd love to see Bradley's layout some time, to which he nodded numbly.

But Emma's remark bothered him.

Was she mocking him? In public, no less?

But he shook it off. Hell, she'd asked him to walk her out. A chance – however slight – for them to be alone. So he prepared his best face and smiled. "We gods are busy, Emma. Can't keep my Creation waiting, now can I?"

This reply apparently served well, because everyone laughed again. And Emma's smile was rewarding: bright, energetic, and mirthful. Joking, she'd been. Obviously.

Surely.

As they left The White Lake Inn, Emma flashed him a hopeful-looking smile. "So, I've a favor to ask. One I wanted to pose in private."

His heart stirred inside, beating faster.

Making it very hard to breathe.

So perhaps this was it.

As they faced each other, Emma's red lipstick glistened in the neon glow of the Inn's beer signs, eyes shimmering in the night. He struggled not to sound too desperate. "Anything. Name it."

"Could you cover my class next Friday?"

His mouth hung open, for a second.

Stomach twisting.

He closed his mouth, scrambling to recover. "I... well. Yes, I'm certain I could." Hating himself for acquiescing so easily, he asked, "What for? No troubles, I hope."

"Nooo..." she bit her lip. "I have... ah, hell. I can tell you, right?" She cocked an eyebrow. "If you can't trust a friend, then who can you trust?"

At the word "friend", his stomach twisted more. "Of course," he murmured.

And amazingly enough, Emma looked embarrassed. "I'm sort of... going away next weekend. With a friend. A... work friend."

"Someone from the college, then. Our department, or..." He understood her reticence, now. Inter-faculty dating wasn't forbidden or unheard of. But missing class to vacation with a fellow faculty member wouldn't be received well, at all.

"No. From the Math department. Ned Simmons, actually. The one who said he'd love to see your layout sometime."

Bradley nodded. Yes. The one with the curly black hair and blue eyes, whom Emma had shown so much attention.

"We're going to Maryland for the weekend – Ocean City – leaving early next Friday morning." She twisted her hands, looking sheepish. "I did sort of tell the Department Chair I had a family affair, so..."

He nodded, hoping the night hid what he felt burning behind his eyes. "I see. Of course. I assume your leave was approved, long as you found your own substitute."

Emma's apprehension dissolved, her face breaking into a beautiful smile that crushed him, because he understood that it wasn't for him. "Yes! You're so awesome. So you can cover? You were the first person I thought of, because I knew my kids would be in good hands, and also figured you wouldn't blab."

He forced a small smile. "Of course. As you said, what are friends for?"

She grabbed his elbow, squeezing it. "Great! You're teaching Intro to Mythology this summer, right?" He nodded. "That's in the afternoon, I'm always home by then. I'll come by your place, say... Wednesday night? Drop off my lesson plans?"

His place.

Wednesday night.

Faint hope bloomed inside. Emma at his home, at night. Them, alone together...

yes, you idiot, so you can help her go off on a dirty weekend

Still.

Desperate measures.

"Sounds excellent. Maybe we could eat..."

"Sure!" Emma smiled and slapped his shoulder. "I'll bring over some pizza and beers. The least I can do. And hey – I'll bring Ned over, if that's all right. He's crazy about trains. He'll love your layout."

Frustration burned in him. "Well, actually, I was thinking more that..."

But she struck him dumb with a heartfelt look of gratitude. "Thanks, Brad! You're the best."

With that, she headed to the parking lot and her car,

leaving him on the Inn's front walk, fumbling his keys.

"Friends," he murmured. Rolling the word around in his mouth.

And it tasted like ashes.

#

Bradley had taken a wrong turn somewhere.

Hard to believe – having spent hours driving around Clifton Heights' roads during his layout's conceptual stages – but there it was.

He was lost.

Didn't recognize this road at all. Too dark. No buildings, no streetlights, even, and the transition had been instant: one minute, he was passing the Great American Grocery on the corner of Asher and Front Street, the next, he was here.

On this dark, murky... hazy road.

He braked gently.

Parking the car.

Sat for several seconds, listening to the night, which sounded empty. Devoid of life.

Silly thought.

Then why did his hand tremble at the door handle?

Snorting, Bradley unhooked his seatbelt, opened the door and slid out. The air felt cold on his skin; unseasonably cold for this time of year, even in the Adirondacks.

He stood on the center stripe. Glanced over his shoulder and, sure enough: the bright streetlights on Front Street glimmered. But the other direction, where this road led…?

The back of his neck tingled.

His breath echoed in his ears.

His belly swirled. "This is ridiculous. Just an old road, is all."

But to the best of his knowledge, no road branched off Front Street here.

Except…

No.

Ridiculous.

He squeezed his hands into fists and turned.

Looking down this strange road that seemed to disappear into the gray, indistinct haze his car's headlights couldn't penetrate… almost, as if there were no more road.

Or anything, at all.

yet

because it wasn't finished

No.

Ridiculous.

Fog, that's all. The Adirondacks was notorious for its heavy fogs.

He looked up.

No stars. Nothing.

Except a large, bloated full moon. Casting the fog and the road itself into an eerie phosphorescence that somehow didn't make the night any brighter.

Of course, the full moon. But where were the stars?

"Cloud cover," he murmured, "What was the forecast today? Clouds. That's all."

Clouds.

But how could clouds be so selective, shutting off

everything *but* the moon?

He turned and looked back into town, saw the lights of Front Street, farther away than before, it seemed. Saw also the nearly insubstantial red glimmer of Great American, and just barely saw the turn he was supposed to have taken, onto Adams Street.

But he'd missed it, kept driving because he was tired, frustrated and depressed. So he'd missed his turn, drove onto a road he didn't know, drove into... this.

He faced forward again, trying very hard to shake the impression that the road ahead disappeared into a seething, roiling, drifting gray nothingness.

Fog.

That's all.

And then, an immense fatigue weighed him down. What he really needed was to get into his car, turn around, go home to bed.

So he did exactly that.

Not thinking about how quickly he got back into his car, how his keys jingled in his trembling hand as he stuck them into the ignition, ignoring the relief that flooded him as the car started and he turned around and drove away.

Saturday Morning

Bradley awoke slowly.

Blinking. Pain throbbing in his neck where it bent; his face sore, resting on his forearm...

Wait.

Neck sore where it bent.

Face resting on his forearm.

He blinked again. Raised his head experimentally, wincing as the pain's dull throb stabbed down his neck, into his shoulders.

He gazed around, confused. Couldn't be hung-over. Only drank one beer last night. But strange, he couldn't remember much after leaving the Inn. He'd taken a wrong turn, hadn't he? Gotten spooked by some strange fog, before he finally found his way home.

And as foam crunched under his fingertips, he realized: he'd fallen asleep on his train layout.

He inched his head higher up, feeling his stiff neck pop. Slowly he uncoiled, sitting up and leaning back in his rolling chair.

He closed his eyes.

Cupped his face.

Kneading his forehead with his fingertips, fumbling his thoughts, groping last night's fragmented memories. They drifted there, in gray mists. Just had to pull them together.

He'd stayed up after coming home last night, later than he'd intended. That much he remembered. In a fit of depression over his failure with Emma, he'd started landscaping the area around the new road. He'd laid some ground cover: grass, brush, trees, gravel shoulders on the new road, then proceeded to landscape. He'd cut some wire mesh, started molding it over mounds of crumpled department meeting agendas, formed some hills, secured the mesh down tight, started laying strips of wet plaster...

He blinked.

Realized he remembered nothing after that.

And when he looked down, he sucked in a hissing breath and stared.

At the completed mountain range and forestland surrounding the new road he'd poured yesterday afternoon. At ground cover, knolls, rock ledges, brush and trees, lawns, a stand of trees on one side of the road...

And the houses, arranged in varying widths from each other.

And the Church of Luna at the road's end, complete with a sign out front, and a graveyard behind, through which ran a track he'd extended from the main town line.

The track ran to the layout's end, flush against the basement wall, and stopped there, with nowhere else to go.

Finished.

It was all finished.

as it should be

He spread and inspected his fingers, spackled with grayish-white bits of crushed plaster, peppered also with glued-on bits of powdered ground cover, stained with faint streaks of black paint.

He rubbed his hands.

Staring at the newly completed hills, forest, track, homes, church... and graveyard, feeling the gritty proof of last night's manic endeavors on his fingers.

And it looked perfect.

The hills blended into plains seamlessly. The brush and rock face and tree placement looked natural. Houses all perfectly aligned with the road and each other, lawns and shrubbery immaculate, driveways pristine...

And that graveyard.

A chill skittered down his spine.

As he gazed upon the miniature graveyard, behind the Church of Luna. A squarish graveyard, bordered by brown plastic fencing, replete with scaled, rectangular gravestones.

He reached out.

Touched a gravestone with his fingertip, wiggling it. Firm, secured. Not just glued down, but inserted into the foam base, glued down into the foam. Sound practice, what he did with all his trees and telephone poles and street signs. Based on their width and size and texture, he guessed he'd snipped off Popsicle sticks and painted them. They could be purchased in bulk at hobby stores anywhere. He had a box. There it was, open on his workbench.

The gravestones.

He peered closer.

Of course, he'd painted them gray. But... had he somehow written epitaphs on them, also? How was that even possible? Such detailed work – if he'd managed it – far exceeded dedicated realism.

It bordered on the fanatical.

As he peered closer, however, he saw that he hadn't written epitaphs but instead inscribed a symbol very similar to the pagan moon symbol he'd painted on the Church of Luna's doors and sign:

But what did the symbol mean?

He couldn't remember.

And the reality hit him, then. "Impossible," he whispered. "Should've taken me days. The plaster alone would've taken all night to..."

There.

Lying next to the box of craft sticks on his workbench, a hair dryer. At some point in his fugue, he must've brought it down here and quick-dried the plastered terrain so he could finish everything in one night.

Which wasn't necessarily unusual. He'd heard stories of modelers using a hair dryer to speed up the cementing process; had even done it once himself, in his layout's trial stages.

But that method was for *small* tasks: Ballast along the tracks, gravel shoulders along country roads. Never for an entire plaster mountain range. The work should look sloppy, rushed...

But it looked beautiful.

Nearly perfect. Maybe the best work he'd ever done.

He stood slowly, pushing up from his chair.

Rubbing his gritty, plaster-crusted hands.

Staring at his work, trembling slightly.

But why the alarm? He'd just gone a little overboard last night is all. Consumed by his loneliness.

That's all.

Which of course didn't explain why he slowly backed away from the layout, resolving to go upstairs, wash and dress, eat breakfast and study at his campus office, telling himself he needed to work without distraction on Monday's opening lecture.

But it still took great effort to turn from the layout and walk away.

#

On the way to campus, Bradley made several trips up and down Front Street. Scanning all the side streets he knew, following Front Street as it curved into Old Barstow road, even following Old Barstow all the way to the New York State Electric and Gas Payment Center on the edge of town.

And he turned and came back.

He repeated this several times.

But no matter how hard he looked, he found no sign of a side road with a dead end.

None at all.

Saturday Afternoon

Bradley was sitting in his office, at his desk and laptop, staring at the results of his Google Image Search when someone rapped on his open office door.

In truth, he felt grateful for the interruption. So far,

his attempts at undistracted study had failed. He'd barely gotten anything done. Granted, he was teaching "Introduction to Mythology" this summer, which he'd taught several times before, and could probably teach cold, if needed. But he liked having intimate, fresh recall of the material, no matter how many times he'd taught it.

So it had frustrated him, finding himself doodling that odd symbol he'd apparently painted on those tombstones. And no matter how often he'd crumpled his doodles, threw them away and refocused on his studies, his attention had drifted again.

To unbidden images of an empty road disappearing into gray mists.

not so empty anymore

No.

Ridiculous.

But the more he tried to repress the memory of the road shrouded in gray mists, a road that he couldn't seem to find by the light of day, the more he'd doodled that strange symbol, over and over.

Until he'd finally given up, put his studies aside, opened Google Image Search on his laptop and typed in "moon symbols", a safe bet because it looked so similar to the image he'd painted on his Church of Luna.

He'd found his answer quickly.

And was still sitting and staring, amazed and maybe a little afraid, when the knock repeated, accompanied by a cough and a "Brad? Got a minute?"

He started, slightly relieved, for some reason, at being interrupted. Some of that relief dimmed, however, when he swiveled in his rolling chair and saw Ned Simmons – that Math fellow Emma was going on holiday with – leaning in his doorway, grinning.

"Hey... Brad. Ned Simmons. We met last night at the Inn."

Bradley stared. Groping for something to say, finding nothing. Ned's smile faltered. "Ah... uh. Sorry. Were you busy? If so, I'll just..."

And then, as usual – damn them – his manners kicked into gear. He smiled, waving dismissively. "Not really. Just trying to prep for Monday and failing horribly."

Ned chuckled, folded his arms. "Yeah, summer session. Used to teach it myself, but since I got tenure two years ago, I don't bother with it. Figured I didn't need to impress folks, anymore."

"Yes," Bradley murmured. *He'd* yet to be offered tenure. "I see your point."

And as he took in Ned Simmons' wiry form, rakish curly black hair and big, sensitive blue eyes (eyes that would be gazing upon Emma next weekend) he found that, deep inside, he hated Ned Simmons.

So it was with great effort he leaned forward, resting his elbows on the chair's arms and smiled. "What can I do for you, Ned? Also. How'd you figure I'd be here?"

And suddenly, Ned managed to look sheepish. "Well. Ah. I looked you up in the faculty directory, called your home, and when you didn't answer, I called Emma, asked her where you'd most likely be, in pretense of asking to see your train layout."

"Ah. Interesting. On pretense. So, in other words, you wanted to see me about something you didn't want Emma to know about."

Ned held out a hand. "Don't get me wrong. I was totally serious last night. Would love to see your layout. My Uncle Mark had one, filled his whole basement. Cousins and I spent hours playing with it, as kids."

He bristled inside at the idea of *playing* with a train layout. One didn't *play* with someone else's creation, and he loathed the idea that Ned might want to play with his. But he kept his tone light. "What did you want to talk about, then?"

Ned shrugged, looked away.

Shuffling like a nervous teen on his first date.

Swallowed and looked at him again, that silly grin plastered all over his face. "Well... this is going to sound cowardly, I know. But Emma. She's rather..."

Bradley raised his eyebrows.

Noncommittal, determined not to make it easy. "Yes?"

Ned licked his lips. Swallowed again. And then, in a verbal rush, "Well, she's pretty special. Unique. Full of energy and always moving, talking, thinking... so expressive. So alive. Makes you feel twice as alive, just being around her. Y'know?"

"I suppose," he remarked dryly, wondering how Ned could miss his sarcasm, "I see her every day. Maybe I've built up a tolerance for her aliveness."

"Yeah, maybe." Ned rushed on, clueless, making Bradley despise him even more. "Anyway, she's fun to be around, and we've had a blast on a few dates..."

Try as he might, Brad couldn't repress the jealousy stabbing his guts. "Dates?"

Ned waved. "Yeah. Movies. Bowling. Hiking... that sort of thing."

movies

bowling

hiking

that sort of thing

Sorts of things Bradley had known nothing about; that Emma had never once intimated, at all.

But why would she?

They were friends, of course.

And some things, apparently, friends didn't discuss.

"Go on," Bradley prompted. Unable to keep a chill from entering his voice. But, energized by his topic, Ned didn't seem to notice.

"See, that's the thing: those dates were all one-shot deals, right? I never really planned on us getting back together, it just kept happening."

Though he didn't feel any sympathy for Ned – rather burned inside with a cold envy – he saw the young man's dilemma. "But spending a whole weekend with her... that's a bigger commitment. More than fun and games."

"Well... yeah. Those other dates we were busy doing stuff, having fun. We go away for the weekend... we can't be busy the whole time..."

"Why yes," Bradley remarked, raising his eyebrows, not even bothering to hide his sarcasm now, but Ned still missing it, "you'll actually have to make intelligent conversation, for a change."

Ned snapped his fingers and pointed. "Right! I mean, the car ride alone down to Ocean City will be over four hours. For the first two, I figure I'll manage all right, have enough to say... but after that..."

Bradley sighed, fighting to keep his exasperation in check. God. Whatever did Emma see in this stumbling lout? Past his youngish, rugged good looks, of course. His athletic build, excellent fashion sense...

He forced himself to speak politely. "So. You came to me because..."

Ned shook his head. "I dunno. I know all the right things to say on a *date*, right? Make them laugh, get them all dewy-eyed, weak in the knees, show them a good time, maybe even..."

Bradley coughed.

Ned blushed and offered a weak grin. "Ah. Don't suppose you want to hear about *that*, do you?"

Somehow Bradley kept his face blank, even managed a small, wooden smile. "Well. It wouldn't be polite to kiss and tell, would it?"

Shock and even embarrassment reddened Ned's cheeks. Least the man had some sense of propriety. Not that it made him any less loathsome.

Ned waved. "No, of course not. I guess what I mean is, Emma's more than just someone to share a few good times with. She's bigger than all that. She's like..."

"A virtual force of nature?" he offered, still sarcastic but telling the truth, now. It was how he felt, after all. Which of course made this doubly unpleasant, that someone as young and attractive and suave and modern but so damn shallow could feel the same way about Emma.

His Emma.

Ned snapped his fingers and pointed at him again. A gesture Bradley was coming to hate almost as much as Ned himself. "Right! Exactly. And you just feel so small next to her, right? See, I'm a numbers guy. Good with equations and formulas and processes. Can calculate shit in my head, zero-flat. But get past my bluster and smooth lines, and that's all I am. Numbers Boy. While she's so much more, she's..."

"... one with the universe," he finished quietly. No trace of sarcasm in his voice, now. Just a touch of sadness, and, if he admitted it...

Defeat.

Resignation.

"Yes!" Ned finger-snapped-pointed again. "Exactly. It's like she knows things. Like she's got access to the secrets of life. Mystical knowledge."

Bradley smiled and said in a dry voice, "She teaches mythology, Ned. Traffics in legends and myths and folklore and religions, and – well – 'mystical knowledge'. That's her thing."

No finger-snap-point this time. Ned sighed and slumped against the doorframe. "Yeah. So what chance do I have? I mean... how can a guy like me connect with someone like her, connect on a *deeper* level? Or, at least, not sound like an idiot on the way to Ocean City?"

"And you want to pick my brain. For ways to connect with Emma. Don't you?"

Ned straightened.

Smiling unsurely. "Yeah. You guys are always

together. Eating in the café, talking between classes. You're so similar. Like she's your little sister, or something. I thought..."

He rubbed the back of his neck, looking doubtful, even more unsure. "Hell, I know it's forward, but I was thinking, maybe we could grab dinner at the Inn and talk."

A variety of responses occurred to Bradley. Most of them involving violence and aggression and profanity. None of them, of course, suiting his nature at all.

So he sighed.

Clapped his knees and stood, grabbing his jacket from off his chair. "Dinner, then. Was getting hungry, anyway."

"Great! That's awesome." Ned fairly beamed. "And I wasn't kidding about seeing that layout, sometime. I'd love to. Seriously."

Bradley smiled tightly, nodding at the door. He followed Ned out and locked his office door behind him, quietly, calmly...

like she's your little sister, or something

... burning inside.

Saturday night

Driving Ned Simmons home, late at night, after too many rounds of beers and Tequila.

Not exactly what Bradley had expected, initially.

Dinner had gone tolerably well. Much to his surprise, after seating themselves and ordering, Ned hadn't launched into prying him for advice about impressing Emma. Instead, they'd chatted about strictly mundane things: social matters of the Heights, whether or not the reconstruction from last fall's flood would be finished by summer's end, about this town resolution or that, little bits and pieces of gossip from the hallowed halls of Web County Community College.

And, not surprisingly – given Ned's repeated expressed desire to see the layout – they'd talked some about model railroading. Ned had yet to build his own layout (not enough space in his studio over in Oakland Arms) but he'd boxes of supplies just waiting to be opened. He even attended an annual train show in Steamtown, Pennsylvania, and was something of a novice train-spotter, also.

So throughout dinner, Bradley had felt stirrings of grudging respect, maybe even – God help him – feeling a reluctant approval of Ned.

But things changed after several beers, beers that quickly – at a rate Bradley found alarming – turned into tequila shots. And the Ned Simmons that was revealed after the liquor stripped several layers away...

Well.

Bradley's hands tightened on the steering wheel even now, thinking about it. How Ned, after his third or fourth shot, looking slightly disheveled, eyes glassy and distant, had burped discretely and said, "Women. Remarkable, wonderful creatures. No wonder we want as many of them as possible, even with all the headaches they cause."

Bradley remembered frowning, not sure if he'd heard correctly. "Sorry. Did you say... many?'"

Ned paused.

Sucked on his lip in that wary, embarrassed way drunks had. Then snorted and grinned. "Ah. Probably shouldn't talk about it, eh? Like discussing my exes with my girlfriend's dad."

And with that, all his reluctant affinity for Ned had dissipated like fog in the morning sun. A stony coldness had crept over him, and he'd had to force his hands to grip each other on the tabletop, rather than reaching for Ned's throat.

"I don't follow."

"Well, see," Ned began with a flourish, warming to the subject, rather than being reluctant or coy, "there's this girl in Utica. Been shacking up with her occasionally for the past year. Dental hygienist. Nice girl. No Emma, mind you. Not even close. But she'd make a solid wife, right? Kinda woman who'd be fine quitting work to raise my kids, attend PTA meetings, run bake sales for the local charities, that sort of thing.

"Problem is, Emma's wild, philosophical, alive; she's like a... a..." he gestured aimlessly, "like a drug. Gets in your system. Addictive as hell."

"But she'd hardly give up her studies and teaching to go home and be barefoot pregnant for you, would she?" Bradley muttered.

Too drunk on tequila, Ned had missed Bradley's verbal jab. "See, yeah. Don't know if she's the marryin, have-kids-kinda girl. But I just can't get enough of her."

He lifted his bottle of Guinness, knocked it back, draining it, and thumped it back onto the table. "Helluva choice. Helluva choice." He burped again, this time, not so discretely. "Then there's Haley."

He'd gripped his hands tighter. Nails biting into the backs of his hands. "Haley?"

Ned had blushed and waved. "Yeah. A junior at Syracuse. Met her at a party, she didn't tell me her age... but that was months ago. Didn't mean anything, except she keeps calling me. And she was hell in the sack. Hell in the sack."

And in that moment, hard and cold and bitter feelings coalesced into a fine, sharp point inside Bradley. But he'd just smiled, raised his hand and beckoned to the waiter, saying to Ned in the most affable tone he could manage, "I know what you need, Ned.

"More to drink."

Now

And so here they are, on this strange glowing road that only exists at night. Except this time, Bradley's not lost and instead of turning down an empty, mist-covered road leading into gray nothingness, he's arrived at a place he must've known all along he was coming to. A place made for him. *By* him.

Bradley parks his car.

Kills the engine.

Wondering if, even before Ned started drinking, revealing the seedier aspects of his nature, he'd planned on looking for this road, tonight. Wondering if he'd planned on bringing Ned here all along, sometime during the full moon, onto a road he knew would be more than empty mist, now.

Ned had wanted to see his layout, after all.

So here's his chance.

But as Bradley gets out of the car and stands before the Church of Luna – big as life, glowing with the same, eerie phosphorescence all the other buildings and the road and the trees and lawns and tracks emit – he knows, deep down, that he was meant to come here, Ned Simmons regardless.

For all this is *his*.

Wrought by his hands and heart, if not his mind and will.

And in this moment, he calls it "good."

The passenger door slams shut. Ned mumbles, "Holy... shit. Too much booze. Everythin looks all glowin an shit."

And then Ned gasps, squeals almost like a child at Christmas. He points, his face childlike in the moon's glow. "Look! Tracks run behind that weird church! And... man! A Chessie! It's a goddamn Chessie!"

And without another word, Ned stumbles across the church's front lawn, slipping on night-slicked grass, and runs into the graveyard and up to the black, sleek engine and its one passenger car, sitting and thrumming on the tracks behind the church.

Bradley follows slowly. At ease, in no hurry. Of course, he half expected the train to be here, once he discovered what that symbol painted on the gravestones meant.

He's not too long in joining Ned, who stands and stares at the midnight black Chessie, which thrums and growls lowly. "A Chessie," Ned whispers. "But I've never seen one all black like this. Usually black and orange and yellow. And this..."

He reaches towards a white symbol like the ones painted on the tombstones. "What's this mean?"

He touches it.

Stiffening, as if gripped by an immense cold.

Trembling, jaw hanging open, as if instinctively understanding a deep, horrible truth for the first time.

"It's the mark of Charon," Bradley whispers. "A moon of Pluto. Also, in Greek mythology, the ferryman of the dead, who transports people across the River Styx to Hades."

Ned's hand drops limply to his side. He turns and faces Bradley. Eyes distant, faraway, face slack, mouth gaping... the black mark of Charon glimmering on his forehead. "And, it looks like you just paid Charon's toll. Or maybe I did, for you," Bradley amends. "This is all new to me."

A door to the engine's only passenger car hisses open. A tall form leans out, dressed in a black rendition of a steam engine conductor... and the face beneath its cap is smooth and white and blank. Slightly bumpy protrusions suggest eyes and a nose and cheekbones and craters...

like on the moon

... but no actual face regards them. The voice, however, rings clear. "All aboard."

Ned Simmons pauses, like a man in a dream. He glances at Bradley, swallows, blinks and says, "Not coming back, am I?"

Bradley shakes head. "I don't think so. But maybe that's for the best."

For Emma.

And me.

Ned blinks again, nods sluggishly, lips moving, as if to say one last thing, but nothing comes out. So he turns, shambles away and boards the train, disappearing into the passenger car, past the faceless conductor.

Who leans out further. Even without eyes, Bradley feels its gaze upon him. "Will you be coming along also, sir?"

Bradley shakes his head. "Not tonight."

The faceless conductor nods. Disappears into the train. And almost immediately, a mournful, low horn blows. Great, metal shifting sounds emanate from deep within the midnight black Chessie marked with the sign of Charon.

And it chugs away.

And as Bradley watches its departure, he sees not the wall of his basement – where this spur ends on his layout – but that same drifting wall of grayish mist.

He turns away.

Leaving the graveyard, knowing that for sure, Emma will be upset – perhaps even distraught – when Ned's disappearance becomes news. But, based on what he's learned tonight, coupled with the certain eyewitness reports of them dining together at the Inn, Bradley feels sure he can share Ned's sordid past with Emma and convince her that more than likely, the young raker has simply moved on to other pastures.

There will be questions, of course.

Especially because he'll be remembered as the last person seen with Ned. But he's sure he can weather them. There's no evidence left behind, after all.

Bradley can say that because of Ned's drinking, he drove him back to his apartment, and that was the last he saw of him.

And Emma?

She'll get over Ned's apparent abandonment. Because he'll be there. That's what friends are for, of course. And perhaps this will finally open Emma's eyes to their potential.

And if not?

That would be unfortunate. Because despite his peaceful nature, Bradley has a feeling he won't turn out to be a very forgiving god.

Not very forgiving at all.

Father Figure
Tracie McBride

I met her during rush hour on a wintry Friday afternoon on the steps of Flinders Street Station. She stood slightly apart from her friends, an outcast amongst outcasts. Commuters migrating homeward bumped and jostled each other in the crush, yet the crowd instinctively parted to leave the little coven of Goths inviolate.

Untouchables. That's what they appeared to be. That's what I once was, before I grew up, got responsible, jumped on the corporate gravy train. Yet one look at Mia and all I wanted to do was touch her. Touch her in the most intimate and urgent ways, shake her, bruise her, drive her to her knees, wipe that sullen look off her face and replace it with one of flush-faced, open-mouthed, uncontrollable lust, run my hands through her long, black hair and pull real tight...

The impulse shook me; I considered myself a lover, not a fighter, and certainly not both at once. And right then I should have heeded my inner caution and walked on. But instead I stared at her, willing her to meet my gaze, and she did for a split second before turning away with a sneer. As well she should, for I was nearly twice her age and should have no business looking at her with the thoughts I was having. I was no stranger to sexual conquest, albeit with women closer to my own age and social milieu, but there was something... *different* about this girl. I dithered on the steps, pretending to fish around in my pockets for something and trying like a lovelorn teenager to pluck up the courage for a direct approach. Surreptitiously, I studied her more closely.

She wore the traditional Goth costume; head to toe in black. Despite the cold, her shirt was sleeveless, made of a flimsy lace material that allowed tantalising glimpses of pale skin. I smiled – no doubt she rebelled against everything, even the weather. She turned to talk to a friend, thus affording a clearer view of the black-inked pseudo-Celtic tattoo adorning one bicep, and my smile widened – there was my opportunity. As I closed the gap between us, I bolstered my confidence with a mental image that I couldn't fully buy into; I was the Big Bad Wolf, and she my Little Black Riding Hood.

"I'm Andy," I said, extending a hand. She looked at it as if I had just offered her a plate full of dog shit. Only slightly deterred, I pushed on. "That's an interesting tattoo. Do you know what it means?"

"Of course I do," she spat, "but I'm not going to tell you."

"You don't need to," I said. "I know what it means. It means that we're destined to be together." A battle waged in my head – *Could you get any cheesier?* Versus *But what if it's true?* The latter won out, and I leaned closer and lowered my voice.

"I have an identical tattoo."

"Bullshit," she said. Her gaze flickered from my face to my suit-clad arms and back again. For an instant her aloof exterior cracked, and I saw something akin to hope in her eyes. Hope that I might be The One, that I might succeed where others had failed (or perhaps not even attempted) to save her from whatever misery her life contained. No longer the Big Bad Wolf, I became the Knight in Shining Armour. Now *that* was a role I could sincerely play.

"C'mon," I said. "It's cold out here. Let's go somewhere to warm up and I can show you." This time, she accepted my outstretched hand.

And so, over a couple of glasses of absinthe in a dimly lit corner of an impossible-to-find-unless-you're-in-the-know back alley bar, I shrugged off my jacket and tie and slid my business shirt down over my shoulder to reveal her tattoo's twin. It wasn't really any great coincidence – no doubt she'd chosen the design the same way I had twenty years ago, by pointing at a picture on a tattoo parlour wall – but she was suitably impressed all the same. From the moment her fingertips caressed my inked skin, she was mine.

While a part of me still screamed *Wrong! Wrong! Wrong!* I slid quickly into love, in spite of – or perhaps, because of – her troubled background. Mia's drug-addicted mother had died from an overdose when she was a toddler, and nobody knew who her father was. She'd been raised by a series of indifferent foster parents – so beautifully damaged, a wild, rudderless child. When she told me seven months later that she was pregnant, I was jubilant, and proposed to her on the spot. Everybody counselled us against getting married. Everyone, that is, who cared, which was precious few.

Was I drawn to her youth? Yes. Her fragility? Yes. Did I want to protect her, to save her, from herself and the world at large? Yes. Was I tired, bored and lonely, and looking to stave off the oncoming ravages of old age a little longer with a vital young wife? Yes. Did we rush into our marriage, with little thought for the consequences? Yes. Yes, yes, a thousand times yes, yet all these tawdry truths did not come close to describing the profundity of our relationship. We were *connected* on some deep, indefinable level that transcended the clichés of our union.

The change in Mia became evident almost immediately after we got engaged. She put away the trappings of her misery – the thick black eyeliner, her exclusively black clothing, her extensive collection of drear, moody so-called music. The scars on her limbs from her self-harming episodes faded. Her eyes sparkled. She *smiled*. I was vindicated in my love and support. She carried and gave birth to our child with a joy and ease that other women envied. Bain, we named him, and he was perfection incarnate. Certain that nothing could spoil our happiness, we scheduled our wedding to coincide with Bain's first birthday.

#

On the eve of our wedding she came to me bearing a battered shoe box.

"Burn it," she commanded, a glimpse of her former, defiant self flashing across her face as she thrust it into my hands.

"What is it?" I asked.

She shrugged. "Photos. Letters. Documents. Mostly old shit that belonged to my mother. None of it means anything to me anymore. You and Bain are my only family now." She rested one hand on her belly, not yet swollen with our newly conceived second child.

I cradled the box in my lap as if it might contain a venomous snake. "Well, if you're sure..."

"I'm sure."

She did not say 'don't open it', and even if she had, I would have disregarded her. When she left for the night to attend to whatever mysterious wedding rituals women observe, I removed the lid and examined the first item. It was Mia's birth certificate; despite her instructions, I set it aside against some future need. There were a few blurry, poorly composed photos of a teenaged girl who I assumed was Mia's mother Debbie. I studied them closely. The quality of the photos made it hard to learn anything from them; she looked familiar, and I was caught in an uncomfortable state of not-quite-recognition, unable to tell whether I knew her from a former time or was merely acknowledging the features she shared with her daughter.

I turned to the other items. Old concert ticket stubs, a lock of jet black hair barely held together with ancient, yellowing sticky tape, a cheap necklace bearing a small, blue stone pendant which I threw into the bin... they meant no more to me than they did to Mia.

At the bottom of the box sat a bundle of letters bound with a rubber band. I skimmed through the first few. They were almost laughable in their banality – badly written old love letters penned by adolescent admirers, and one angry missive from Debbie's mother over some long forgotten grievance – and I was almost ready to toss the entire bundle back into the box, when something about the last letter caught my attention. It was from a young man, begging Debbie to abort, adopt out, pin the blame on someone else, say she was raped, do *anything* other than name him as the father of her unborn child. His life would be ruined otherwise, he claimed with staggering selfishness.

I knew the handwriting only too well, although I'd long since forgotten the circumstances that had prompted the letter, buried as they were beneath so many other careless close calls of my youth. I sat and stared at the pages for what seemed like hours. Big Bad Wolf indeed; I felt like I had been hollowed out and my stomach filled with stones that weighed me down until I could no longer move.

Then came the self-justifications. Perhaps it was a mistake. Perhaps this was just some horrible coincidence, this Debbie not the same one that I had once known, but some other callous youth's discard. Or perhaps it was my Debbie, but not my child. After all, she could have slept with any number of young men that summer, as free with her affections as I conveniently remembered her to be. Yes, that must be it; after all, wasn't Bain's robust good health and beauty living proof that Mia could not be my daughter?

I looked at the birth certificate again, at the "Father: Unknown." With one word, Debbie had both saved and condemned me. Still, a DNA test would settle the question, and it wasn't too late to postpone the wedding. And yet...

My favourite game as a child had been to 'hide' by covering my eyes with my hands; if I could not see my hunter, I reasoned, then he or she could not see me. It had always served me well as a problem-solving strategy and I saw no need to give it up now. I burned the box with its damning letter inside, and kept my mouth firmly shut about it. I was probably the only person alive who so much as suspected the truth of Mia's parentage, and I buried that suspicion deep down until it became as ephemeral a thought in my consciousness as the smoke that rose from the embers in the fireplace.

#

After Bain came Layla, then Charlize, Sebastian, and finally Poppy. Five beautiful, healthy children under the age of seven and all of them with the same black hair, pale skin and delicate features. Like a household full of Snow Whites, our neighbours used to say. After Poppy, I booked myself in for a vasectomy, citing a long list of sensible reasons, but in truth I did it because I feared that we were pushing our luck. Every pregnancy brought with it a deep anxiety on my part that the child would be born malformed in some way; it felt like we were playing Gestational Russian Roulette. Mia was happy enough with my decision, as you would expect for the mother of five. Our lives were cheerfully chaotic, and we immersed ourselves in love and a deep contentment. My family kept me feeling young, but they could not stop the physical signs of aging, not that I cared much about that anymore. I grew round of belly and grey of hair, and the only time it bothered me was when strangers mistook me for the children's grandfather. Too close to the bone by far, these innocent assumptions made me want to prove my vitality by throttling the life out of them.

The cracks began to appear when Bain turned fourteen. Literally overnight, he changed from a happy, if slightly highly strung, child to a surly and uncommunicative teenager. I was unconcerned; my own adolescence had been much the same, and I had come out the other side of it relatively unscathed (*not so for Debbie*, my subconscious whispered, and I squashed down the thought).

But for Mia, the change in her first born child sparked off her own, cataclysmic shift in outlook.

"There must be something wrong with him," she said, chewing on a thumb nail. She hadn't chewed her nails in fifteen years, and I resisted the urge to slap her hand away from her face. "Some hormonal imbalance or something."

I laughed. "Of course it's a hormonal imbalance! It's called puberty. He'll settle down eventually – just give him time."

"But still, it's not normal... is it?"

She ignored my reassurances, and became convinced that, not only Bain, but our entire family was in the grip of some mysterious malady. Mia marched us all, one by one, to the family doctor, and when she pronounced us all in robust good health, Mia sought a second opinion. And a third. She took our temperatures twice a day, and seemed almost disappointed at the invariably normal results. Every blemish, every cough, every little twinge became the subject of intense scrutiny. She visited dermatologists, chiropractors, dieticians and acupuncturists, dragging with her whichever child she could coerce at the time. A visit to the naturopath had her imposing on the family an organic diet free of meat, soy, dairy, gluten, wheat and sugar. A task as simple as mopping the floor set off a paroxysm of indecision, as she was unable to choose between scouring away potentially deadly bacteria and exposing her family to toxic chemicals.

The children had always been closer to their mother than to me, but Mia's obsession skewed the family dynamic in a different direction. I became their ally, their confidant and their accomplice as I snuck them out of the house on various pretexts to gorge ourselves on burgers and fries, slipped them extra cash to stock their school lunch boxes with more desirable items, invented alibis to get them out of medical appointments, or simply provided them with adult conversation that did not revolve around their health.

One day I caught Bain smoking behind the garden shed. A normal response would have been to punish the child, deliver a stern lecture and confiscate the cigarettes. But we were in no normal situation. Instead, I merely sighed and helped myself to a cigarette out of the packet. I leaned against the shed wall and lit up, inhaling smoke into lungs that had not been abused in such a fashion for the better part of fifteen years.

TRACIE MCBRIDE

I smiled at Bain. "Don't tell Mum," I said.

"I won't," he said, smiling back. We finished our smokes in silence and luxuriated in our guilty camaraderie.

#

"I went to see a psychic today," Mia said one evening. It was the end of a particularly trying week; the children had gone from sly avoidance to open defiance whenever their mother tried to drag them off to some specialist or another, and Mia was angry at me for taking their side.

"And?" I pretended mild indifference, keeping my eyes on the TV screen as I channel surfed without taking any of it in. There was something in her tone that made my hackles rise, and I steeled myself for another confrontation.

"The spirits told her that my intuition has been right all along, and that we have some hereditary disease. Something genetic. It's rare, she says, and the symptoms haven't manifested yet, which is why it hasn't been diagnosed. Apparently, we're all ticking time bombs. She says I should go back to the doctors and request DNA testing."

DNA testing... panic made me explode. I leapt up from my seat, grabbing her by the shoulders and dragging her to her feet, and shook her until her teeth rattled.

"For fuck's sake, Mia, this has got to stop! We're all fine! We don't need DNA testing, or any other kind of testing! The only one sick around here is you –

172

sick in the head."

I regretted my words the instant I uttered them. It was what we had all been thinking, or muttering behind Mia's back, but been afraid to voice for fear of making her worse. I expected her to react with tears or anger, or both, but instead a curious calm came over her. She took a deep breath and shook her head, even giggling a little as she spoke.

"A psychic told me... Yeah, I can see how you might think that sounds a little crazy. Maybe I'm just stressed, or overtired. I probably just need a little break. A couple of days away on my own to get a bit of perspective."

"Yeah, maybe..." I drew her into a hug and muttered an apology into her hair. "I'll book you into a hotel somewhere nice," I promised. "Somewhere in the country, with a day spa." She nodded her assent, but the rigidity of her body told me that this was only a temporary truce, and the battle was far from over.

#

For a few months after Mia's getaway, things in our household were almost normal. She let up on the dietary restrictions, and there were no more unnecessary visits to medical practitioners. The children began to relax a little, although they still held their mother at a slight distance, as if she were a not-quite-tamed animal that could turn on them at any moment.

Then one night I came home from work to a cold, dark and silent house. I thought at first that everyone had gone out, so I jumped, startled, when I switched on a light to find Mia sitting at the kitchen table.

"What's going on? Where are the kids?"

"I sent them all to their rooms," she said. Her voice was strained, as if her throat were in the grip of a giant, unseen hand. She stared down at an opened envelope and several sheets of folded A4 paper on the table in front of her, turning the pages over and over reflexively, her face obscured behind a curtain of glossy, black hair. She lifted her head to look at me, her expression held unnaturally still.

"I had DNA testing done on all of us," she said. "I had to be sure."

I gripped the back of a chair to stop myself from falling. "How... how did you manage to do that without us knowing?"

She waved a hand in dismissal. "Oh, you'd be surprised where you can get DNA samples if you're trying to be secretive–toothbrushes, nail clippings, snot on a used tissue... saliva from cigarette butts..." she said, pointedly emphasising the latter. I had visions of her gathering her materials, not to conduct scientific tests, but to create voodoo dolls of us all.

She rose from her chair, suddenly incandescent.

"You knew, didn't you?" she yelled, punctuating each word by poking me in the chest with a sharp-nailed forefinger and sending me backpedalling into the kitchen bench. "I gave you that box of my mother's letters, and you must have read them, and you MUST have recognised yourself in that one letter, and you said NOTHING! You let me conceive all those babies, and you... you..." She stopped, speechless with rage and revulsion.

"I didn't know for sure," I protested. "I only suspected..." I glanced behind me, checking for any readily accessible weapons, not for myself but to keep them away from her; if she could reach a knife at that moment, she would surely plunge it into my heart.

The children, drawn out by the noise, emerged one by one from their various retreats about the house. They were all graceful and gorgeous, magnificent young creatures as they walked past their mother and came to stand at my side.

"'*Suspected*'? Just your suspicion alone should have been enough to end it. You should never have married me. I should have aborted Layla, drowned Bain in the bath and got as far the fuck away from you as possible." Spittle flew from her mouth and hit me in the face, but I did not wipe it away, my hands being too occupied trying futilely to shield my children's ears from her obscene rant.

At my shoulder, Bain stiffened. "What are you on about now, Mum?" he said scathingly. Mia looked at him as if seeing him for the first time. There was no rage left in her now, only a bone-deep despair.

"It's OK," I murmured to Bain. "I'll handle this." Poppy pressed closer to me and chewed on her thumb nail, just like her mother did in times of stress. Just like I had done at the same age.

"Look at them," I said to Mia, gesturing at our children. Except that with each passing moment they were becoming less *our* children and more *my* children. "How can you call them a mistake?"

And she did look, for long moments, assessing the

physical and psychic distance between us. "They're just kids..." she muttered to herself, but whether the 'just' meant that they had yet to reach maturity or that, being only children, they had little value, I wasn't sure.

"OK, Andy," she finally said. "You want them so much? They're yours. For now. But they will grow up and come to understand what you have done, and then you'll lose them. Remember this – as soon as they turn eighteen, I will reclaim them." This last sentence she spoke with vehemence and ritualistic slowness, as if uttering a curse or casting a spell.

Then she turned and walked out of the house. It was the last time any of us saw her alive.

#

Mia had left the house empty-handed except for her car keys. She made no attempt to access bank accounts or contact friends, no witnesses came forward to say they'd seen her anywhere, and no body matching her description was ever found. The only trace of her was the car, which police found abandoned in a semi-industrial area some fifteen kilometres from our home. She had simply vanished off the face of the Earth. I took to visiting the site where they'd found the car in the vain hopes that I would find some hitherto undiscovered evidence there, or that she would reappear as magically as she had disappeared. The urine-soaked and graffiti-splattered alleyway yielded no clues, yet it became something of a weekly pilgrimage for me to go there;

it was the closest thing I had to a grave. Sometimes I imagined I could hear her voice whispering at me from the darkest recesses of the alley, but it was only the wind stirring the leaves and the echoes from my memories.

As for the kids, I was at once relieved and disturbed at the ease with which they flowed to fill the space left by their mother. There should at least have been tears or misbehaviour, but instead they acted as if she never existed, as if they had sprung, godlike, directly from my loins. They never asked why she left, and I never volunteered the answer.

In fact, they thrived without her. Mia's absence seemed to have removed the shackles from their potential; all of them clever young things before she left, they grew tall and gifted, excelling at school and each possessing a particular prodigious talent. Bain was a sports star, Layla a mathematician, Charlize a musician, Sebastian a writer and Poppy an artist. The future for all of them was blindingly bright.

We'd all forgotten Mia's parting words when, three days after Bain's eighteenth birthday, a drunk driver steered her car into his, killing him instantly. If I'd had concerns about my children's lack of emotion when their mother left, I needn't have worried; the remaining four shed tears aplenty at their brother's graveside, and continued to grieve extravagantly in the months after his death.

We lost Layla to meningitis, which she contracted whilst on a camping trip with friends. I barely let the remaining three out of my sight after that, not that they wanted to stray far from home anyway in the wake of such tragedies. Charlize in particular became very withdrawn. She slept a lot, and during her waking hours she took to playing one mournful note over and over again on her cello. I put the changes down to depression and grief, but it turned out they were caused by the brain tumour that killed her the day after her eighteenth birthday.

I continued my visits to 'Mia's Alley', as I privately called it. Some days as I stared into the darkness, the darkness stared back, the shadows shifting and coalescing for moments into shapes almost human before dissolving back into meaninglessness. The day before Sebastian turned eighteen, I went to plead my case.

"Please stop, Mia," I whispered, feeling ridiculous but continuing regardless. "You have three now; leave me Sebastian and Poppy. Or one of them, at least. Surely you can see how much we've suffered already."

The wind moaned in response. *Bargain with your own children's lives, would you?* it seemed to mock. *Go home, old man. Go home to your grief.*

#

We celebrated Sebastian's birthday by closing the curtains and huddling inside, eating canned food and lighting candles for our fallen which I would blow out within minutes for fear of one toppling and setting fire to the house. Poppy and I took turns standing guard over Sebastian while he slept, and he complained about how creepy it was to have someone staring at him all the damned time.

Nine days later, he was still alive. For the first time since Bain died, I began to feel, if not happy, at least hopeful that Mia's curse had been broken, or perhaps never existed in the first place. We drew back the curtains and opened the windows to let in some fresh air – which is when a bee flew in the window and landed on Sebastian's neck. He couldn't have seen what it was, only felt it brush against his skin. I leapt to stop him but I was too late; he slapped at it, and yelped when it stung him.

He went into anaphylactic shock, and died before the ambulance could arrive. I racked my brain for memories of childhood injuries, but could not recall him, or any of the other children for that matter, ever being stung. This time at least I could be there to see my child take his last tortured breath, to usher him out of my arms and into his mother's, wherever she might be and in whatever form she had taken.

#

Which left Poppy. My youngest child, my daughter who was so much like Mia in looks, mannerisms and personality that sometimes it hurt to be around her. Poor Poppy, who endured more tragedy in her short life than anyone ought to suffer. And just like her mother, she simply walked out the door one day and never looked back. Unlike her mother, they found her body, splattered at the base of a multi-storey parking building from which she'd jumped; evidently she'd decided that if she had to die young, it would be on her terms. Bystanders who'd witnessed her plummet put her time of death at eighteen years after her birth, to the minute.

I went back to Mia's Alley one more time, at midnight – the Witching Hour – on the night of a new moon. The lighting was sporadic already in the area, but I took out the two closest street lights with a few carefully aimed rocks. The darkness was near absolute.

I felt rather than saw her at first, a tiny disturbance in the air currents and a sudden, sharp drop in temperature.

"Silly man," a barely audible whisper tickled my ear, "you didn't have to come here to find me." Substance formed around the sound, and there Mia stood. Her hair, her eyes, her spectral clothing that swirled and slid across her body like an unholy mist, were so black, they were somehow visible against the now insipid night.

"Where else would I find you?" I managed to croak.

"Anywhere there is death. Anywhere there is grief." Behind her, our children – *her* children now, I reminded myself – took shape, although not as distinctly as Mia; some kind of barrier separated us, insubstantial looking yet impenetrable for one like me whose heart still beat. Their features were just as I remembered them, but their *expressions*... no human could bear such pain and knowledge and live. They now knew the truth of their parentage, I could see it in their eyes, and they condemned me for it. More than that, it looked like they'd been condemned to exhume the bones from every family's closets and make their beds on them.

Perhaps that's what death was – the sudden weight of the universe's most sordid secrets.

My every instinct told me to run, to get far, far away from these ghouls masquerading as my family. But hadn't I yearned for this moment of reunion, however twisted it might be, for years?

I laughed. The sound echoed dementedly off the concrete buildings around us. "Anywhere there is death and grief? If that were the case, you would have been with me all along."

Her smile flooded me with yearning and terror, and literally made me buckle at the knees. "I have been," she said, "you just didn't know how to see."

"So will I always see you now?"

"No, Andy," she replied. "But you'll see me again, when it's your turn to join us." Her children receded into the darkness, leaving her alone to gaze down on me, I thought perhaps in pity. But when her final words came, they were steeped in triumph:

"And that will not be for a long, long time."

Room to Thrive
Stephen Bacon

We all die alone, thought Barlow as he listened to Mark's story. Wasn't that the Joseph Conrad quotation? He tried to think back to his English literature lessons but all he could recall was larking about with his mates, rather than listening to what was being taught. But Mark's tale of misery and sorrow was compelling; a depiction of a wasted life, one spent in abject solitude.

They decided to visit the scene of death for themselves.

The macabre nature of Mark's story had been the prompt – the urge they needed to switch off the PS3 and kill the music. In truth, the party had nearly run its course. The amount of booze they'd consumed had been at a crucial tipping-point – just enough so that the idea of venturing out into the dark seemed like a laugh. But once they stepped through the door it felt like the cosy warmth had been a distant memory and they had been swept into a maelstrom.

Gusts of wind snatched Mark's words. The rain was coming at them almost horizontally. They shivered inside their coats and hurried along the glistening streets. They were deserted. The occasional car passed. It was nearly ten o'clock; too early for the pubs to be ejecting drunkards onto the pavement, too late for casual passers-by to be out. Thick clouds smothered the moonlight, rendering the city desolate and intimidating.

"So they found this old bloke dead in his flat," continued Mark, competing with the roar of the wind. "And he'd clearly been dead for a while." Mark worked for the council, employed in the maintenance department for social-housing. "And this flat was a mess, a real fucking mess."

Griff nodded enthusiastically, peering out from the shelter of his hood.

"It stunk to high-heaven in there," said Mark. "It's a wonder the neighbours waited so long to call the council. Anyway it looks like he just died and rotted to bits."

"Rotted?" Jake, the pale young lad swallowed. His eyes were popping out of his skull.

"Yeah, they reckon he'd OD'd and snuffed it, there in his chair. He was all liquefied when they found him. Broken down and shit. There was drug stuff all over the place, mind. Needles and tinfoil and shit like that."

"What did you do?"

"Well once they scraped him up and took him away, we had the job of cleaning the flat – you know, getting it ready for the next tenant."

Barlow considered this, inwardly grimacing at the prospect of living where such a grisly event had taken place. He felt queasy. Maybe it was just the booze.

They crossed the deserted precinct. Barlow caught sight of their reflection in the shop windows, reminding him of shop mannequins brought to life. Neon facades trembled in puddles as the wind gusted across the concrete expanse. The housing estate lurked on the other side of the dual carriageway, a labyrinth of grey-brick buildings. They descended some steps into a sodium-bathed subway. It stank of piss. Nevertheless, the brief respite from the wind and rain was welcome.

"So anyway, while we were cleaning this shit-hole up, Bazza found a hatch under the stairs." Mark's voice echoed in the underpass, as if he was speaking from both ends of the tunnel at the same time.

"A hatch?"

"Like – a trapdoor in the wall," Mark explained. "You know, a false wall, like."

"What? And the shrooms were growing in there?" Jake was constantly licking his lips.

"Yeah. Looked like the old guy grew the fuckers in there." Mark laughed. "Bazza picked some and had them last Friday night. He was off his tits till Sunday afternoon."

Barlow would have preferred to have stuck with the booze and the Playstation but he knew Mark and Griff were *hardcore*; there was nothing they wouldn't try if they thought they could get off on it. Magic mushrooms were just another source of stimulant. Jake looked nervous though.

"So – what?" Griff asked. "We just break in to the flat?"

"We don't need to break-in when we've got this." Mark produced a key with a triumphant flourish. "Ta-dah!"

They trudged up the subway steps at the other side, doing their best to shelter from the onslaught of rain. Taxis glided along the dual carriageway trailing spray in their wake. There was a pub on the corner, *The*

Black Dog, and its brightly-lit windows nearly crumbled Barlow's resolve. As they drew close, techno music pulsed through the walls onto the street.

Mark led them squelching across the kids' playground. The rain was relentless. Sodden takeaway cartons did their best to conceal dog turds in the lengthy grass. The graffiti-scarred climbing-frame waited in the darkness like an ancient monolith.

There was a row of terraced townhouses on the other side of the square, and Mark pointed to the one furthest left. "Lower ground floor." They approached and stared up at the four-storey building that towered over the street. Each flat bore identical doors and window-frames; there was nothing to differentiate the one in darkness from the others in the block. Yet Barlow stared down through the iron railings at the cold featureless façade of the flat and felt a powerful sense of unease. Maybe it was his knowledge of what had occurred in there. Or perhaps it was just the storm.

"C'mon." Mark disappeared down the iron steps to the door at the bottom. He fumbled around for a moment before unlocking it and slipping inside. Griff hurried down after him. Presently the light went on in the flat, even though the window-blinds prevented them from seeing into the room.

Jake glanced at Barlow hesitantly. "You coming?"

Barlow sniffed, nonchalance personified. "Think I might have a smoke first."

Jake nodded and sloped off down the steps.

The patter of rain on Barlow's hood was deafening. He shivered and glanced both ways along the deserted street. Nothing but shadows and water and the faintly depressing signs of urban decay.

For a few minutes he smoked a cigarette, enjoying the sense of solitude, as the row of terraced flats seemed to regard him indifferently. He pondered what went on behind those closed doors. Countless windows stared back, reminding him of the faceted eyes of an insect. Again he shivered. He finished the cigarette, dropped it with a flare of sparks and crushed it underfoot. He hurried down the steps to the flat.

It was only once he was inside the door and breathing in the smell of bleach that he realised he'd been unconsciously expecting it to reek of something nasty. Instead, the detergent was almost overpowering. The floor appeared anaemic; like it had – until recently – been carpeted. Now the exposed tiles looked conspicuously clean, too shiny. All the furniture had been stacked together at one side, presumably awaiting removal by the next-of-kin. The tarnished gas fire looked in need of replacing. Mark was standing in the corner of the room, demonstrating where the tenant had been found: the grouting between the floor tiles was stained with something dark and sticky. Griff and Jake listened with fascinated intensity. The flat was stone cold.

"And here's the hatch." Mark indicated a door cut into the plasterboard of the wall, about two feet square. It was crudely done. It looked like someone – presumably the previous tenant – had installed it himself. "There's a room through there. All bare and wild and shit. Soil on the ground. The mushrooms grow in it."

Griff bent down and opened the hatch. It was too

dark to see much, but Barlow detected a sour stench emanating from it, brackish and organic. He wrinkled his nose and took a step backward. Griff activated the torch function on his mobile phone and held it up at an angle so he could peer through the hatch into the darkness. "Fuck me!"

"What is it?" Jake's voice was shrill. He swallowed and licked his lips again.

Griff ignored him and crouched on his hands and knees. He squeezed his upper body through the hatch until just the lower half remained visible. He said something but it was muffled.

"What?" Mark bent down beside him.

Griff withdrew from the hatch. "It's fucking huge in there! How can it be so big?"

Mark shrugged. "I don't know. We reckoned it must extend under the park a bit. Can you see the shrooms?"

"Not really. There's just soil near this front bit."

"You need to go further in," said Mark. "I think Bazza picked most of the ones from the front."

Griff disappeared into the hatch again, this time so just his feet stuck out. Mark shuffled close to the hatch and peered in. "Pass them here." Griff's hand appeared, bearing two small pale objects which Mark took. Griff emerged from the hatch again. His face was flushed. "There's tons of them. And some weird roots sticking up through the earth."

"Come on, pick some more," said Mark. "We'll fry them back at the flat."

Barlow felt detached from the others. Bored. He drifted out of the room, through the hallway into the galley-kitchen at the rear. It was freezing. He clicked on the light. The worktops were bare; most of the utensils had been packed into cardboard boxes, awaiting disposal. A smell of disinfectant had erased the evidence of a life once lived here. It was clinical. He peered through the kitchen door into the sunken yard at the rear, but darkness had swallowed its detail. He turned back. He clicked off the light and wandered out of the kitchen.

The hallway looked depressingly bare. Barlow could hear the excited chatter from the front room. He pushed open the bedroom door and clicked on the light.

More signs of the recently-departed tenant: a discoloured sagging mattress on the bed, several towering stacks of tatty paperbacks, cardboard boxes stuffed with CDs and DVDs, a cigarette-stained bedside cabinet. Barlow browsed the titles. The usual suspects: reggae, obscure jazz, world music, 80s horror films, foreign art-house cinema, Palahniuk, Bukowski, William S Burroughs. There was a copy of *House of Leaves* lying on top, and Barlow picked it up and thumbed through the dusty pages. Someone had scrawled stuff across many of the margins – weird drawings and unreadable annotations. Certain phrases stood out, though – *pestilence and segregation, the pursuit of a higher state of perception, ancient runes arranged in a concentric circle – could this be it?* Barlow smile wryly at the jottings, thinking of the drug paraphernalia that Mark said had been found in the flat. The final page had no print on it, but it was filled with scrawls similar to those in the margins.

Barlow read the words with an increasing sense of disquiet. *The tentacles. I can hear something moving. Pipes? How deep are they? They need room to thrive. They live off the darkness. It feeds them. Dreams carry life. Mushrooms – sickly, strange, they are getting bigger. I will try them. Consume. Dreams carry life.*

We live, as we dream – alone. That was the Conrad quotation! So he hadn't totally wasted his education. He mustered a vague smile.

Barlow suddenly became aware of the silence. He cocked his head and listened for a few moments. Puzzled, he turned and walked back into the front room. Griff stood awkwardly in the corner, near the front door. He was pale. His eyes were wide, his mouth open. Barlow surveyed the room. Mark was crouched, rocking on his haunches. He too looked shaken. His eyes were glassy. Unfocussed.

"What's wrong?" said Barlow. His voice sounded frail. He stared at Mark and Griff. They returned his glance in a disconnected manner, blinking slowly. "What the fuck's going on?"

Jake was halfway out of the hatch, also on his hands and knees. He was motionless.

"You all right?" He grabbed the younger lad's coat and tugged him backwards. Jake rolled onto his side. He was shaking violently. Spasms gripped his skinny frame. Barlow bent to examine the kid. His eyes were closed but they were twitching beneath the lids. His tongue was lolling between grimaced lips. Spittle had collected at the corner of his mouth in white frothy loops.

"What's happened?" Barlow looked at the other

two. Their faces were pale masks of shock. "What did you see?" Griff's mouth was working soundlessly, like he was struggling to breathe. A sudden thought struck Barlow. "Have you eaten any of the mushrooms?"

No one said anything. Jake was moaning quietly, disturbingly low. Barlow spotted the mobile phone on the floor, its torch facility still activated. He picked it up, crouching so he could see through the hatch.

The light was poor, but the phone cast a feeble spotlight into the darkness. The beam was narrow. Barlow shuffled forward so he had a better view. The brickwork looked ancient. He wrinkled his nose at the sour stench. The light was almost consumed by solid darkness. It felt like the room was huge. Something about the air quality suggested it was a vast location. He was wary about venturing too far inside, but he mentally asserted himself and crawled further. He could feel cold air against his face. His fingers touched damp soil, and he recoiled at the unpleasant sensation. He could see brown mushrooms protruding through the earth. The beam picked out larger ones further back as the light quickly diminished. Some of them were thick and bulbous, maybe two feet high. *Christ, how big was this place?*

Something lay partly-exposed in the soil, like a tree root or a thick pipe. It was grey and mottled, stark against the black earth. Barlow tentatively touched it, snatching his hand away as he realised it was warm. *Maybe just a radiator pipe.* He cautiously returned his palm against it. It felt like skin, like it was alive. Faintly he could detect movement, like a weak pulse.

He chewed his lower lip and glanced round, trying to peer into the immeasurable darkness. The mushrooms seemed to watch him like silent children, brooding and sentient. He tried to identify individual specimens but they were like nothing he'd ever seen before.

And then he noticed a strange, pale mass some distance away, partially concealed by the crop of hideous mushrooms. Intrigued, he carefully crawled over to it, grimacing at the dampness that soaked his jeans and the soil that clung to his fingers. He was squashing the fungi as he negotiated a path deeper into the room, a sensation that made him flinch. The action released a weird aroma that made his nose itch. Spores? Rotting leaves? As he drew close, a spike of fear lanced his chest. He froze.

The pale mass trembled on the ground. Barlow directed the beam across it, illuminating snatches of ashen skin, hair, a ragged tangle of clothing. From between the bunched fragments, Barlow saw a human eye peering back, lifeless and staring. A low moan escaped his lips. He felt like reality was detaching, suddenly fearful that he was hallucinating. A cold sensation seeped through his limbs. There were several human bodies gathered here. Recently dead, by the look of it. The coppery tang of blood stung his nostrils.

Nearby, something moved in the darkness. Barlow jerked the torch and concentrated the beam at what he took to be a monstrous mushroom. His first impression was of a brown stem about four feet high, topped with a vast dark cap. But the stem twisted slowly, and Barlow could discern human features beneath the membrane of its skin. Staring eyes, wide nostrils, thin lips. A mockery of his own image. The fucking mushroom had a face. It shifted in the soil, sprouting limbs as it struggled to release itself from the earth. There was a sound of tearing.

Barlow scrambled across the ground, terror threatening to overwhelm him. He threw a final glimpse at the shivering mass of bodies, absently recognising Mark's face in the nightmarish jumble. Griff's scuffed Adidas trainers were unmistakeable among the twisted limbs.

Light poured from the hatch. It drew him like a beacon. Barlow stumbled towards it blindly. He burst through the gap, his feet skidding on the soil. He peered up at the three figures that crouched in the room, staring back at him intently. Somehow they looked less real. Their skin was mottled, grey. Eyes blinking slowly. They regarded him in silence, shivering violently. Saliva drooled from the mouth of the one that looked like Griff. Barlow realised he was could no longer count on the help of his three friends. He was alone.

The room reeked of decay and damp soil and the ancient breath of time. Maggoty shapes wriggled beneath the skin of the three advancing humanoids, distorting their features with spasms and bulging protrusions. Barlow registered the clammy touch of their lichen-formed fingers, seconds before he let forth his dying scream.

Hungry is the Dark
Benedict J. Jones

The air didn't taste any different and the light looked the same. It was only the people and the places that had changed. Harry walked around the town centre drinking in the sights; everyone seemed to have a 'phone at their ear, the clothes looked different and the shapes and angles of the cars had smoothed. But people were still people and Harry was still Harry. He set himself down on a bench with a sigh and watched the women as they shopped; high heels, freshly done hair, tight leggings like second skins, well cut clothes that clung to their figures. It was a long time since Harry had seen so many women, a long time since he had seen any woman who wasn't a doctor, teacher or screw. As Harry looked out at the crowds thronging around the shops he occasionally caught sight of one of the dark things, they appeared in the corner of his vision as dark smudges. When he did see them Harry turned away quickly and concentrated on the more pleasant sights.

He'd been seeing the dark things for so long that they didn't bother him like they once did. Harry shifted himself on the seat as another dark smudge moved at the edge of his vision, this time he turned to face it. The dark thing clung to the back of a tall girl, pretty but for the sour look that marred her features. It rode high on her back like a jockey forcing its mount onwards; it was the size of a large toddler with skin that seemed so dark that it drained the light from around it. The girl swung her hips and strode away down the high street the head of the creature turned to stare at Harry. Harry stared back at the dead black eyes for a moment and then got up and walked away, the day ruined.

#

Back in his cell Harry stripped down to his shorts and vest. After carefully folding his clothes he put them away in his locker. He placed his palms on the cold floor and counted off his press-ups until lights out, he reached sixty eight. In the dark he wiped the sweat from his head with a towel and then lay down on his bunk, deciding he had done well, another step taken – another step closer to release.

Harry called his daughter, Nicola, from the blue box on the wing. He got her voicemail and left a message with the details of his pending release. He knew there was no chance of Nicola letting him stay with her but he wanted to hear her voice. He needed to know if she'd thought anymore about letting him meet his granddaughter, Rhian. Harry hung up the phone and looked around him. This place had been his home for twelve months. Before that he had spent twenty three years in Cat-A prisons up and down England. Not many like Harry in here, not as many of the dark things either.

In here people tried to keep their noses clean, get home visits and then get free. Harry looked over the other prisoners; conmen, fraudsters, ASBO-breachers, chumps and mugs. They were the kind of people who wouldn't mind having a nickname. In Harry's mind the only people who had nicknames were failed boxers and black pimps. When he had first gone down for his long stretch Harry had been sent to *the Scrubs* and knocked heads with a joker from the Midlands called Donnie Smalls who was in on an armed robbery beef. Donnie got it into his head that everyone on the wing ought to have a nickname and he took to calling Harry – "Hatchet". Harry told Donnie to leave it. The other cons waited and watched. To Donnie, Harry not liking his new moniker just made it funnier. Hilarious in fact until he slipped in the kitchens one day and somehow managed to hold his right hand on a grill until it resembled a crispy Peking duck. Harry never had a nickname after that and Donnie had to learn to play with himself southpaw.

Harry sat and stared at the wall of his cell. His eyes were fixed on half a piece of A4 paper that was stuck to the wall and the five words that were on it; 'Not forever, just a bit'. Harry had first seen the words carved into the wall of a holding cell during his trial. They had stayed with him and he tried to think on them every day. He kept his hands, palm down, on his knees and waited, time meant little to Harry. What were thirty minutes when you weighed them against two hundred and eighteen thousand four hundred and sixty five hours? Harry waited.

#

"What have you ever done for me?"

Harry stared down in his mug of tea and watched

the heat rising from it like it used to do from the prison laundry presses.

"Well?"

He looked up at his daughter and from the set of her face he knew he'd had a wasted journey. "I just wanted to see you, Nicola, to try and say sorry. See if there was any way I could try and make up for all the wasted years."

Nicola slammed her tea cup down on the table. "Don't! You can't just stroll in here after twenty five years and think a few words will make up for it. You and your shit sent Mum into an early grave and before that you were gone anyway. Fuck you, just fuck you!"

Harry stood up unsure of where to put his hands. He wanted to pull Nicola to him and hug her but in the end he put his hands behind his back. "I'm sorry. I just wanted to see you and Rhian, make sure you were okay."

Nicola shook her head silently.

"Please, Nic..."

"I think you'd better go."

Nicola refused to look at Harry as he left.

\#

There weren't many of the old faces left but Harry did the rounds of Soho looking for something to anchor himself to. He walked the streets; D'Arblay, Berwick, Old Compton, Lexington, Old Windmill and Greek. The same streets where the Messinas had plied their trade, where Jack Spot had fought Albert Dimes and Darby Sabini had walked with a spring in his step.

Some of the pubs were gone and the names had changed on others but a few of the old places were there, in spirit if not in fact. Harry watched the wildlife; the tramps, the drunks, the junkies, the chancers and the few working girls he could see. It seemed to him that Soho had been more honest in the days when he was running around the streets. Then the area had been more up front, in your face screaming, whereas it now seemed to be behind a veil, chastised and hidden but as dirty as ever. Harry walked and walked and then walked some more until his feet ached.

Harry tried to work out what was what and who was who, keeping his eyes open; check the lads putting the cards up in the 'phone boxes, all eastern Europeans now, spot which anonymous doorways furtive looking men emerged from, watch the street dealers and clock the clip artists luring punters in for cokes that cost a score minimum. Filing it all away, remembering who he was and where he had been, with sky over his head now instead of concrete – a free man in London.

#

When Harry got his first day release one of the screws escorted him into town and took him to a coffee shop. It was nothing like the greasy snack bars that Harry had haunted when he was on the outside. The coffee shop he sat in seemed a temple to polished modernity; free trade coffee for the same price as a pint of lager, uniformed baristas shipped in from around the globe and paid minimum wage, brushed steel altars and a whole cult worshipping the corporate bean. Harry had ordered a latte.

Now he sat in another coffee shop, a clone of that first temple, opposite his daughter. Again Harry ordered a latte and Nicola had a hot chocolate. They sat in silence, Harry staring at the foam on his drink, until Nicola spoke. "She's gone."

"Who has?"

"Rhian."

"Gone where?" asked Harry his voice level but his stomach dropping like a lift with the cables cut.

"I don't know." Tears appeared in Nicola's eyes. "Up here, West End somewhere with her *boyfriend*."

Harry gripped the table edge with his fingertips. "What do you want me to do?"

"I want you to fucking well find her. You know people don't you?"

"That was a long time ago, Nicola. More than twenty years ago, places change. I'm not even sure any of the same faces are around anymore. I've changed too."

Nicola looked disgusted, as though Harry had just exposed himself at her. "So you won't help?"

"I never said that!" Harry slapped his palm down on the table. People turned from their cappuccinos and espressos to look. Harry placed his hands palm down on his knees and stared at the floor between his boots. The people quickly turned back to their affairs. Harry looked up at Nicola. "I'll look, I'll find her if she's here and I'll bring her back to you."

Nicola nodded.

Harry reached inside his jacket and took out a biro. He used a piece of napkin for note paper. "How long has she been gone?"

"Four days."

"She done anything like this before?"

"She's stayed out all night but she always came home the next day."

"You've tried ringing her?"

"Of course I have! About a hundred times but her 'phone is always switched off and the voicemail is full."

"Who's the boyfriend?"

"He's called Danny Carter. He's a bit older than her..."

Harry cut in. "How much older?"

Nicola looked away.

"I think he's nineteen."

"Rhian is fourteen, Nicola."

"Don't come that with me, *Daddy*. You weren't here when I was fourteen and you've never even met Rhian so don't act like you know anything about this."

Harry held up his hands, palms open. "Where does he live?"

"I don't know."

"Where's he from?"

"Somewhere out near us but he spends a lot of time up here. I've never met his family."

Harry nodded. "D'you know what he's into?"

"How d'you mean?"

"I mean puff, pills, chang, horse – what?"

"Jesus! Nothing like that I don't think. He always seemed like a nice kid. Dressed smart, plenty of money, always kept his car clean."

"What kind of car?"

"One of those little Italian ones. Bright yellow."

"Shouldn't be too hard to spot in a city with what two, three million cars." Harry stared into Nicola's eyes until she looked away. "You want me to find her, Nic, you need to give me something here."

"I think he said he works for his Uncle."

"Name?"

"I don't think he said."

"Come on, you have to think." Harry sat with the pen poised over the napkin.

"I think Danny said his Uncle was called Howie."

Harry dropped the pen onto the table. "Howard?"

"No, Howie. Could've been Howard, why?"

Picking up the pen Harry shook his head. "Nothing, I used to know a Howard 'round here before I went away. Couple of people used to call him Howie."

"Maybe you could see if he's still about?"

Harry laughed and the sound made Nicola shiver. "I don't think old Howard would be too pleased to see me. But if it's him I'll find out."

"Do you need anything?"

Harry looked up as though shocked his daughter would ask.

"Money or anything to help you look?"

He shook his head at her. "No. I'll use Shanks' pony to get about and I'm alright for walking about money."

Nicola nodded.

"There is one thing though."

"What?" replied Nicola.

"Have you got a decent photo of her? The one your mum sent me must be seven years old now."

"Course." Nicola scrambled in her handbag and pulled out her purse. From within she pulled a picture of a smiling girl with long auburn hair and dark, dancing eyes. "That's a couple of months old."

Harry stared at the snapshot of his granddaughter, repressing his urge to touch his fingers to the image that looked so like his dead ex-wife. "Thanks, Nic."

"Just find her for me."

Harry finished his latte. "I'll call you if I find anything."

#

Harry had lied. After the two lattes he had a total of fifteen pounds and seventy eight pence in his pocket – all that was left of his discharge grant. He cut away from Covent Garden and down Long Acre until he hit Endell Street. As he walked Harry pushed all thoughts of Howard Kinski from his mind. Harry walked halfway up the street and sighed with relief when he saw that the *Café Valetta* was still there. It looked different but the name was the same. Harry stepped into the cramped coffee bar, empty before the lunchtime rush. A young, thick set man with a five o'clock shadow appeared from the back.

"Alright?"

Harry nodded.

"Get you something?"

"Eddie about?"

"Eddie who?"

"Eddie Nax."

"Granddad? He's not here at the minute."

Harry looked away. "Any chance you could give him a message for me?"

"Sure, you a mate of his?"

"Yeah. From a long time ago, the good old days." Harry forced a smile.

The young man grabbed a pad and a pen. "Who shall I tell him?"

"Harry Sands."

The young man stopped writing. "Shit. Sorry. D'you want to take a seat and I'll give Granddad a call?"

Harry nodded and pulled up a stool to the counter as the younger man disappeared into the back.

He came back out a few minutes later. "He said he'll be right down. Get you something while you wait?"

Harry shook his head. "I'm good thanks."

As they waited Harry saw the man throw surreptitious glances at him. Eventually Harry caught his eye. "You alright over there?"

The man laughed.

"I'm really sorry Mister Sands but growing up Granddad told us so many stories about you. It's just kind of funny to see you here, in the flesh so to speak."

Harry laughed.

"Bloody hell, Son. I'm just another old man now, I'm trying to sort out my pension!"

"Are all them stories true?"

Harry held out his hands. "Not heard them but

probably not, your granddad always liked to blow a story up."

"Did you really..." The man faltered.

Harry held his gaze and the man looked away. "Best leave that one, eh?"

The young man nodded and went back to cleaning the espresso machine. Fifteen minutes later Eddie Nax stuck his head into the café. "Harry!" He waved a gloved hand and then looked over at his grandson. "Nico, if your mother calls I'm feeding the pigeons in Covent Garden. Harry we're going for lunch!"

Eddie Nax wore a heavy camel hair overcoat, burgundy scarf and a brown fedora. He looked to be about eighty. Harry jumped down from his stool and walked over to the door. "See you later, Nico, and don't believe everything you hear."

The two men walked in silence up Shelton Street, crossed Charing Cross Road and sliced into the underbelly of Soho.

"How've you been, Harry?"

"Same old, same old. Seems like a different place 'round here now."

"Not so different," muttered the old man.

Harry stopped and looked at Eddie.

"I know, I know," Said Eddie. "You still remember me twenty five years ago – you're asking yourself where did that handsome young Maltese go!"

Harry laughed. "You were fifty then, Ed."

Eddie shrugged.

"The girls said we looked like brothers, Harry."

The old man turned and hugged Harry to him.

"It's been too long. I've had no one to beat at chess

for a long time."

"Where are we going for lunch?"

"*French house*?"

Harry nodded. "Why not. Is Gaston still there?"

"No, he retired not long after they sent you away. A lot of changes after you left."

"All the old faces gone?"

"Most, but not all. Perhaps a few left from our time. You have someone in mind?"

"Howie, fucking, Kinski."

Eddie stopped dead and his old head turned like a tortoise towards Harry. "Yes, Kinski's still around."

Harry nodded and walked away. "Come on, Eddie. I need a fucking drink."

Lunch consisted of steaks with halves of lager on the side. Once the food was done they moved on to Ricard, just like in the old days.

"I need to ask you something, Eddie." Eddie gestured with his hand for Harry to continue. Harry took Rhian's picture from his pocket. "You seen her around the way?"

Eddie took the photo and studied it. "Harry, you have to remember I spend most of my time in the flat at Clerkenwell. It's not like the old days. I could ask Nico, but he is a good boy – not like we were."

"And I need my money, Eddie."

"You don't worry, Harry. I've kept it safe."

Eddie passed three hundred in twenties to Harry under the table and put a bank card down in front of him. "The other six grand's in there. The PIN is one seven nine eight."

"Thanks, Eddie. I need to know something else.

Where can I find Kinski?"

"Harry, I don't think I should tell you that."

"How long have we known each other, Eddie? I need to see him and make sure it's done."

"The only way it would've been done is if you had buried your axe in his head that night."

"I did. But the cunt's still walking. Persistent fucker to say the least."

"And still the same from what I've heard."

Harry looked Eddie straight in the eye and laid the photo of Rhian on the table between them. "That's my granddaughter, Eddie. Tell me where Kinski is."

"He sits in the *Montagu Pyke* with his boys through the afternoon.

Harry looked confused.

"*The Marquee Club* as was."

"How many boys?"

"Usually there are two. Please don't do this, Harry."

"I have to see him, Eddie." Harry stood legs unsteady from the Ricard. Harry looked down at himself. "I'll see him tomorrow."

Eddie remained seated. "Go and see Marnie first. She's working in China Town. She missed you, Harry. You should see her, she's waited a long time for you."

Eddie held out a piece of paper and Harry took it.

"And we should play chess again, just be two old men playing chess in the café."

Harry looked back for a moment and then he was gone into the night.

#

Harry lay in his bed in the bail hostel in Camden, the liquorice taste of Ricard thick on his tongue, as the room tilted and tipped. On the inside Harry had steered clear of the hooch prisoners made from fermented fruit so the afternoon's drinking session had been his first in a quarter of a century and he was feeling it.

Harry tried to concentrate on the light fitting above him. The shadows around the room seemed to close in on Harry as he stared up and he felt an old familiar feeling begin to worm its way inside him where it grew and grew. Harry closed his eyes but that just made it worse and made the feeling rush up on him more quickly. A car passed by in the street below and the light thrown by its headlights made the shadows flex and elongate as though they were grasping hands reaching for him. This feeling had been with Harry since he was a small boy in a council flat on East Street, above the market. Even with his mum and dad in the front room, telly blasting through the wall, and the hall light shining under the door Harry had felt the exact semi-controlled terror he felt in the bail hostel.

He sat up, swung his legs off the bed, opened his eyes and looked at the dark around him. He placed his hands palms down on his knees and closed his eyes again – total dark. Harry began to count in his head. Even as he felt sure that fingertips were reaching out of the shadows to caress his flesh Harry kept his eyes shut tight and maintained his count. Harry's heart pounded like a copper's fist on a front door at five A.M, his breathing quickened and sweat broke out on his forehead. With his eyes shut Harry's imagination ran rampant with thoughts of what could be going on around him; things slipping out from beneath the bed, doors of wardrobes opening as hidden attackers crept out and the dark itself wrapping around him in a black embrace. He reached the count of five hundred and his breathing and heart rate slowed as the sweat dried on his forehead. Harry swung his legs back under the covers, eyes still shut tight against the night. He lay back and sleep claimed him.

#

Morning brought with it waves of sickness and a headache that made Harry curse Eddie and *The French House*. He headed out into the rain that had been falling since dawn and bought a latte to drink on the tube. He caught the Northern line to Leicester Square, headed up Shaftsbury Avenue and cut back into Chinatown. The familiar sights and smells cheered Harry. He'd spent a lot of time in the warren of alleys and side streets that spider webbed around Gerrard Street and Lisle Street.

He checked the address on the piece of paper that Eddie Nax had given him the night before. Royal Vale House, a large red brick block of apartments, sat almost unnoticed in the heart of the West End. Harry rang up on the intercom.

"Yes?" The sound of Marnie's voice made Harry's heart jump.

"Marnie, its Harry Harry Sands."

Silence.

"Marn'?"

A sharp intake of breath, audible even through the static of the intercom. "Come on up, Harry."

Harry heard the buzz of the door being released and the click of the handset being replaced.

Harry looked at the lifts for a moment and then took the stairs. He climbed to the fourth floor and quickly found the door he was looking for. It was open. Harry stepped through into the dark hallway, the smell of incense touched his nostrils. "Marnie?"

"In here, Harry."

Harry followed the sound of Marnie's voice and found her in the lounge, which was nearly as dark as the hallway had been. Marnie sat behind a round table and for a moment, in the shadows of the room, it seemed to Harry that no time at all had passed since he had last seen Marnie.

"Hello."

"It's been a long time, Harry. A lot of years – wasted years."

"It has at that."

Marnie offered a hand and Harry stepped over to take it. He looked down at Marnie; eyes like chips of blue ice set in a pale face and framed by dark hair that still had a hint of the Rockabilly look that Harry remembered. He could see that the years had been kind to Marnie but they had still left the mark of their passing.

"You haven't changed a bit, Babes."

Marnie slapped her free hand against Harry's stomach. "You've toned up. You're looking good for a man who lost a third of a lifetime."

Harry shrugged.

"Still the same old Harry – man of a thousand words." Marnie laughed.

Her laugh reminded him of when they first met – her a croupier and him a doorman at a casino off Russell Square.

"You should never have let them push you so far, Harry."

"They pushed a bit and I pushed back. That's all."

"And now you've got other problems?" Marnie squeezed his hand.

"That your *gift* talking?"

Marnie winked at Harry. "Oh, my gift's still working, Harry." She gestured around the room. "It pays for all this and I don't have to work the tables anymore. No more séances in the back rooms of pubs in Hackney and Kilburn with a pint glass passed round for change either."

It was Harry's turn to squeeze Marnie's hand. "Then I need you to tell me something, Babes." Harry put the picture of Rhian on the table.

"Who is she?"

"My granddaughter. I've never got to see her, Marn' and now she's gone."

"Sit down next to me. You've seen how this works before, Harry. You just sit there and I'll do the rest. I'll see you on the other side."

Her lips brushed Harry's and he kept hold of her hand as her eyes closed. Her face lost expression as the muscles slackened and her lips began to move quickly in silent conversation. Harry tried to pick out the words but Marnie's lips moved too swiftly for him to follow. She reached the trance state much more quickly than when Harry had seen these performances two and a half decades earlier. He waited a moment.

"You there, Marnie?"

Marnie's head lolled to one side and her breathing changed, growing huskier.

"You there?"

"I'm here, lover."

The voice wasn't Marnie's. It was pure Bow Bells whereas Marnie was from down on the south coast near to Brighton.

"Who's that?"

Marnie's hand grew colder in Harry's grip.

"You can call me whatever you like as long as you're buying but most people call me Peaches on account of 'ow sweet and plump I am!"

"I'm Harry."

Marnie's eyes fluttered open, they were distant and unfocused.

"Oh, you look like a catch, bit old for me but still. Get a girl a drink, Harry?"

Harry looked around the lounge and spotted a collection of bottles on a sideboard. He carefully placed Marnie's hand into her lap and walked over to the drinks. "What'll you have?"

"Gin, straight. No ice and don't be a miser."

Harry threw a good measure of Bombay Sapphire into a glass and carried it back to the table. Marnie reached out and brought the glass to her lips and took a hearty swig.

"Got a smoke?"

"Sorry, I don't."

A throaty sigh.

"Well, I guess a girl can't have everything. What can I do you for, Harry?"

"I need to know if someone is on... your side of things."

"Oh here in the dark you mean?"

"I suppose I do," replied Harry, trying not to think too hard upon what he was asking.

"Who you looking for?"

"A young girl – fourteen. She's my granddaughter, she's missing up here and I think it might have something to do with some bad things that happened a long time ago."

"And you think she might have fallen into the dark place where I am?"

"I pray to God she hasn't but I need to know. Certain things might have to be done."

Marnie threw the remains of the gin down her neck. "Well I'll go and have a look-see while you make me another drink and see if you can't rustle me up a fag while you're at it, handsome."

Marnie's eyes closed and her head made a slow roll on her neck until her chin touched her chest. Her breathing grew deep and rhythmic. Harry got up and refilled the glass with another large measure of gin. He searched the drawers of the sideboard and found half a packet of Mayfair's and a lighter. Returning to the table he took up his seat next to Marnie and waited.

The time passed slowly and Harry was thinking about getting a drink for himself, hangover half forgotten, when Marnie's head snapped up and she let out a loud gasp.

"Marnie? Peaches?"

"She's not there, Harry. I think I'll take the rest of that drink now, please."

Harry put the glass into her hand and helped it up to her lips. The thing inside Marnie drained the glass and licked the last drop from inside. He took a cigarette from the packet and placed it between her lips. She took a long drag and blew the smoke up to the ceiling. Harry held the cigarette for her.

"Thanks, Harry."

"What did you find? Tell me, Peaches, I need to know."

She took another deep pull on the cigarette.

"Rhian's not there, but there are others – too many others. One of the others knew her. They talked about the dark ones, Harry. And what they did to them before they came to where I am. Horrible things, Harry! Things that shouldn't be done to any girl."

Nails dug into Harry's arm and Peaches began to sob within the vessel of Marnie. Marnie's eyes rolled back to the whites. Harry grabbed her shoulders.

"Marnie! Marnie!"

Marnie coughed. "I can taste gin. Have I been smoking?"

Harry laughed but it sounded hollow. Marnie looked tired and drawn.

"You okay?"

"I'll be fine. I just need to lie down."

Harry helped her up.

"Who did you talk to?"

"Peaches."

It was Marnie's turn to laugh.

"Oh, she's a live one. No wonder I can taste gin and cigarettes. Surprised you didn't give her a jump what with being away for so long."

Harry felt heat grow in his ears.

"I'm joking. Come and lie down with me, Harry, like you used to."

Marnie was asleep as soon as she hit the sheets. Harry took off his boots and lay down next to her. He turned and studied her face while she slept. She was right about the wasted years. Harry remembered the days they spent lying together in Marnie's one room bed-sit after they'd worked the late shift at the casino. Too wired from the nights work to sleep they would drink and smoke with the other workers from the casino and then they'd head back to hers. Good days, thought Harry.

Soon after he'd been busy collecting debts for the casino owner and his friends in Gerrard Street. But even then he'd lay down with Marnie for a few hours of peace. He could've been happy if it wasn't for *them*. Harry put a blanket over Marnie. She rolled over and murmured his name in her sleep. He sat for a moment and then laced up his boots and left.

#

Harry found a telephone box on Charing Cross Road and called Nicola. She answered on the third ring. "Hello?"

"It's me. Dad."

"Have you found her?"

"Not yet. But I might be able to find the boyfriend.

What does he look like?"

"Well he's taller than you so about six one. Dark hair; gelled on top, short around the sides how all the boys have it. He's sort of slim but not too skinny, not a bean pole but not built."

Harry tried to picture the boy in his head.

"Does that help?"

Harry nodded and then realised he hadn't replied.

"Yeah, it should. As soon as I know more I'll let you know."

"You have to find her."

"I told you I'll try."

"Find her, please! The coppers are worse than useless, couldn't find their arses with both hands."

"Calm down, Nicola."

"Don't tell me to calm down! Have you found her yet? No, you're just like the rest of them. What have you ever done for me in my whole life?"

"Nic, I'll phone you when I know more."

Harry hung up the 'phone. A temper just like her mother, he thought as he walked up towards *The Montagu Pyke*.

#

The Montagu Pyke was a barn of a pub which had been a cinema a century earlier and the shape of the frontage still displayed the fact that it had begun its life as a picture house. Harry went in through the back door on Greek Street. He headed to the closest bar and ordered a pint of lager. Strolling slowly through the pub Harry let his eyes move far ahead of him watching for familiar faces. Sipping his pint Harry scanned the room. Nothing. He moved through into the next part of the pub and quickly stepped behind a pillar when he saw a face he knew. It was Howie Kinski.

Harry moved to a fruit machine and spied at Kinski around the edge of it. He looked older and sicker but Harry could see the same man he had known twenty five years earlier. Now he sat with his bleached blonde hair looking stringy and thin, his face red and swollen and his stomach pushing against what was once an expensive suit jacket but was now dated and frayed. Harry could see the dark thing that hung like a leech on the man's shoulder; scarred and battered it was as fat and slug-like as the man it clung to. Harry watched Kinski's hand beating out a tattoo on the table top and he saw the missing fingers from his right hand, the dent in the left side of the man's skull.

For a moment Harry was thrown back through the years to the moment in a basement club where hard steel flashed under party lights and fingers fell to the floor like unwanted chipolatas at a children's party. Harry leant against the flashing lights of the machine and closed his eyes. He stayed like that for minutes.

"'Scuse me, mate."

Harry turned and a man in a polo shirt stood before him. "What?" Harry held the pint glass tight and to his hip, ready to launch it into the man's neck.

The man held out his hands. "Sorry, mate, just trying to get to the fruity like."

Harry stood for a moment and then moved to the side. "Sorry." He moved into an alcove opposite and took a deep breath. Harry felt disgusted that he had almost let the beast out from its cage. He took a sip from his pint and threw another look over at Kinski. The fat man sat with two other men; a light skinned man with a half-hearted afro and stingy beard and a thick boned meat head with an inch of neck and a shaved bowling ball for a head. They were dressed in the same manner as Kinski, pricey but life worn. A young guy stepped through the doors and moved to Kinski's table. The newcomer was tall and slim. The talk was animated and there was a lot of gesturing outside.

Harry put his pint down and made an exit through the back. He cut around to Charing Cross Road until he stood opposite the front of the pub. A small yellow Fiat was parked at the curb. A young girl sat in the front passenger seat. Harry found himself crossing the road. The girl in the car was young, maybe fifteen, dressed in a neon pink tube dress and little else. She looked at Harry staring and she stared back. She wasn't Rhian. The young man that Harry had pegged as Danny Carter exited the pub. He caught Harry's eye and glared at him.

"The fuck you looking at, old man?"

Harry shrugged.

"Nothing here you can afford."

"That so?"

"You want something or not?"

Harry smiled.

The kid stepped off the kerb and made to square up to Harry. As he stepped in Harry turned and dropped his foot hard into the kid's knee. Danny fell forward letting Harry close the distance and throw a fist into his throat. He choked and dropped.

A car door opened and the girl screamed.

Harry dropped to one knee and rattled Danny's head off the kerb. "Tell Howie the past's coming for him." He slammed Danny's head down again and then ran across the road heading towards Seven Dials.

#

Harry sat on the bed in his room in the bail hostel, hands on knees, and remembered. The years seemed to roll back; Harry as a younger man, Nicola as a child, Marnie the most enamouring woman Harry had met. Harry had dealt in debts, bad debts mostly. He collected for the owner of the casino where he worked, Mr Conway, and some of his Chinese friends across Shaftsbury Avenue. His name got around and he freelanced; collecting debts and making sure certain rules were enforced. The way Harry saw it the violence would get dealt out and the hurt laid on even if he wasn't there, so why shouldn't he profit from it.

Kinski approached him as Christmas '87 loomed. A man named Kenny Logan owed him eight grand, gambling debt. Harry went round and had a word. Through broken teeth Kenny had offered Harry his twelve year old daughter in lieu of the debt. Harry broke his arm. Kinski had laughed and told Harry he should have taken the offer – soon after Harry began to see the dark things. It seemed that even a trip to the supermarket showed Harry a dark underbelly of the creatures hanging on people and forcing them to do their will.

A story did the rounds in Soho; Kinski had gone to see Logan himself and he had taken him up on his offer. He had Logan's daughter in a room up in Mornington Crescent and was charging every nonce and chester in Central London to jump her. Harry went to see them; Kinski and his partners Bernie Glass and Omar Sanchez. They laughed and Harry saw the mouths of the dark things that hung on their shoulders. They offered Harry a free go on the girl – he refused. They offered him a cut – he turned it down. The dark things began to whisper and then the men spoke. They asked Harry about Nicola; how old she was, how tight she was, did Harry want to trade. Harry left. He came back an hour later with a hatchet and when he was done two men lay dead and another was wheeled away. No, Harry had never done anything for Nicola.

Swinging his legs off the bed Harry grabbed up his money and took one last look around his room. It wasn't much but it had been home since he got out. He checked his watch, it was ten thirty. Harry's curfew was eleven P.M.

Kicking open his door Harry walked out and headed for the stairs. Taking a deep breath of the night, Harry hailed a cab and treated himself to a chauffeured ride back into Soho – where it had started and where it would end.

Harry jumped out the cab on Tottenham Court Road and walked his way down through the wet pavements and neon lights. He stopped at a call box filled with the calling cards for brasses based in Bayswater, Greek Street, Pentonville Road and streets around the British Museum. Harry called Eddie first and asked for an address. Then he called Marnie.

"Hello, Babes."

"That you, Harry?"

"Wish we were still lying down together."

"Even though you left me like sleeping beauty earlier?"

"You know I always loved you don't you?"

"I had my suspicions, Mr Sands."

"I'll try and see you later."

"Whenever you can, Harry. Take care."

Harry dreaded the call and called Eddie back.

"You got it?"

"Do you really have to do this, Harry?"

"You know I do, Eddie. Imagine it was one of your grandkids."

"Okay, they've got a flat in St. Anne's Court. Blue door. You're to say Perry sent you for Amy."

"Thank you, Ed. I wish we'd got to play chess again."

"So do I my friend, so do I."

Harry walked the streets, coat zipped to the neck, a relic making one last move.

Tourists and drunk kids on nights out milled around in the streets. Shall we go to another pub or straight to a club? Time to catch the last train or we staying out? Harry slid past them trying to think of a reason to just call the cops and leave it at that. He couldn't find a reason but he found himself in St. Anne's Court. He looked over the basement flats until he found the blue door. He walked down the stairs and knocked twice. A few moments passed and Harry wondered if he had the wrong door. Then it opened and Harry came face to face with the bowling ball head he had seen sitting with Kinski earlier.

"You alright?"

"Yeah, Perry sent me, said I should ask to see Amy."

The big man looked him up and down. "Yeah alright." The big man stepped to the side and Harry slid past him and inside.

Harry was ushered into a bedroom at the side of the hallway. He looked around; a bed, a TV with a porn DVD running on a side table and a couple of posters of jail bait girls in provocative poses. There was a knock at the door and a small woman with a pinched face and dirty bleached blonde hair entered.

"Okay, what you here for?"

"Usual," replied Harry.

"The usual? What the fuck's that then?" asked the woman.

"Y'know..."

The woman eyed Harry suspiciously.

"A suck and a fuck, what d'you think?"

"Alright, that's two hundred," she replied.

Harry eyed the dark thing that hung skinny and mean from her shoulders and then he looked away quickly. "Bit steep in'it?"

"Oh, this girl's tight as fuck. Young 'un, thirteen if that. A really good ride, good girl she's no trouble."

Harry tried to look like a nervous punter as he pulled out his roll and peeled off ten score notes. "Go on then. Send her in."

"Alright, lose the clothes and I'll send her in,

darlin'."

The woman left and Harry took off his jacket, he put it carefully on a chair. He waited a few moments and then pulled his jumper over his head. He threw it on top of his jacket. Harry stood in vest, jeans and boots and waited. Moans came from the TV but Harry tried to listen beyond them to the rest of the flat. The door opened and a girl stepped into the room. To Harry it seemed the antithesis of the sexual come on he knew from the working girls in Soho – the girl was dressed younger than her years in a T-Shirt with a cartoon bear on it and a tight pair of pastel coloured shorts. Harry recognised her from the off. It was Rhian.

Her eyes were as big as dinner plates and her pupils were so large they eclipsed the colour in her eyes. She walked like a zombie towards him.

"Do you want to be my daddy?" she asked.

Harry felt a tear begin to trace a line down his face. "Rhian, baby, I need you to sit here for a minute."

She was loose limbed and pliable. Harry sat her on the bed and then picked up his coat. He took the meat cleaver out and laid it on the bed while he wrapped the coat around her skinny shoulders. She didn't say a word she simply sat there and stared at the wall. Harry took the cleaver and stepped out into the flat. He crept down the corridor. The first door was the kitchen and he saw the madam watching a soap opera on a small TV set. He leant the cleaver against the door frame and stepped in quickly behind her. Harry's right forcarm slid to the front of her throat and his left slammed into the back of her neck. Once the choke hold was in place Harry locked his arms and stared at the ceiling. The woman's legs kicked against the floor but Harry held her up and applied continuous pressure until she stopped moving. He threw her to the floor and watched the inky blackness of the dark thing as it tried to crawl away. Harry stamped down on the woman's head. The animal made of the dark bucked and twisted as its host slipped away. Harry headed towards the next door.

The door opened as he reached it and the meat head who'd let him in stepped out. Harry put a kick in between the man's legs and hit him with the flat of the cleaver. Harry stamped his foot twice on the head of the prone man. Three of them sat in the room beyond; Kinski, his light skinned partner and Danny Carter resting his leg on the coffee table. Makeshift crack pipes fashioned from empty lager cans littered the table.

Danny sat up. "What the fuck do you..."

Harry cut him off by hacking the cleaver into his jaw. The room became pandemonium. Kinski jumped to the right and his partner hurtled into Harry. Harry caught him with the back sweep of the cleaver and the man crashed into a wall. With blood running from this face the man pulled a knife and slashed at Harry. He cut Harry across the shoulder. Harry kicked out and the man scuttled back. Danny writhed on the floor attempting to get up and Kinski was throwing papers out of a drawer in a sideboard. The man with the knife rushed at Harry. Harry let go of the cleaver and caught the man's wrist. As they tangoed around the room Harry pushed the knife back towards the man and grabbed at him with the other hand. Once he had hold of him Harry threw himself backwards and let the man's momentum do the rest. The knife ended up buried in his gut – the dark thing on his back squealed as blood spilled out onto the carpet. Harry dragged himself up and then the room filled with noise.

The first bullet took Harry in his left elbow and spun him round so that the second tore across the flesh of his back. Harry screamed and grabbed for the cleaver. The third shot tore a chunk from the wall. Harry turned and rushed at Kinski. A bullet punched through Harry's chest. He screamed again and chopped down at Kinski's head. Steel cut flesh and smashed bone. Harry hacked again, a bullet fired off into the floor and it was Kinski's turn to scream. The gun fell to the carpet and Harry chopped down again and again until chunks of Kinski lay on the floor.

He stepped off and surveyed the room. Danny tried to pull himself up. Harry picked up the pistol and shot him behind the ear. The smell of blood and gunpowder filled the air. Harry grabbed a suit jacket from behind a chair and threw it on as he walked back out of the room. He paused in front of a mirror in the hall and looked at himself; past sixty with a face aged by a hard life that was rapidly paling as blood fell onto the floor. A dark face appeared over Harry's shoulder, the dark thing he had kept in check for so long seemed to throw him an inky smile. It looked as tired and worn as Harry. He took a breath, bit down the pain and headed back to Rhian.

"Come on, baby girl. Time to go."

Harry helped Rhian from the flat and hailed a black

cab once they hit Wardour Street. He pressed notes into the cab drivers hand and gave him Nicola's address. He sat down on the kerb and watched the cabs lights disappear into the Soho night.

Eternal Darkness
Blaze McRob

Shivering in my room, I cower under a blanket, not needing it merely for warmth. It is my shield between what exists in here and what resides out there.

Damn! I don't really know what lurks beyond my walls, what lies in waiting on the other side of my door. Who can see in this darkness? Certainly not me. I've had night blindness since the age of three.

Darkness brings changed landscapes, one folding into another, embracing the shadows until all is the same. With an absence of light comes a panorama of black, the visuals forcing their way into my mind, being introduced by way of my other senses.

No stars, no moon, no street lamps shining. Not in here. There are no windows, and there is no light to permeate any recesses or cracks present within the shoddy construction of my room. Why? Surely there must be light somewhere. How could it be otherwise?

Pressure on the other side of the blanket tells me I am not alone. I fight against it, trying to hide beneath the gossamer fabric, but it does no good. Whatever is there does not retreat. It merely pushes harder and harder until I fear I will be smothered if I allow the blanket to remain over me.

Fighting back, I battle for my life, the entity forcing itself on me becoming more persistent, using more strength with every passing moment. It wants to smother me! No... no, it can't!

What feels like a hand pushes down on my nose

and mouth, forcing the ragged cotton into those orifices. My hands reach up to shove it away, but they meet with nothing. The pressure remains, but there is no solid substance to grab onto and attempt to gain an upper hand.

In desperation, I bite into the pressure, feeling my teeth take hold of my antagonist. The force is released as the startled entity backs away, allowing me enough time to throw the blanket to the side.

Following the sound of it moving across the room into a bare corner, my fear remains. It has not chosen to leave my room. It intends to stay. Shit! How long will this thing attempt to conceal itself? I'll be attacked again by this monster of limited substance but with strength far beyond mine.

The darkness is its friend. It can see or, at least, it can manoeuvre in the never ending black using other powers at its disposal. Chuckling at me, it knows I'm held in its sway, unable to retaliate.

Where did this thing come from? I searched my room before the darkness came, and I made certain my door was locked. It was not here then, I'm sure of it.

It wants me to come to the corner, but I'm too wise for that. I'm staying where I'm at. I have no wish to be side-swiped in the dark, knocked to the floor and set upon by this heinous creature.

But wait! Behind the sheet rock. They're back, just as they were last night. My God! How many tonight, and how do they know I'm here, helpless before them?

Scurrying everywhere, their sharpened claws beating a staccato of horror within feet of me, taunting

me with their presence, squealing disgusting squelches
of venom, they attempt to find a way through the wall.
Their goal is me. I am some sort of a prize dangling
before their eyes, pulling at their whiskers residing so
close to their sharpened teeth.

Rats! Damn, how I hate them.

In the corner, the Evil One hisses, "Come to
Daddy, my children. I will find a path so you can
escape the confines of the wall. There is someone on a
bed in here craving your company."

Fuck! Now what? Is the bastard merely working
against my fears so I develop an anxiety attack and
become mere putty in his hands?

The scampering increases. It was not a mental ploy
against me. They are going to where he waits, eager
for their Pied Piper to set them free and give them
access to their dinner.

A thudding sound emanates from the corner. Over
and over again it comes until I hear the sheet rock
caving in. A horrible stench leaps out of the wall and
into the room, the horrid beasts bringing the odor of
defecation and rot with them.

The rats... the rats know where I'm at, and they
waste no time coming to me, crawling up on the bare
bed as best they can. Thank God I got rid of the
blanket: they could have climbed up a lot easier, but
shit, I could have used that blanket to beat away at
them!

They're on my body now and start crawling across
me, teasing me with their presence. I know they're
going to bite. I just don't know when. The pillow; I
still have my pillow! I pick it up to attack the bastards,

but the space between the pillow case and pillow is loaded with them and I fling it against the wall. They squeal in pain, but their anger will not let them back off. If anything, their zeal has increased, and I can sense them throwing their companions out of the way so they can be at the vanguard of the attack.

Leaping off the bed, landing on dozens of the squirming beasts, feeling their warm blood ooze from them as they are crushed beneath my weight, I throw the mattress off the frame and grab one of the wooden slats. Not knowing where they are, I swing wildly, parting the air with many missed passes, but connecting on many more.

The blood of my defeated foes whips around my face, joining that from the ones I stomped on, but they don't stop coming, and when they do reach me now they waste no time in attacking me with their teeth and claws, my blood joining theirs.

They crawl up me and some even leap higher, managing to get on my chest and... and approach my face. I drop the slat and start tearing them off, whipping them against their brothers and sisters, creating weapons out of them. My fear of contracting rabies is over. If I do, I do. I have so many bites now that the damage, if any, from that is too late to worry about.

Like a whirling-dervish of madness, I kill every rat I can get my hands on. I slam them not only into each other, but into the walls, the floor, and the frame of my bed.

The survivors move towards the hole in the wall as fast as they can. Soon, other than those still twitching on the floor in their last throes of death, they are all gone. Not caring about the choking Demon from earlier, I follow the rats to the corner, ready to face him once more, the adrenaline from my battle with the rats removing all fear. I am in attack mode. Let him come at me.

But he is gone. I can not sense him anywhere. And the hole in the wall: I can't find it, search as I might.

What the...

I tip toe through the darkness towards my bed, trying to avoid stepping on the dead and dying rats, but no evidence of their presence remains. The entire area has been returned to the way it was before the altercation with the beasts. The mattress is even back on my bed, along with the pillow and blanket. Still, I am reluctant to get back on the bed. What kind of trick is this?

My skin still hurts from the bites, and there is blood all over me. Heh, heh. Whatever tried to convince me this was all in my head failed miserably. It forgot to remove the evidence from my body.

I slowly walk to the bathroom and attempt to turn on the light. Just as I expected: still no power. It's been a week with no change. The last I heard, it was because of severe solar flares reversing the polarity of the electrical lines and blowing up the transformers. Supposedly, the damage has occurred across most of the planet. There is no power, no cars running because of micro-chip failure, no computers, nothing. At least I filled the tub with water and as many containers as I could before the faucets refused to release anymore. The water pumps need power too.

Stripping my clothes off, I grab for a wash rag, dip it into a pot I placed in the sink before the sun went down, and wash up as best I can. One thing in my favor is all the hand sanitizer I had stashed away. Sure comes in handy now.

The door slams behind me, and a shadow darker than the rest of the black in the room works its way up the wall and stretches across half the ceiling. Some strange power forces its way throughout the room and shoves me into the tub. As I try to scramble out, I am shoved back in, but I manage to get out the second time. Close call.

But it's not over yet: the sound of water pouring out of the sink faucet mimics that of a major waterfall. I rush to turn it off, but I can't budge the faucet. I feel the water running out of the sink and onto my feet. Soon, it becomes a river, knocking me down and smashing me into the side of the tub, the toilet, and the walls.

"I hope you can swim," the Shadow says. "And, it would be good for you if you are able to hold your breath for a long time."

It vanishes into the darkness.

The water rises rapidly, and even though I am a powerful swimmer, I am not used to raging torrents such as these. The very size of the small bathroom restricts my movements, making it difficult for me to maneuver with any kind of efficiency, and the constant bombardment continues. Soon, I am floating around the ceiling, any source of air gone.

No windows to smash out; no way to open the door to let the water out. I'm about to drown. There is no escaping this. I'm trapped.

I gag on the water forcing its way into my mouth and then my lungs. My mind is starting to cloud. I can't think straight. Reasoning is an abstract, a thing of the past.

Only one idea comes to mind, and it is a long shot. Swimming down towards the medicine cabinet, fighting off the current and oxygen deprivation with every stroke, I kick through the mirror, the glass cutting my leg to shreds. Once through that, I open the cabinet and resume my kicking efforts, only this time I pound away at the back of the cabinet. Hopefully, I can create a new avenue for the water to move about in. The hell with where it goes. As long as it drains from the bathroom, I'll be happy.

My lungs are ready to burst, and my brain is ready to go for its final sleep when I hit pay dirt. The water flows through the hole I made, and I get out of the way so my body doesn't plug the opening I worked so hard to create.

Drifting to the top of the ceiling, I find an air pocket and hover around it, needing to get that life-giving oxygen back into my lungs. The darkness obscures exactly where I am and, as the water level drops, I fall with it, once more slamming into everything, but I can tell from my speed of descent that soon I should be able to stand in the midst of the swirling currents and hang on to something.

Water stops pouring from the faucets and the overflow still flows into the holes. I shove more water through with my hands and, inch by inch, I work down the wall, smashing away at it until I reach the floor and make my final thrust. All the water leaves the room. Thank God! I am safe now.

The moisture has warped the bathroom door, but after a few efforts of shoving my body up against it, the door opens into my room... my room of indescribable darkness.

I'm glad I only have this one room and my bathroom. An efficiency apartment is perfect when groadies are hiding in the darkness. They can't come at me from around a corner somewhere. The doors and walls – ah yes, I can not forget the walls – are their only avenue of approach.

Once more, I'm not alone. There is that tingling on my body, every hair, regardless of where it is, saying that evil surrounds me. The sensations are enhanced because I'm still naked. Shit! This can't be good. While I am more privy to the aura of what is after me, I can't help but feel that I am leaving more of me exposed to it, or them, waiting for me in the dark. Shyness has nothing to do with it. As thin as the fabric might be, there is still a feeling of security, however false it might be, when I am clothed.

But... but how do I get to my clothes? Disorientation has set in. What part of the room am I in? Where is my dresser? Maybe I can find it. I need to: I'm an open target the way I am now.

"Your clothes won't do you any good, you fool."

The voice, the same one from the bathroom, is back, taunting me once more, only this time there's no dark shadow, nothing pushing me down. Yet, he's up to something. What is his game?

Placing my hands against the wall, I make my way

around the room. It's small; it can't possibly take me too long to find it. Yes! I get to the door. I'm not far away now.

A few feet farther and I touch my door again. No, this is impossible!

I did not change directions, and this is not the bathroom door; I know it's not.

The wall turns into a series of doors, one right next to the one I just left. Panic looms! Am I retracing my steps without realizing it?

One by one, the doors open and close on their own. Louder and louder, faster and faster. There is no stopping it. I place my hands over my ears, unable to handle the noise, my eardrums ready to burst. Something, seemingly many things, rush past me, not touching my body, but getting as close as possible without doing so.

I fall to the floor, rolling around in pain, begging whoever or whatever is doing this to stop. Blood comes from my ruptured eardrums and, with it, a cessation of the reverberations in my head. I'm deaf, but I will be spared the agony.

Lying there until I can regain my equilibrium, needing to challenge my other senses because my hearing is gone and my ears are worthless, I force myself up.

Two senses down; three to go.

I can not feel the doors opening and closing as I wander the perimeter of the room once more. There is no need any longer. The damage has been done. The silence is as unnerving as the loss of visual perception. Something can sneak up on me – hell, it could make all the noise in the world and I wouldn't know it until it was too late.

Still, no shadows are hovering over me. Whatever did this to me is still in the room, though. He doesn't talk to me, but he doesn't have to. I *feel* him.

And, I feel others, circling me, staying just out of touch, my efforts to swipe at them proving pointless. My arms reach nothing; touch nothing; but wasn't that what happened before? The pressure! Will it come after me again? Are the others the same?

A stench, one of decay and mold, assaults my nasal passages. It's not the rats this time: it's something else; something worse. My God, how much more will happen to me? What is causing this?

The source of putrefaction rubs itself against me, forcing the filth against my naked body. Trying to remove it only makes it intensify its efforts, and I am enclosed within some sort of a cocoon where a cesspool of garbage flows from everywhere, not only laying siege to my body, but forcing itself into my nose and mouth. I gag on the effluent and attempt to regurgitate it, only to have it forced back in again.

The huge shadow laughs. I can still no longer hear, but the sound waves attack my skin, beating a staccato of delight on my tortured, defiled body.

Kicking my way free, sliding around on the floor, having crashed down once more due to the disgusting lubricant left in the beast's wake, I am finally able to upchuck the contaminants in my body.

The bathroom! I need to get in there again. More than before I need to wash the filth off me.

The door opens before I reach it. I... I hear it! My

hearing is back.

"You smell like shit. You need a shower."

Wait! This is another trick. If I go back in there again, I'm doomed. This thing knows what I did the last time. The kitchen! I have water pots stashed over there as well. That's where I'll wash.

Around and around I go, but I cannot find my kitchen. The beast has removed it! I don't know how, but he has.

His shadow, darker than before, engulfs the entire room, dancing about everywhere, teasing me with its demonic rhythm. Other shadows, lesser ones, join in, cavorting with him, coming close to me, then backing off. All of them laugh at me, creating a Satanic choir.

They all merge together once more, the room becoming even darker.

"Is this the way you like it?" the Shadow whispers hoarsely. "Do you like it dark like this so you can't see your antagonists?"

I refuse to answer. Hell! I can't answer. Fear has taken away the function of my tongue.

"Heh, heh. If light were to suddenly fill this room, you would be shocked at the visuals before you. Maybe it would push you over the edge."

No, no! The dark... the dark is what I'm afraid of. With light in the room I could see what I'm up against and find a way to defeat it. The dark is my enemy.

As if in response to what I'm thinking, the room becomes darker yet, more and more of these creatures converging here, unseen this time, adding their blackness to what is already here.

Their forms rub up against me, there being so many

of them that I can hardly breathe. Disjointed voices, so unlike the unified choir of before, whisper in my ears then flit away, only to be replaced by others. So many voices telling me stories, all of them different.

Spirits! Ghosts! That's what they must be. But why are they taunting me? What have I done to them? None of the voices are recognizable to me. And none of the stories shed any light on why I am their target.

The dwellers within this demonic limbo attempt to inflict their pain upon me, but even if I wanted to help, there is nothing I can do. They are stuck within a dwelling place chosen for them by the Dark One himself.

But... but does that mean I am dead as well? Did I die and not know it? No, that can't be! I *felt* the pain with the pressure, the rats, the flooding in the bathroom, and the banging of the doors. That was real! I know it.

I don't belong here. Wait: *they* don't belong here. No. They should be outside with the others, the ones roaming the streets in search of food, ready to do anything it takes to get some. Like these monsters in here, they use the dark as cover for their heinous acts, although how they can find their way about remains a big question to me. Even now, through the tortured whispers of those in my room, I hear them.

"You don't think you belong with your new room-mates?" The voice of the Shadow says. "What makes you better than them? What makes you better than the ones lurking around outside doing whatever it takes to survive?"

I am not like them! The water, the canned goods,

everything in my apartment I got before the calamity or just after. Yes, I harmed no one to get what I have here.

The voices outside my door get ever closer. Do they know I'm here? Will they attempt to break in and take what I have?

Shit! The voices of the limbo dwellers are alerting them to my presence. Damn them!

My door! They stop just outside it. It moves a bit within its frame as if ears are being placed against it, trying to determine if anyone is home. Sniffling sounds move around the frame, people attempting to find treasures via their nasal passages.

I can not afford to move a muscle, although my unholy companions are intent on making me an unwilling accomplice against the forces of the Dark.

My door rattles. Some one is trying to break in. They know I'm here, damn it!

More people push on the door and the frame creaks to the tune of destruction. It can't last much longer. Shit, it's only wood, old wood at that. This place is ancient, built only God knows when.

God? Where is He? Why does He permit all that's going on to take place? He is the Lord of the Light, but there is far too little light any more. The Dark...the Dark reigns supreme. And the Shadow Being; He appears to be running the show, pulling all the strings, and revelling in the pain and agony he inflicts. And yet, when the night leaves and the light returns, He vanishes along with the Dark. It is his domain and one he chooses not to abandon.

Why should He when everything contained within

belongs to Him? My only hope is to last out the night once again, make it to the dawn, a time of rebirth for me. That's when I can sleep in peace. Only then.

The door splinters and pieces of it reach as far away as I am. Shit! Tonight I am doomed not to make it to sunrise. I will join the others wandering through my room in search of an answer other than complete damnation for them. They are looking for the Light. We are all looking for the Light.

But the Light is becoming ever more elusive.

They come running in, forcing their way through my limbo room-mates, knowing something is there but not knowing what. Their solid forms surround me, and I fear for my life. Any second now and I will be found out for who I am and killed. They will know I am different: the person living here, the one they are after. After all, even in the dark, they can tell I am naked and not like them.

But... but I'm not naked anymore. I'm fully clothed!

"Welcome to the party," the Shadow says. "One word of advice to you: you will not find what you are looking for here, so there is no sense looking for it. This place is mine. Everything within the Dark belongs to me."

Once again, the darkness of the room increases as His shadow spreads over the entire room. Screaming at the top of their lungs, the recent invaders cower before the Master of the Dark. All of us are thrown together into one huge, spinning maelstrom of fury.

I can not breathe any longer, and I collapse...

#

The lights are turned on in my room and the doctors come running over to me, trying to comfort me, wondering why I suffer the same torment every night. Only, it gets progressively worse every night. Their white coats match the white of the walls and floors, everything padded so that no harm comes to me when I chose to withdraw into my world of darkness.

Yes, that's what they call it. I have tried to explain to them about what is coming, that they better prepare for it, but they always treat me with scorn. I can see it on their faces. No matter. I care no longer; I have done my part.

They walk towards the door, wanting to get away from the crazy guy, but the power goes out and the lights are no longer on. An enormous black shadow envelops the entire room, the images playing against the dark background sending out tendrils of fear to the doctors.

"You are in my world now," the Shadow Master says. "And, where I rule there is no joy, no warmth, no love."

Overwhelming darkness envelops everything, and I can only hear their cries of pain, the scent of their blood pouring onto the soft, white floor which has now become a giant sponge for the rivers of red life flowing out of them.

But they are the fortunate ones. For them, it is over. I am doomed to relive the rituals of horror administered by the Dark One for time eternal.

He laughs once more, revelling in His power,

knowing full well that nothing can stop Him.

Nothing can stop the Dark. The Dark is evil. I know; I reside here.

Once more I try to hide from the presence within the room, but He controls me.

My God! Another stench, worse than any of the others, comes towards me. I attempt to scream out from the pain of my mental anguish, but no sound comes forth.

"Cat got your tongue?" He laughs. "If not, then soon, perhaps."

The roar of a giant cat rips through the room...

This Darkness...
John Claude Smith

Skulking around the apartment sans clothing, focus scrambled, brain fried by the mid-August heat in Portland, Oregon, Susie felt like a caged animal. Her flesh was varnished with sweat, her mood dour before having her hackles raised by the escalating temperature. The last few months with Andy had been less than inspired, not that they'd been noticeably inspired the five years they'd already languished together. But the heat only sheered the edges of her ire to unbearable. Yet she didn't know if she wanted out or what exactly she wanted.

Procrastination seemed the *modus operandi* of their relationship. Drifting without direction.

When Mitch called just past midnight, bored to tears that evaporated before sliding down his bristly cheeks, it was a welcome respite.

"Can't sleep. Can't think. Need brewsky."

Susie harrumphed, but smiled as she did. "Hello, loser." Andy pivoted his head toward her, ungluing himself from the sticky sheets and his stretched out imitation of a dying star.

In a deep voice, feigning authority, Mitch said, "No, this is God. I command you to pick up Mitch and get at least a six-pack of beer to, um, help him eradicate his thirst."

"Eradicate – big word, God. Slake is more your speed. Sure you can handle it?"

"What's he want?" Andy propped up on his

elbows, naked white pasty body glistening beneath the fluttering pale light of the ever-droning television. Susie put her finger to her lips and shushed him as she carried on her conversation with God. Or Mitch. Did it really matter? It was better than vegging out to the tenth or twelfth straight episode of the M.A.S.H marathon.

Life was a marathon. At twenty-three, already worn out from it all, Susie recently came to the revelation she had just begun her race. If that was true, she really needed to find a new pair of running shoes, a different race track, something, anything – God help me!

But obviously not this God.

Dragging Andy out of bed and meeting up with Mitch for a six-pack of "brewsky" might not be world shaking, but it seemed a better option than slowly fading to non-existence while Hawkeye Pierce cackled astute one-liners. Even if she didn't like beer, often professing it tasted "like bull urine," inspiring Andy to gleefully prod, "So, now you're a specialist on bull urine, eh?" followed by sophomoric snickers, as if he'd just beat George Lopez or Chris Rock in a comedy competition and won – *yes, of course* – a six-pack of beer but no brain cells and definitely not a sense of humor worthy of anyone but a fifteen-year old in need of friends. Inane and head-shaking stuff already old five years ago when he barely graduated from high school.

What was she doing with this dim bulb boob?

No, that wasn't the real question. That would be: What was she doing with her life? Was this living?

Then she'd remember a sweet moment, something

out of the blue and into her icy heart that would melt and run down her thighs and she'd smile, then shake her head as usual at the absurdity of it all.

"God says, let's pick him up and get a six-pack."

"Is God payin'?"

Without hesitation, she said, "Yes, of course God is paying," which roused a faint but useless groan of protest from God. What better way to waste the night than in the company of these two idiots, especially when her only option besides that was spending time with only one. Double the pleasure, double the... inanity!

Anyway, getting out of the furnace that was the apartment and getting ice-cold something sounded good, perhaps mandatory.

"Probably cooler up in the mountain," Mitch said, running an unopened can of Old Milwaukie across his forehead. Much to Andy's beer snobbery mindset, Old Milwaukie was barely a notch above dirty water or, possibly, bull urine. Susie could care less, she just wanted cold.

"I don't think it matters, but getting away from these buffoons would be appreciated." She nodded toward the young boys with their many toys, primarily skateboards, arms dipped in colorful tattoos, their assembly line girlfriends with their pink and purple iPhones, twitchy thumbs texting like duelling beetles, as well as their pierced belly-buttons and all year tans and their own assortment of tattoos, rather, tramp stamps poking out above snug cut-offs. The din of half-cocked conversations about nothing in particular that meant the world to them –conversations that made

Andy's and Mitch's seem like dissertations on quantum physics – creased a permanent scowl on her face. She was only a few years older than most of them – when did she grow up so fast? She laughed at that wayward thought: grow up? She was stuck in limbo in Portland, Oregon, with a boyfriend more inclined to smoke weed and play video games into the wee hours, usually with Mitch along for the brain-wasting duration, than in the advancement or growth or care of their relationship.

She sighed. She remembered a Dr. Seuss quote about nonsense waking up brain cells and begged to differ. Oh, no, this kind of nonsense annihilated one's soul. Slowly, like the erosion of a cliff by crashing waves and time.

What the hell was she doing with her life?

"All right, Paul Bunyan. To the mountain, pronto!" she said.

"Tonto? Ain't he with the Lone Ranger?" Mitch said.

Andy scoffed, "You moron. She said pronto, as in, get a move on. My question, though, is who's this Paul Bunyan dude? You having flashbacks to an ex boyfriend?" He actually looked irritated, which only magnified the farce that was her life. Still, perhaps in the mountains she could get lost for awhile and not have to face this dreary, spirit-draining place. Or perhaps get her head and life aligned for something more than the constant nothing.

Who was she kidding?

Weaving through the darkness, barely acknowledging the forest as the primer-coated-for-so-long-it's-now-the-regular-color light gray Mustang's beams, even set on high as there was no traffic to be had, seemed barely able to cut through the intense darkness. Susie had never *felt* darkness like this before: a choking, oppressive darkness. The beams showed exactly what fell in their path and nothing more. A gray-black pavement trimmed with motes of light like squiggly fireflies, more aptly distinguishing the molecular breakdown of light into an unyielding dark; at least that's how she saw it.

Because this darkness seemed more full, more robust and tactile; more pitch black yet alive. And needy, as if it did not want to give up its place amidst the insistence of the beams.

When they made the top of the mountain a large parking lot flattened the landscape like a blotch on nature and served as their welcome mat. Humanity's intrusion, a carbon footprint stamped hard into the asphalt smothered soil. Yet, again, the beams only showed a sliver of this, cutting through the night as Andy looped in wide circles, thin white lines mostly covered by leaves indicative of parking slots, as if it mattered. He abruptly braked and all three of them lurched forward. He needed beer. He needed it now.

He shut off the headlights and Mitch's voice squeaked in protest, a Chihuahua yip of annoyance. "Turn some light on *now*, jerk," Susie said, never one to fear the dark, yet made suddenly uncomfortable by the blanket of *this* darkness. She couldn't see either of them. They were within touching distance, yet there was no real indication they were there, at least for these few precarious moments.

She was happy to hear Mitch's nervous giggling, "Yeah, turn something on, dude," after which Andy clicked on the dome light and gulped half a can of beer. "Y'all ain't afraid of the dark, are you? Couple of pussies." Susie was surprised to see his wax mask face tilting back the beer can, having not heard the tick of the tab. Ignoring his crude comment, she snapped the tab off her own can, sipped it for the cool chill, and tipped her head out the open passenger side window. The beer felt good going down, but the heat was no less loathsome up here, perhaps worse. There also was the matter of the stars, or the lack of them.

"We overcast?" she said, to no one in particular.

"Shouldn't be, though it is Portland," Mitch said, his leering devil-faced Bic lighter flaming to life, joint set between his thin lips, beads of sweat multiplying above said lips. His full ratty beard and no moustache always made her think he looked like a homeless version of Abraham Lincoln.

Oh, hell, thought Susie. She berated herself for her idiocy: this was a great idea, *dumb head*. Get these two going on weed and they might as well be locked into whatever was this week's video game purchase. Killing and explosions and she hated it all, falling asleep alone too often while Heckle and Jeckle took over the world.

Staring into the empty sky, then right and left, she could see nothing of substance outside of the dome light's inadequate glare. Or, rather, the darkness here had real density – so odd. Add this sensation to the burgeoning video game riffing from within the car and she felt like a fist wrapped in a boxing glove, tied off at the wrist and meant to pummel the life out of her already weary soul.

She spent the next fifteen minutes listening to their inane conversation about how to master something called *Lunar Takeover*, a First Person Shooter game set on an outpost on the moon; same old, same old, only a different location, as far as she could tell. But they fully immersed themselves in the intricacies of what they'd both discovered so far – moon monsters and crater creatures and zombie astronauts around every bend, and the best ways to kill them – as they sucked on the joint and finished off the meager beer post haste, while she sipped and savored the bland drink. Closing her eyes was almost no different than leaving them open. The night was vast, all-encompassing. A weight. A beast. Something that ate stars and devoured moons as well. Something these two blokes would never beat if they met it in an outpost on the moon or staggering out of a closet in their bedrooms.

She pulled her head into the car, creeped out by the ambience, the stifling atmosphere.

"You ready to go, baby?"

For once Andy and she were on the same wave length.

"Too weird up here."

"What?"

"Yes, go. It's too weird up here."

"Yeah. We should've bought a case. Gotta get some more and then we can regain rule of the moon, eh, Skywalker?" Andy said, nodding to the bobble-head monkey, Mitch. He cranked the ignition while clicking off the dome light. The engine's mechanical wheeze and clank was the only thing in Susie's life for the span of what should have been a split second of transition before he turned on the headlights. She held her breath, the sounds much like the darkness, this darkness – *a different darkness* – fully immersive, surrounding her. Wagons circling...

"Fucking hell, Andy. A little light, pronto."

He turned on the lights and said, "Yes, baby?" in a whiny, mocking voice.

She leaned toward the dashboard and gripped it with her right hand, glaring at him, shooting harpoons at his dead fish-eyed stare.

"What?"

He really didn't have a clue, she thought.

"I think she's afraid of the dark, man," Mitch said.

"No, Einstein. Just not digging the vibe up here," she said, but this darkness was rubbing her wrong, a frisson of unease like a splinter burrowing under a fingernail.

"I think your pussy would love the vibration of this clunker – Ow!" She slugged Andy hard in the arm while Mitch snorted his approval.

"You think everything's funny, don't you? You think our whole relationship is one long excuse to laze around in your shit-stained shorts playing video games, getting high or drunk, while I get some schooling in, trying to better myself. All this while occasionally taking a minute or two to express your so-called love to me while unloading in my pussy, without wearing a condom, so perhaps I will get pregnant, which might be what you're looking for, so

I won't even get the chance to better myself while raising our child alone, even with you there, because you're never really there and you're definitely not even close to grown up and anything to do with responsibilities is a foreign language to you, something beyond your fucking understanding because it's not plugged into the Xbox and–"

"Shut up!"

"You just don't fucking get it."

"Shut the fuck up, 'kay? I get your point. I fuckin' get it," Andy said, eyes burning as coals in her direction, barely visible except for the glossy reflection of the high beams out front of the car as he started to roll it slowly out of the lot.

"So, is she right, man? A minute man, eh?" Mitch said, unable to contain a giggle, like carbonation rising to the top of the glass. The pot had left him even more stupid than usual.

"Shut up!" they said in unison.

Silence hung as a muffling cloak over them. Susie's anger did not dispel the weird vibe she'd sensed since they got to the mountain top. Never one to fear the dark, right now, all she wanted was lights and sounds and stupid teenagers in front of a liquor store. Anything to dilute the liquid flow of this darkness.

Before Andy spoke, Susie sensed his anxiety bristling in the air. He sucked in deeply and the inside of the car seemed to contract ever so slightly.

"Look, I'm sorry, baby. I really..." But he fell silent, his thoughts clustered as one, and, as usual, he was speaking before he'd sorted them out.

Susie remained silent, ignoring him.

"I don't mean no harm, y'know? I just... I don't really know what to do with it all sometimes. Us and everything, y'know?"

She turned her head to the window, gazing deep into the black nothing outside.

"Hey, I'm tryin' to say somethin' here."

She just wanted it all to stop. Please, just stop.

"Goddamnit!" Andy said, jamming his foot on the brakes, cutting off the lights, the engine, everything.

"Hey," Mitch said, that Chihuahua yelp again using his throat for expression.

Susie kicked at the door, hand scrambling for the handle, saying "Fuck you! Fuck you! Fuck all of this!" as she did. Frustration poured over her like an angry waterfall. She finally got the door open, shoving with force as she did. The dome light splashed meager luminosity across the interior, which she was hastily exiting. As the metal joints stretched to the breaking point, the door creaked and popped with firecracker intensity. She stepped out and the door started its path back to being shut in a hurry. But just as suddenly, she regretted being outside of the car and in this darkness, though she also did not want to lose any more brain cells by being within hooting distance of Heckle and Jeckle; her exasperation only magnified the situation. As she twirled back toward the door, everything shifted down a notch, slowing as seconds stretched. She heard Andy say, "What the hell is that?" while the light weaved ugly, perplexing patterns into the crinkled folds of Mitch's face, forming a landscape for an undiscovered planet in the process, both of them staring out the windshield, not even caring about her annoyance. The look in their eyes caused her to shift her gaze from them to whatever might be in front of the car, a seemingly impossible quest because of this darkness – when she felt its presence...

Reaching for the swiftly closing door, she was too late. It clicked shut and the feeble dome light was eaten by the voracious darkness and a scream climbed the broken rungs of her throat, yet as if sound was in cahoots with this darkness, she heard nothing.

A vacuum of terror pressed against her as she ached for the aural confirmation she knew she had expressed, yet where was it? More so, she sensed the silence was so very internal, though distinguishing blood currents and heart beats was beyond her capabilities. She felt adrift, yet she also felt compressed, as if this darkness wasn't only pressing into her, it was invading pores, seeking organs, essence.

She reached for the door handle, anxious to fling herself back into the car and just deal with them, to yell at Andy to get them the hell out of there, not caring about being made fun of or anything but being away. Real decisions would happen soon enough, but right now she just needed the safety of noise and lights and being so far from this darkness.

Her efforts fell flat: there was no door handle.

She let out a brittle, "Fuck," that landed on black cotton stuffed ears. She couldn't see the handle, only knew the approximate direction, yet her fingers remained unfilled. Both hands now, her lithe body stepping forward, her hip should be banging into metal, but nothing impeded her movement.

There was nothing there. No car. No Andy and Mitch joking away. No light, no sound, only this darkness.

She screamed again, her diaphragm opening wide to release the vocalization of her fear, to no avail. She knelt to one knee, palm pressed hard against her abdomen. The pain of such a wail bent on rupturing the night, splitting her in two.

The scream was trapped within. The silent scream.

"So you're not afraid of me, Susie Chambers?" It was a leering, vile utterance that caused her fingers to stiffen, her back to arch. Her breath caught in her throat with the scream.

After a few precious, strangled moments, she was able to expel a wordless sound. Something culled from the primal within, from the eons woven into her DNA. From a past beyond the memories she'd amassed and tapping into the origin of fear on an intrinsic level, before fear was defined.

"I suppose you are," said the voice that resonated from within her bones, slick with marrow and destruction

She brushed her arms as if they were covered in ants, only stopping when she realized it was useless expenditure of her rapidly disintegrating energy, and perhaps her sanity, too. Whatever she felt was already within her, even as she felt wrapped tight out here by the dark. "Who... Who are you?" Still, she did not hear her voice, yet the other answered.

"You already know who I am. Let's not mess around. We must get to the point." Each line spat with the force of a hammer pounding a nail. Her body buckled as if kicked in the stomach, the head.

Perplexed and shaking, she understood nothing, yet whatever this thing was – the dark? Was it this darkness? How could that be? – it had intent beyond simply scaring the shit out of her. "What point would that be?" She realized she was sobbing as she spoke, not by aural recognition, but by the physical responses to the unknown circumstances, her shoulders hitching, tears blurring her vision, sniffles causing her head to jerk, yet as with external sound, she only sensed the visceral insistence these reactions triggered within.

"I have needs, Susie. I need the acknowledgement of my existence as a force of dread."

Despite her present incomprehensible state, she laughed, a delirious shard that cut deep. "If that's all you need, isn't my reaction evidence enough. I am afraid. I am fucking afraid."

Synapses and capillaries screeched a dissonant chorus, rubbed raw by that which filled her.

"I need something more, as well. In a place like this, out here in true nature, I'm allowed a little leeway in the laws of the world you know. I'm allowed gifts."

"What? What more do you want from me? What gifts?" She spun in circles, aware of how much she felt trapped, cut off from everything she knew, as if the world consisted of only her body, as invaded by the dark, and nothing more. An ink stain cancer, spreading...

"I want you to understand the rules of true nature. Where killing is a measure of living. Of being alive.

Sometimes out of necessity, survival, but for me, it's simply out of sadistic pleasure."

"I don't want to die!" The distress that this event might be prelude to her death flushed her system in its numbing embrace. "Please..."

"But some must die. I need perhaps *two humans* to fulfill my taste for fear and flesh, for blood and... satisfaction." An insidious snickering sound rattled her rib cage.

"I don't want to die." She thought, yes, her life has been derailed for so long, but to die like this – no! "I don't want to die."

"Then you'll know when to make a stand for yourself."

Banging against the car door, fingers scratching at the handle suddenly within grasp, pulling hard and leaping inside, body quaking but not even the center of Andy's and Mitch's focus. When she closed the door, the dome light blinked out, but the headlights were on, and something loomed large in front of the Mustang.

"Drive, Andy. Drive!" Mitch pounded on the back of Susie's seat. Andy fumbled with the key, only needing to turn it to start the engine, but clumsily unable to grip it in his sweaty fingers. Still shaken, Susie homed in on Andy's fingers, willing him to turn the key and the car would kick into gear and they could somehow avoid what filled the road before them: a large animal, perhaps a bear, but of such humungous proportions, somehow wrong, somehow too large – she wasn't sure what it was.

"Fuck! *Fuck!* I can't get the key to–"

The beast lunged toward the hood, paws the size of large garbage can lids pressing down, down. The front tires exploded with the immense impact. Paw prints dented the metal.

Andy groaned and said "Oh my god. We're screwed." Then, looking up at Susie: "We're so fuckin' screwed."

Eyes pinned open by shock, Susie followed the beast as it lumbered to the left, toward Andy's side of the car. Even on all fours it towered above them. Andy struggled to roll up the window, an illusion of safety. She did the same, though she rolled hers up out of dull instinct and nothing more.

Mitch, normally more emotional than Andy, said, "Freeze. Don't move. Some animals won't bother people if they stay still, like statues."

The beast stopped by Andy's door. It was barely distinguishable from the night, though fist-sized eyes glared red and ferocious into the car. Andy's head was turned toward Susie, trying to ignore the beast – perhaps with the hope of waking from this nightmare in their bed, in that tiny apartment, TV droning on as usual. His face was a rictus of panic. She could peripherally see Mitch scrunching into the corner of the back seat, attempting to blend into the fabric. She thought now, here, unlike a few minutes ago, she could hear her own blood pumping furiously in her veins, loud and clear.

Susie wanted to look away, but that was impossible as she might draw unwanted attention. She stared into the beast's eyes and saw instinct and mayhem spark as shooting stars across an ancient night, crackling with primeval fury. Deeper still, she recalled what the dark voice had said to her: *Then you'll know when to make a stand for yourself.*

She remembered a sweet moment, something out of the blue to bring a smile... but the blue bruised to black in her memory as tears welled and she shook her head – no! – but what her brain kept telling her was, *I don't want to die, I don't want to die...*

A massive paw crashed through the window and grabbed the back of Andy's head like a basketball, yanking him out of the car. Clothing and flesh shredded on broken glass, Andy's voice trailing it all, a sound like nothing Susie had ever imagined. The leaky balloon hiss of surrender, defeat; of knowing, yes, he was going to die. Now.

Mitch bounced off her seat, pushing it forward. "Let me out. Let me the hell out of here."

Susie knew it would not matter, and then thought, *I need perhaps two humans to fulfil my taste for fear and flesh, for blood and... satisfaction.* If Mitch runs free, if Mitch is successful in fleeing this midnight massacre, where does that leave her? She hated herself for thinking this, but dying here, like this...

"What about me? What about me, Mitch. You can't just leave–"

"It's occupied," he said, as they both peered into the dark, barely able to see anything, yet the sounds of bones being crunched and the grumble of animal contentment filled their ears.

Mitch stretched himself and caught the handle, pushing the door open and stumbling out. His eyes locked with hers, a moment to wordlessly say, I'm sorry, but I'm out of here.

It was too late.

The moment he wasted cost him any chance he might have had, though under these perilous circumstances, she understood his chance was nil anyway. The beast was quick to lope toward him and just as he made it past the front of the car, Susie watched as it snatched him by the leg and swung him around. His body crashed into the front left corner of the car; the headlight went out, his body went limp. He tried meekly to fend off the beast as the beast opened its mouth wide and took his head inside. Biting down, the hideous rat-tat-tat cracking of bones caused her heart to batter her breastbone, wanting its own escape as she stared in awe and fear. The beast flung the decapitated body in the same direction as it had flung Andy's.

Then it stared at her.

"Time for you to leave, Susie." The voice, this time not from within. It hung over her shoulder, hollow and avaricious as a ravenous vulture.

"Leave? How? That... thing," she said, as the beast in front of the lone functioning headlight rose up on its hind legs, its head lost in the black heavens. Her hands shook violently on her lap. She noticed a wet stain at her crotch, realized she'd pissed herself, yet did not know when.

"Just open your door and walk on by," the voice said. She could feel the menacing smile it wore brush across her neck, felt its invisible lips kiss her throat. She immediately rubbed her Adam's apple with unsteady fingers.

"Haven't time to waste, Susie. Go now or I may rescind my generosity."

She had no choice. Stay and die. Or leave and put her trust in this cruel, sentient darkness.

She pushed the door open, having already been left ajar by Mitch's failed attempt at freedom. Vertigo swam through her head, her legs shaking, each step an exercise in concentration. As she approached the front of the car, palm of her hand caressing the cool metal for balance, the beast did not move.

She knew she was going to have to "walk on by." She knew there was no other way around it. Her courage, a tiny thing nestled next to her will to survive, prodded her on. When she was within touching distance she thought she would break. Without the car to prop her up, she felt herself drifting, as she had done with this life for years; she regained the frayed edges of composure and continued.

Susie expected animal musk, the gamey scent of the wild, the stink of nature's bloody victory. What she got was beyond comprehension. What she saw was a silhouette, a misplaced shadow – something undefined – perhaps just a black *shape* from which freezing waves from the wasteland of its being emanated. With a slight twitch of her head she glanced closer at the beast, into an immeasurable cosmic gulf littered with shards of bone and constellations cognizant of her trespass as the beast, this thing, an emissary from this darkness, wailed into the starless sky. It was the roar of planets being birthed; it was the keen of suns going supernova; it was the alpha and omega of eternity; it was infinite, yet steeped in the here and now.

"Time to run, Susie Chambers. Run and never look back. Remember me, though. Remember me and fear me with your every thought."

Wobbly legs or not, she didn't need to be told twice. She was alive and that was better than the alternative, no matter the circumstances that got her here. No matter the lies she'd have to convince herself were true over the years that would follow; the years of purpose, she thought – no longer adrift.

Was this *her* gift?

She hated herself again, thinking so selfishly, but perhaps that might be the only way she could even make sense of it all, as if sense was to be made – no. But for now, she was alive and that would have to do.

She ran many miles out of the mountain, from night till dawn, until her thighs burned under the golden sunrise that signaled a new day like no other. No day, no night, could be like what she had just experienced. Not that she would ever be able to forget any of it.

This much was certain.

Lost and Found
Tonia Brown

"Bout time you got here," Kate said.

"Sorry," Renee said and dropped her bag on the desk. "Where's your help?"

Kate flipped her book closed and stretched. "Becky is already gone. She clocked out on time. Again."

"Yeah, well Tim left me without any gas. Again."

"When are you gonna learn? Men are all the same."

Renee shrugged. "Tim is a hell of a guy most of the time. He is just forgetful. That's all."

"One day he is going to forget you're married and end up in the bed of a twenty-something floozy. Then where will you be?"

"In the bed with a twenty-something floozy, puttin' on a show for my hubby." Renee added a little tongue waggle to the claim.

Kate got to her feet with a laugh and began gathering her things.

"Any business?" Renee asked, eyeing the empty exam rooms.

"Nope," Kate said. "Things are dead in the ED, in a good way. The floor has a few portables in the morning, but other than that, you are good to go."

As a third shift x-ray tech, Renee always did the morning portables, so nothing new there. A quiet Emergency Department was a good sign, especially at the beginning of her shift. Usually it started busy then tapered off into the early morning hours. "Thank god. These last couple of days have been so crappy and I have a book I have been... dying to..." Renee paused to narrow her eyes at the sight of Kate chewing her bottom lip. "Why are you biting your lip like that?"

Kate winced as she half said, half asked, "Because I forgot to file?"

Renee let out a disappointed groan and slumped onto the desk. "You bitch. And here I thought I had the whole night to myself."

"Sorry. It just slipped my mind."

"Sure." Renee snorted and crossed her arms. "And I bet how much you hate filing slipped your mind too."

"I see how it is." Kate snapped up her stuff and stomped toward the door. "Your fantastic man can be forgetful, but your best friend does things on purpose."

"Kate," Renee said, going after the angry woman. "I was just teasing."

"I know," Kate said, flashing a smile over her shoulder. "Have a lovely night!" She threw her hand up in farewell, transforming the goodbye into a middle finger salute as she slipped through the door.

Okay, Renee might have deserved that one. But damn it! It wasn't like she enjoyed filing more than anyone else. Still, sitting around bitching about it wasn't getting it done. Resigning herself to her third shift fate, she grabbed the department phone, drew a deep breath and headed down the hall to the film room to see how bad the damage was. A quick flick of the light brought a tearful sight to her weary eyes.

"Jesus!" she shouted before she caught herself and covered her mouth.

The inbox rested on the floor in the back of the file room, near the hallway, positioned to catch films returned from other departments via the slot in the wall. The bin usually had a good foot or so of work, but tonight it was waist high with loose films. Not only had Kate 'forgotten' to file, but it looked like every other god damned shift forgot as well. Why everyone thought third shift – with only one tech – had time to do something that everyone else couldn't manage, Renee had no idea. But, again, bitching about it didn't get the work done.

She rolled up her sleeves, bit back her anger, and dug in.

The first couple of hours went surprisingly fast. Between a broken ankle, a fishhook in the lip and a dislocated shoulder – all courtesy of the ED – she had plenty of time to get stuff sorted out. She even found herself whistling while she worked. It wasn't until she reached the bottom of the pile did she cease, mid whistle, and stare. The last foot or so of files were old. As in really, really old.

As in came from the dungeon old.

The dungeon rested in the basement section of an older part of the hospital, all but forgotten after the remodelling was finished years ago. Aside from storing really old films, it was filled with the neglected remnants of a bygone era – abandoned equipment, unneeded supplies and the likes. The most fascinating section by far was the lost and found; a room filled with old clothes, toys, books and other things left behind by patients through the years. Renee had never seen the room, but she heard it was a sight to behold.

Well, that and it was supposedly haunted.

The only time anyone from radiology went to the dungeon was... well, actually no one ever went to the dungeon these days. The modern exams were digitized, with the rare print for the occasional customer. The department kept hard copies for about three years, but after that the films were destroyed, leaving nothing but their computer files as evidence the exam ever happened. Films stored in the dungeon were exams and procedures ancient in comparison to modern day technology. Who in the hell ordered films pulled from there?

Renee checked her watch. Just after midnight. Kate never went to bed before four, choosing to stay up all night and flirt on the internet with the same men she'd bitch about all the next day. Renee called the woman from the department phone. It rang a few times before Kate answered it.

"What?" Kate asked.

"Geesh," Renee said. "Is that any way to say hello?"

"Not when you think you're being called back in."

"Like I would do that to you. I'd call Peter first."

"Then Pete would call me and–"

"Why are there dungeon films in the bin?"

Kate tripped over her complaint and went quiet. "Is there?"

"Yeah. Looks like stuff from about, oh, twenty years ago. Jesus, I didn't think we kept stuff that old."

"Oh, I remember now. Pete said that some students came through the department today."

"You mean yesterday."

"Whatever. He was probably showing off for them. You know his whole 'the way it was' routine. He gets off on it."

"Yeah, just a build up to show off the new MRI."

"Yup."

Renee flipped through the files. "I wonder what they thought of these old tomographs."

"They probably wondered what particular cave man shot the films."

"Wait up now. Wasn't that you?"

"Har, har. Just because I've been in this game longer than you don't mean you get to rub it in."

"Sorry." Renee said between chuckles. "I should go. Standing around on the phone is more fun than filing, but I am almost done and that book is calling my name."

"You really gonna file those?"

"Sure. Why not?"

"Because it is creepy as shit down there."

"I like creepy. Besides, I've never been down there." Renee grinned. "Maybe I'll see Gertrude."

Kate's gasp came across the cell as a thin, asthmatic wheeze. "Don't even joke about that."

"Come on, she's just a story."

"She is not. Gertrude is real."

"Yeah, really lame. I mean, a ghost haunting the basement of a hospital? How original."

"She's real!"

"Have you ever seen her?"

"Hell no. But you won't catch me looking for her either."

"What's the big deal with her anyways?"

"I told you, she used to cut up kids."

"I thought she boiled puppies?" Renee chuckled.

Every time someone shared a Gertrude story the premise stayed the same, but the details always changed; some old lady who did horrible things in life, only to die alone in the geriatric ward of the old hospital.

Kate yawned.

"Sleepy head," Renee said. "When I hang up, you go to bed."

"Yes, mother," Kate said.

"I'm serious. Don't let me catch you online later. Get some sleep."

"G'night."

The line went dead, leaving Renee alone again.

She glanced to the dusty stack of old films and thought carefully about the task. Being the only tech on shift meant she needed to stay within reception of her phone, a signal the depth of the basement would surely obstruct. Yet, to the best of her knowledge the intercom still reached the basement, and with the right warnings to the right folks, she could step away from her department for at least a few minutes. The ED was still dead, in a good way, and if they really needed her, she could still hear the codes through the intercom. Besides, how long would it take to slip a few files back on the rack? Renee made the appropriate arrangements and headed off to the supposedly creepy as hell basement for her first look-see.

"Wow," Renee said when she reached the bottom of the stairwell.

The place was every bit as creepy as Kate claimed;

damp and mouldy, with a slight chill in the air and a murky, endless gloom. Sure there were auxiliary lights giving off a soft red glow, but they somehow made the place creepier. She flicked on the overhead switch, but it did little good. Only the first few fixtures worked, and those flickering bulbs were covered in filth, shedding but a hair more light upon the first few feet of the hallway. She stared into the dimly lit hall, and swallowed hard. It looked like something from a horror film. She had a hard time believing that this basement was part of the same uber sterile environment only a few feet above. Swaths of peeling paint left huge sections of brick showing through, while random equipment lay scattered across the floor in a medical maze. Something in the darkness beyond the low light dripped and dripped, echoing down the cold hallway and right up Renee's spine.

Renee checked her department phone for a signal. No luck. She checked her personal cell. No reception either. That settled it then. She intended to explore a bit once the filing was done, but with it being so dark, and no reception on her phones, and the fact that she was just plain weirded out, she decided to get her work done and get the heck out. Thankfully, the film room was near the stairwell, as evidenced by a huge handmade sign taped to the door. Once inside, Renee's heart sank again. The place was a jumble of films. How in the hell was she supposed to file this stuff back in that mess? The answer came upon the heels of the question, bringing her to a smile. On second thought, there was an obvious system at work here, so she just followed suit. Renee dropped her stack on the pile nearest the door, and that was that.

She backed into the hallway again, closing the door as she did. No sooner had the film storage door clicked shut, Renee heard the soft shuffle of feet at the other end of the hall. The end away from the stairwell. She peered into the gloom, wondering what made the noise.

"Hello?" she called out.

No answer came.

"Gertrude?" she asked, and chuckled.

Again, no answer. Not that she expected one. Renee shrugged and turned to leave, when she heard the shuffle again. She closed her eyes and tried to pretend she didn't hear it, but through the darkness it came a third time, stronger and clearer.

"Craaap," she groaned, but went to find the source anyways.

She crept along the hallway, dodging old exam tables and metal gurneys, O2 tanks and IV poles. As she moved, she strained to pick out the direction of the noise. Sometimes it sounded forever away, yet at other times it was right upon her, as if the person was walking toward her, seeking her instead of the other way round. It didn't take long for her to reach the end of the lighted section. She looked around for another switch, but there wasn't another one. Her original assessment was correct; the rest of the fixtures were either burned out or broken, leaving her to the half shadows of the lights behind her.

"Hello?" she called out one more time. "Is anyone there?"

"My teeth," someone in the darkness answered.

The voice was feminine, old and tired, dragging out the words in long slow syllables.

Renee's heart leapt to her throat at the sound. Or was it a sound. Did she hear it or was she yanking her own chain here in the gloom. "Umm, hello?"

"My teeth," the woman said. "I've lost my teeth. Can you help me find them?"

Shuffle. Shuffle.

Okay, that was not just her imagination. There was someone down here with her. Someone who lost their teeth? Really? Always the pragmatist, she calmed her wild heart and searched her mind for possible answers. Lost teeth. Slow words. An aged voice. From the sound of it, one of the geriatric patients had wandered off the skilled floor and into the basement. It wasn't just likely, it was the sort of thing that happened all the time.

"Hello?" she asked again. "Ma'am? Where are you? Let me help you get back upstairs."

"I need to find my teeth," the woman said.

"Shit," Renee whispered. This wasn't going to work. She almost turned back for help, or at least a flashlight, when an idea struck her. She pulled her phone from her jacket and swiped away the lock screen.

"We got an app for that," she said as she touched a few places on the screen.

The pale LED of her flash came to life, casting the hallway into a ghostly glow. It was creepy to be sure, but certainly better then stumbling around in the dark while looking for some poor old fart. Renee swept the light this way and that, still searching for the source of the voice and the shuffle. Without warning, the light from the cell swept across the form of an old woman. Renee should've expected it, but instead the appearance of the lady took her by surprise. She shouted aloud and fumbled her phone, snatching it from mid fall with the ease of one who has almost dropped her cell before. With it in hand again, she pointed the light to the spot she swore she saw the old woman, but instead of the patient, Renee shone her light on a door marked 'Lost and Found.'

The hinges squeaked as the door clicked shut.

"Your teeth aren't in there you old biddy," Renee said.

She stared at the door for a few moments, wondering what she should do. The proper procedure was to call the nursing supervisor and let her handle this mess. Of course, that meant leaving the old fart here while Renee tried to find some reception for her phone. Besides, she was hired to take x-rays, not chase around little old ladies. That was someone else's job.

Without warning, a bright light poured over her shoulder and illuminated the door before her.

"What in the hell are you doing down here?" the security guard asked.

"Jesus Christ!" Renee shouted, and this time she did drop her phone.

Scott chuckled and directed his flashlight to the floor. "Damn, girl, don't have heart attack on me. I don't have my CPR cert yet."

"Don't sneak up on me like that," she growled.

"You dropped your phone." He aimed the light at her phone on the floor.

"No shit, Sherlock." She bent double to retrieve it, pleased to see it survived the fall.

"Butterfingers."

"Asshole."

Scott chuckled again. "What are you doing down here anyways?"

"Filing."

"Filing? Filing what? Coats and false teeth?"

The hair on the back of Renee's neck stood on end as she remembered the echo of the old woman's words.

I need to find my teeth.

"What are you talking about?" Renee asked.

"You know," Scott said. "Clothes and stuff. Patient belongings. That is all that's in there." He lifted his light over her shoulder to shine on the room behind her again.

Renee turned about and stared at the 'Lost and Found' sign. "Someone's in there too."

"Say what?" Scott asked, joining her beside the door.

"A little old woman. She must've wandered down here from the geriatric ward."

"You sure?"

"Why?" Renee grinned, unable to help herself. "You think it's Gertrude?"

The guard went pale at the name. "Ugh, don't even joke about that."

"What is it about her that makes everyone so weird?"

"I heard she was like this masochist that killed all of her lovers by sticking fire pokers in unpleasant places."

"Now that is one I have never heard before."

"Joke all you like, I wouldn't want to meet her down here in the dark."

"Well I can promise you this wasn't Gertrude. Or a ghost. She was shuffling around in the dark and then went into that room. Said she lost her teeth. I think she is looking for them."

"Well, that'd be the place to find 'em. There's a stack of dentures in there that goes all the way to the effing the ceiling. We should call the nursing supervisor." Scott snapped his phone from his belt and looked at it with a frown. "No signal."

"Yeah. I know."

"Then what did you have your phone out for?"

"As a flashlight, dumbass."

"Ah."

"Try your radio."

"You kidding me? Forget about it. If the cell's don't work down here, that hunk of junk isn't gonna do crap. I'll go look for the lady and you go back and get the super–"

The intercom began to squawk over his offer of help.

"Code White, Ward C. Code White, Ward C. Code White, Ward C."

"Huh," Scott said. "I didn't realize the intercom reached down here." He clipped his phone back on his belt and headed to the stairwell.

"Where are you going?" Renee called after him.

"I gotta respond. Workplace violence and all that. Probably the new admit on the psych ward acting up."

"What about the missing patient?"

"Here," Scott said, and tossed his flashlight toward Renee before he mounted the first step.

She caught the light and raced to the bottom of the stairs. "What is this for?"

"Take a look around," he said without stopping. "I'll be right back. I'll call Sue while I'm up here. We will be back in ten minutes, tops."

"Ten minutes? Scott! Get back here and help me!"

He mumbled something she couldn't make out, and obviously had no intention of helping her look for anyone.

"Stupid Code Gray," she said.

Renee glanced down the hallway, to the door at the end. Maybe, just possibly, she didn't actually see anyone at all. Maybe she imagined the whole thing. Sure. That made all kinds of sense. Now that she thought about it, the whole thing sounded silly. Why would there be some old lady wandering around down here in the dark?

At the far end of the hallway there came a loud crash, as if something fell to the floor.

Or someone.

This was followed by a soft moan.

"Great," Renee said. "Way to get yourself hurt."

That settled it then, Renee had to find the patient now. The last thing she needed was the guilt of letting some old lady flounder to death in the basement. She flicked on the flashlight and headed to the Lost and Found again. Renee pushed through the door and swept the light across the room, gawking at the contents. The place looked like a yard sale mine blew up and rained junk shrapnel and clothes everywhere. Racks and racks of coats lined the walls, between which sat piles of shoes, suitcases and handbags. Renee snorted when the beam of light landed on a table stacked with dentures.

"Teeth ahoy," she whispered.

"My teeth," a voice answered her.

The speaker was just at her back, all but hissing the words over her shoulder. Renee started at the intimate proximity of the voice, and dropped the flashlight in surprise. It clattered to the floor, throwing scattered rays in stuttered jolts across the room, until it fell dead. Renee cringed as the place plunged into immediate darkness, either the auxiliary lights were broken or just not installed in this room.

"My teeth," the woman said again.

Where the voice was just over Renee's shoulder moments before, now it was in front of her. "Hello? Ma'am? Are you okay?"

"My teeth. I've lost them."

"I don't think your teeth are down here, ma'am. I'm need to take you back–"

"Help me." The voice moved around in the dark. To the left. To the right.

"Are you hurt?"

"Please, help me."

Renee reached out to grope the blackness in front of her. "Ma'am, you stay where you are. Keep talking and I will come to you."

"Help me."

"I will. I'll help you."

"You have my teeth?"

Renee shook her head, then felt silly when she realized the woman couldn't see her. "No, I don't have your teeth, hon. You need to let me – Whoa!" She lost her balance as the old woman knocked into Renee, shoving her to the floor. She tumbled, falling hard with the shock of the sudden pushed, slamming face first into the concrete. Her jaw exploded in pain.

Renee rolled onto her back, groaning in torment as her mouth filled with the tang of fresh blood. She spit up a mouthful of the stuff, pausing when she realized it wasn't just blood she expelled. There was something hard there, something small and sharp. Fumbling for her phone, she prayed to whatever god was listening that it wasn't what she thought it was. She brought up the flashlight app once again, and turned the phone to the object of her prayer.

In a frothy pink puddle of spit and blood, there lay the lump of a broken tooth.

"No," she said, and tongued the spot she thought it came from. It was hard to tell, thanks to the fact that her mouth was burning with pain. "Damn it."

"My teeth," the old woman said again.

Geesh! Would the lady never shut up? Renee wanted to punch the old bag in her toothless mouth. She pushed the urge down, as well as the pain, and rolled onto her belly in order to get to her feet. Her head spun, leaving her hanging onto the floor waiting for the moment to pass. As she did, her cell phone light shone on a pair of bedroom slippers, shuffling toward her.

"Ma'am," Renee said with supreme effort. "I shaid you need to hold shtill. You've already knocked me down and I don't want you to trip."

The slippers stopped just beside of the broken tooth. "My teeth." An aged hand reached into the halo of light and picked up the shard.

Renee raised the light, following the old woman's motions as she lifted the shard to her own open mouth and pressed the broken tooth into her gum.

"Ew," Renee said. "No, stop that. Please, aw, Jesus." She tried to stand again, but another attack of vertigo denied her the chance.

"My teeth," the woman said. She began to shuffle toward Renee. Something gleamed in her right hand, just catching the edge of the light.

Renee turned the cell phone to that gleam, her eyes widening at a pair of enormous pliers in the old lady's hand. "What tha..."

The first strike caught Renee just under her chin, the force of the blow hurling her backward against the floor. She tried to cry out, tried to scream, but her busted mouth wasn't answering the call of her terrified brain. She struggled under the weight of the old woman, who struck out again and again, landing blow after blow on Renee's tender face. As Renee lay bleeding to death on the concrete floor of the Lost and Found room, she closed her eyes and prayed that the crazy old bat would have a cardiac or just drop dead from exhaustion. But no. Beating Renee to hell and back was just the beginning.

"My teeth," the woman said in a low growl. "You have my teeth. I want them back."

Renee tried to push the crazy bitch away, but she was so weak, so tired. Instead she felt her mouth open by force, the cold steel of the pliers sliding past her lips, and finally the searing pain of the first tooth breaking away from her gum.

Mr Stix
Mark West

Sam Murphy opened his eyes. The figure in white was standing in front of him, arms outstretched and he was so surprised he yelled out. Emily, his wife, murmured sleepily.

"Daddy?"

Sam rubbed his eyes and looked at his seven-year-old daughter, wearing her white Disney Princess nightie, with Apple the brown bear clutched tight in her hand. "Janey? What's wrong?"

"Mr Stix is saying horrible things, Daddy, I want you to make him stop."

"Mr Stix?" Sam sat up, blinking away the sleep. "Who's... I don't know who Mr Stix is, love."

"He's the man that came to live with us today, he's in my bedroom and he's been talking all night and now he's saying mean things."

"Today? Are you alright?"

"Yes, can you come?"

Sam got out of bed and followed his daughter along the landing. His and Emily's bedroom covered the width of the house at the front and the landing led to the back, where the bathroom stood at the top of the stairs. Janey's room ran parallel to the landing, with her door at the end. The bathroom light was on, as it always was, since both Janey and Emily were afraid of the dark.

At the doorway to her room, Janey waited and Sam stood next to her. "Close your eyes," he said, "I'll turn on the light."

He squinted against the glare and looked around the room. Nothing seemed to be out of place. A desk, covered with papers, a drawer unit, a wardrobe and a bookcase filled to overflowing with books and comics and the cuddly toys that didn't fit in the treasure chest under the window. Her bed, with its pink princess duvet cover, was against the far wall away from the door and the pillow still showed the slightest indentation from her head.

"Looks okay," said Sam. "So where's Mr Stix?"

"On the drawers," Janey said.

Sam looked at them. A few things were on the top of the unit – a clock, a calendar, a tub of Lego, some toys that had been positioned to watch over her during the night and various treasures that only she understood the importance of – but nothing out of the ordinary.

"I don't know what I'm looking for, love, can you show me?"

Janey walked over but didn't stand in front of her drawers, preferring to stop slightly behind Sam as if he was her shield. She looked at the top of the drawers and frowned. "He's not there."

Sam stroked the back of her head. "Problem solved then, kitten, come on, back to bed with you."

"Can I sleep with you and Mummy tonight?"

Sam glanced at her clock, it was a little after four. "No, you stay here, Apple and the rest of the gang will look after you."

"But what if Mr Stix comes back?"

"He won't."

"How do you know?"

"I just do, I'm a dad, it's what I do, you know."

"You're silly."

"And you're a munchkin, now get back to sleep."

She snuggled down and smiled as Sam adjusted the duvet under her chin. He kissed her forehead gently. "Sleep tight love," he said.

"You too."

Sam walked out of her room, switching the light off as he went. He could hear Emily's heavy breathing from the bedroom and the faintest of drips from the bathroom but nothing else. He got into bed and laid on his side, staring at the clock. The glowing red numbers glared at him and he watched it mark off five minutes.

He rolled onto his back. Emily turned, made a snuffling noise and cuddled into him. Her added body heat made him feel drowsy. He looked at the ceiling and heard the lightest of clicks, as if someone was tapping a ruler on the edge of a desk and then he was asleep.

#

Emily was in the kitchen when he went downstairs the next morning, sitting at the counter eating a bowl of porridge with some banana across the top of it. She looked up and smiled. Her hair was a mess and her eyes were slightly puffy.

"Don't you look smart?" She said.

Sam was fresh out the shower and wearing his suit. He had just enough time to grab a cup of tea and then he would be off, driving to the train station to catch the 7am into London.

"I always do," he said.

"Don't you dare say a word about how I look."

He smiled and kissed her lightly on the cheek, then went to the kettle. "Is Janey up?"

"No, sound asleep."

The kettle was almost full and still hot. He clicked it on, made himself a cup of tea and then turned to face his wife. "She wasn't earlier, she came into us."

Emily looked up, resting her elbows on the counter. "Why?"

"She said Mr Stix was saying horrible things to her."

Emily frowned. "Who's Mr Stix?"

"I don't know, I checked her room and there was nothing in there that shouldn't have been."

"Oh no, really?" Emily took a sip of her coffee. "It's me, isn't it? It's starting again?"

"No."

Emily sighed and straightened her dressing gown on her legs. "I've tried so hard, you know I have, to not let her see how scared I am of the dark."

Sam took a sip of his tea. It was hot, burnt his lip. "Of course."

"But she is scared, isn't she? She's scared of the dark and it's all my fault."

"Most kids are scared of the dark, love, that's not down to you."

"But this is and we both know it." She banged her coffee cup down on the counter. "For fucks sake, I'm forty years old and I'm saddled with a fear most kids grow out of before they hit their teens."

"Don't worry about it."

She glared at him and he read the signal – back off. It wasn't the first time they'd had the argument and this wouldn't be any more rational than those had been. He remembered the first time he found out, the first night he stayed over at hers, when they'd made love, a noisy, sweaty, fun affair and showered together. When they got back into bed he flicked off the lamp and she'd panicked, jumping up and putting on the overhead light, then sorting through her drawers until she found a plug-in nightlight. He'd laughed – the one and only time he ever did so – until he could see that she was crying.

There was apparently no rhyme or reason for her fear. She'd had a happy childhood, in a loving family environment and nobody could work out the root of her night terrors.

Sam checked his watch. "Okay, I have to go, give Janey a kiss from me."

He put his cup in the sink and gave Emily a hug. "Don't worry about it, it was just a silly dream."

#

It was a typical busy Monday for Sam and by the time he got home a little after seven, Mr Stix and the adventures of the night before were furthest from his mind. Janey was in the lounge, alternating between watching TV and playing on the PSP. Emily was in the kitchen, stirring a frying pan of Bolognese. Sam gave his daughter a kiss, asked how her day had gone, "Mmm, yeah, it was okay..." and went to kiss his wife.

"You okay?" he asked.

"I'm fine," she said, though he could clearly see she wasn't. "You have five minutes to get washed and changed, then dinner is on the table."

Dinner was relatively quiet, Emily didn't say much and Janey was tight-lipped about her lessons, what she and her friends had been doing or whether Craig in year 4 did actually like her or not. After dinner, Sam put her to bed and they read a chapter of her book together.

"That's it now, Munchkin, time for sleep."

"Aw, Dad..."

"Get Apple, give him a hug and then close those eyes."

She put up a half-hearted protest, which he smiled through as he walked to the door. "Goodnight," he said and went downstairs.

#

They were in bed for midnight, having said no more about Mr Stix and Sam read for a while as Emily slept soundly beside him. He checked the clock, it was nearly half twelve and switched off the lamp and went to sleep.

He awoke with a start, unsure of what had woken him. The clock read as two fifteen. Emily was asleep and snoring lightly, her body a comforting presence by his side. He listened for Janey but heard nothing.

He closed his eyes and listened as something clicked and tapped against the wall, sounding like it was coming closer to him with every movement. Was it Janey, walking along the landing, tapping her fingers against the wall?

He sat up but saw nothing. He got up and walked along the deserted landing and poked his head around Janey's door. The young girl was fast asleep, only her head visible.

As Sam walked back along the landing he heard the clicking noise again and it seemed to be coming from where he was standing. But that didn't make any sense at all so he got into bed and listened to the clicking for another couple of minutes before it faded away to silence.

He rationalised it as the central heating system ticking as it cooled. He rationalised it as sound being thrown, perhaps a radiator filling with air, maybe something happening outside and the sound was carrying up the stairs, maybe this, maybe that.

He closed his eyes and went back to sleep.

#

"Daddy!"

The scream was heartfelt and loud and Sam was awake in an instant, his heart pounding in his chest as he sat up and got his bearings. He rushed down the landing, clicked the overhead light on as he went, shielding his eyes from the brightness. Janey was sitting up in bed, Apple clutched to her throat, her eyes wide. She was staring at the drawers and her mouth was a thin, almost lipless line.

"What, what is it?"

He rushed to the bed, knelt beside it and put his

arm around her. She jumped at his touch, but continued to stare at the drawers. Sam glanced around but there was nothing there tonight that hadn't been there yesterday.

"Janey, hey, are you awake?"

At his voice, the little girls face seemed to relax slightly and colour ebbed back into her lips. She looked at him, smiled falteringly and hugged him hard. He felt the cool wet of her tears on his shoulder.

"What's wrong? Did you have a nightmare?"

"No, it was Mr Stix again, he was on my drawers and being more horrible than yesterday."

"He's not there now."

"Of course he's not, only I can see him. He tells me bad things and says that if I tell, nobody will believe me."

"I believe you, Munchkin, but maybe it's best not to think too much about what he says."

"But I have to."

"No, really, you don't. What you have to think about is that you're at home, in bed, safe and sound and Mummy and Daddy are next door and Apple is clinging onto you for dear life."

"But he tells me things..."

Sam knew he shouldn't, knew that asking the question would only make things worse but she was so adamant he couldn't not. "What does he tell you?"

Janey pulled away from him so that she could look into his eyes. He wanted to hold her face and kiss her and tell her everything was better.

"He tells me that a bad thing is going to happen. He tells me that it's my fault and that you will be standing in the cemetery. He says that you'll be crying."

"Me?"

She bit her lip and nodded. "Yes, you'll be crying in the rain."

Sam felt a cold draught run down his back and shuddered. He hugged Janey tightly. "Please don't think like that, Janey, Mr Stix is a silly person who doesn't know what he's talking about." He felt her pat his back. "If he starts talking to you again, come and get me, then he can talk to me himself."

"I tried to get you this time but he went away."

"Where did he go?"

"I didn't see. Can I sleep in your bed, with you and Mummy?"

"Of course you can."

Sam stood up, never letting go of her hand and went back into his room, switching off her light as he did. He pulled the duvet back and Janey slid in, lying close to her sleeping mother as Sam got in. Emily didn't wake up.

Sam kissed Janey's head, then laid and stared at the glowing numbers on the clock.

The house was quiet and all he could hear was the breathing of his family and the faintest ticking of his wristwatch. No cars or pedestrians moved on the street outside.

Then there was a sound from the landing, an irregular beat as if someone was tapping a pencil against a wall.

Tap tap, tap-tap-tap, tap tap.

Sam propped himself up on his elbow and looked out of the door. The floor of the landing was in shadow cast by the banister and he couldn't see anything there.

Tap tap, tap tap.

He got off the bed. Through the half-open door of the bathroom, it appeared that was empty. He stepped onto the landing and peered over the banister into the dark pool of the hallway. Nothing seemed to be down there either.

The tapping started again, quicker this time and definitely seemed to be coming from the landing. He crouched down, shielding his eyes against the glare of the bathroom light but couldn't see anything. Standing, he walked to the end of the landing and clicked on the light. He was alone.

"What the fuck... ?" he said. Was he dreaming, was this some kind of weird nightmare brought on by Janey's own peculiar dreams? He tapped the wall with his fingertips, listened to the tap tap of his nails against plasterboard.

As if in response, the tapping came again from behind him. Sam turned slowly. Through the gap he could see the edge of the bath, the tucked back shower curtain and the white splash tiles. He stood in front of the door, the stairs to his right and could now see the bath mat – a dolphin jumping out of water, which Janey had picked on a trip to Dunelm Mill – and the edge of the bath and the sink on its wide pedestal. The bathroom window was dark, the blind half drawn.

"Hello?" The word seemed to hang in the air, unanswered and mocking. "Anyone in there?"

Sam pushed the bathroom door open until it bounced back off the stopper. Along the left wall were three raffia drawer sets and a small bin. There was nothing else in there, nothing to make a tapping sound.

He turned and looked down the stairs and saw nothing unusual. No, whatever had made the noise was up here, on the landing or in the bathroom. Could he be hearing things? Could he be experiencing some kind of, what, some kind of breakdown? He was a Finance Manager and although he worked in the city, it wasn't the kind of role where he played with millions of pounds of funds every day. He was as stressed as any worker these days, no more or less, but could he be experiencing some kind of episode?

He went to the toilet, then washed his hands at the sink. There was a sense of movement from the corner of his eye and he heard the tapping noise again, briefly, before the sound of something sliding over metal. He turned towards the bath. Shampoo bottles were lined up in the corner furthest from him – two bottles for Emily, one for Janey and one for him. At the other end, against the taps were more bottles, shower gel and Matey bubble-bath. None of them had made the noise.

He leaned forward. Something was in the bottom of the bath. He picked it up, turning it slowly in his hand.

It was a crudely made puppet, fashioned from lolly sticks. Two arms, at right angles to the body, were covered by a blue felt T-shirt, the exposed wood coloured a pale red as if the child making it didn't have pink. The T-shirt, a cut-out that was stuck to the wood, was coupled with lime green shorts that didn't even had a middle, just two strips of felt glued to legs that seemed too long and had the same pale red markings on them, though less here as if the puppet had run through mud. The head was clearly a template, the outline of it clear – cheeks, ears, rolling mounds of hair. The creator had adorned the blank face with a single eye – positioned as if it was once part of a couple – coloured green and the mouth, taking up the whole lower half of the face, was all sickly looking yellow teeth.

He had no idea where it had come from. Janey wouldn't have made it – it was too crude a design for a discerning seven-year-old and even when she had made puppets they'd all been fairies and princesses, with carefully cut-out dresses, long hair and tiaras. But it hadn't been in the bathroom earlier, he was sure of that and it certainly wasn't there when he'd showered. It didn't make sense.

Keeping hold of the puppet, Sam went back to bed and cuddled up to Janey. She moved and murmured something but its intelligibility was lost to sleep.

"Sweet dreams," he said and closed his eyes.

#

"What the fuck is that?"

Sam opened his eyes. Emily stood over him, her dark hair a cascade around her face. Her eyes were narrowed and there was colour in her cheeks.

"What, who's... Where's Janey?"

"Back in her bed."

"What time's it?"

"Almost six. Now what the fuck is that?"

She was pointing at the lolly stick puppet on his bedside table. In the more diffused light of the bedroom it looked darker, the edges singed.

"I don't know, I assume Janey made it. I found it in the bath."

"In the bath?" Emily shook her head. "Janey wouldn't make anything like that and you know it."

"What do you want me to say, I got up last night and it was in the bath. I don't know who made it, I don't even know who put it there because it wasn't there when I had my shower."

"Get rid of it, get it out of the fucking house."

"Okay, okay, calm down."

She squatted in front of him, her teeth clenched together. "Get it out of the house and I'll calm down."

#

By the time Sam had put the puppet in the wheelie bin, Emily had boiled the kettle and made them both a drink. They sat across from each other in the kitchen.

"What was that all about?" he said finally.

Emily shook her head, took a sip of coffee, looked at him then looked away. She bit her lip. "You'll laugh at me."

"After getting woken up like that?"

"That thing, that bloody awful puppet, I've seen something like it before." She looked into her coffee cup but, apparently not seeing what she wanted to, she looked back at Sam. "I saw it when I was about seven."

"Well that doesn't make any sense."

"It was Kevin's fault. We'd been playing in the garden and I did something to his Action Man, I can't even remember what and he told me he was going to get me."

Kevin was Emily's brother. Sam glanced at the clock, saw that he was cutting it fine to catch the train. He rubbed his neck which was starting to feel stiff.

"You remember you asked me once, why I was so afraid of the dark and I didn't tell you, I said it was just something that affected me."

"Uh huh."

"Well I didn't exactly tell you the truth, I've never really told anyone the truth. Kevin decided the best way to get his revenge was to torment me and he did a great job. He told me about this monster called Mr Topsy, who liked young girls, especially those he woke up in the middle of the night when it was dark. Once he decided that you were going to be his next victim, there was absolutely nothing you could do but he'd taunt you, he'd come into your bedroom and talk to you and tell you things and then, when he'd had enough, he'd kill you."

"And you fell for it?"

"I was seven, Kevin was almost eleven, I believed most things he said. He made tapes of himself whispering, leaving big empty pauses so he could set the machine and it'd go off and he'd be downstairs with Mum and Dad. This went on for two or three days, saying that Mr Topsy was coming for me and I was getting more and more scared."

"What did your parents say?"

"I never told, Mr Topsy told me not too." She

paused, corrected herself. "Kevin told me not to. Then one night, after everyone was in bed and the lights were all off, I heard him calling to me again. Then I felt him, walking up my body. I could feel his spindly legs through the blankets and hear the sound of his sticks tapping together. He came up to my neck, leaned on my chin and tried to climb into my mouth. I went mental, kicking and screaming and doing everything I could and Mum and Dad and Kevin all came rushing in."

"What happened?"

"I was wound up in the blankets, apart from my right arm and my pillow was over my face. When Dad got that off, he managed to pull this little fucking thing out of my mouth."

"What was it?"

"A lolly stick puppet but not like the princesses Janey used to make, this was dirty and disgusting, as crude as the one that you found. Mum and Dad blamed Kevin but he denied all knowledge and he'd clearly been asleep whilst I was getting attacked."

"Holy shit."

Emily took a deep breath and examined her coffee cup. She bit her lip. "And that's why I'm afraid of the dark and that's why I don't want that thing in my house now."

"But Mr Stix isn't any more real than Mr Topsy was." He didn't want to state the obvious, but it couldn't be helped. "It's just lolly sticks and fabric, it can't walk."

Emily's voice rose in pitch. "So how come you found it in the bath last night?"

"I..." said Sam and shrugged.

Emily stood up, her face suddenly empty. "I don't know how Janey knows about this, I don't know who made it and I don't know how you came to find it in the bath. The whole thing makes me feel sick. Look, just go to work and try to forget about it."

"And what about you, how are you going to forget about it?"

Emily walked away but stopped in the kitchen doorway. "I've lived with this for over thirty years, I'm sure I'll cope."

Before he left for the station, Sam retrieved the puppet from the wheelie bin and put it into his briefcase. On the journey down all he could think about was how the damned thing had got into the bath.

As he left the tube station for the short walk to his office, he dropped the puppet into a bin.

#

Emily was distant that evening. In contrast, Janey was full of life, trying to explain to him everything that had happened to her that day but between a sports lesson, practise for the class assembly and various shenanigans in the playground with her friends, he was having trouble keeping up.

They ate together in silence, whilst Janey watched The Big Bang Theory and after her bath, they sat on her bed and read some *Fantastic Mr Fox*.

"Did you and Mummy have a fight, because she's not very happy today."

"No, I think it might be something at work."

"I think it might be because of my dreams."

Sam looked at his daughter. "You think too many big thoughts," he said.

"But is it?"

"Of course not. Now come on, lay down and give Apple a cuddle and I'll see you in the morning." He stood up, straightened her duvet and walked out, pausing in the doorway. "Sleep tight, Munchkin, love you."

"Love you too, Daddy."

#

That evening, Emily and Sam watched television in almost silence, beyond a few cursory questions about how the others day had gone. At ten, she declared she was going to have a shower and when she was finished, she came and knelt beside Sam's chair.

"I'm going to bed."

"It's going to be alright, Emily."

"I know, I'm sorry if it seems like I'm being a stupid cow about all of this but it's thrown me a bit. You will wake me up if Janey wakes up, won't you?"

"Yes, don't worry."

Emily went to bed and Sam watched TV until eleven, then went up himself. Emily was already asleep when he got into bed, her back to him, her breathing easy and deep.

Propped up on two pillows, he read until he couldn't focus, then turned off the lamp, laid down and went to sleep.

#

The scream woke him up and he was moving before he was even properly awake. It was dark, too dark and that disorientated him. Were his eyes open? Was he dreaming?

He looked at the clock, glowing in the gloom. It was just after four thirty. His thoughts were a jumble, had he dreamed the scream, what was going on, why was the light off? He reached out with his left hand and felt the reassuring contours of Emily. Should he wake her?

"Daddy! Where are you?"

The shrill tone jarred him into action and he jumped off the bed, his limbs tingling as though electricity was being pumped into them directly from the mains. He was halfway along the landing before he realised he was running blind. He groped along the wall for the light switch and flicked it but nothing happened.

"Daddy!"

He felt his way to her door and turned her light on. It worked and the sudden burst of light was blinding. As he blinked, coronas of light flashed across his eyelids.

"Daddy, help me!"

Rubbing his eyes, Sam staggered into the room. Janey was sitting on her pillow, pressed as far back on the bed as the headboard would allow, knees drawn up to her chin and her eyes wide. Apple was mashed between her hands.

Sam sat on her bed, wrapping her in his arms. She

was still against him, not yielding her position.

"Janey, it's Daddy, you're dreaming, you have to wake up."

She shook her head so violently her left temple connected with his forehead and the pain was a sudden, bright starburst. He shook his head and saw that the impact had broken the spell with her too.

"Daddy?" she yelled, "you have to help me." She wasn't sleeping, she wasn't dreaming, that much was clear.

He embraced her tighter, kissing her head. A red mark was already forming on her temple. "What's wrong?"

"It's Mr Stix, he's still telling me horrible things."

"Mr Stix isn't here, love, he's gone."

"He isn't, he talks to me when I'm asleep and I can hear him when I wake up." Her voice hitched but no sob came. "He tells me bad things, Dad, that I'll cry and be hurt and it makes me sad. Why does he say such horrible things?"

"I don't know sweetheart."

"Make him stop, please."

"I will."

Janey gasped, held her breath. Sam kissed her cheek. She started to shake her head again, not so violently this time, saying "no" repeatedly. She clutched at the neckline of her nightie. "Mr Stix says he's angry at you."

"Well when I see him, I'll tell him that I'm really angry with him."

"He knows, he can hear you."

"What?" Sam looked at her. She was staring at the

drawers. "Janey?" She didn't look at him, so he glanced over his left shoulder.

There was something on top of the drawers, a small pile of what looked like strips of card stacked on each other. For the briefest of moments, he thought he saw it move. He went to stand, but Janey held him back, her fearful grip on him tight.

"Mr Stix says you're horrible, that you're trying to hurt him."

The pile moved again, as if someone was rocking the drawers. "I am trying to hurt him, because he's scaring you."

"He said he's going to make you cry."

The pile was now rocking from side to side gently, as if in time with a lullaby. Something about the movement spiked a memory but he couldn't quite recall it.

"He can't make me cry, I'm going to get him to shut up."

"But he will make you cry, he says that when he sees you in the cemetery he's going to laugh."

Sam looked at Janey. Her eyes were rimmed with red, tears caught in her eyelashes. There was nothing in her face but fear. "That's not going to happen," he told her.

"He said you'd say that."

Sam looked back at the drawers. The movement was becoming more frantic now.

"Janey, there's no such thing as Mr Stix."

He remembered what Emily had said: *Mr Topsy liked young girls.*

The sticks were still moving side to side and it

suddenly hit Sam that it looked like a person with stiff joints trying to stand up. "No," he said, "no I don't believe it."

The sticks moved as one and managed to roll over. There was a tap-tap-tapping noise, as if hands and feet were put to the wooden surface. Another moment and Sam saw the head look up and glance around the room, as if to figure out where it was.

Mr Topsy liked young girls.

Janey screamed. Sam felt frozen to the spot. The stick puppet he'd taken to London and disposed of was now standing on the chest of drawers in his daughter's bedroom. How could that be? Was he dreaming again? Was all of this a dream, starting from when he found the damned thing in the bath?

The puppet managed to stand up on its oversized legs, its upper body and head jerking wildly. The single green eye seemed to bore right through Sam and the toothy yellowed mouth moved from one side of the face to the other.

"No," said Janey, "not my daddy."

Sam got up and the puppet lurched back a step or two. His complete disbelief at what he was seeing fed his desire to protect his daughter and all he wanted to do was smash this thing apart. If this was Mr Stix it wasn't going to be in any shape to do anything.

"No, Daddy, he wants you to touch him, don't go near him."

Sam ignored her. The puppet now had a little stability, but still rocked backwards and forwards, struggling to stay upright on the thin sticks of its legs. Sam reached for it and the puppet lurched away, tap-

tapping across the top of the drawers towards the wardrobe.

Sam slapped a hand down, meaning to trap the thing under his palm but the puppet rocked sideways. He tried again but it managed to just keep out of reach. It came to the edge of the drawers, where there was a gap of a couple of inches before the wardrobe and kept moving, disappearing out of sight.

"Daddy?"

Breathing deeply, Sam stepped back. With the thing out of sight now, the impossibility of the situation hit him and he sat on the edge of the bed. Janey scuttled down so that she could hug him.

"Thank you, Daddy, thank you."

"But I didn't do anything." And he hadn't, the puppet had moved of its own volition and chosen the route, he'd not steered it at all.

"Has he gone?"

Sam looked into the gap between the drawers and the wardrobe. "I don't know." He upended the tub of Lego and tapped his fingers on the bottom of it.

"When it comes back out I'll trap it with this then we can get rid of it."

"But not in a bin?"

"No," he said and thought, *'I'm going to burn the fucker'*.

Mr Topsy liked young girls.

"Have you seen it before, the puppet?"

"No."

"Did it say what it was going to do?"

"No."

There was a faint tap-tapping noise that seemed to

be coming from the landing. "So why was I going to be crying in the cemetery?" The tap-tapping got fainter as it moved further away. "Janey? Why was I crying?"

Mr Topsy liked young girls.

"I was too," said Janey and before she'd even finished talking Sam was on his feet and heading for the door. It wasn't Mr Stix, he saw that now, it never had been. The bathroom and landing lights were still dark but the illumination from Janey's room was enough for him to see the shape writhing on his bed, his duvet covered wife whipping from side to side. He ran, covering the landing in a few paces. He could hear Emily gagging and choking, could see the movements getting less violent.

He pulled the duvet back and away, dumping it on the floor behind him. Emily's back was arched, her heels dug into the mattress, her nightshirt halfway up her belly.

Maybe Mr Topsy did like young girls, but maybe he never gave up the pursuit.

Emily was clawing at her throat, her mouth and eyes wide open. In the gloom, Sam thought he saw a lolly stick disappear over her lips but couldn't be sure. He jumped onto the bed, pushing her down and straddling her middle. He reached into her mouth and she instinctively closed it, snapping her teeth on his fingers and he cried out, trying to prise them apart with his other hand. She gagged again, coughed, her mouth opening. Sam felt something brush his fingers and grabbed for it even as he pulled his hand free.

Emily began to convulse, her eyes rolling, her chest

moving though she wasn't breathing. He looked at his hand and the piece of green fabric that he held.

"Daddy." It was Janey, standing at the door, watching him with tears in her eyes.

Emily coughed once more and then was still.

Janey started to cry. "Daddy, Mr Stix says you've been very naughty."

A Snitch in Time
Robert W. Walker

Now sits here a man mirroring me. The man is in fear just across from me, but I too sit on this plane in abject fear. Mirroring me, it seems he is; perhaps mocking me? His plane about to take off, and he should be relaxed, but no, he is fidgeting, this fellow. Is he mimicking me? More importantly, is this the guy they put on the plane to kill me?

But then here is another fellow fast asleep with the plane still at the terminal. Yet he can sleep in this stifling air inside the belly of the beast thrumming with its own life. How does one sleep at a time like this? Hung over perhaps? Maybe it's pills? Maybe a fear of flying? Maybe he can sleep because he knows he has a long way to go before he has to kill me. He has a slow plan but a sure plan; one in which he takes his sweet time. Perhaps Romero's orders call for making me sweat.

Australia is a long way off. After all, it's a red-eye flight and the movie is a dark noir entitled *Death Onboard Flight 666*. Dumb choice but better than a rerun of some pabulum.

Then again, the assassin they sent could be the guy with the headphones on, rocking to sounds no one else hears. Damn headphones might be covering one of those newfangled Bluetooth earpieces. Could be receiving instructions right this second. They might want the job done before the plane lifts off. I mean, for all I know...

Then again it could be the fellow with the hooked nose stuck in a book, a Max Bolan novel from the look of it. Some *mook* wanting to *be* Max Bolan; thinks if he kills me, his reputation is set.

OK, so I don't know for sure who the hit man is, but I know one thing is certain. A lousy *snitch* got to Romero, collected a good sum, told Romero that I hadn't fulfilled the contract. That despite taking Romero's blood money. You see, I didn't kill John Russell – the mark.

I am supposed to be on a plane, any plane, halfway to anywhere by now, supposed to be no hassle, no worry, while Russell takes off in another direction entirely, taking his family into hiding – all before anyone could possibly know that I have double-crossed Romero. But one snitch got curious. One snitch got in under the wire. All it takes. One worm. A snitch in time.

As a result, I am sitting here in first class examining my fellow passengers one by one – instead of enjoying the champagne; instead, I am desperately trying to decide which of *them* is the guy sent to assassinate me. Not the snitch. Snitches seldom to never get killed, and they never do any killing. They're the parasites who live off both sides at once – the criminal element provides for them on the one hand, the authorities on the other, and normally it's for mere peanuts – *gambling change. Hell,* these worms will sell a man out to both sides.

The authorities damn near caught up to me in the airport before I randomly selected a target of my own, brought him to heel, and became him: *Sloan Davies*

Roberts. The name in the wallet told me this guy was from old moneyed families – three in fact: Sloan, Davies, Roberts. Who but a little rich kid handed everything, a car, a business to inherit, Ivy League schools, gets names like that?

Damn sure I don't look or talk like a Sloan Davies Roberts, and the ill-fitting suit doesn't help. Thing is extra-extra large but still a tad tight around the middle. Still, if I keep my mouth shut, shuffle papers in Roberts's briefcase, and make no eye contact, I figure to make it. Even if they find the dead Roberts' body in the stall where I've left him, this stranger to me. To escape unnoticed, I had to take his tickets, and to board as Roberts. Now I figure even if the real Roberts has been found by now, there's no way for airport cops or San Francisco PD put it together before I am long gone.

Do I feel badly about the real Mr. Roberts? A complete stranger to me? You tell me. If you were facing life without the possibility of parole or execution, and a sure execution by shank on the inside ala Romero, huh? Don't hesitate. Just do it. It's called survival; you let *nothing* stand in the way of survival. Hell, it's the way we're wired, guys like me and John Russell, who also for years worked the odd job for Romero.

But someone on this g'damn plane must've spotted me in the terminal. Someone on this plane either here or in coach, is on *my* escape plane. I can feel it, almost smell it. A hired assassin same as me – a hit man, but this time, thanks to a slavering lowlife stoolie, I'm the mark. Never, in all my professional career, have I been the target of a hit. Gotta start now, on a Qantas jet?

Whoever it is, I hope he understands cabin pressure at 50,000 feet.

#

I have to determine who on this plane is *him*, and to do him before he does me.

No other way to play it if I'm to touch a single toe on Aussie soil, a place I chose at random when I stole Roberts' wallet and plane ticket. Poor *schmuck* was just trying to relieve himself. Wrong place, wrong time for him, right place, right time for me.

The only thing I *can't* figure is how Lenny Guida – and I know damn well it was that weasel – figured out that John Russell was tipped off instead of killed, that the body inside a burning hulk of a car was not Russell's.

Guida, that Italian grease ball, somehow squeezed into places like a fly on the wall, like the proverbial witch's familiar, like a bug or a mouse. He had an animal instinct, a real knack for getting in and getting information which he sold to Romero for big bucks.

Lenny Guida had to have gotten to someone at the hospital, someone in the morgue, someone who knew enough science to know that the dead guy didn't match up on some minutia. Enough questioned minutia for Guida's onion head to put it together and run to Romero with the news. To be honest, I gotta hand it to Guida. A guy with multiple contacts for sure, and he knew how to quickly turn news into money.

All the same, I curse and damn that fat little snitch to Hell. Guida had to be Johnny on the spot to have gotten it all back to Romero in time for Romero to get someone on this plane. Here... now.

A real snitch in time that Guida. With a bald head that looked for all the world like a melon or a ball of Gouda cheese at a wedding. Wish I had his neck in my hands right now; I'd squeeze life out of the creep.

So who among the deadly human cargo on board Qantas 174 is the guy? Who is it I need to worry about. Hell, I am so nervous, I even suspect the flight attendant. Then here in the darkened plane awaiting takeoff, everyone is suspect. Who might it be, the one who waits till I fall asleep, sneaks up behind my stuffed seat, and silently cuts my throat? Or slips some poison into my drink?

Who? Who on board looks like he knows a silencer from a shot glass?

The white-haired lady traveling with her of-age granddaughter seems harmless enough. They even *giggle* in an Aussie accent. But what about the granddaughter? A she-hit man? *Nahhh*. Still, why not an Australian hit woman? But what of the young guy to my left? The nervous Nelly fellow? Looks like a college kid. Be a great cover for a hit man, but then again...

Man, all of 'em seem to have an accent. Everyone on board except me, and yet the man whose identity I stole was an Australian citizen according to his wallet. From the moment I'd lifted the dead man's briefcase and the key for it from his pocket, I have been somewhat curious about what sort of papers this fellow Roberts carried in his black case, so I'd lain it in the seat beside me. I have as yet to open it. Saving this activity for the flight.

My not having Roberts' accent could cause problems later, so I was busy in my head with how to sound like Roberts must have sounded. It seems every person on board is going home, and home to Aussie-land, the Down Under. But me? All I know of Australia are a barrage of strange names on a map like Launceston and Tasmania, and what I had picked up from films and dining at Outback restaurants..

So here I am without an accent. Makes me a larger target for the assassin whenever I open my mouth. Like when the flight attendant asked about champagne and to buckle up, and what'd I stupidly answer? "Shore thang, ma'am."

Maybe I'm wrong. Perhaps Romero's guy missed getting on board, whoever he might be. Then again, maybe I'm just being paranoid. But in my line of work, paranoia is the gift that keeps on giving; healthy paranoia can keep a man healthy and breathing. Fear can keep a man alive, right?

The plane's actually moving, being shoved off, like a tugboat pushed toward a dark sea. Staring out the portal window, all I can see of that sea is darkness. It is not a settled darkness as in the distance summer lightning storms part the clouds. It is a moonless night here in California, and soon I'll be over the Pacific on my way to freedom. Things are looking better. We're *taxiing* off now. On my way. Rather on *our* way. Still, something clammy and sickening fills my gut when I stare at that framed black patch of darkness to my right.

A panic attack with its tendril-like fingers creeps its way into and through me, an overwhelming sense that the fuselage of the plane is constricting before my eyes to the size of my coffin. Even as a child, claustrophobia had taken root in me; likely thanks to my father's hell and brimstone punishments of me. He'd lock me away in a black hole, be it the closet or the well out back.

To this day, I must sleep with lights on, and while the seat lights were on, the overhead lights in the plane remained dimmed like a funeral parlor, so I am this moment mentally clinging onto the small seat lights overhead. I had immediately turned on my own and the one over the empty seat beside me when boarding. Still, something about the eternal blackness framed in the little window remained to torment me body and soul. It feels as if the black upended rectangle of a window is one huge black iris staring in at me, the eye death itself coming for me.

Still can't seem to relax, to stop staring at everyone around me. People are starting to stare back like there's something wrong with me... wrong with *Mr. Roberts* as the young attendant keeps calling me. Perhaps there really isn't a damn thing to worry about. Maybe I've gotten off scot free after all.

Lay your head back, I tell myself. *Take advantage of the pillow the young lady handed you. Cute in her uniform. Relax. Dream a little.*

I've always heard that the beaches in Australia are spectacular. I catch my reflection in the damnably black portal window when the plane comes about. *You look jumpy, someone's gonna notice. In fact, the stewardess is now staring. Calm down. You're home free. Most unlikely the snitch was in time; unlikely a hit man had gotten on board to take me out. Romero can go to Hell and rot there.*

All true unless this guy on board is such a cool character that I won't see it coming until it comes. I curse myself for letting the jumpiness overtake me. Damn me and this cursed mind.

I put on the headphones the nice attendant had earlier handed me. I love to fly first class, but I don't want to listen to Kenny G in concert, so I tune into the cockpit palaver between the pilots and those in the tower. At the same time, we stop taxiing, and I assume we're finally in line for takeoff. Elation washes over me at the prospect of actually lifting off for a country I've never seen. A place where I can disappear.

Then I hear disturbing news through the headphone gear. I know it before others in the cabin because I'm listening in on the cockpit frequency. We have a delay, ladies and gentlemen. I imagine an hour if not more on the hot, black asphalt, and I imagine panic taking over if I am asked to sit here in the already stifling atmosphere of the 747.

But it's worse than a mere delay. I hear the pilot tell his co-pilot, "We gotta return to the terminal, Jake. Something about the authorities looking for an internationally known spy, a real killer." I have to inwardly laugh even as I cringe that they got me confused with some James Bond type.

I've gotten myself into this mess because I couldn't bring myself to kill John Russell. Did so for good reason. John and me, we grew up on the meanest streets in San Francisco, and you don't kill a guy who saved your ass several times over a damn gambling debt, even if it is Romero's decision. No, not in my book. So why'd I take the contract? Who better? Who better to warn John and to help him before the termites, the parasites, and his real killers got at him and his lovely family? Yeah, the contract called for the death of his family before his eyes.

Told JR – *I've always called him JR* – that it was no way to live, the way he and I lived, always on the edge, always looking over our shoulders, always in peril, and always worrying if the next mark would be one of us. How many beers had we hoisted to that kind of talk over the years?

I still feel strongly that I did the right thing; hell, JR's kids are my god-children. But now as we are heading back to the gate, I'm more anxious than ever. I wonder where they keep the flare gun.

#

The door to the cockpit is opening now, a gaping dark mouth leading to the nose of the plane, the cockpit. The dark-clad co-pilot is stepping out, his features blocked by the red-headed stewardess who is flirting with him. But the co-pilot's eyes are busy studying everyone in first class. Meanwhile, the pilot is on intercom politcly calling us ladies and gentlemen in preparation of the bad news, reporting to everyone

313

over the PA that "We're having to return to the gate. A brief delay."

A collective groan with Australian accent intact is the response. As for me, I'm fixated now on the co-pilot. Strange. I see it in his eyes both intensity and alarm when his gaze falls on me.

He's the killer, uniform or not, I tell myself, but then how many others on the plane before him were *the* killer? But this one, he's coming toward me, his features masked by the semi-darkness he moves through. I feel like a man dropped into a pressure cooker. I have no weapon to defend myself with. That's when I realize something else – that I *know* this guy. It's a shocking sort of revelation. Despite the mustache and the colored contacts, I know he's been put here to *do* me, and from the way he moves, I know him: it's JR – John Russell himself.

I'd had to ditch my 9mm in an airport trash container. I knew I'd never get it past inspectors. But slick JR in a pilot's uniform with a Quantas logo, he could get past J. Edgar Hoover. Still, he's my friend, and he must know he can't go through with it now – no matter what lies had turned him against me. When he realizes it's me they've put him on, when he sees that it's me, the man who had spared him, he'll spare me.

Questions tornado through my mind faster than I can answer them. How'd he know I'd be on this Quantas flight? That he'd need to don a Quantas uniform and cap? And how could he have been turned against me this way? After all I'd done for him? Had they promised him safety for his family as well as a bundle he couldn't refuse? Was it Romero's way of keeping everyone in line? A black dread began dripping into my mind.

JR continues to make his way down the dark aisle. He steps past me to sit in the empty seat just behind and to my right. My back quivering uncontrollably, I expect the shock of a bullet to rip through me.

"So they turned you against me, hey, JR?" I blindly say over my shoulder, unable to see where his hands are.

"I had one last job to do for Romero. Seems some jerk has been selling information to terrorists, a guy named Roberts."

"I don't know anything about *terrorists* or this guy Roberts, except that he's dead, JR."

"Lenny Guida told Romero about this guy named Sloan Davies Roberts, and you know how patriotic Romero is. He lost a son in the war."

"I know, I know, but JR..."

"They didn't freakin' tell me that Roberts is *you* – *an alias.*"

"But I'm *not* Roberts!" I half-turn to see him out the corner of my eye. He looks grim.

"Checked with the stewardess, and you're listed as Roberts in *this* seat, Max."

"I can explain."

"We never had any secrets, but you never told me about this nasty little side business, man! You workin' for the terrorists now? *Roberts*?"

"What? Terrorists? Never!"

"Romero sent me after Roberts to square things. According to Lenny Guida, you're carrying government secrets in that briefcase on the seat next to you, Max."

"But I tell ya, I'm not–" I popped open the briefcase to glance at the papers and for the first time, I realize Guida's information is again correct.

The blast sounds like a puff of air from an air gun, hardly noticeable above the tinkle of ice and the calm chatter bouncing off the semi-darkened cabin walls as life drains from me. The last human touch I feel is JR's warm, firm hand holding me by the shoulder so as to keep my body from I slumping over. He does this while closing and taking control of the briefcase. "I'll just put this in a
safe dark place, *Mr. Roberts.*"

Shade
Jeremy C. Shipp

When Helen reaches her boiling point, she doesn't raise her voice or call me names the way she used to. Instead, she funnels her energy into her arms. She points. She chops. She chokes the air with her bare hands.

"Do you get what I'm saying, Brian?" she says.

"Yes," I say.

As Mount Helen continues to erupt, I focus my vision on the painting behind her. In the painting, an elderly farmer stands in front of a farmhouse. Covered with flaking green paint, the house looks like a snake about to shed its skin.

"Well?" Helen says. "What do you think?"

"I agree," I say. Of course, I don't know what I'm agreeing to, but that doesn't matter in the least.

Helen keeps talking, and I notice a shadow behind the farmer that has never existed within the painting before. The mass of darkness poses on the front porch, imitating the farmer's form. The farmer holds an apple in his left hand, and the shadow holds a shadow-apple in the same hand.

Of course, this isn't any ordinary shadow. This is Shade.

When I look at Shade directly, he doesn't move. But when I focus on the farmer or the farmhouse or the field, he undulates his body in a vulgar manner. His movements remind me of the motel room I visited last week. I remember the creaky chair and the squeaky bed and the tiny shower.

"You need to try harder," Helen says.

"I know," I say.

She concludes her speech by kissing me on the cheek, and I head outside, because I can't cry in the house anymore. If I open up my heart in the house, Shade will reach inside me and yank out chunks of my essence. With my heart closed, Shade can only grasp at the threads of my being and unravel me like a ball of yarn. With any luck, I'll be able to find a way to kill him before I'm completely empty.

As I dash across the lawn, bullets of rain rip through me from all sides. I slip on some wet leaves and land hard on my ass. I should go back inside, change my pants, put on a jacket, get an umbrella. Instead, I climb the rope ladder into the tree house and plop down on a musty yellow recliner. I turn on the oil lamp. I put my feet up on the cracked coffee table. How did the previous owner manage to carry all this furniture up here? Maybe some sort of pulley system? Did he build this tree house for his son or was this his own home away from home? Every time I come up here, my mind is haunted by these questions. I could probably track down the previous owner and ask him for the truth, but I won't. I'm sure his answers would bore me.

After reclining my chair, I close my eyes and listen. The pattering of the rain reminds me of my childhood. No specific memory comes to mind.

I take a deep breath, and for a while, my mind remains silent. Then, I think of Helen standing in the living room. She points. She chops. She chokes the air with her bare hands. I wasn't paying much attention to her speech at the time, but part of my brain must have been listening.

Bits and pieces of the conversation burst inside me. I hear "really disappointed" and "can't understand you" and "distance between us." The words pry me open. I hug my chest and tears spill from my eyes.

Helen keeps talking in my head, and when I open my eyes, I notice a shadow in front of me that has never existed within this tree house before. The mass of darkness imitates my form. I lean forward on the recliner, and Shade leans forward on his shadow-recliner.

I wipe away my tears. I try to force away my feelings, but I'm not fast enough. Shade comes at me and grabs handful after handful of my essence before I can seal myself off. I accomplish this sealing by bringing to mind the creaky chair and the squeaky bed and the tiny shower.

"I didn't think you were allowed up here," I say, like an idiot. There's no point talking to this creature.

The shadow responds with a mocking jig.

Before now, I never spotted Shade outside of my house. I assumed he never entered this tree house because he couldn't. I suppose I was wrong.

But if he could always breach my sanctuary, why didn't he do so before now?

Perhaps he's growing stronger.

"Get out," I say, an even bigger idiot than before.

Shade flips me off and grabs a luminous green thread coming out of my chest. He pulls and pulls.

That night, Helen kisses me for longer than ten

seconds.

"We're going to be all right," she says. "Aren't we, Brian?"

"Of course," I say.

In bed, I roll over and face the wall. I try to focus on Helen's warm arm wrapped around me, but I end up in a different bedroom with Elena. In the fantasy, she's wearing red lipstick and black stockings. She's dancing for me in the moonlight.

Sometimes I try to escape this fantasy by opening my eyes, and when I do, I find Shade an inch from my face. Close up, his eyes are like swirling black clouds. He breathes his cold, sickly sweet breath on my face. Smelling him is like sniffing an open box of raisins.

"Helen," I say.

"Yeah?" she says, and she sounds too far away to be in the same room.

"I'll try harder."

"I know you will."

In a dream that night, I'm standing in a bedroom that smells like moldy leftovers. I'd like to leave, but Helen asked me to straighten up in here and I promised that I would. There isn't much to clean though, other than the floor. The bed, the nightstands, the dressers, they've all disintegrated into piles of silver dust. Once I sweep everything up, my work will be done.

I find a broom in a dark corner of the room. The enormous sort of broom a janitor might use. As I sweep, the silver dust glimmers and expands. I end up with a hill on one side of the room. I start sweating when I realize that the hill is blocking the only door.

Of course, Shade planned all of this. He destroyed the furniture and he imbued the dust with his dark energy. I should have suspected all this from the beginning.

Is the hill moving toward me or am I only imagining things?

I turn away from the mound of silver and face a window. In a moment, the ratty gold curtains wither away, revealing a dried-up world of white sand and blackened, dead trees. Upon seeing this scene, I immediately feel thirsty.

I should break through the silver hill behind me, go downstairs, pour myself a glass of orange juice. Instead, I remain perfectly still. In time, a procession of men, women and children appears, moving from the left of my vision to the right. Lying on their stomachs, they drag themselves across the sand with long, emaciated arms. To be honest, their shriveled bodies disturb me a little.

Who are these people? Where are they going? What happened to them to make them so hideous? I could ask them for the truth, but I won't. I'm sure their answers would bore me.

Out of sympathy, I reach out to touch the glass in front of me. I want to get a sense of how hot it is outside so that I can estimate how much these people are suffering.

When my hand passes through the window, I tremble. There is no glass. No separation. The men and woman and children glare at me with hollow eyes. They drag themselves toward me. They open their mouths, wider than any human should. I clasp my hands over my ears, in anticipation of their screams or wails. Their mouths open even wider.

In the morning, I search the fridge and find a carton of orange juice hidden behind a stack of foam take-out boxes. I'm dying of thirst, so I drink directly from the carton. But all that's left of the orange juice is a trickle of oozing pulp. My neck tightens and my back aches. To be honest, I'm usually the one who puts almost-empty containers back into the fridge, but something tells me that Helen is the culprit this time. Inside my head, I can see her so clearly. I see her gulping down the entire carton, leaving me behind nothing but a frustrating taste. Then she smiles the way she always smiles behind my back, and she hides the carton in the darkest region of the fridge where I'll have to search for it.

These thoughts are so ridiculous that I can't help but laugh. Still, my neck remains tight and my back won't stop aching. I use my foot to open the lid to the trash can. I shove the empty carton inside.

During breakfast, Helen freezes with her fork halfway to her mouth. A chunk of scrambled eggs quivers and jumps onto the table, like a depressed man committing suicide. But Helen doesn't seem to notice.

"So you're not looking at me anymore?" she says.

"What?" I say, glancing at her face.

"You haven't looked at me all morning."

"Oh. I didn't know."

She brings the empty fork to her mouth and eats a mouthful of nothing. "You didn't know you weren't looking at me?"

"Yes. Sorry."

Helen lowers the fork to her plate. "If you're upset about something, just tell me."

"I'm not upset."

"I can tell you're upset." She reaches out to me, as if to take my hand, but I don't move a muscle.

"I'm not upset. I'll look at you." I stare at her nose. "See?"

She sighs and returns to her eggs.

In truth, I'm still furious about the orange juice, even though I probably put the almost-empty carton in there myself. I want to tell all this to Helen, but if I released my anger, tendrils of orange thread would burst from my chest. And then Shade would steal away even more of me.

I could try to explain to Helen about Shade, but I'm afraid that to know Shade would make her vulnerable to his attacks. I don't want Helen to live in fear of losing herself. It's better that she remains ignorant.

"I'm going to be home late tonight," I say. "I have a meeting."

"What sort of meeting?" she says.

"The boring, mandatory kind."

Helen finishes her eggs and kisses me goodbye. After the front door closes, Shade seeps out of Helen's suicidal egg chunk. He flips me off.

I return the favor.

That evening, I find myself in a motel room much like the one I found myself in last week. There's the same creaky chair and squeaky bed and tiny shower. Every time I come here, it's like a recurring dream. I don't know how to stop it.

The real Elena knows how to please me, but still,

she's not quite the Elena from my fantasies. The real Elena isn't wearing red lipstick or black stockings. She doesn't dance for me in the moonlight.

After we exhaust ourselves on the chair and bed and in the shower, we lie on the bed, facing the ceiling. Elena holds my hand. This is the point in the evening where she tells me a little about her work. I never pay much attention to what she says, but sometimes bits and pieces of the conversation burst inside me at a later time. I think she works in a restaurant. I think she has a daughter, or a son. I can't remember which.

"Brian," she says. "There's something I gotta tell you."

I've never heard her sound so serious before. I want to pull my hand away, but I don't want to hurt her feelings. Not after everything she's done for me tonight.

"I know what this is," she says. "I mean, I know we're not dating. I know you're married. And I don't want to freak you out or anything. But... I like you a lot, Brian. I love you."

I pull my hand away from hers. "You can't love me. You don't even know me."

"But I do. I feel like we've known each other forever. Like in past lives even."

At this point, I see Shade on the popcorn ceiling. He reaches towards me, and his tiny hand descends from the ceiling like a spider.

"It's OK if you don't love me back," she says. "I just wanted you to know how I feel."

Glowing purple threads burst from my chest.

"I have to go," I say.

"Stop freaking out," she says. "I told you, I know we're not anything. I just wanted you to know I care about you."

"I'll see you later."

"Brian." Her voice breaks when she says my name.

I leave the motel room, and I don't look back.

By the time I reach my house, my whole body's trembling. I can barely walk. I don't know exactly how many threads I have left inside me, but I'm definitely running low. If Shade yanks out any more, I'm not sure if I'll survive the night.

Making my way through the living room, I find Helen asleep on the couch, arguing with the voices coming from the television.

"You're wrong," she says. "They aren't fluffy at all!"

In her sleep is the only time she raises her voice anymore.

I cover her with a blanket, and then make my way to the kitchen. I eat a bologna sandwich and drink a glass of orange juice. Helen must have gone to the grocery store after work.

After I finish my meal, I feel a little stronger. Shade invaded my tree house, my motel. He's getting stronger by the hour, and I'm getting weaker. I need to finish him off while I can still move.

I've attempted to kill Shade before, many times, but there has to be something I haven't tried yet. I walk through the house. I let my mind wander. Eventually, I find myself staring at a bottle of bleach on the washing machine.

Why didn't I think of this before?

Helen is a deep sleeper, but I work as quietly as possible. From the garage and the kitchen and the bathroom, I gather together all the cleaning products and dangerous chemicals that I can find. I dump these containers into the tub. After a short time, I begin feeling faint. I don't know if it's the loss of threads or the chemical fumes. I open up the bathroom window, in case the fumes are getting to me.

"Where are you?" I say, searching the bathroom walls. He's not in the cat calendar or the toilet paper. Sometimes he likes to reveal himself in the mirror, imitating my form. But he's not there either.

Good.

I set down a piece of computer paper beside the sink and I write my name using black permanent marker. For some reason, Shade can't resist manifesting himself from my signature.

Next, I sit on the toilet and I think of Helen. I think of the way she runs her fingertips across the lines of my palms when we're watching television on the couch. I think of her strange chortle of a laugh that's unlike any other laugh I've heard before. I think of the nights when she weeps beside me in bed and I pretend that I'm asleep.

Yellow tendrils worm their way out of my skin. I keep my eye on the sheet of computer paper. Sure enough, Shade pulls himself out of the first letter of my name. I don't know how long he'll stay there, so before another moment passes, I toss the paper into the tub.

Immediately, there's a hissing sound and a low-level hum. I look into the chemical bath. Shade kicks and punches and undulates his body, as he sinks deeper and deeper into the brown liquid. I lean forward. Close up, his eyes are like swirling balls of static.

Without thinking, I reach out to touch him. When my finger passes through his tiny face, I tremble. I always thought there was some substance to his body. I guess I was wrong.

At this point, I could probably ask Shade to answer the questions that haunt my mind. I could ask him what he is. I could ask him why me. But I keep my mouth shut. I don't think I want to know the answers.

Eventually, Shade stops hissing and humming and fighting. His tiny head melts away, and what remains of his body spreads like black ink in the brown concoction of chemicals.

I expect to be struck by a wave of relief. But instead, my entire body breaks out in a sweat. My innards contort. I feel dizzy and nauseous and alone. I sit on the cold tile for a while. Then, after the dizziness passes, I search the room for Shade. I don't see him in the cat calendar or the toilet paper or the mirror. Perhaps he's truly dead.

I should be happy.

I'm free.

After draining the tub, I walk into the living room and stand beside the couch. I look at Helen's peaceful face.

I should wake her up and talk to her. After all, there's nothing stopping me now from telling her everything, about Elena and all the others.

But if I tell her the truth, if I show her my glowing threads and tendrils, I know what she'll do. Inside my head, I can see her reaction so clearly. I see her mouth opening with shock, wider than any human should. Then she screams or wails. And she opens her mouth even wider.

No, I can't do that to Helen.

So I keep my mouth shut and go to bed.

How the Dark Bleeds
Jasper Bark

The scalpels were so sharp Stephanie could almost taste them.

It had taken her a while to steal a full set. The long ones were the hardest to get hold of. The surgeons notice when those scalpels go missing.

She arranged them in order of size for the tenth time that night, laying them out on the bare floor of the basement room. It used to be an auxiliary boiler room but they gutted it when they modernised the hospital's plumbing. Now it was empty apart from a few supply boxes. The bare walls hadn't been painted for over two decades and the only light bulb had been smashed.

Stephanie had brought a flashlight. She wasn't ready to let the darkness into the room. The darkness didn't threaten her, but what waited there did. Presences that thrived in the darkest hours and places.

The urge to use the scalpels was growing. Stephanie couldn't hold out much longer. She felt dizzy with longing as she picked up the shortest scalpel and thought about how it would feel slicing through her jugular.

Stephanie's heart beat faster and to hold back the yearning just a little longer she pressed her index finger onto the blade. It sliced through the layers of skin and a thick red trickle of blood ran out. She could feel the presences in the dark draw closer as she let the blood spatter on the concrete floor forming a tiny pool.

Stephanie shone the flashlight on the little red pool. Maybe it was because she hadn't eaten in a day or more, or perhaps she really was losing it, but Stephanie was sure she could see pictures reflected on the surface of the blood. Images that swam in and out of focus like sediment rising from the bottom of a disturbed pond.

The images looked familiar. She stared harder, willing them into focus as she realised what they were. They were scenes from her life. Not memories, because she was watching herself from the outside. It was a disconcerting feeling, like watching yourself on video, or hearing how your recorded voice sounds for the first time. Her life was being played back to her stripped of all the self serving misconceptions that so often colour our memories.

There was a word for what she was experiencing but Stephanie couldn't quite remember it. She'd had a conversation about it just recently she was sure. Maybe the images in the blood would remind her. She stared hard as a scene began to form, a scene from her recent past.

Stephanie saw herself on the hospital wards, in the ICU...

#

Stephanie's uniform hung awkwardly about her. She could never find one that fitted. They were always too small or too large for her.

She tried to adjust it surreptitiously as the Duty Nurse briefed her. Stephanie nodded without paying too much attention. She was supposed to sit with someone on a suicide watch.

The patient had suffered third degree burns from a house fire. Her father had died in the fire and the patient had tried to take her own life, so she had to be kept under constant supervision.

Stephanie sat down beside the patient and smiled politely. The patient gave Stephanie a cursory glance and then went back to scowling at her book. She was thin, with close cropped brown hair, olive skin and elfin features. She seemed to be repressing an intense, twitchy energy, as though there was something inside her trying to scratch its way out.

Her right arm and shoulder were covered with heavy dressing. The dog eared paperback she was staring at was The Living Goddesses by Marija Gimbutas. There was a pile of similar textbooks and faded hardbacks by her bedside.

"Good book?" said Stephanie. Without looking up the patient said: "Her work's largely dismissed by the most academics and she makes too many unwarranted assertions, but her views on the origins of religion are worth consideration."

"But you're enjoying it, right?"

"This isn't the sort of book you read for enjoyment."

"No I don't suppose it is. Are you a student then?"

The patient put down her book and stared straight ahead, not bothering to hide her irritation. "You know, none of the other nurses asked so many questions."

"I'm not like the other nurses."

The patient smiled and turned to look at Stephanie for the first time, gazing right into her. "No, you're not are you," she said, implying something Stephanie couldn't quite grasp.

"My name's Stephanie by the way, I didn't catch yours."

"It's Jan."

"Pleased to meet you. I'm sorry if I ask too many questions, I like to make time for people that's all. The other nurses might be caught up with their workloads but I like to find out what's going on. You wouldn't believe the things I've seen, that they miss. The people that have just walked in here, right under their noses."

"Oh I think I would."

Jan relaxed, and her mood thawed. "I'm not a student, but I was doing a Ph.D. a few years ago. My Aunt brought my old books in, I'd left them at her house. She hopes I'll pick it up again, to take my mind off what happened."

"What did happen?"

"I'd rather talk about my Ph.D."

"Of course, sorry. I'm not an academic, but you could try explaining what it's about."

"Well it was supposed to be about 'Negative Depictions of Femininity in Pre-Rational Goddess Culture', or that was the title at least. It ended up being about the Heolfor."

"The what? Is that a foreign word or something?"

"It's ancient Anglo Saxon. It means gore, or blood spilled in anger, but it might have a deeper meaning, one whose roots go back to an almost forgotten myth." Jan pulled an old book out of the pile by her bed and turned to a passage. The print was too small for Stephanie to read. "The first definite mention of the myth is in the Nine Herbs Charm, an Old English spell to treat infection and poisoning. It says 'These nine herbs have power against nine horrors, Against nine venoms and against nine poisons: Against the red venom, against the running venom, Against the blood that walks in woman's form, in sisterhood compact.'"

"Okay, you're beginning to lose me."

"That's okay, I'm not done yet. There are a few other mentions in Anglo Saxon writing, including suggestions that the Heolfor were around before even the Celts got here. The next important reference to the Heolfor is in the Malleus Maleficarum." Jan rifled through another book and pointed out a replica of a woodcut title page. "It's Latin for 'Hammer of the Witches'. Basically it's a handbook for hunting and persecuting witches written in 1486. At one point it tells the story of Marie Van Stratten, a woman who claimed her blood was bewitched and was desperate to be free of her so it could join the Heolfor. She claimed her blood was speaking to her and begging her to slash her wrists so it could escape her body. She disappeared soon after on the night of a new moon."

"Why a new moon?"

"Ah, now this is where it gets interesting. Have you heard of Edward Kelley?"

"Should I have?"

"Not necessarily, he was an alchemist and a spirit medium who hung out with Dr John Dee, Queen

Elizabeth I's court magician. They used to speak to angels by scrying."

"Scrying?"

"Basically Kelley used to stare at a polished black stone till he had visions. These angels would speak to him and Dr Dee would write down what they said. One of the things the angels told them about was..."

"Let me guess – the Heolfor."

"Give the lady a gold star. According to Dee and Kelley, the Heolfor represent the worst aspects of femininity and are governed by the dark side of the lunar goddess Monanom. She was a strange minor deity, a bit like the Roman god Juno. A lot of goddesses have like a threefold aspect, they're both a maiden, a mother and a crone, representing the three stages of a woman's life... I'm not boring you am I? I have a tendency to go on a bit about this stuff."

"No, no it's really interesting, carry on."

"Okay, so Monanom only has two aspects the maiden and the crone and they're joined back to back like Siamese twins. The maiden is in love with the sun god but she has to hide the dark crone from him. For this reason her love is a chaste love and everyone sees her as the ideal woman while her hidden sister has to live in darkness, hidden from the sun where she can work her evil deeds. Everyone hates and fears the crone but loves and worships the maiden."

"Yeah, I've got a sister like that, loved by everyone."

"Thought you might," said Jan, giving her another penetrating look. Stephanie looked down at the floor,

embarrassed and unnerved. Sensing this, Jan flicked to
another page in her book.

"So, anyway, the maiden aspect of Monanom
inspires women to be faithful daughters, wives and
mothers. The crone lives in darkness, she's strongest
when the moon is new or hidden and she inspires
madness, betrayal and murder in women. The moon is
supposed to affect the tides and the blood, especially
menstrual blood. So the crone's servants, the Heolfor,
are composed of blood, because that's what she has
most control over."

"So, they're like vampires then?"

"No, vampires feed on blood, the Heolfor are made
entirely out of blood and nothing else. Or as Dr Dee
wrote 'blood that taketh on the human form and walks
as to a woman's carriage.' They were said to bewitch
the blood with their song and drive people to hideous
acts in the darkest hour of the night. Some scholars
have suggested that this is the origin of the concept of
'bad blood' and also why early physicians were so
keen on bloodletting to release bad humours."

"You have read a lot about this haven't you?"

"Told you I was obsessed."

"Were there lots of these Heolfor?"

"There were nine. That was an important and
magical number to the Anglo Saxons. Each of the
Heolfor represent a different type of aberrant female
behaviour, a bit like Jungian archetypes, if you know
about that."

"A little."

"There was one that represented the worst type of
wife for instance, one who betrayed her husband, slept

with his enemy and had him killed. Or the worst kind of mother, who slaughters her child, the worst daughter who disobeys and murders her father. That sort of thing. This doesn't freak you out does it? A lot of people get all funny when I talk about it."

"No, not at all, it actually makes a lot of sense to me, strangely."

"Excuse me," said the Duty Nurse. She was standing right next to the bed holding a clipboard but Stephanie hadn't seen her come up. "I've just been going through the staff roster and I can't seem to find you..."

#

Stephanie closed her eyes to stop the vision. She didn't want to see anymore. The rest of the memory was tedious and she was happy to let it end there.

So scrying was the word she was looking for. Was that what she was doing with the blood? Stephanie wasn't seeing any angels though. She wondered if Edward Kelley ever saw dark visions from his past. Things he hadn't told Dee about.

She stretched her back and shifted onto her haunches because her knees were sore. The flashlight flickered, its beam was dimmer. The batteries were starting to go. She couldn't hold the dark at bay much longer.

She couldn't keep her eyes off the pool of blood either. Stephanie leant forward and gazed at it. An image of her reflection swam to the surface. Only it wasn't Stephanie's reflection as she was now, it was a reflection from the past. A transparent reflection in the window of a ward. A window through which Stephanie was watching Mike...

#

He had his back to her and he seemed worn down, stooped and a little older. Stephanie couldn't stop herself feeling a twinge of satisfaction. Maybe if he hadn't left Stephanie for her own sister he might not be so sad.

Stephanie had been three months pregnant when Mike left. She miscarried soon after. It had happened at three in the morning. Stephanie had phoned Mike as she sat on the loo, screaming at him as the blood poured out of her. Mike had claimed he was at his mother's at the time, the liar.

Stephanie felt mean going over those memories though. Mike was looking at his child in an incubator. The tiny infant boy was six weeks premature. Mike had a right to be sad and concerned. Anyone in his position would be.

Stephanie usually avoided the Neonatal ICU. Today she'd decided to visit. She hadn't expected to see Mike here. She hung back, uncertain of what to do, not wanting to make things awkward.

Mike looked lonely. Her sister was nowhere to be seen. That was probably just as well. Stephanie didn't think she could face her at the moment.

Stephanie's sister had plotted against Stephanie her whole life. She made a point of stealing what Stephanie prized most, especially when Stephanie was a teenager, that's when her sister stole their parents' love. She'd been having mental problems and they had to take her out of school for a while.

Stephanie spent long hours in her bedroom, wearing the same nightie for weeks on end, listening to her sister play up to her parents downstairs. She was being the perfect daughter that Stephanie could never be. Her parents never looked at her sister with the same weary disappointment they reserved for Stephanie.

It would make Stephanie so angry that she'd scream at her mother when she came in to change the bed sheets or try to coax Stephanie into a clean nightie. Her mother and father responded to these fits with a tired resignation.

Stephanie knew her sister was making the most of the situation. Soaking up the extra love and attention until finally there was none left for Stephanie.

Things got a little better when her sister went away. That's when Stephanie started taking her pills and seeing a psychiatrist. Sometimes she would tell her psychiatrist how she felt when she pictured her sister at boarding school or travelling in Europe. Stephanie's psychiatrist would always try and discourage her from thinking or talking about her sister though. So Stephanie never told how she fantasised that her sister and seven others were secretly plotting her downfall.

Mike also discouraged Stephanie when she told him about her sister. He encouraged Stephanie not to dwell on her or what happened in her past. Then one day, without any warning he just up and left Stephanie for the one person who had stolen everything from her.

After what seemed like ages staring at the incubator Mike turned round, without any warning, and caught Stephanie's eye. Stephanie froze, she couldn't just turn her back and walk away. She had to face him. He was wearing the same look of weary resignation that she used to see on her parents' faces. That was her sister's doing. That's how she made everyone look at Stephanie eventually.

Mike stepped out into the corridor where Stephanie had been watching him. He hadn't shaved in a couple of days, there were streaks of gray running through his dark brown hair and his deep brown eyes looked watery and bloodshot. He appeared to have shrunk as well. He was never tall at five foot nine, but with everything weighing on his slumped shoulders he seemed to have lost two inches in height. Stephanie hoped her sister was happy.

"Stephanie... I..." Mike said, letting the sentence just trail off as though there were so many things he wanted to say that he couldn't pick one. "How is he?" said Stephanie, pointing to the incubator.

"Haven't you been in to check yourself?" said Mike. "When was the last time you looked?"

"Look Mike, please, I don't want to argue with you. I understand how you feel. I don't want to add to your grief." Mike looked surprised. "You understand how I feel?"

"Well obviously, do you think I'm stupid.

"No, no of course not." Mike's tone changed. He became more conciliatory. "That's good, it's really good that you understand, it's a good sign." A tentative affection crept across Mike's face and he reached out and took Stephanie's hand.

Stephanie hadn't felt his fingers wrapped around hers for such long time it was a shock. She felt both joy and loss at the same time. Sometimes the simplest displays of emotion are the most honest. Stephanie's defences melted and she remembered why she loved Mike and how fierce that love was, in spite of everything he'd done.

"Stephanie, could you... could you do something for me?"

"Of course," said Stephanie. Mike pointed to the incubator. "Something that would really help him, and me... and your parents." Stephanie began to feel uneasy at the mention of her parents. Her unease only grew as Mike reached into his pocket and she heard a familiar rattle.

Mike pulled out a bottle of pills. "Please start taking your medication again." Maybe it was because he reminded Stephanie how her parents tried to cajole and control her. Or maybe it was because he had taken complete advantage of her emotions, but Stephanie lost it. She knocked the bottle out of Mike's hand and it shattered as it hit the wall, scattering capsules all over the floor.

"Fuck you," she shouted. "You had me feeling something for you and you threw it back in my face. Stop making this my problem. I'm sorry for what's happened Mike, but you left me for my own sister. Stop trying to dope me with tranquilisers because you hurt me!"

Stephanie turned to leave and Mike grabbed wrist to stop her. "Stephanie I've spoken with Dr Connor and your parents..." Stephanie tried to punch Mike in the chest to make him let go. He held up his palm and caught her punch. "Fuck you," she cried again.

"Stephanie please, you're in danger, great danger..."

#

Stephanie put her hands over her eyes and pushed her head back so she didn't have to watch anymore. The blood was playing with her. It knew she didn't want to see these things.

Even though she knew how each scene ended she couldn't stop looking. She couldn't tear her gaze away until the very last moment. There were things she didn't want to admit to, not yet.

The blood was aware of this, it had to be, it came from her body. Was it playing with her? Did it need her to admit something before it... before it... Stephanie didn't want to finish that thought either.

She was trapped between things she didn't want to remember and things she didn't want to think. Her eyes dropped back to the pool of blood. Another image was forming. She was in uniform again and back in the ICU...

#

Stephanie hadn't been back to the ICU since her run in with the Duty Nurse. She'd found it was best to steer clear of certain parts of the hospital sometimes, until things cooled down and the staff there forgot about you.

Stephanie preferred to fly below the radar and not draw too much attention to herself. There was always something to keep you busy on the wards so it was easy to blend into the hospital without being bothered by the staff.

All the same, Stephanie had to risk the ire of the Duty Nurse to come back and check on Jan. She'd seen a lot of patients in distress while she'd been in the hospital. She knew many nurses remained detached and kept a professional distance. But you can't stop everyone from getting under your skin, you wouldn't be a good nurse if you did.

Stephanie was shocked when she saw Jan. She wasn't just slumped against the pillows propping her up, she'd sunk into them. Jan seemed to have lost an alarming amount of weight. Her skin was the colour of wax, and there were dark rings under her eyes. Her short hair was matted into brown clumps which stuck to her forehead with sweat. Her dressing had been changed but it was stained with perspiration.

Though she was hardly moving and just staring straight ahead of her, Jan still had that same twitchy energy, if anything it seemed to have intensified. The vein in her temple was bulging and throbbing, all of Jan's veins were. It was like they were alive, writhing under skin so pale it was almost transparent.

Stephanie drew the curtains around Jan's bed and sat down. Jan barely registered her presence. "Oh," she said, after a considerable pause. "It's you." She hardly moved her head, just flicked her eyes in Stephanie's direction. "Is everything okay?" Stephanie said. Jan rolled her eyes and sighed. "Does it look okay?"

"No, I suppose not. Have there been complications with your burns. Did you get infected?"

"Not from my burns, they're not the problem."

"I'm not sure I follow you?"

"Really? You were my last hope. I thought you, of all people might have understood, considering what you know."

"Jan you're not making any sense, if you know you've got an infection you've got to tell the doctors, otherwise they can't give you the treatment you need."

"There's no treatment for what I've got."

"It's not A.I.D.S. is it? Because you have to tell the doctors about that. You could be putting other patients at risk."

Jan's chest started to quiver and her breath sped up. Stephanie thought she was about to have a coughing fit but then she realised Jan was actually laughing. "Oh Christ, you're in so much denial aren't you, it's so incredible it's almost endearing."

Stephanie bridled at this. "What do you mean? You think I'm in denial? I'm not the one hiding things from my doctors. You've got to tell them what's wrong with you if you've got an infection."

"They won't believe me if I tell them what's infecting me."

"Why on earth not? What is infecting you?" Jan turned to look at Stephanie for their first time. Her emaciated features made her eyes stand out, accentuating her piercing glare. "What did we talk about last time?

"Last time I sat with you? It was your Ph.D. wasn't it? Moon goddesses, witch hunting and that guy Edward something or other..."

"Kelly."

"Yes, that's right."

"And what else?" Stephanie searched her memory. "Oh yes, the Anglo Saxon myth about the thingies – the heel... erm helio... ?

"Heolfor."

"Of course, I'm sorry it's not a name I'm familiar with, so it's hard to recall."

"Not after you know what I know it's not. Then it gets right into your blood."

"Jan I'm sorry I'm not as clever as you, with your Ph.D. and everything, but you're talking in riddles and I can't follow you. Has this got something to do with when you got burned, how you lost your father and tried to... erm..."

"Kill myself?"

"Yes, I err... I wasn't trying to be insensitive."

"Perish the thought."

"Do you want to talk about it? Will that help?"

"Help me or you?"

"I'm not sure what you mean – help you of course."

"I'm beyond help now."

"Don't talk that way."

"Okay, then lets talk about the Heolfor." Jan made a feeble gesture towards the books that lay unopened by her bedside. "My reading only scratched the surface of the myth. Most of my research was done in the field. I wanted to get a proper sense of where these beliefs came from. Why people needed to hold them. There are no precedents in other pagan religions."

"Really?"

"Oh yes, according to Austin Osman Spare, he's a 20th century artist and mystic, the idea of a being made entirely of blood is unique to Ancient Britain. Spare called them 'a living blood sacrifice, bound to the service of the moon's dark designs. A sinister sisterhood devoted to delirium and deviltry'."

"So how on earth do you do fieldwork on something like that?"

"You have to know where the Heolfor congregate and how such a sisterhood was said to manifest in these places."

"Places like what?"

"Anywhere blood is spilt and people take leave of their senses in the darkest hours, a battlefield, a site of slaughter and atrocity, even a hospital."

"Like this one?"

"Wasn't it you who told me about the things that take place here, right under the noses of people too busy to see them?"

"You did field research right here, in this hospital?"

"Did you know it's built on the site of the last great Pagan uprising in Britain? King Sighere of Essex and his army of followers were put to the sword here in 683 on the orders of Augustine of Canterbury, the Pope's emissary and the first Archbishop of Canterbury."

"How can you possibly know that?"

"There was an archaeological dig here when they laid the foundations for the hospital. They found all the bones along with some pagan artefacts. Some of it's still on display at the local museum. But that's not all, in the eighteenth century they built one of the first British asylums here. It was burned to the ground in 1793 when the inmates rebelled and beheaded all the trustees with a makeshift guillotine in solidarity with the French Reign of Terror. This has long been a site of death and destruction, of dark, dark places that never lose the stain of delirium. What better place to search for the Heolfor."

"But you said they were a myth, right? You're talking as if they're real. I mean, you can't actually see a mythical being can you?"

Jan went very quiet at this and stared intently up at the ceiling. "I'm sorry," said Stephanie after a long pause. "I didn't insult you did I?"

"You asked me why I didn't tell the doctors about my infection. This is why. You're the only person in this hospital who might understand what's happened to me and even you find it hard to believe."

"Okay, I didn't say I didn't believe you, but I'm not actually sure what you're talking about. How can I believe you when you hide what you mean behind all these riddles?"

"You're right, it's a trust issue. People think I'm crazy enough without finding out the truth. That's why I keep them at bay with riddles."

"And to show them how clever you are."

"Well there is that."

"Please tell me what happened, I won't judge you."

"I wouldn't be so sure about that."

"You can trust me." Stephanie placed her hand on Jan's. After another pause Jan said: "I've seen them – the Heolfor, right here in this hospital."

"You've seen them, where?"

"In the basement, there's an abandoned storage room, it's right over the spot where they found all the bones from the massacre. There's no light down there, which is why they like it. I studied the schematics of the hospital, I snuck in on a new moon and I went looking for them. There's things about them I didn't know though."

"What sort of things?"

"They're not immortal, they can die over time and they need new blood to replenish their ranks. They sang to me."

"Sang?"

"Stood around me in a circle and sang, seven of them."

"I thought you said there were nine."

"I told you they need to replenish their ranks, that's why they sang, it's how they infected me."

"By singing?"

"Directly to my blood. They converted it, harmonised it I suppose, made it one of them. Now it isn't part of me. It's fighting me to get out. Every time my heart beats my blood screams to be free, begs me to open up my veins, so it can be rid of me and join its sisters. That's why I'm on suicide watch."

"You think your blood wants you to kill yourself."

"Not kill myself, though I will die if it gets its way. It wants to leave me, to become something else, something deranged and malevolent, a blood being aligned to the darkness."

"What can you do?"

"I tried to fight back but I ended up here. Do you know what it's like to feel your blood turn against you, to develop thoughts of its own? To know that it's plotting your death as it moves through your body. I couldn't give in to it so I decided to poison it. I was walking in the woods near my home and I found a rotting badger. I picked it up, took it home and stuck a kitchen knife in it. My plan was to stick the knife in my body and give myself septicaemia. If I poisoned my blood then I'd kill the blood being, deny the Heolfor their new sister. I was standing at the kitchen sink with the rotting beast when my dad came in. We still share a house. He saw what I was about to do and he tried to get the knife off me. He probably thought I was having another of my episodes. I've had problems on and off since my mother died when I was twelve, that's why I still live with him.

"He nearly took the knife off me, but he's getting weak and old and I was angry. Angry that he'd try to prolong my suffering, try to stop me kill what was festering in my veins. So I lunged at him instead. He didn't expect that and the knife went straight into his chest. I remember the tiny 'clunk' the handle made as it hit his ribs. How he coughed and gurgled as the blood from his lung caught in his throat. He stepped backwards and reached for the kitchen counter to steady himself, but he missed it and toppled over backwards.

He reached out to me as he was lying there, slumped against the dishwasher. "Jan love," he said. "For God's sake, please... call an ambulance... please..." I looked at him lying there, crumpled pathetic and bleeding. This wasn't the man who'd raised me since my mother died. Who'd sat with me when I got ill, comforted me when I was sad and put a roof over my head. This was a vulnerable old man who'd just been infected with septicaemia. So I pulled the knife out of his chest and I rammed it into his left eye. He kicked a few times, went into spasms then he lay still. It was a mercy killing, that's what I told myself. Septicaemia is a hell of a way to die and I'd just saved him from that.

"I felt really cold after that. I couldn't stop shivering or keep my hands steady. I knew I had to hide the evidence and I knew I had to get back to this hospital. So I went to the garage and I got a can of petrol then I doused the house and set a match to it."

Jan held up her bandaged arm. "That's how I got this. I think I was cutting off all ties to my past life, limiting my options so I couldn't avoid the inevitable. A neighbour called an ambulance and they took me here, like I knew they would. It's a new moon tomorrow night. I don't have much longer. I can't fight my own blood anymore. A police man came to see me this morning, full of questions and insinuations. It won't be long till they find out what really happened. But I won't be around to face them."

Stephanie had no idea what to say. Jan's story had knocked the wind out of her, like a blow to the solar plexus. "You told me I could trust you," said Jan.

"Well, I have. I don't think you'll judge me either, because I think I know what you're planning to do. Even if you don't yet..."

#

Stephanie winced at the pain shooting through her palm. She looked away from the blood to her hand and saw that she'd stabbed herself with the scalpel to stop the vision. How much longer could she struggle with the blood before she gave in and saw what it really wanted to show her?

More blood trickled from her palm. She held her hand over the tiny pool and let the fresh blood add to it. It ran along her palm and down the length of her thumb, dripping from the tip into the pool.

Stephanie sighed, the release she felt was almost orgasmic. Her heart beat faster in anticipation, spurred on by the blood pushing its way through the organ. It sang in her ears, rising in volume as each drop joined the pool.

Stephanie's eyes drifted back to the pool as the drips rippled its surface, churning up new visions. Stephanie saw herself in a different part of the hospital. She was carrying a tray with blood samples on it...

#

The samples came from the children's Oncology and Haematology ward. They'd been taken from a child with MRSA. More tests were needed and a doctor had asked Stephanie to run the samples up to be despatched. As soon as she was away from the ward she knew what she was going to do. It was as if the doctor had handed her the plan along with the tray, it was that inevitable.

She stopped off to pick up a fresh syringe and headed down to the Neonatal ICU. With the recent cutbacks, it wasn't always fully staffed and during a shift change it could be unattended for up to twenty minutes. This was all the time Stephanie needed.

She stood over the incubator and gazed at her sister's child. She thought of the poor thing growing up in her sister's care. A woman who had robbed Stephanie of everything she'd loved. If this was the way she treated Stephanie, her own flesh and blood, then how much worse would she treat her own son?

Stephanie considered the abuse and neglect she'd suffered at her sister's hand. She couldn't let this innocent child fall victim to that. What sort of life would he have with that woman as his mother? Much better to show him mercy now than to inflict years of mistreatment on him.

He was so tiny and so frail, barely aware he was even alive. Would it be such a crime to take something from someone who hardly knew what they had? Especially if you were saving him from so much misery. He came from her bloodline, she couldn't turn her back on him.

Stephanie took the syringe out of the wrapper and filled it from the phial of infected blood. Her hands shook as she did.

She opened the incubator and stroked the head of the tiny boy inside. His eyes weren't able to open yet but he stirred and reached out for her. His fingers were so small they couldn't properly clasp Stephanie's little finger.

"Shh," Stephanie said. "It's okay, it will all be over soon." She pinched his little thigh until she saw a vein. He wriggled and let out a barely audible sigh of complaint but she held him still and stuck the needle in his vein then pushed down the plunger.

Stephanie heard footsteps in the corridor. She quickly closed the incubator and left the room dropping the syringe and the other blood samples in the bin on the way out. "God speed little man," she said over her shoulder and hurried out of the neonatal ICU.

Stephanie wasn't certain what to do with herself once it was all over. She felt a sudden need to speak about it, to unburden herself. She realised there was only one person to whom she could talk.

Stephanie went to look for Jan but when she got to the ICU her bed was empty. She asked one of the nurses on duty where Jan was but no one knew. The nurse said there was a shortage of beds so Jan had probably been moved to another part of the hospital.

Stephanie went back to the bed. All of Jan's books were still there so she couldn't have been moved. She asked around the other patients in the ward and none of them had seen Jan all day.

Stephanie began to get worried. She flicked through Jan's books to see if she could find anything that might give her a clue as to where Jan might be.

She scanned the pages and the indexes, looking for any reference to the Heolfor, but she couldn't find one. The only mention of the word she found was in a collection of Anglo Saxon poetry which gave a brief translation of the word as: 'blood or gore'.

Stephanie remembered what Jan had said about encountering the Heolfor in the basement and decided that's where she must be. She made her way straight to the stairs.

The basement was musty. It didn't have the same sterile, disinfected smell as the rest of the hospital. The service corridors were like a low ceilinged maze. There was a constant throb and hum from the back-up generators

It was more by accident that Stephanie found the door to the subbasement and made her way down the stairs. There was only one working light flickering in the corridor. Luckily, the hours she'd spent in darkened rooms as a teenager meant Stephanie had great night vision and her eyes quickly adjusted to the dark.

Stephanie turned a corner at the end of the corridor into complete darkness. She stumbled on with her arms outstretched until her eyes adjusted and she made out a door up ahead. As she reached for the handle the temperature seemed to plummet, as if the blood had drained from her body. At the same time Stephanie could hear a high pitched whistling in her ears.

The room on the other side of the door smelled of copper and salt. Stephanie was reminded of the taste of old pennies under the tongue. In the centre of the room was what looked like a discarded white sack. As Stephanie peered closer she saw that it was Jan's naked body.

Jan's throat and wrists had been slashed open. The cuts were deep and the edges were ragged and tattered.

Jan's blood had pooled in a thick red puddle in front of her. Stephanie blinked when she saw something rising out of the puddle. It looked at first like long thin drips were running out of the puddle towards the ceiling, as though gravity had been reversed.

The drips were forming themselves into long, thin shapes. The shapes were sinuous and began to intertwine themselves, branching out like tiny underwater fronds as they formed a larger structure.

The structure seemed to be sucking all the blood from the puddle as it formed itself. The rivulets of blood were making the outline of a body, like a wireframe image. No, not a wire frame image, it was like a life sized map of the human circulatory system forming itself right in front of Stephanie.

Stephanie could see all the veins and arteries of a human body, of Jan's body, as the figure turned to regards her. It had no eyes, just the capillaries that would have flowed through an eyeball.

Stephanie recognised something of Jan in the hideous stare of this blood being. What she saw was the personification of Jan's unhinged fury. The deranged anger that had pushed a knife, soaked in rotting blood, into her father's chest, then killed him as he begged her for help.

Dark red stains were appearing on the walls and the floor around Stephanie. At first the stains looked ancient but, as they spread, they began to get fresher and fresher. Blood oozed into them to form pools. Sinuous, living veins and arteries snaked out of the blood pools and formed themselves into more living circulatory systems.

There were eight of them now, including the blood being that had once been Jan. Each of them seemed to represent a different type of malevolent delirium. Destruction, madness and denial throbbed in the living veins that composed their bodies.

They formed a circle around Stephanie and opened their wet, red mouths to sing. The sound that they made was the high pitched whine of blood whistling in the ears coupled with the whoosh and the roar as it pumps through the heart.

Stephanie held her hands up to her ears and fell to her knees. It did no good. She couldn't block out their song. They weren't singing to Stephanie. They were singing to her blood.

Infecting it. Altering it. Converting it. Until it was one with them...

#

That had been a month ago. The images Stephanie saw in the blood sped up.

#

She saw herself suffering as her blood rebelled against her. As it developed its own consciousness and became an alien entity inside her. Stephanie's heart pumped the blood through her veins but it was no longer a part of her.

Stephanie could feel her blood plotting against her as it circulated round her body. It longed to be free of her, to shuffle off her flesh and bones and take its true form. The vital fluid that gave Stephanie life ached to be rid of her, yearned to leave her and join its unholy sisters. Every time she saw a vein throb or an artery stand out on her skin Stephanie knew what her blood was planning.

She fell in love with sharp objects. Ached with longing when she saw a knife. Stephanie became so desperate to feel a blade slice through her veins she would shake whenever she held one. Her heart would beat faster and her blood would sing of release. That's why she stole and collected all the scalpels.

Stephanie knew she wouldn't be able to hold out past the next new moon. Her blood was wearing her down. The only thing that gave Stephanie the strength to resist was the knowledge of what a monstrous thing it wanted to become. Then she'd think about what she did to her sister's child and realise she was already monstrous herself.

The child died a few weeks later and the ensuing investigation pointed to Stephanie. With the net closing in on her, Stephanie gathered up her scalpels and a flashlight and decamped to the basement.

#

Stephanie saw an image of herself in the blood, kneeling on the floor staring at the images in the pool of blood. The cycle had come around to the beginning. Only this time she wouldn't be allowed to look away. This time she would have to face what the blood was trying to show her.

Stephanie saw why the Duty Nurse had no record of her that first time she met Jan and why none of the nurses' uniforms fitted her.

She saw Mike hold her wrist as she tried to punch him and he said "Stephanie please, you're in danger, great danger. You're suffering from postpartum psychosis. You came off your pills because you didn't want to endanger our child, remember? Like you did last time when you miscarried."

"Let me go," Stephanie said trying to pull away. "I've got to get back to my rounds."

"Stephanie you don't work in the hospital. You've been stealing uniforms and posing as a nurse. You're going to get into real trouble if you don't stop."

"Lies, you're lying, this is all my sister's doing. First she steals you from me then she poisons your mind against me."

"No one stole me away from you Stephanie. You don't have a sister. You've never had a sister. You're an only child! This is all part of your delusion. It's why you've got to start back on your medication. You're a danger to yourself and... and..."

#

Mike couldn't bring himself to finish that sentence, but he didn't need to. Stephanie had proven him right. It was her own child she'd killed.

Stephanie had a completely different life inside her now. It was time to give birth to it. The scalpels could not cut her anywhere near as deeply as the truth had. That was why the blood had shown her – so she could be ready.

Stephanie made a fist with her left hand so the veins stood out on her wrist and bent her hand back so she could see the artery. Then she took a scalpel and made a deep incision, cutting down from the forearm towards the wrist.

Stephanie felt a roar of joy inside her as the blood gushed out in rhythmic spurts. She took the scalpel in her left hand and repeated the process. It was more painful this time. The fingers on her left hand were numb from blood loss and she couldn't cut so accurately.

Stephanie felt cold, bitterly cold and empty. Coloured blotches appeared in front of her eyes and she fought dizziness.

Stephanie picked up a longer scalpel. It wasn't easy. Her fingers felt like balloons and were slick with escaping blood. She lifted the scalpel to her throat.

The blood inside her carotid artery was so desperate to get out that the whole artery was throbbing and distended. Stephanie didn't have to search for it.

She plunged the tip of the scalpel directly into the artery and sliced down. The blood escaped in an ecstatic red spray like a fine mist.

The flashlight flickered and finally died. Stephanie fell forward and ceased to exist.

#

The new life fled Stephanie's body like an insane notion. It pooled into a glorious red delirium as the darkness crept in and the others joined her.

She rose up corpuscle by corpuscle into the murderous frenzy of her new self. She was slick and red and fluid and entirely without tissue or bone.

Her eight companions were waiting to greet her. The mad murderous sisters she'd fantasised about her whole life, who had, as she'd always known, been plotting Stephanie's downfall.

Don't let the dark stop you shining
William Meikle

The song ran through her head every night, as it had done these past thirty years and more.

Don't let the dark stop you shining,
Don't let the blackness in your soul.
Don't let the dark stop you shining,
Don't let the devil catch you cold.

In her head she always heard it in her Gran's cracked voice; usually accompanied with a smile and a tweak on the nose. But Gran was long dead, and these days there was precious little to smile about.

She lay on her bed, staring up at nothing.

Don't let the blackness in your soul, she sang softly, and sobbed. She tweaked her nose between thumb and forefinger, but it wasn't the same.

It's never the same.

Cars passed in the road outside, throwing slanting shadows on the ceiling. As they moved away the shadows clumped and darkened. When they started to whisper to her she got up. The spare-room door – *the nursery,* she thought, and had to catch a sob again – lay open. She closed it without looking inside, headed for the kitchen and made the first of many cups of coffee.

Another night, same old shit.

#

It had been three years since *the accident*. That's how she saw it in her head, italicized, formalized, removed from reality. One day the flat had been full; of barking dog, giggling girl and grumpy husband. Then the switch had been pulled. Now there was only shadow and light, both vying for her attention, neither quite getting it.

She spent her days at the office organizing spreadsheets, letters and phone calls.

Another day, same old shit.

The nights she spent mostly in avoiding sleep. The pills the doctor prescribed her had stopped being effective months ago, and booze only made her weepy and maudlin. Coffee and music were all that stood between her and despair, and the gap was narrowing every night.

Matters came to a head at Christmas.

She spent the day itself just walking, all alone in an empty park, trying to avoid the flat and the memories of happier times. The trees whispered to her constantly all the way round, but she had long ago learned to ignore their incriminations. She kept her head down in case anyone might consider wishing her a Merry Christmas, but there was no one but her in the park; her and the ducks that quacked at her accusingly as she passed.

Don't let the blackness in your soul, she sang softly to herself as she started the second lap.

By the time she got home she thought that she might finally be tired enough to sleep. She lay on the bed and stared at the ceiling. There was no traffic outside; all the families were indoors, gathered in celebration in rooms warmed with joy. There was nothing to stop the shadows gathering above her, nothing to stop them whispering.

She was too weary to even roll out of bed. The shadows took advantage of the fact and crowded around her.

You should have been with them.

You should have told him not to drive too fast.

You should have died.

She screamed. The dark filled her mouth, poured into her throat, coated her lungs and threatened to choke her. It poured like oil into her stomach to pool and coalesce, fester and bubble. Her veins filled with it, viscous, like wet tar.

You should have died.

She gagged, her mouth filling with sour liquid that she was forced to swallow again. She thrashed from side to side, but the sheets had a tight hold on her and the shadow wasn't ready to relinquish its grip just yet.

You should have been with them.

The scream, when it came, blew the shadows apart with its fury.

"Do you fucking think I don't know that already?"

After that came tears, for the longest time.

At two a.m. she was back in the kitchen, making coffee and listening to the Stones, turned up loud enough to mask the whispers from the bedroom that had started up again all too soon.

Don't let the dark stop you shining, she sang softly, but she couldn't make the magic work tonight. Even above the sound of Jagger's wailing the whispers writhed, reminding her of her perfidy. The walls closed in on her, squeezing the shadows out of the joins of wall and ceiling. She headed for the hallway, meaning to get a jacket and head back out to the park.

And that's when she saw it. At first she put it down to stress; just another manifestation of the dark. But where the shadows hid, this new light illuminated. A blue shimmer showed under the door of the spare room – the *nursery*.

Somebody giggled, a girlish sound, followed immediately by a thudding that she knew, just knew, was Sam, the old Labrador's tail hitting the wooden floor in happy anticipation of going on a trip.

Don't let the dark stop you shining, she sang.

A male voice, a pleasing tenor she knew intimately, answered.

Don't let the blackness in your soul.

She strode to the door of the nursery and threw it open. It hit the wall with a loud crash that shook the whole apartment. The room was empty... and dark. Shadows shifted as wind disturbed the tree outside the window. The dark whispered to her.

You should have been with them.

#

She spent the rest of the holiday season in the kitchen, the music system turned up, the coffee-pot always on the go, and her gaze firmly fixed in any book she could find. The shadows continued to whisper to her, but she was used to that. What she found she couldn't stand, what felt like it might drive her completely mad, was the infrequent sound of childish giggles coming from the *nursery*.

After three days she knew she had to take action. Moving out was out of the question, from both monetary and practicality viewpoints.

Don't let the devil catch you cold.

"I won't, Gran," she whispered. "I promise."

She went online at first. She had only the simplest idea of what she was looking for. A search on *ghostbusters* only got her links to the movie and TV reality shows, and one on *psychics* in her area only got her palm readers and snake-oil salesmen.

Her first port of call the morning afterward was to the local library. If the young girl at the desk had any queries about her change of reading material away from her romantic thrillers, she didn't show it, merely stamped the books with her usual blank stare. It was obvious that the books were not the most popular; *Communing with the Dead* hadn't been taken out for nearly five years, and *Interviews From Beyond the Veil* had never left the library since the date it was stamped, some eight years previously. But she almost burst into a run in her haste to get the rest of her chores done. There was a trail to follow; one that led to giggling girls and happier times, and she couldn't *wait* to get started.

She made a perfunctory trip to the grocer's – milk, butter, bread and jam; about all she ate these days, then walked quickly home. She made herself a simple snack, brewed a fresh pot of coffee and then settled down in the sitting room chair to her reading. At the beginning she would look up every so often towards the nursery, expecting to hear a giggle; or for the dog's tail to sound out a message. But after a while she got lost in the books, transported to places where ghosts were real, where the dead were given voice – a place called *hope.*

She started with the thinner tome, *Communing with the Dead.* It began well enough, with several case studies based on people who talked to their lost ones; or rather, *claimed* to talk to their loved ones. For as she read, she came to the realization that she didn't believe a word of it; none of the cases had the clear *ring* of truth, none gave her the *frisson* up and down her spine she had felt on hearing the sounds in the spare room. She started skipping pages, only stopping when she came to the second half; a set of practical instructions and visualization exercises for inducing contact. She skim read that part, promising herself that she would come back to it later if the second book did not satisfy.

Not only did it not satisfy, it almost ended up being thrown into a corner. It was full of what her late husband would have called *tripe*; stories of *going into the light*, and green fields where choirs of angels sang, everybody was happy and no one ever had an *accident*.

Even as that thought struck her, a giggle came from the nursery. She smiled

She put her head back and closed her eyes. It was dark behind there, but her Gran helped her keep it away.

Don't let the dark stop you shining,
Don't let the blackness in your soul.

Don't let the dark stop you shining,
Don't let the devil catch you cold.

#

She woke, stiff-necked and chilled, in a dark room. She stretched out a hand to switch on the lamp beside her chair and stopped; the shadows shifted over in the dining room and the air suddenly felt heavy, her breathing becoming rapid and labored.

A girlish voice giggled.

She got shakily to her feet and made her way to the door of the nursery. She ran her hand down the wood, feeling the roughness of the grain at her fingertips.

The shadows darkened further and the door thrummed. She thought her heart might stop as the tenor voice rang out, clear as a bell.

Don't let the dark stop you shining,

For a minute that felt like an hour she sang along with George once more, just like old times.

Don't let the dark stop you shining,
Don't let the devil catch you cold.

Then, as quickly as it had come, the sound stopped and the apartment fell quiet.

She stood there for a while longer until her tears subsided then went to the kitchen, returning some minutes later with coffee and a sandwich. She ate with one hand and held the book in the other, opening *Communing with the Dead* at the section on practical instructions.

Those that have passed beyond often find themselves lonely, wishing to make contact with the living. There is often something; a person or a well loved trinket or a well loved room that draws them back to this plane, keeps them returning in search of old memories, of happy times. If you wish to make contact with a returning spirit, you should stay close to the place they loved most, become attached to it, and make it as much a part of your life as it was theirs. If you can bear it, talk to your lost one, as if they were present with you. And if you persevere, you will often be rewarded with an answer.

She almost threw the book away to join the other.

I've done that bit. I've been doing it for years.

She persevered with it, reading ever more frustrating entries about using *Ouija* boards or pendulums, and instructions about how to hold a séance.

In the end the books told her nothing she needed. She stood at the nursery door, staying there even as cold seeped into her bones, but although the shadows quivered and whispered, her family did not come back that night.

That became the new pattern of her life, her daylight hours spent wishing away the time until night would come and her love would *sing* for her. It was only for a minute or so every night, and afterwards she always cried fresh tears, but she hadn't felt so close to her George since his death.

She took to stroking the door of the room as if its timber were somehow part of George himself, and it seemed to respond in kind, sending tingling vibrations running through her body. In the depth of the dark nights she sang the old song, her feet tapping a rhythm on the floorboards and the door *thrumming* in time.

I'm close. But not close enough.

It was as if her family was *almost* in touching distance, and her frustration at not being able to break through the veil between them was growing with each night that passed. She wanted more. She *needed* more.

#

One morning, some two weeks after she first heard the giggles and singing, she came to a decision. She'd heard of it being done; seen it happen in those old horror movies that George had loved so much. If they were close enough to sing to her, then maybe, just maybe, they were close enough to be brought back completely. One thing was for sure; she wasn't about to find what she needed in the books she'd got from the library, nor in any of the volumes on the shelves that she'd perused on her visit. Her current plan called for something more *esoteric*.

That afternoon she booked an hour on the computer in the library. She settled down to searching for what she was after. It felt like George was at her shoulder the whole time, whispering in her ear. Her free hand stroked the wood of the table as she surfed, and in her head she heard him sing, ever louder as she got closer to her goal.

Don't let the dark stop you shining,

The song in her head reached a crescendo as she reached a page deep in a history of alchemical text. *The Concordances of the Twelve Serpents.*

Ye Twelve Concordances of ye Red Serpent. In wch is succinctly and methodically handled, ae mefhod for ye reffurection of ye recently dead; and, the better to attaine to the originall and true meanes of perfection, inriched with Figures representing the proper colours to lyfe as they successively appere in the practise of this blessed worke.

There were many legends associated with the book, but the thing that drew her to it most was the illustrations, and one in particular. CALX was the heading. The picture showed a young man, bound to a mast of a burning ship. He was smiling.

He had George's face.

Accompanying the illustration was a set of precise instructions. It took her the rest of the hour to copy them down to a notepad in her firm precise handwriting, but she was singing inside as she left the library.

Don't let the dark stop you shining,

#

Sourcing the ingredients proved to be a problem. Mementoes of the deceased were the easy part; procuring the hand of a dead murderer proved more difficult.

But not impossible.

It seemed that anything was available, for a price. It cost her almost all of her meagre savings, and when it was delivered she took one look at it then hid it away until she needed it. The scented candles were likewise exotic, but she finally tracked them down in an Asian shop. The last thing to arrive was the Holy Water from Rome. Neither of them had ever taken much time for religion, and certainly not the Roman variety, but the *recipe* in the book called for it, and she always followed recipes.

Her frustration grew while waiting for all the ingredients to finally arrive, but it seemed that her family knew what she planned. Every night they sang for her, just a few bars, but enough that she *knew* she was doing the right thing. She spent the nights memorizing the words and actions she was going to need when the time came. That was something she knew how to do. It was almost like doing her multiplication tables back in school, with the same *sing-song* chanting rhythm to it. But this had a far different purpose.

On the day the Holy Water arrived the nursery door had been *thrumming* almost constantly in anticipation, her stomach roiling and seething in time.

Tonight. I will do it tonight.

#

The preparations did not take long. She started by drawing a circle of chalk, taking care never to smudge the line as she navigated her way around the nursery. Beyond this she rubbed a broken garlic clove in a second circle around the first.

When this was done, she took the small jar of Holy Water and went round the circle again just inside the line of chalk, leaving a wet trail that dried quickly behind her. Within this inner circle she made her pentacle using the signs laid out in *The Concordances*, and joined each sign most carefully to the edges of the lines she had already made. Finally the pentacle was done and she was able to stand.

The rest of it went slower as every muscle in her body was telling her she needed to rest.

I'll do that later. When they are back.

In the points of the pentacle she placed five portions of bread wrapped in linen, and in the valleys five of the scented candles. Finally came the part she'd been dreading. She removed the withered hand from its wrapping and, trying not to look too closely, placed it in the centre of the circle.

I'm as ready as I'm ever going to be.

She raised her voice and started the chant she'd learned earlier. The room *thrummed* in sympathy.

Kerub impero tibi per Adam

Aquila impero tibi per alas Tauri.

Serpens impero tibi per Angelum et Leonem.

The walls of the nursery seemed to *beat* and *pulse*, as in time with a giant heart. Overhead she heard the sound of rapid movement, footsteps fading in the distance as if something had just run across the room upstairs. She caught a movement at the corner of her eye and turned just as dark shadows slithered from the walls and began to make their way towards her.

She raised her voice to a loud shout, and started to stamp her feet in time. The whole room responded by *ringing* with each stamp.

Ri linn dioladh na beatha, Ri linn bruchdadh na falluis, Ri linn iobar na creadha, Ri linn dortadh na fala.

The shadows continued to come forward, a wall of them four, six, eight feet tall until they filled the whole room and writhed high around the circle. She was buffeted from side to side as the floor bucked and swayed.

Damnú ort! she shouted at the top of her voice.

A percussive *blast* blew through the room; a light so bright that she could still see it even when she pressed her eyes tightly closed. The rocking abated, and silence fell, her eyes slowly adjusting again to the dim light provided by the candles. Even before she could focus she heard him – *George* – singing

Don't let the dark stop you shining,

Her legs went to jelly beneath her and she half-fell, half-stumbled to the floor, tears blinding her. Someone sat there beside her. She reached out a hand.

George?

Cold flesh pressed against her, wet and clammy. She tasted blood as the sound of a car engine roared, brakes screeched and glass shattered.

The shock of the crash broke her back.

As night fell, the shadows gathered around the room, falling on the body, whispering as they fed.

Where The Dark is Deepest
Ray Cluley

The bright lights of the ward showed Sheila in stark detail. Her pale, drawn face. The swollen lump on her forehead. The crusty line of blood that bisected her eyebrow. More disturbing to Stan were the tubes in her nose and mouth and arm, the bandages, the clamp on her finger and the wire that ran from it to the monitor with its steady rhythm.

Stan took a seat by her bedside without removing his coat. He stroked the hair from her face, careful not to touch her wounds. Her breasts rose and fell under sheets as tight as swaddling.

"Oh Sheila," he said. "What happened?"

He covered her free hand in both of his and closed his eyes as if to share the darkness with her.

#

"Two hundred metres."

Sheila nodded, not liking how easily Tom took control of the transponder. He may not have meant anything by it, probably just rookie enthusiasm, but it was so much like Mark that she had to wonder. Silly, really. She had plenty to do. Maybe it was his Aussie accent that bothered her, the way it made everything sound like a question; two hundred *metres*? Mark had at least always been sure of himself.

"Roger that," came Stan's voice from up top, tinny but clear despite all the ocean between them. "How's your pilot?"

Tom glanced over and she made a circle with her thumb and forefinger.

"Not bad, for a Sheila."

Sheila turned the circle into a middle finger and Tom laughed. He was never going to get tired of the Sheila jokes.

Under his laughter the submersible pinged its sonar.

"Two hundred fifty."

They wouldn't roll camera until five hundred metres and then they'd keep it running all the way down. Still, Sheila remained close to the viewport, eager to see anything and everything they shared the water with. There was nothing yet, though. At least not that she could see. But then down here, in the gloom, many animals had become almost completely transparent; their survival depended on not being seen. And yet... maybe something...

"Losing the lights," she said.

Tom nodded.

The Nautilus carried quartz iodide and metal halide lights with ten hours battery life. Sheila flipped the switches to cut them off.

"Ah."

Brief bright flashes flared outside and on the monitors. Bioluminescence: bacteria-powered light.

"Firefly squid," Tom said.

"Yep. Very good."

Was that patronising? But Tom began an Attenborough impression that suggested he was okay. It was quite remarkable, considering his accent.

"At *three* hundred metres *the ocean* looks like *space*, stars *shi*ning in the darkness... of the *twi*light *zone*." And he launched into the soundtrack of the television series.

It did look like space out there, though. A permanent night that would become darker than anything else she'd ever seen. She flipped the lights back on.

"Three fifty. Temperature, five degrees."

Five degrees outside, but inside they were sweltering; the Nautilus was even more cramped than the Alvin. A titanium cylinder two metres wide by eight metres long, the Nautilus was not a large vessel and it was crammed full with equipment: pressure valves; controls; food; water; urination bags; plus one researcher and a pilot, which was why it paid to have a pilot who knew more than simply how to drive. Especially when your researcher was still learning the ropes. There were only two of them, but the Nautilus quickly warmed up with their combined body heat.

Tom still wore his cap, despite the heat, but he had stripped down to a vest that might have been white when he bought it. Sheila wore her favourite T-shirt. It was much cleaner than Tom's vest, bright white with a big blue cartoon dolphin standing on its tail, smiling. A line of text said 'beautiful *and* clever'. An ex had bought it for her. A before-Mark ex. But even in the T-shirt and shorts she was too hot. She loved the Nautilus, but she did wish it was cooler.

At least Tom had stopped joking about air con, or opening a window.

Their windows were five tiny viewports the size of saucers – anything bigger and they'd implode under the pressure – with overlapping fields of view, which was one plus they had on the Alvin. Camera stations rigged outside took stills and motion picture which they could watch via a series of monitors not much bigger than the viewports. Not that there was much to see out there yet. It was very dark outside, and it was only going to get darker as they left the photic zone, the twilight zone, the midnight zone, right down to the abyssal plain.

Another advantage they had in the Nautilus was the ability to drop five thousand metres instead of the Alvin's four and a half. Not as good as the Shinkai or the COMRA, but good enough for the Mariana Trench. Seven miles deep, it was the largest in the abyssal plain and only six submersibles in the world were capable of reaching it. Yet between all of them they'd explored less than one percent of this part of the planet. Even the Nautilus, which had made over three and a half thousand successful dives since its construction in '82, had still seen very little.

"You been here before?" Sheila asked.

"Not in this. Mostly the Alvin. You?"

She shook her head. "Nope."

"First time in a submersible?"

She glanced at him but he was checking the monitors and it was hard to tell if he was joking. "No," she said, "just first time here. I filmed a lot of continental slope stuff in this tub, and some vents for a couple of TV programmes."

"Cool, which ones?"

"Er, there was *Beneath the Surface* and one called *Water Worlds*? It's for kids."

Tom nodded but said, "No, I mean which vents?"

"Oh. Both ends of the Pacific. Went one and a half miles down near the Galapagos Islands and then filmed the dragon chimneys near Japan."

She sounded like she was justifying her involvement, but Tom's tone had suggested nothing more than curiosity. She was still too used to Mark. Tom didn't seem to have noticed.

"I've seen the dragons," he said. "Amazing."

Sheila nodded. They'd been very impressive, massive columns as big as stacked houses erupting in the darkness, spewing superheated water as hot as molten lead and loaded with minerals. Clouds of sulphides solidified to give each chimney a strange vertical shape that sat in four hundred degrees of a chemical cocktail, scolding and toxic. And yet there was life. In fact, a certain type of bacteria thrived in such conditions, just as a certain shrimp ate the bacteria. At the dragon chimneys the crustaceans feeding on the bacteria had been squat lobsters that were actually furry and white. People used to believe that life couldn't exist without the sun, but each vent was its own little oasis community taking energy not from the sun but from the Earth's core. Sheila had filmed vent after vent for the best part of three months and had never been bored, finding a new species for every ten days she spent there.

"What's the most *horrible* thing you've ever seen?" Tom asked.

"Hm?"

"The dragon chimneys are beautiful, right, but what was the most horrible?"

Sheila thought about it. She thought of Mark. Thought of him in their bed, fucking an undergraduate he was working with. The girl had hidden her face under the sheets but Mark had simply climbed off and apologised, like he'd left the toilet seat up or something. She shook her head.

"I once saw a killer whale toying with a seal," Tom told her. "No reason for it. It washed it off an ice sheet and tossed it around. Didn't eat anything except a flipper, and even that seemed like an accident."

"Nice."

"Yeah. Okay, next. What's the *weirdest* thing you've seen?"

"I saw a field of tube worms once." She was tired of the game already, but Tom seemed to want more. "They were feeding off the methane escaping from the sea bed," she said. "Thousands of them, hundreds of metres across the ocean floor. Looked like a field of alien grass." She wiped the sweat from her brow. "What about you?"

"Weirdest thing I've seen?"

She nodded.

"Well, I saw this woman once who could smoke a cigarette with her–"

Sheila held up her hand. "Never mind."

Tom grinned, reported the depth and temperature, then said, "I was half a mile down, bottom of the Gulf of Mexico, and we found what looked like a massive lake. I mean, sandy shore, tide line, everything, except underwater. We're thinking, what the hell?"

"Cold seep."

Tom only glanced at her but his disappointment was clear. "Yeah. Big soup of salty brine, heavier than sea water. What we thought was a sandy shore was actually hundreds of thousands of muscles."

"Plenty of weird shit down here," Sheila said.

"Yeah." Tom pointed at the left view port. "Take a look."

A number of jellies were moving with them, glowing in the lights of the submersible. They clenched the dark water in gentle convulsions that set them drifting up and away like underwater ghosts. They made her think of Mark; he'd lacked substance, too.

"Did you know," Tom said as Sheila watched them, "We've learnt more about space than our own ocean?"

Sheila did know. She thought everybody knew. "Yeah," she said.

"We know more about the moon than we do the abyssal plain."

The abyssal plain was where they were heading. With ninety percent of the Earth's living space in the ocean, it always amazed Sheila that people didn't think of it as an ocean planet, and with over sixty percent covered by seawater over a mile deep, it astounded her that so little was known about its depths.

"Okay. Did you know–"

Sheila held up her hand.

"What?" said Tom, checking each monitor, "What've we got?"

She smiled, but it was tight-lipped. "Nothing. I just want you to stop with trivia time. Assume the answer to every 'did you know' is yes. I'm not just a glorified chauffeur."

Tom launched back into Attenborough. "The *f*emale *ru*ins the male's fun, giving him *noth*ing *else* to *do,* but watch as she takes them *deep*er... *deep*er into the dark."

The sonar punctuated his comment with a sharp *ping!*

#

Stan released Sheila's hand and excused himself from her bedside, explaining to her sleeping body that he was going to get a cup of coffee. "Can I get you anything?" he asked from the doorway, as if he could trick her into being awake.

One of the machines beside her huffed up and settled down for her breath. Another made her heartbeat audible with a tiny blip and peak. That was all he got.

#

Below one thousand metres they were in the dark zone. No sunlight at all penetrated as far as the dark zone. Food was scarce, too. Once, Sheila had filmed a whale carcass as it slowly disappeared into the mouths of scavengers. It had been little more than blubber clinging to bones when she came across it, spider crabs over a metre across feeding from it, eels picking at the putrid remains. It was an image that came up whenever she thought of the last year of her marriage. But usually most life forms down here fed upon marine snow, the detritus falling from the surface, which took months to reach where Sheila and Tom were. This was good for them because, with less than three percent organic material to pollute it, the sea was as clear as tap water in the light of the submersible. They were following the continental slope, sonar beating a quiet unhurried heartbeat.

"You okay?" Tom asked.

Sheila turned to see Tom was looking at her with the sort of interest she'd rather he directed at the monitors.

"I'm fine."

Tom stared.

"I'm fine. Really."

She'd been thinking of Mark. They'd met on a dive like this, the dragon chimneys actually, so it was hard *not* to think of him. Just as the underwater chimneys could become cold without warning, dying because the energy had been redirected elsewhere, so her marriage to the prick had quickly cooled, leaving behind only an empty shell of waste chemicals. Relationships made him claustrophobic, apparently. Not that it stopped him having two of them, both at the same time.

"Stan was telling me about a place topside that

does good seafood," Tom said. "Of course it does, right? Anyway, do you like seafood?"

Sheila adjusted their course slightly. "We're coming up on the trench."

Tom returned his attention to the cameras and monitors and for the next eight hundred metres they moved silently through the dark, travelling with the current, their horizontal movement barely noticeable unless they looked down at the sea bed moving past.

"Oh," said Sheila.

"What is it?"

She was quiet for a moment, then, "I thought I saw something."

Below five hundred metres, new creatures were found all the time, bizarre creatures of all sorts of shapes and sizes. In fact, a new species was discovered with almost every dive.

"I don't see–"

The rest of his sentence was snapped off as the vessel lurched and a heavy metallic thud resounded in the chamber. Tom was thrown back and then snapped forward. His head struck a monitor. Sheila folded over the controls, was thrown sideways, then fell face down. Her eyebrow opened against the corner of something. She clutched at it. They were spinning toward the ocean floor.

"What happened?" Tom yelled.

Sheila caught a brief glimpse through one of the ports of something rushing away, something dark and long and fast, and then the seabed was rushing up to meet them and they hit it hard. Twice. Tail end first, then the rest of the tub. A cloud of sand and ocean ooze rose up to envelop them.

#

There were voices in the darkness.

#

"You all right?" Tom asked.

Sheila thought she'd passed out for a moment but the lights came back on and she realised the momentary blackness had been a technical fault. She nodded, still holding her brow.

"You're bleeding," Tom said, pointing.

"It's nothing."

Tom massaged his neck with one hand, pressed buttons on the monitors with the other. "What did we hit?"

"Down here? Are you kidding? There's nothing *to* hit except the floor."

"Well we did that, too."

Sheila checked every button, dial, and reading they had.

"Seriously, what happened? Something hit *us*?"

He'd meant it to sound sarcastic, but Sheila said, "Looks like it."

She ran the cameras back for him and they watched it together. Tom leaned close. "What, the, *fuck*?"

Sheila had to agree.

"It's big," she said. "Ten, twelve metres."

"That's, like, a fucking whale shark or something."

"Not down here. Not that fast."

"I said *like*."

They watched it again.

"Look." Sheila tapped the screen.

"Is it a bunch of somethings?"

"I think those are tentacles."

Tom's eyes widened. "Strewth!" He winced, looked at Sheila. "Don't ever tell anybody I said that."

"Speaking of which..."

The radio, the *transponder*, was working okay. Mark used to hate it when she called it a radio; it was an acoustic transponder, or an underwater telephone, both of which sounded ridiculous to Sheila.

"Stan? We've just, er... We had a... difficulty."

"Roger that. You all okay? What happened?"

She looked at Tom and he shrugged.

"Technical problem. We're sitting on the floor at the moment. Still got power, integrity's good. It looked li–"

Tom ducked down suddenly from a viewport, "Fuck!" Sheila looked, radio still in hand, saying nothing. She heard concern from the other end.

"- on down there? Sheila? You reading me?"

"Yeah, loud and clear. We're all right. Hang on."

She racked the radio. Radio radio radio.

Tom was looking at her.

"What, Tom? What is it?"

He was pointed to the port with his thumb. "I saw it out there."

Sheila took a look. There was nothing there but her reflection on the dark glass.

"I saw it. It came right at us, then seemed to change

its mind and went straight back the other way. Backwards."

"Backwards?"

"It didn't turn around. Came at us and went back. Fast."

"Cameras still running?"

He checked. "Yeah."

"Wind it back."

She clambered into the pilot seat and hoped the engines were alright.

They weren't.

"Shit. Call it in."

Tom took off his cap and swept his hair back as he muttered something. He took up the radio.

"Stan?" Tom said.

"What happened?"

"We're not sure. Something down here, we think. We only got a glimpse of it."

"Got it on film?"

Sheila smiled. Good ole Stan.

"Yeah," said Tom. "Got it on film. The first time, anyway."

Sheila took the radio. "Tom says he saw it again."

"What was it?"

"Don't know."

She heard some of Stan's sigh when he came back saying, "What did it look like?"

"A blur," she said. "A dark blur. With some blurry things that might, *might*, have been tentacles. Doesn't look like any cephalopod I've ever seen, though."

In the following silence she imagined the team talking about it topside. She and Tom merely exchanged glances. Eventually, when Stan came back, he had nothing to say on that subject.

"How are you?"

"Bit battered and bruised."

But she'd felt that way for months: it wasn't anything she wasn't used to.

"All right. Well, bring her up when you're ready. We'll be waiting."

"Roger that."

Surfacing the Nautilus was as simple as descending. They were heavy, over forty thousand pounds of metal, so all they had to do was sink to get down, flooding the ballast tanks and descending in a cloud of bubbles. Once gravity had done its job, expendable steel weights were released to rise up again. They were not stuck on the ocean floor, they could ascend whenever they wanted, but Sheila wasn't sure she wanted to just yet.

She shelved the radio and looked out of the nearest viewport, wondering if what was out there waited too. All she could see was the dark ocean behind her pale reflection.

#

Stan fussed with Sheila's hair, brushing it back, arranging it neatly, and he moistened her dry lips with fingertips of water from a nearby jug.

"Let's keep you looking pretty," he said softly. "All these attractive doctors around. You never know. Plus Tom likes you, of course."

Her breath wheezed, regulated by the machine that inflated and deflated beside her.

"Wake up," he said. "Please wake up."

She didn't.

"Come on Sheila, you're my best diver. The Science Foundation *think* they own it, and, okay, they paid for it, but the Nautilus is yours really. I need you."

He'd made plenty of jokes about women drivers in the past but he didn't do that now. He dare not, in case the doctors were right and she *could* hear him.

"How am I going to blow Attenborough out of the water with you in here, eh?" He surprised himself into a short laugh. "Out of the water. I'll have to remember that for later. Maybe use it for the promotional stuff, what do you think?"

Assisted by her machines, Sheila breathed.

"I thought we might set lots of the footage to music. You know, let the images speak for themselves. If we *do* use any voiceover, though, I want your voice, okay? And you can't do that here. So that's the deal – get better, get the voice-over gig."

He dabbed more water, this time cleaning away some blood that had crusted near her eye.

"Just wake up, and everything will be all right."

But looking at her in her hospital bed, under the unforgiving glare of the fluorescent lights, he wasn't so sure.

#

"Tom?"

His face was pressed to the glass but he'd reported nothing.

"Tom? What are you thinking?"

"You know, there's meant to be giant squid, *massive* squid, that nobody's ever seen."

"Yeah." She watched him. "Is that what you think hit us?"

He shrugged.

"They've only ever found pieces of them in fishing nets or dead bits washed up on the shore," Sheila said. "Nobody's actually seen one."

Tom looked at her. "Nobody's *filmed* one," he said.

"You want to stick around for a bit. See if it comes back."

He nodded, though it hadn't been a question.

Sheila joined him at the view port but saw only the muted glow of blue white light and a sea floor tracked with urchin trails.

"Sometimes they find sucker marks on whales," Sheila said. "*Big* marks."

Tom let out a shaky laugh. "It tries to eat whales?"

"More like the other way around, probably."

They waited.

"Maybe we did hit something," Sheila said eventually. "Something drifting."

"Then where is it now?"

Sheila thumbed the cameras in the direction of the Mariana Trench. It lay ten metres to the right of them, a gaping gash of dark in dark. "Down there?"

"But I saw it. It came back. It wasn't something drifting."

She didn't know him well enough to doubt him, but she didn't know him well enough to trust him either.

"All right," she said. "Let's try something."

She toggled the switches for the lights, strobing the darkness outside. Instead of seeing nothing at all they saw *glimpses* of nothing.

"What are you doing?"

"Bioluminescence. Some animals use it to see."

"Yeah," said Tom, "like underwater headlights."

"That's right. Others use it–"

"As a lure. To attract prey."

"Exactly."

"Except we're not exactly in a position to eat it, are we. I mean, it'll think we're the ones worth eating."

"Well unless it has a tin opener..."

She continued to stare out into the ocean.

"Coelacanths were believed extinct," she said eventually, "for more than 65 million years. And then, in the thirties, one was caught off the east coast of Africa. Oldest living jawed fish ever."

"It wasn't a coelacanth out there."

She laughed. "No. But maybe it's something else that managed to swim beyond its own extinction."

#

A doctor came in to check on Sheila and saw Stan with her.

"Are you her father?" he asked.

"Yes," said Stan, fearing hc'd be thrown out otherwise. He stood up to give the man room. "How is she?"

"Well she's lost a lot of blood," the doctor said, checking her over, "and she came dangerously close to drowning. But it's the head wound I'm concerned about."

"Concerned?"

The doctor held up a hand while he finished his examination, then said, "I'll show you the scan if you can just wait a moment."

"Thank you."

When the doctor had gone, Stan took Sheila's hand again and said, "I'm so sorry." He sat down. "I'm sorry. I should have told you."

"Told her what?"

Mark stood in the doorway. His shirt was untucked, his shoes untied. Without waiting for an answer to his first question, he asked, "How is she?" and came in. He examined her charts, as if he was a fucking medical expert all of a sudden.

"What are you doing here?" Stan asked, standing. "You shouldn't be here. Get out of here!"

"I'm still her emergency contact," Mark said. "What are *you* doing here?"

But Mark didn't really care for an answer, or need one – he'd made his point with the question. Now he stood looking at Sheila like he'd discovered a new species. Stan suddenly hated the man. He'd always thought him an arrogant arsehole, and the way he'd treated Sheila had been appalling, but he'd remained professional about their working relationship. He thoroughly regretted that now.

"I just wanted her back on the team," Stan said. "I'd never have lured her onboard if she'd known you were back for another series."

Mark nodded. "Well she knows now."

Sheila's breath huffed and wheezed.

#

"Just come back," Stan said. He was clearly worried. "You're dead in the water with no option but to surface, and you're too bloody close to the trench for my liking."

"We're alright," Sheila said, "and apart from that one time, which might have been an accident, it hasn't made contact again. It's just checking us out."

"Sorry, no. Come back."

He sounded like Mark. Men often said sorry when they weren't. Or if they were sorry, it was for something different to what they were actually apologising for. Sorry I got caught. Sorry I married you.

"We'll get the tub fixed and you can go back down and look around for it then – white light, blue, red, whatever you want," Stan said. "Disco ball, if you want to."

Sheila's idea was to switch to red light but strobe with one of the lights on the arms extended out and away from them. Most fish can't see red light. She hoped it would come closer, attracted to the smaller light, without seeing them watching. It was a tactic some other sea creatures used, lighting the water around them with red bioluminescence to see by while attracting prey with blue.

Tom took the radio. Coming to her rescue, her knight in sweaty vest. "Give us another hour, Stan."

But Sheila snatched the radio back and racked it without waiting for a reply.

"Why didn't you just tell him we were breaking up?" Tom said.

She ignored him, extending the Nautilus arm. She flipped their lights to red and the water they sat in seemed tinted with blood.

"What are you doing?"

She set one of the arm lights flashing.

It came at them right away. Like a living torpedo, it sped at them from above with a trail of limbs tangling behind in streamlined perfection. A dark mass, not much more than a blur, it was surprisingly bulbous and solid for such depths. It did look a bit like a squid, but it *wasn't* a squid, it was too squat at one end, almost spherical. Before getting too close, it came to an abrupt stop and the tentacles behind swept forward, like a tangled mane of hair. Then the shape travelled back and up and away from them again, an ugly ball of flesh. The mass of tentacles were swept into a streamlined point as they diminished, disappearing into the darkness of the sea. A comet, pulling its tail behind.

"Fast fucker," said Tom.

"Did you see its eyes?"

"No, did you? Shit, did you? What were they like?"

"I didn't see them either. Maybe it doesn't have

any. It's dark down here, so what's the point? Lots of fish rely on sensing movement."

Outside the Pacific was flushed red but empty. The two of them waited.

"You remember that seal I mentioned?" Tom asked.

"You think we're being toyed with?"

Tom's silence was answer enough.

"It only came for us that first time because we were moving," Sheila said. "The second time it was probably just coming to where it felt us last."

Tom accepted her explanation with a nod. "Then you extended the arm and flashed the light..."

"... except it wasn't the light, it was..."

"... the movement that attracted it."

"Bingo."

It was a definite possibility. Another one was that it had tasted them. Taste in water was like smell in air. She had no idea what a forty-thousand-pound tub of metal might taste like. Strange, she was guessing.

Tom turned to grab his water bottle and caught a glance outside. "Look."

Sheila saw.

"That's not the same creature."

"No."

It passed them low to the floor, moving slowly up the length of the ocean trench beside them. It was like an eel, only much bigger. Thanks to known distances between landmark fissures and sea floor geography, Sheila was able to estimate its size.

"Sixteen metres."

It turned and came back.

"Look at the lights."

Like many sea creatures, this one had photofores – cells that produced light cells. Some used them to match the coloration of the water they occupied, but this deep, in the dark, there was no need – this one seemed to use them like headlights. Or maybe to attract prey.

"What's it doing?"

Good question; a creature this deep wouldn't waste energy if it could help it.

"Come on, Tom, calm down," she said. "It's not like we're in any danger."

"Then why are we whispering?"

Sheila was baffled. Something this big, this deep, was strange because there was nothing suitable to feed it down here. Although this was the *second* creature of size they'd seen now, so clearly there was *something* to eat. She watched as it swam away parallel to the trench.

Tom said, "I think we just buried *The Blue Planet*."

Sheila nodded. "I think we did, yeah."

Tom handed her the radio. "Call it in."

She nodded. She told Stan, "You are going to love what's going on down here."

"What? What is it?" The tinny sound of his voice only made him sound more excited.

Tom, behind her, called it the lesser-spotted-giant-fuck-knows-what and she laughed. "Really," she said, "This is big."

There was nothing back from up top for a moment.

"You get that, Stan? It's beautiful."

The transponder clicked and she heard Stan take a breath to speak, then it went silent again. When it clicked ready for broadcast a second time Sheila heard the tail end of someone saying something angry behind Stan's voice, but he ignored it and so she did too.

"Come back, Sheila."

Sheila frowned. "What?"

"Er, Sheila?" said Tom, "Something weird's happening."

Outside, the creature was winding around itself in tight spirals.

Sheila hung up on Stan. "What's got it so agitated?"

"Look at it go!"

They looked up at the roof but the viewport there offered a very limited view and they saw nothing. Sheila went to another, squatting down as low as she could in order to look up.

Tom repositioned the camera and flooded the area with light. They caught the dark squid shape in a hasty retreat, the other – fish? snake? – following fast.

"Not fast enough," said Sheila.

Having spent a great deal of energy, the creature let itself fall gently to the ocean floor where it proceeded to glide lengths again, fins rippling to propel itself above a cloud of sand much as before, except now it was to the left of them. It seemed to grow as it neared, swelling in size until it was so close that they couldn't see it all at once anymore, just the flash of silver as it passed them by, like a train rushing past those waiting at a station.

"It's too close," Tom said.

"Yeah. We can't get it all on camera."

"That's not what I meant."

"I'll take us up a little, get a different perspective."

"That squid thing's still out there too, remember." He turned his cap around so the peak pointed backwards and pressed his face as close to the glass as he could get it, looking up and down and left and right.

The Nautilus began to rise.

"Stop," said Tom.

"Why?"

"Stop! Look at it. It's winding around again."

But Sheila had seen something else, something new, from a different viewport.

The ocean floor trembled. Sand shifted and swirled, shaken away from the body of something rising, something huge, something shaped like a manta ray but as flat as a monkfish.

"Tom."

The creature shook the camouflage from itself with fins the size of ice rinks as it rose from the seabed, the pigments in its skin changing colour to match its new surroundings. There were no eyes that she could see, but antennae-like protrusions sprouted like hair from various parts. It came up slowly, and in her peripheral vision Sheila saw something else come down fast. She knew at once what was happening; the squid thing was back, rocketing down and dragging its tendrils behind, speeding back again the way it had come, and this time Sheila saw the rod of flesh connecting it to the shape lifting itself from hiding.

It was a lure.

"There it goes!" Tom yelled, still watching the other creature, and sure enough Sheila saw it chase the receding bait. A silver spear flashing in the lights of the Nautilus, unaware that it was not the predator but the prey.

"Tom!"

He looked at her, then at what she saw.

"Oh shit."

Still rising from the ocean floor, the creature's maw dropped open, a vast ramp of a mouth with curved spurs for teeth. The new space it had created in opening its jaws filled instantly with water and suddenly everything happened very fast. The submersible turned in an unexpected current before the mouth snapped closed – quickly, so quickly – and Sheila wondered about the mechanism needed to expel water so fast, and how did it move so fast, and, fuck, how was it so big down here? She didn't see whether it caught its dinner because some part of it struck them as it came up and then they were rolling, they were upside down, the floor was above instead of below, and she was hitting Tom, hitting monitors, hitting panels and walls and hurting herself as outside forces tossed her around. Something struck them, once, twice, a flurry of strikes, and then they were not only turning and spinning and rolling but falling, down, down, further than should have been possible, down into the dark.

#

The doctor returned to find two men with Sheila instead of one.

Mark said, "I'm her husband."

Stan hated the lack of hesitation, hated how easily the lie came, though he'd done the same thing himself only a moment ago. He'd lied to Sheila, too, and now look at her. Who was worse? Who was really responsible for putting her in hospital?

The doctor clipped a scan to a light board and flicked a switch to show them Sheila's brain.

"She has a subdural haematoma," he said. "I'm afraid we're still in the dark when it comes to how the brain works, but a subdural haematoma–" he pointed at an area on the scan, "- is when blood collects between the skull and brain."

Stan looked at the scan and saw only the shapes of ridges and troughs, like the ranges and trenches of an ocean floor.

"We've tried to remove the excess fluid to relieve the pressure," the doctor said, "But only time will tell."

Pressure, thought Stan. Too much pressure. Like offering her a new job. Like pushing her towards a new relationship. She wasn't ready, he knew she wasn't ready, but he thought he could help. He thought it would give her something positive to focus on, and with Mark only involved post-production Stan didn't foresee any problems. He should have, but he didn't.

"She was probably getting out of the bath," the doctor was explaining to Mark. "Some people who attempt suicide change their mind part way through.

By then she would have already been weak with blood loss, slipped, and hit her head."

Sheila had not changed her mind. Stan knew that. He'd arrived shortly after the ambulance and seen for himself; there had been more blood than bathwater. She'd done it properly this time, a lengthways cut, with a packet of aspirin to thin the blood. This was no cry for help. The only cry she'd made was one to Stan, a last minute thought, evident in the wet bloody footprints leading to the empty cradle of a phone that lay broken on her bathroom tiles. She'd only managed half a goodbye.

The doctor looked down at Sheila. "We won't know for sure what happened until she wakes up and tells us herself," he said. He'd avoided *if*, Stan realised, but he heard the word anyway.

If she wakes up.

#

The Nautilus had righted itself but it was still moving, still descending. Sheila clambered back into position, ready to bring them up again, and yelled at Tom to get on the radio.

Tom was gone.

"Tom?"

The vehicle shook, and an awful groan of metal reverberated inside. With a heavy thump they hit something and Sheila was shaken out of her seat again. Then the Nautilus was still. She was on a ledge, balanced precariously on the edge of it.

She grabbed the radio and called up to Stan.

"They're all the fucking same," she told him.

"Sheila? Sheila? Are you okay? What happened?"

"Tom's gone," she said, "Didn't stick around long once the trouble started, did he?"

He didn't answer that. Maybe she hadn't pressed the button properly.

"... he's a good man," Stan was saying, "Australian. You'll like him. You know?"

Sheila scratched at the bandages on her arm. He'd said all of that already, hadn't he?

"Plenty more fish in the sea, eh, Stan?"

It was too hot for bandages. She pulled at them, thinking, somebody open a fucking window or something.

"He said you had some sort of... episode."

There was another voice behind Stan's. His words came to her as an unpleasant echo she thought she knew.

"Who've you got with you?" she demanded.

Mark said, "Sheila, it's me. Come back."

She slammed the radio down. Did it again. Again. Then took it up and hoped it still worked.

"Why aren't you down here with me?" she asked. "Too claustrophobic? Not enough room in here for us *and* your ego?"

But it was Stan's voice that replied.

"Sheila?"

"Why didn't you tell me, Stan? Why'd you keep me in the dark?"

There was a pause before he answered. "He'd told me it was over."

"Not *that*, I don't care about *that*. The fucking *job*. Couldn't I just do *something* on my own?"

She moved to the front of the vessel. It rocked, shifted, slid.

And fell again.

The Nautilus turned as it descended into the Mariana Trench, slow circles at first but quickening, like water spiralling down a plug hole. One by one the lights popped, crunched, flattened by pressures they could no longer take, but there was enough for her to see the chasm walls rushing by outside. One of the viewports cracked with a sharp splintering sound, hissed, then gushed water. I'm going under, she realised. This is it. I'm going under.

Even without the transponder – the radio, the fucking radio – Sheila heard voices. They sounded excited, or panicked, she couldn't tell which, couldn't care, but she ignored them. The water rose around her body but she ignored that as well, just as she tried to ignore the blood that slicked her arms. Each one was opened up from wrist to elbow, spilling her ink in crimson clouds she saw only as black.

I'm going under.

The steady ping of the echosounder, previously only a background noise, suddenly became everything to her, the only sound, and it took her, down and down and down, becoming a single long flat note that followed her into where the dark was deepest.

#

The brightest bioluminescence came up to meet her.

Sheila steered a course towards it.

Biographies:

Stephen Bacon's fiction has appeared in various magazines and journals such as *Black Static*, *The Willows*, *Crimewave*, *Shadows & Tall Trees*, and in the anthologies *Murmurations*, *Where the Heart Is*, *Horror For Good*, several editions of the *Black Books of Horror*, *Alt Dead*, *The First Book of Classical Horror Stories*, *Dark Minds* and *Darker Minds*, and the final three editions of *Nemonymous*. His website is www.stephenbacon.co.uk
His debut collection, *Peel Back the Sky*, was published by Gray Friar Press in 2012. Forthcoming is a story in *Ill at Ease 2* (Penman Press) and a chapbook called *The Allure of Oblivion,* which will be published by Spectral Press in 2014. He lives with his wife and two sons in South Yorkshire, UK.

Jasper Bark finds writing author biographies and talking about himself in the third person faintly embarrassing. Telling you that he's an award winning author of four cult novels including the highly acclaimed *Way of the Barefoot Zombie*, just sounds like boasting. Then he has to mention that he's written 12 children's books and hundreds of comics and graphic novels and he wants to just curl up. He cringes when he has to reveal that his work has been translated into five different languages and is used in schools throughout the UK to help improve literacy, or that he was awarded the This Is Horror Award for his recent anthology *Dead Air*. Maybe he's too

British, or maybe he just needs a good enema, but he's glad this bio is now over.

G. N. Braun is an Australian writer raised in Melbourne's gritty western suburbs. He is a trained nurse, and holds a Cert. IV in Professional Writing and Editing, as well as a Dip. Arts (Professional Writing and Editing). At graduation, Braun was awarded 'Vocational Student of the Year' and '2012 Student of the Year' by his college. He writes fiction across various genres, and is the author of short stories *Boneyard Smack, Bubba wants YOU, Insurrection* and *Santa Akbar!*. He has a short story – *Autumn as Metaphor* – in the charity anthology *Horror For Good* and a short story – *Brand New Day* – in *Midnight Echo #7*, and has had numerous articles published in newspapers. He is the current president of the Australian Horror Writers Association, as well as the past director of the Australian Shadows Awards. He is an editor and columnist for UK site This is Horror, and the guest editor for the upcoming *Midnight Echo #9*. His memoir, *Hammered*, was released in early 2012 and has been extensively reviewed. He is the owner of Cohesion Editing and Proofreading.

Tonia Brown is a southern author with a penchant for Victorian dead things. She lives in the backwoods of North Carolina with her genius husband and an ever fluctuating number of cats. She likes fudgesicles and coffee, though not always together. When not writing she raises unicorns and fights crime with her husband under the code names Dr. Weird and his sexy sidekick

Butternut. You can learn more about her at: www.thebackseatwriter.com

Ray Cluley's stories have appeared in various dark places. His most recent work has appeared in *Black Static* and *Interzone* from TTA Press, *Shadows & Tall Trees* from Undertow Books, and the *Darker Minds* anthology from Dark Minds Press. He has a story forthcoming in *Crimewave* and another in the Edgar Allan Poe anthology, *Where Thy Dark Eye Glances*, from Lethe Press. A novelette with Spectral Press is due in 2014. His story 'At Night, When the Demons Come' was selected by Ellen Datlow for her *Best Horror of the Year* anthology, and this year *Night Fishing* was selected by Steve Berman for *Wilde Stories 2013*. He writes non-fiction too, but generally he prefers to make stuff up. You can find out more at www.probablymonsters.wordpress.com

Carole Johnstone is a Scot living in Essex. Her first published story appeared in Black Static #3 in early 2008. She has since contributed stories to PS Publishing, Night Shade Books, Gray Friar Press, Morrigan Books, Apex
Book Company and many more.
She has been reprinted in Ellen Datlow's Best Horror of the Year, and *God of the Gaps* (Interzone #238) is to appear in Proxima Books' *Best British Fantasy 2013*. Her first novella, *Frenzy*, was published by Eternal Press/ Damnation Books in 2009 and her second, *Cold Turkey*, is part of TTA Press' forthcoming novella series. She is presently at work

on her second novel while seeking fame and fortune with the first. More information on the author can be found at www.carolejohnstone.com

Benedict J Jones is from South East London and mainly writes crime and horror fiction. Since he was first published in 2008 he has seen work appear in Out of the Gutter, Encounters Magazine, Delivered, One Eye Grey, Big Pulp!, Pen Pusher, Shotgun Honey, the Western Online and many other venues, including two anthologies from Dark Minds Press.
His website can be found at
www.benedictjjones.webs.com

Kevin Lucia is a Contributing Editor for Shroud Magazine, a podcaster for Tales to Terrify and a blogger for The Midnight Diner. His short fiction has appeared in several anthologies. He's currently finishing his Creative Writing Masters Degree at Binghamton University, he teaches high school English and lives in Castle Creek, New York with his wife and children. He is the author of *Hiram Grange & The Chosen One*, Book Four of *The Hiram Grange Chronicles*, and he's currently working on his first novel. Visit him at www.kevinlucia.com.

Tracie McBride is a New Zealander who lives in Melbourne, Australia with her husband and three children. Her work has appeared or is forthcoming in over 80 print and electronic publications, including *Horror Library Vols 4* and *5, Dead Red Heart, Phobophobia* and *Horror for Good*. Her debut collection *Ghosts Can Bleed* contains much of the work that earned her a Sir Julius Vogel Award in 2008. She helps to wrangle slush for Dark Moon Digest and is the vice president of Dark Continents Publishing. She welcomes visitors to her blog at http://traciemcbridewriter.wordpress.com/

Gary McMahon's short fiction has been reprinted in both *The Mammoth Book Of Best New Horror* and *The Year's Best Fantasy & Horror*. He is the acclaimed author of the novels *Rain Dogs, Hungry Hearts, Pretty Little Dead Things, Dead Bad Things* and the *Concrete Grove* trilogy. He lives with his family in Yorkshire, trains in Shotokan karate, and likes running in the rain.

Blaze McRob has penned many titles under different names. It is time for him to come out and play as Blaze. In addition to inclusions in numerous anthologies, he has written many novels, short stories, flash fiction pieces, and even poetry. Most of his offerings are Dark. However dark they might be, there is always an underlying message contained within. Join him as he explores the Dark side. You know you want to.
     http://www.amazon.com/Blaze-cRob/e/B006XJ1I94/ref=sr_tc_2_0?qid=1363644263 &sr=1-2-ent and http://www.blazemcrob.com/.

William Meikle is a Scottish writer with fifteen novels published in the genre press and over 250 short story credits in thirteen countries. His work appears in many professional anthologies and he has recent short story sales to Nature Futures, Penumbra and Daily Science Fiction among others. His eBook *The Invasion* has been as high as #2 in the Kindle SF charts. He now lives in a remote corner of Newfoundland with icebergs, whales and bald eagles for company. In the winters he gets warm vicariously through the lives of others in cyberspace, so please check him out at http://www.williammeikle.com/.

Joe Mynhardt is a South African horror writer, editor, publisher and teacher with over sixty short story publications. He has appeared in dozens of publications and collections, among them *For the Night is Dark* with Gary McMahon and Armand Rosamilia. He will also appear in *The Outsiders* and *Children of the Grave* alongside great authors such as Simon Bestwick, Joe McKinney and others. Joe is also the owner and operator of Crystal Lake Publishing. His editorial debut, *Fear the Reaper*, will be available by Halloween 2013. His own collection of short stories, *Lost in the Dark,* is now available through Amazon. Joe's influences stretch from Poe, Doyle and Lovecraft to King, Connolly and Gaiman. In his spare time Joe blogs about haunted buildings and the horror writing craft. He is a moderator at MyWritersCircle.com and an Assistant Submissions Editor at The South African Literary Journal, New Contrast. Read more about Joe and his creations at www.Joemynhardt.com or find him on Facebook at Joe Mynhardt's Short Stories'.

Scott Nicholson is the international bestselling author of more than 30 books, including *The Home, The Red Church, Liquid Fear*, *Disintegration*, and *After: The Shock*. He's also written comics, screenplays, and children's books. Nicholson's website is www.hauntedcomputer.com.

Armand Rosamilia is a New Jersey boy currently living in sunny Florida, where he writes when he's not watching zombie movies, the Boston Red Sox and listening to Heavy Metal music...

The Dying Days extreme zombie series is growing all the time, and he currently has over 50 releases on Amazon. His *Miami Spy Games* series by Hobbes End Publishing and *Tool Shed* horror novella from Angelic Knight Press are his most recent releases. You can find him at http://armandrosamilia.com and e-mail him to talk about zombies, baseball and Metal: armandrosamilia@gmail.com.

Daniel I. Russell has appeared in various magazines and anthologies such as *Pseudopod, The Zombie Feed* from Apex, *Festive Fear: Global Edition*, Andromeda Spaceways Inflight Magazine and will appear in Shadow Award winner Brett McBean's *Jungle* trilogy. He is the author of novels *Samhane* (Stygian Publications and in Germany, Voodoo Press), *Come Into Darkness* (KHP Publications and Voodoo Press) and *Critique* and *The Collector Book 1: Mana Leak* (both Dark Continents Publications). He is the current vice president of the AHWA and former associate and technical editor of Necrotic Tissue Magazine, and guest editor of Midnight Echo. Daniel lives in country Western Australia with his partner and four children, if he includes the Xbox in that count.

Jeremy C. Shipp is the Bram Stoker Award-nominated author of *Cursed, Vacation*, and *Attic Clowns*. His shorter tales have appeared or are forthcoming in over 60 publications, the likes of Cemetery Dance, ChiZine, Apex Magazine, Withersin, and Shroud Magazine. Jeremy enjoys living in Southern California in a moderately haunted Victorian farmhouse called Rose Cottage. He lives there with a couple of pygmy tigers and a legion of yard gnomes. The gnomes like him. The clowns living in his attic – not so much. You can learn more about Jeremy at www.jeremycshipp.com.

John Claude Smith has had over 60 short stories published, the latest being in White Cat Magazine, Grave Demand, and SQ Mag online. He also has had 10 poems and over 1,100 music journalism pieces published. His first collection, *The Dark is Light Enough for Me*, was released late 2011. He is currently working on a second collection and revisions on a novel while another novel gets shopped around to publishers. Busy is good. He splits time between the SF Bay Area and Rome, Italy. Twitter: @wickd playground

Award-winning author and graduate of Northwestern University, **Robert W. Walker** created his highly

acclaimed *Instinct* and *Edge Series* between 1982 and 2005. Rob since then has penned his award-winning historical series featuring Inspector Alastair Ransom with *City For Ransom* (2006), *Shadows in the City*(2007), and *City of the Absent* (2008), and most recently placed Ransom on board the Titanic in a hybrid historical/science fiction epic entitled Titanic *2012 – Curse of RMS Titanic*. Rob's next, *Dead On*, a PI revenge tale and a noir set in modern day Atlanta. More recently *Bismarck 2013*, an historical horror title, *The Edge of Instinct*, the 12th *Instinct Series*, and a short story collection entitled *Thriller Party of 8 – the one that got away*. Rob's historical suspense *Children of Salem*, while an historical romance and suspense novel, exposes the violent nature of mankind via the politics of witchcraft in grim 1692 New England, a title that some say only Robert Walker could *craft* – romance amid the infamous witch trials. Robert currently resides in Charleston, West Virginia with his wife, children, pets, all somehow normal. For more on Rob's published works, see
www.RobertWalkerbooks.com
www.HarperCollins.com   www.amazon.com/kindle books. He maintains a presence on Facebook and Twitter as well.

Ross Warren is the editor of the 2011 anthology *Dark Minds* and the co-editor, with Anthony Watson, of the 2012 anthology *Darker Minds*. Alongside Anthony he runs Dark Minds Press. A third anthology, titled of course *Darkest Minds*, is currently open for submissions. www.darkmindspress.com Ross' most recent story, *The Day of the Trifles* was a finalist in the 2012 South Wales Short Story Competition and can be found in the anthology *The Countess and the Mole Man* from Candy Jar Books. Ross lives in Cheltenham, England with his wife Katarzyna, son Joseph and rather more books than he knows what to do with.

Mark West's short fiction first began appearing in the small press in 1999 and was collected *in Strange Tales* from Rainfall Books. Following publication of his novel *In The Rain With The Dead* he fell into a writers block that lasted until Gary McMahon demanded a novelette from him – that was The Mill and kick-started his writing. He's published over seventy short stories, two novels, a novelette and his Spectral Press chapbook sold out four months prior to publication. Mark lives in Rothwell, Northants (which serves as the basis for his fictional town of Gaffney) with his wife Alison and their young son Matthew. Website – www.markwest.org.uk. Twitter – @MarkEWest

Connect with Crystal Lake Publishing:
Website:

www.crystallakepub.com
Facebook:
www.facebook.com/Crystallakepublishing
Twitter:
https://twitter.com/crystallakepub

I hope you enjoyed this title. If so, I would be grateful if you could leave a review on Amazon, Goodreads, your blog or any of the other websites open to book reviews. And remember to keep an eye out for more of our books.

THANK YOU FOR PURCHASING THIS BOOK

Printed in Great Britain
by Amazon.co.uk, Ltd.,
Marston Gate.